Disruption

by
J. B. Jamison

Author's Website: jbjamison.com

ImagiLearning, Inc.

ISBN 978-0-9988885-2-1

Printed in the United States

Here's What They're Saying about Disruption

"A page-turner, conspiracy-soaked saga. Chilling…"
- Doug Evans, Colorado Mountain Writers' Workshop.

"A well-researched and intriguing thriller…"
- Dr. James Lynch, Florida Southern University.

"Fast-paced, engaging, action-packed thriller…"
- Lesele Rose.

"The only thing I can say is that I hope you make a series…"
- Judy Anable.

"An extremely tense, powerfully enjoyable ride…you won't want the journey to end."
- Geoffrey Smith.

OTHER BOOKS BY John B. Jamison

Six Simple Stories.
Simple Faith?
Time's Up!

To my captains

Chapter 1

With the normal night noises in the warm bayous north of New Orleans, you could barely hear the low rumble of the huge boat as it drifted its way up the Mississippi River. A light appeared up high as the door to the pilothouse opened. The dark shadow of a man moved down the stairs.

"If somebody is getting a blowjob down there, I'm throwing the son of a bitch in the river."

As he walked down the gangway, he could see the ski boat tied alongside the tow. It happened a lot. People wanted to see what a real towboat was like. These dry landers had read too much goddamn Mark Twain and believed that working on a towboat was all romantic and exciting stuff. He thought how he would like to set them straight. He'd like to tell them just what a hellhole life this really was; away from home for months at a time, living with a crew that always included two or three assholes and at least one very nice but completely useless drunk.

The first time it had happened was back when he was still a new Captain. He had walked into the small galley to meet the visitors, and the first thing he had noticed was a thin blonde on her knees, blowing one of the deckhands. Then he saw the brunette sitting on the bench, giving hand jobs to the cook and the engineer. There was another brunette in the kitchen doorway grabbing her ankles, but he couldn't see just who else might be involved there. And in the corner, some slicked haired guy in sunglasses was counting a wad of bills in his hand.

As Captain, it had been one of those decision times.

The proper thing would have been to throw the pimp and his girls back into their ski boat and write up the crew for what was clearly a violation of company policy.

Instead, he had stepped back into the hallway, returned to the pilot house, and drove the boat on up the river.

The Captain of a towboat isn't always the most popular guy. The good ones try to be fair, but there are times you just have to kick some ass to get things done. The Captain might spend an entire trip with no one talking to him, and a few crew members always watching for some way to get even with him. In this Captain's defense, he knew of others who had stopped a shipboard party, only to end up with a crew very creative in getting even. So, the Captain had let it go, hoping the little bit of fun might help morale.

What he hadn't counted on was that one crew member – the one with the religious bent; the one who always carried his bible with him, who took personal offense at the mini Sodom and Gomorrah taking place in the galley, who wrote a letter to the head office describing the behavior of the crew and their Captain. It was the second-closest the Captain ever came to actually losing his job. The letter the bible thumper had sent to the Captain's wife caused a bit of a stir as well.

That afternoon long ago was one of the reasons he was ready to get off these damn boats. He was tired. The magic that pulled him to the river instead of attending his high school graduation had faded. Too many lazy crewmen. Too many days and nights away from home. And now all of those pain in the ass, politically correct rules and regulations from the home office. It just wasn't the same anymore, and he was counting the days until he was done with it all.

So tonight, as Captain Charlie Graff moved down the gangway to meet the visitors from yet another ski boat, the one thing he was certain of was that he was not going to let these disloyal bastards risk his job again. Not this close to retirement. He had his Captain's voice ready as he pushed his way into the room.

Fortunately, there was no blonde on her knees, brunette on the bench or bent over in the hallway.

There was, however, a big guy standing in the middle of the room, another in the doorway and the third sitting on the bench. He then noticed that the big guy in the middle was holding an automatic rifle. The crewmembers in the room looked less relieved than the ones that last time.

As he took it all in, the man on the bench spoke up like an old, long-lost friend.

"Captain, welcome. I want to thank you for your hospitality for inviting us to join you on your boat."

"What the hell is going on here?"

"Captain, please. We mean you no harm. We simply want to borrow your boat for a little while; oh, and your crew, and you."

"Borrow my...? Look you son of a bitch, I don't know who the hell you think you are but you'd better..."

The Captain stepped forward, and the guy with the gun turned to face him, targeting the Captain's more than ample belly.

"Captain, please. I strongly advise you to stop and listen to what I have to say. I'm afraid that my men are a bit more tense than I am, and having something happen to you would create problems for our plans."

"I don't give a goddamn about your plans...this is my boat, and this is my crew."

"Not for a while Captain, no. As I said, I am borrowing you for a while, until we complete our mission here. Once we are finished, I will return your boat to you, and your crew."

"Mission...what mission? Nobody comes onto my boat and tells me what they are going to..."

"Captain!"

The leader slowly got up from the bench. He was tall and thin, and had a smile on his face, but not in his eyes.

"Captain. I am sorry you are so upset. But I must tell you that I don't have the time to discuss this with you right now. We have taken control of your boat, we will be with you for a few days, and then we will give your boat back to you. You have my word. But just to show you that I am sincere in what I say, it may be necessary for me to give you a little demonstration of that sincerity."

The leader motioned to one of his men, who grabbed Danny, the youngest crew member, walked him toward the door of the galley, pulled out a small revolver with a silencer, and pointed it toward the back of Danny's head. It occurred to the Captain that the shot sounded a lot like pulling the tab on a can of beer, except for the little puff of pink smoke and Danny's clothing collapsing into a heap on the floor like it was ready for the laundry if it wasn't for Danny still being in them.

"Such a waste." the leader sighed. "I do hope you won't ask me to give you another demonstration Captain. Fortunately, young Danny had no family, had no real friends who might miss him. The river was his life, and today you made the decision that his life was over."

The rest of the crew stared at their Captain, whose eyes slowly regained focus.

"Now Captain, why don't you and I go up to our pilothouse and I will explain what we are going to do. The rest of my men will be aboard shortly to help prepare the crew for their part in the mission. Ah, here they come now."

Before he could speak or move, the Captain heard another small boat pull alongside. The leader motioned him toward the door, and after a brief glance at his crew to tell them not to do anything stupid, Captain Charlie Graff stepped from the galley with his fists and teeth clenched.

Chapter 2

The pilothouse was the top level of the boat; a square room the size of a small kitchen and surrounded by windows. There was a long bench along the back wall, and a big chair surrounded by controls and screens at the front window. As the captain and visitor entered, the glow from the radar and control panels was the only light in the room.

"Well, it looks like we have guests. Giving a little tour captain?" The voice from the chair looked toward the door and noticed the gun. "What the hell..."

"It's ok Frank, just drive the boat. We have a bit of a problem here."

"A bit of a problem?" the leader said. "Now Captain, we'll never get along if you consider us to be a problem. I promise you that we will do our very best to not interfere with your work at all while we complete our mission."

"And Frank, what your Captain hasn't told you is that my crew and I have come to borrow your boat for a while. We require a place we can work, and you are providing us with that place."

"You can't come on board this boat and..." Pilot Frank Maddox began.

"And Frank, what the Captain also hasn't told you yet is that I am quite sincere in my mission. Isn't that true Captain?"

The Captain nodded toward the leader, "They killed Danny; shot him in the back of the head."

Frank hesitated, and then rose from his chair, "What the fuck is going on here?"

"Just do your job and keep us going up river Frank, and I will tell you and your Captain all that you need to know."

Frank paused and sat back down, "And how do you know my name? Just who the hell are you anyway?"

The leader continued as he reached into his pocket.

"But first, just so you clearly understand how important it is that you do work with us, let me give you these."

The leader handed each man a small photo.

The first thought in the Captain's mind was that it was a very nice photo of his wife, one of the nicest he had seen in a while if it wasn't for that set of cross hairs focused on her forehead. "What the fuck is this?" Charlie asked.

"Gentlemen, we didn't just decide to come out and jump on the first boat we found running up the river. We have taken a lot of time to prepare for this mission. We know all about you, and your families; who they are, and more importantly, where they are. In fact, we have friends who are watching your wives, and your children, and grandchildren right now...well, all of the time."

Two men spoke with one voice, "You son of a bitch."

"Our friends mean your families absolutely no harm, and you have my word that nothing will happen to them...any of them...as long as our mission is allowed to continue. Do we understand each other gentlemen?"

Silence.

"Gentlemen?"

"Yeah, I get it," strained out of the mouths of the two men.

"Wonderful. Now. Captain, I'm sure your crew is growing concerned. I need you to go and let them know that everything is fine and that they are to cooperate with us fully. I have photos to give each of them that may help you explain the situation. For now, simply instruct them to go about their work as they normally would. They should do nothing to raise any suspicion that anything is not perfectly normal. Please let them know that if anyone does not follow these orders, I will be forced to instruct our friends to pay a little visit to your families...and I am sure none of us want to see that happen."

Charlie and Frank stared at their photos.

"One more very important thing you need to communicate to your crew immediately. From now on, no one is to go aft of the ship, behind the engine room. This is absolutely off limits from this point on. Is that understood?"

"What are you..." the Captain raised a hand.

"NO! There are no questions about this Captain; it is off limits to every member of your crew, including yourselves. Am I clear?"

"Yeah, fine."

"Trust me, Captain; this is as much for the safety of your men as anything else. My men will make no unnecessary trips to that space during our mission as well. Only the doctor and his team will have regular access."

"The doctor? Who the..." the Captain asked.

"Ah yes, you will meet him later. He will be boarding soon with his team and the, um, supplies."

The leader briefly looked around the pilothouse as if he was thinking about having the place redecorated.

"Captain, we have a long trip ahead of us, so I suggest that we all take a deep breath and go forward like this is just like any other run. We will not interfere with any of your work, and I know you will not interfere with ours. In fact, if we all do our parts, you probably won't even notice that we are here."

As the leader and Captain moved toward the door, the leader turned to Frank, smiled, and spoke in a voice you would use as you leave the room after tucking your three-year-old in for the third time after they keep getting out of bed.

"And Frank, while the Captain and I are down talking with the crew, please do not try to do anything brave like sending any calls for help. We have friends watching and monitoring the boat; the radios, cell phones...honestly, we have thought of most everything...this mission is that important to us. So just drive the boat, and when we come back, I will explain more."

As the leader and Captain made their way back to the galley, the Captain saw the body of the young deckhand being loaded into the skiff, on its way into one of the dark bayous. Between the gators and other scavengers, there wasn't much risk of anyone asking questions anytime soon.

Chapter 3

The seven men were standing in a circle around the crowded galley, staring at the little photos they each hold in their hands.

One finally turned to the leader, "So, you're telling me you have some asshole with a gun following my wife and kid, and if I do anything wrong you're going to have that guy kill them...is that it?"

The leader smiled.

"Well, that's the general idea, yes. You see, if any one of you does anything that might threaten our mission, our friends will...not just one of them, but all of them will do what they have been prepared to do. You see we are all on this mission together. But, I assure you, we have not come here to harm anyone, and you have absolutely nothing to worry about as long as we all do our jobs. When our mission is completed, you get your boat back, and everyone goes on with their lives. You have my word."

The Captain glanced at the floor where Danny had fallen and then at the leader.

"You'll have to excuse us if we have a bit of a problem with your word."

"Captain, I understand your sarcasm, and that's why I will ignore it for now. It was not my desire to harm one of your crew, but you forced my hand. I had no time to spend negotiating with you about our plans, so I had to demonstrate just how serious I was...and am."

"Gentlemen. We will give you more details once we are fully underway, but here is what you need to know for now. We have taken control of your boat, and by default, of you. We have a mission to carry out that involves many people, some of whom have been preparing for many years. You will meet more of our team as we move forward, while others will remain invisible to you. You need to know that not all of those involved in our mission will tell you so; some will appear to be completely unaware of what is happening, and will fulfill their roles by simply watching and listening; going about their days just doing their jobs...wherever they may be."

The leader paused.

"Now, we are adults here, and I realize there is simply no way we can follow you around all of the time and monitor everything you say and do while we are on this boat. But, before anyone gets the idea that they might do something to try and stop us, or to try and get a message to someone, remember that if you do that, the person you are communicating with may well be one of our friends. And the result of that action would be something I truly would hate to see happen."

"I have one other little gift to give you."

One of the leader's men handed each man a small piece of plastic.

"I need you to put these little things on your wrists. I'm sure you've seen things like this before; they're just like the bracelets you get in the hospital. Only ours are a little fancier. You see that thin little wire inside your bracelet? It becomes active as soon as you fasten the ends together."

The group mumbled and squirmed.

"Oh, there is nothing to worry about, they won't harm you. They just work as a small antenna. Every few minutes each bracelet sends a signal to announce that it is still here. As long as you are onboard the boat, your signals will keep everything running smoothly. However, if anyone chooses to leave the boat, or to do something foolish like removing your bracelet, your signal will not be received; and, well, that would be an unfortunate thing."

"If it helps, you will also notice that my friends and I each wear a bracelet. This is a little insurance to see that, if anyone had an idea to do something brave, like throw one of us overboard, it would not be the best path to take. Does everyone understand?"

After a pause and a glance around the room, the Captain sighed audibly, "Ok, we get it, you've made your point. So just what the hell are we supposed to do now?"

"Well Captain, you do whatever you would be doing if I was not here. As I understand things, you will be picking up some barges to move up the river; so I suggest you have everyone focus on their jobs to get that done. Those of you we so rudely woke from your off watch sleep, please just go back to bed. And why don't you all take your little photographs with you as my gift, a little memento of some of the truly important things in our lives."

"And oh, one last thing, to stress something that your Captain hasn't told you yet. From this point on, no one is to go aft of the boat beyond this room; no one. This is for your own safety, so I must insist that you comply."

A deckhand looked up, "So just how are we supposed to work the barges we have to pull?"

"You will push your loads upriver this trip, so there is no need to worry about that."

The Captain turned to the leader, "What you may not understand is that whether we pull or push a load depends on how many barges we have and what's inside them, and we never know that until we get our orders, and those are always changing. Unless you are also in charge of giving us our tow orders now too."

The leader smiled, "Captain, I do understand. You can trust me. You and your crew will not need to go aft of this room during our mission. Now, let's all get back to work."

Chapter 4

Frank Maddox, the Pilot and second in command, was in his chair in the pilothouse, staring at the river. The Captain was sitting on the bench behind him, looking back and forth from the window to the photo in his hand. Over the past half hour, they had several ideas for retaking control of their boat, but each one fell apart as they thought it through. They had received new orders to pick up loads below New Orleans. It wasn't a normal trip, but not much else had been normal that night.

The pilothouse door opened, and the leader walked in as if he did it every day.

"Hello gentlemen, I'm glad to find you together. I want to tell you a bit more about our mission before the doctor arrives; I'm sure you have questions."

He paused and smiled, "And I'm sure you've had time to come up with several great ideas for throwing me off of this boat too, haven't you? But since we're still here, I'm guessing we've done a good job of avoiding that outcome? I don't blame you at all, really. But, I am hoping that after I explain things, you will understand that what we are doing is really a good thing. I don't expect you to fully buy-in, but perhaps it will make the next several days move more smoothly."

The Captain turned from the window, "If you're expecting to come in here and have us..."

"Captain, all that I expect is for you to follow instructions and drive your boat. But, please give me the courtesy to explain why we are here. How you respond to that information is completely up to you." He smiled, "Within reason, of course."

"Gentlemen, what would you say was the number one problem facing our nation today? I mean if you could identify one thing that has done more to harm the people of our nation, and perhaps the entire world, what would that one thing be?"

The Captain and Pilot exchanged glances, "Oh hell," Frank said, "I don't know. You want me to say something like illegal aliens or terrorists, or gays, or liberals, or something like that, is that it? Is that what this is all about? Another protest of some kind?"

"Frank, please, give us more credit than that. Those things are the issues of people who want to fight about things they can never really change. They enjoy the process of protesting; it makes them feel they are doing something, but it will never really change anything."

"Let me ask this instead; have either of you ever lost something? I mean something of real value to you; something that was so important to you, you didn't know if you could survive that loss? Captain, I know that you understand what I am saying."

After a moment of silence, the Captain said, "Ok, yeah, I lost a man on a boat once; Frank was there. He tripped over a line, fell into the water and was caught between the barge and the lock wall; it all happened so fast, there was nothing we could do," the Captain's voice drifted off.

"Yes, Captain, that was a tragic accident. But what if it was not an accident?"

"But it was..."

"Yes, of course, it was, absolutely; and you feel terrible about it almost twenty-five years later. But what if, just imagine, what if that man's death was not an accident, but happened because someone did something that caused it to happen? How would you feel then?"

"You mean what if someone pushed him?"

"Or what if, and this is just an example, what if your man fell from the barge because someone in the home office made the decision that if you didn't take the time to collect all of the lines each time you entered or left a lock, you could get through the lock fifteen percent faster and save the company money? So, he tripped on a line left out because of a rule created by someone sitting at a desk, not on a boat. In fact, that person had never set foot on a boat but was focused on making more money for the company. How would you feel?"

"Well, honestly, I'd probably feel a hell of a lot better, because I would have found that son of a bitch and killed him myself."

"Exactly! If someone was doing something that was risking the lives of your crew, you would do something; because you are the Captain, and because you are a good man."

The Captain stared at the floor.

"Let me tell you a story. My son was nine years old when we discovered he was sick. He was a good kid; not a genius or anything, but just one of those kids that everyone liked, could do most anything he wanted to do, and was always smiling and having fun." The leader paused, looked to the floor, then continued, "We used to go for drives a lot, you know, just exploring the countryside, just the three of us out on our own, looking for new things and enjoying being together. Then we ended up spending our drives running from one doctor to another, one hospital to another, trying to find out how to keep our son alive. And we finally found the answer, and I'll tell you, that was a very good day. Until the insurance company informed us they would not cover the treatment. They called it too experimental. The risk to their money was not worth the risk of saving my son's life. Because of a mathematical formula created by some bean counter sitting at a desk, in some office far away from my son's hospital room, the company made the decision that took my son away from me. There was a cure, but they would not do it. They killed him."

All eyes were locked on the floor; the only sound was that hum from the engines.

"So while that company's leaders sat in their offices receiving their paychecks and living lives that were untouched by their actions and decisions, my...my...world, like those of thousands of others, died."

"Captain, there is a boat approaching port side," the radio announced.

The leader opened the door and said, "Ah, yes. Right on time. This will be one of our supply boats coming out now. I need to go see that everything is going smoothly. But, there is nothing to concern yourself with gentlemen, it is just business as usual."

As the leader closed the pilothouse door behind him, Charlie said, "Business as usual. Right."

Chapter 5

"Frank, what do you make of all this?"

"Hell Charlie, I was just sitting here thinking about that night up near Beardstown when we almost took out the old railroad bridge. With the high water, I still don't know how you got through there. But I remember we both said it was probably the wildest ride either of us would ever take. I'm beginning to think we might have been wrong."

"Hah, yeah, that was a hell of a night. To be honest with you, I don't know how I got through there either; sometimes you just have to stop thinking and do what you do. That time it worked. This time, I'm not so sure."

Frank nodded his head. "This guy just seems to be pissed off and probably has good reasons to be. But I just don't see how it fits here; on a towboat. What the hell is going on."

They heard him whistling before the pilothouse door opened, "All is going just fine down there. You have a good crew on this boat."

Neither man responded.

"Gentlemen, my friends and I believe that we are living in a nation, and a world, that is controlled by people who have so much wealth that they have no understanding of what life is like for the rest of us. They run organizations that decide how we will live, and how and when we will die. Our politicians make grand gestures like publicly accepting salaries of one dollar a year, and then go on to enjoy the luxuries of their family's investment savings, million dollar homes and hidden accounts. These so-called leaders care more about the risk to their dollars than about the risks to their people. And don't tell me that we have rich politicians because we chose them; they have created a system that is open to only the rich; they control that as well."

The Captain and Pilot were silent.

"Gentlemen, these people need to be stopped. We must remove their ability to control the decisions that impact our lives. And we can't focus on individual issues or individual people. The problem is far larger than that. Remove one person, one issue or one company, and another takes its place. That, gentlemen, is why we are on your boat."

Silence.

"What if, just what if, they were to experience what we experience every day? What if their families and safe offices were faced with the things we have faced? What if they had to spend their day focusing on their losses, rather than their gains? That is what our mission is about. To see that those who have enjoyed their safe lives in control of the world, lose that control."

"On a towboat in the middle of the Mississippi River?" The Captain blurted it out as if he had just been told that pigs could fly.

"Yes Captain, on this boat. Exactly. We are going to use this boat to change how this nation operates. We are going to break the connections the wealthy and powerful use to keep their wealth and power and retake control of our own lives. And we start that here by splitting the country in half."

There was a brief pause.

"Wait," the Captain was out of his chair, "splitting the country in half?

"It is exactly what it sounds like. Have either of you heard of something called an RDD?"

No response.

"RDD stands for radiological dispersion device; in simple terms, an explosive device that contains materials that are highly radioactive that are spread around when the bomb explodes, making that area unsafe for humans for a very long time. It's sometimes called a dirty bomb."

"You're planning to launch a nuke from this boat?" Charlie surprised himself with the volume of that question.

"No, no Captain, nothing like that. We don't want to do that kind of damage. All we want to do is disrupt things; we don't want to harm people; that's what we are trying to stop."

Silence.

"Our devices use traditional explosives, things like C4. Don't ask me for much more about that because I don't understand that stuff at all; that's all being handled by the doctor. But, those elements create the explosion that will spread the other materials. And wherever the radioactive materials land, those places will be dirty for fifteen to twenty years, maybe longer."

The Captain's face was tight, "So just how is that not going to harm people? This makes no sense at all."

"No one needs to be harmed, trust me. I would not be here if that was a part of our mission. Let me explain. As we move upriver, we will be placing our devices beneath each highway and railway bridge along the river. When all are in place, they will be detonated."

"So your plan is to blow up bridges," came from the Pilot, "they'll just rebuild them."

"You're forgetting the dirty part, Frank. We don't need to damage them. All we need to do is make the bridges dirty, and to create a dirty space around them that will take a huge amount of time and money to clean up."

A new look came onto the Captain's face.

"No gentlemen, it's not about blowing things up, it's about splitting this nation in half by creating a dead space right through the middle of it. Transportation will be stopped. Cities and industries will be uninhabitable. It is about disrupting a system that serves the wealthy and uses the rest of us as it chooses."

"But to do that," Charlie said, "you'll need dozens of these devices."

"Twenty-seven will do the job. We will target the highway and railway bridges along the river. Just twenty-seven."

The Captain shook his head, and the sharpness returned to his voice, "But I don't see how you can say that you aren't going to harm anyone. You're placing these things right where people..."

"Yes, we are placing them where they could do the most damage. However, no one needs to be hurt. You see, when all of our devices are in place, we will then notify the media of our plan. We will give twelve hours, notice before the devices are used. That will allow time for anyone in the areas to move safely away."

The Pilot joined in, "So, it's basically extortion; you give the country twelve hours to meet your demands, or you will explode the bombs!"

"Oh no Frank, not at all. There are no demands, that does not work. Our devices will explode and will create the dead zone; that is the purpose of our mission. We want to give everyone time to safely move from the area before the devices are used, but the devices will be used."

The leader opened the door and stepped out onto the gangway. The two men looked up from the floor, "Well shit Frank," Charlie said, "I guess this makes that night at Beardstown look pretty damn tame now, doesn't it?"

The leader stuck his head back into the room, "Captain, may I see you downstairs, please? I need to update you on some details."

"Sure, I was ready for a refill anyway." The Captain drained the cold coffee from his cup and walked out the door into the morning breeze.

Chapter 6

Someone new was standing in the galley. At first glance, the Captain thought he looked rather nerdy, and nervous. But what struck him most were the man's eyes. They had the look of someone who wasn't seeing the things in the galley but was looking at things that were someplace else. He thought they were crazy eyes, and he had to admit that the guy made him really nervous.

"Let me guess; this must be the doctor you've been telling us about."

"Very good, Captain, please allow me to introduce you; this is indeed the doctor. His associates are setting up their equipment now so he can begin his work."

The doctor seemed to slowly become aware of them and stepped toward the Captain with an outstretched hand. But the eyes were still not here. As he looked toward the Captain, he was looking through him, not at bones and arteries, but someplace about seven miles behind him.

"I am very happy to meet you, Captain," the doctor said as he shook the captain's hand.

The words came out just as you would expect if you saw the eyes.

"I do trust that our presence will not inconvenience you and your crew too greatly."

The Captain wanted to reach out his free hand and tap the doctor on the head just to see if it would echo. As calm and together as the leader seemed to be, this doctor-guy was the direct opposite; the kind of guy who might shake your hand and then turn around and piss on your leg, and then offer you a towel with the picture of a puppy on it to clean up the floor.

"I am sure we will find a way to do our jobs," Captain Charlie Graff said, in place of, "Holy shit, we're screwed!"

There was a brief hesitation as hands and arms disengaged.

"Doctor, may I ask you a question?" Charlie asked.

The doctor's eyes found the Captain and seemed to take on a sparkle.

"A question? Certainly Captain. I would be happy to hear your question."

"I'm no scientist and don't know a lot about these device-things you're building, but I read a lot, and my understanding is that the stuff you need to put into them is really hard to get ahold of, and you need quite a bit of it to make the things, you know, effective."

"An excellent question Captain. I am happy to see that you are a thinking man, and have an interest in these things. They told me that would be true."

There was a noise, and the doctor glanced toward the door where two men had entered carrying a metal case.

"But I am afraid that I must go and tend to my duties right now Captain. I will be happy to talk again later and will answer any questions you might have. But let me just say that you are correct in your understanding, in most cases. However, when you have the capabilities of a group such as ours, those challenges become minor. Indeed, it has taken us time to gather our resources, but we have been patient, and have done what others have not been able to do. And now please pardon my rudeness, but I must go."

The doctor left with the two men. The Captain did not take a breath from the moment he recognized the case's yellow radiation warning label until the leader touched him on the shoulder, "Captain, why don't you refill that cup of coffee now?"

"Yeah," is all the Captain could get to come out.

Chapter 7

As the Captain poured a fresh cup, the leader motioned for the Captain to join him at the table.

"Captain, I assure you that the doctor is a very capable man. I noticed your hesitation. Understand that he has been under a great deal of pressure recently, getting his work done, and has not had much sleep."

The Captain nodded.

"And speaking of sleep, you are off watch now, and things are quiet for a while. Why don't you get some sleep as well? I assure you that if anything of importance arises, I will see that you are notified."

The Captain looked toward the window.

"Captain, really, it is important that you rest. You are the only one who can make sure that everything proceeds normally, and that no one attempts anything that might, well, we need you to be alert and in control of your boat."

"Captain, I'll tell you what. You go get some sleep, so you are rested, and when you are up, I will answer questions I know you have. But please, you must rest."

"Alright, alright, but I don't see how the hell I'm going to get any sleep; not with you here, and the doctor back there, with his radioactive crap cooking our brains."

"I understand your concern Captain, and I assure you that we have taken every precaution to see that there is no danger to anyone here from the radiation. The elements are safely contained in canisters. And just to take extra precaution, we have placed shielding in the workroom where the devices will be assembled. Plus, we will only have a few canisters on board at any one time."

The Captain looked up from his coffee.

"Yes Captain, that is why we needed to borrow your boat. It would have been impossible to carry all twenty-seven devices around to deliver them. The canisters may still carry residual radiation from when they were loaded, but handling two or three at a time makes that harmless. What we needed was a movable laboratory; a place we could assemble our devices one at a time, and safely deliver them to their destinations."

"My boat."

"Your boat."

"But why..."

"Captain, sleep. We will talk more later."

The Captain dumped his now lukewarm coffee in the river as he walked along the side of the boat toward the ladder to the second deck and his cabin. As he glanced at the shore passing by, he was tempted to just jump into the water and swim away from this nonsense, but the bracelet on his wrist kept him here. Once inside his cabin, he kicked off his shoes, stretched out on his bed, knowing full well he would not, could not, sleep. He pulled out the photo of his wife and unfocused his eyes to make the scope crosshairs disappear. She was really beautiful. She looked just like she did before the kids were born; that time they took off to the Ozarks and spent three entire days and nights doing nothing but...nothing but...

Sleep is good.

Chapter 8

He opened his eyes and thought about a fresh, hot cup of coffee, and began running the daily routine through his mind. Then he remembered. He grabbed his deck shoes, threw water on his face, and ran out the door.

The sun cast a red glow over the water as the boat made the turn to the barges. It was almost an hour before the change of watch, so Frank was piloting the boat. As the Captain entered the pilothouse, Frank explained they were stopping to pick up six barges, all loaded and ready to move upriver; three to Memphis and the others to St. Louis. The Captain found his seat on the bench and stared into his cup of dark roast.

What troubled him was not the dirty bombs. There were other things eating at him right now. First, when he caught the boat a week ago, the office told him he would spend the entire trip on the lower river getting caught up on some loads that had been delayed in the spring floods. But they almost never took a boat this far down river. These barges were south of New Orleans, down in big boat water where the oceangoing ships load and unload. And why did their new orders say they were going back to the upper river; something had changed. But what bothered him most was the fact that the leader apparently knew about the change before the orders came. His eyes lost focus on the cup, and without raising his head, he said: "Frank, there's a snake in the home office."

"I've been thinking the same thing but didn't want to say it. Who the hell could it be?"

"Shit, it could be anyone I guess."

"Well, I can't imagine the old man being involved in something like this."

"Nah," the Captain said. "I mean hell, I've been with him for almost 30 years; and if anyone wouldn't tolerate somebody messing with his boats, its him. And besides, he's got as much to lose in this deal as anybody else. I mean, damn, if they actually blow these things up like they say, it fucks up our river too; we're out of a job, and the old man's company goes under with all the others."

"He can be a real asshole at times," Frank said. "but he's not stupid. Who else are you thinking?"

The Captain stood and walked to the window, "I dunno. Most of them have been around for years; it's almost like a family."

"A fucked up one sometimes."

"Yeah, that's for sure; but not this fucked up. Alma is the one responsible for putting together the orders; she's the one directing all of this. But..."

Frank interrupted, "Alma compiles the orders, but anyone there could come up with reasons to change them; it's not really that unusual you know."

"Yeah, I know. I'm just fishin'."

What about Alex, he's fairly new, just came on about a year ago, wasn't it?"

"Yeah, I think about a year. And he deals with..."

The pilothouse door opened and the leader entered, looking fresh and alert, carrying a plate of donuts.

"Good morning gentlemen, I've brought a little something to start your morning."

Frank turned to stare out the window at the deckhands making up the tow, and the Captain looked at the leader and his plate as if he had just invited them to all put on tutus and dance around the pilothouse for a while.

"Guys, c'mon. I'm trying to make this experience be as painless as possible, really. Ah, Captain, how was your sleep?"

"Just fine, thank you."

"That is good. It's important that both of you are in top shape during our mission. I was able to get a bit of rest myself, though those engines sure do make a lot of noise, don't they?"

No response, as the leader placed the plate on the small table, "Well, anyway, here you go, help yourselves!"

No one moved.

"I see we are picking up the first load. That is excellent; right on schedule. Once you are finished, we need to stay here for another few minutes before we begin to move up river. This is actually one of the more challenging parts of our entire mission, and timing is critical. I will let you know when we are prepared to move on."

No movement, no comment, no nothing.

"In fact, I'll tell you what. We're almost at the end of watch anyway, so Frank, why don't you go ahead and go downstairs and get some rest? I'm sure the Captain won't mind; he and I have some conversation to continue anyway. Is that alright with you Captain?"

The Captain's eyes did not move from the window. "Sure, that's fine, whatever you want, it's your boat."

The Captain glanced at Frank and nodded his head toward the door. Frank scanned the controls to make sure everything was in order and stepped from the pilothouse as the Captain settled himself into the big chair.

Chapter 9

"So, just where the hell are we right now?" the Captain asked as he looked at the GPS and radar screens. "We usually don't come down this far."

"We're just a few miles south of New Orleans," The leader said. "It makes a nice place to do things more unnoticed."

"I don't see..."

The leader's cell phone hummed, he took a quick look, and smiled, "Well that was even faster than I expected. Captain, we are ready to get underway. Please take us up the river."

Charlie glanced at the leader, turned his eyes to the front to make sure his crew was ready, and reached for the controls. They felt the vibration as the huge engines surged, and the leader walked to look out the aft window at the great churning of water caused by the twin, twelve-foot propellers.

"This is an amazing machine Captain; I imagine it must sometimes be quite challenging to control it."

The Captain remained focused; and silent.

"Captain, or do you really mind if I call you Charlie?"

"Call me whatever you want."

"Then Charlie it is. And my name is Dennis; that is my real name, by the way, in case you were wondering."

The Captain stared out the front window.

"I wasn't."

"Charlie, I realize you look at me and see a maniac; some kind of a warped, deranged, evil fool. I can't blame you for that. Five years ago, I would have thought the same thing. But I'll tell you; we're really not all that different; you and me."

The Captain looked out the window.

"Well, Dennis, for one thing, I'm not holding a bunch of men hostage and threatening to kill their families and blow up radiated bombs across the country; and I sure as hell haven't shot an innocent man in the back of the head, so no, I think we're probably more different than you think. And I think it would be better if you just kept calling me Captain; if you don't mind."

The Captain guided the boat into a sharp bend to the left, as it passed downtown New Orleans and its Riverwalk area, just waking up for the day.

"Certainly, Captain. I really do understand. Like I said, a few years ago I would have felt exactly as you do. But then..."

"I know, you lost your son. I can't imagine how hard it was to deal with that, but shit man, how did that end up with...?"

"There was more to it than that, Captain. Yes, my son's death was very difficult. But as I spoke with others, I was shocked at how common that experience was; just how often people who might be made well are allowed to die, simply to fit within the algorithms of an insurance company."

The leader paused while he looked out the aft window again.

"It just ate at me. It wasn't about me anymore; it was about all of those who had their lives destroyed as part of the daily games of those with the wealth and control. And I looked for ways to try and make a difference in the normal ways. I became active in politics, and I studied more about business and law. But they're too well established. They own the businesses; they own the banks, they own education, they own the governments, hell, they own it all. And it's the same in every nation in the world; the rich and powerful taking advantage of the poor and powerless. Don't you ever get tired of seeing this stuff happening Captain?"

A pause as the captain guided the boat under the massive structures of the Crescent City Connection; the twin bridges carrying the morning rush traffic into the city.

"Hell, of course I do. Anyone in their right mind gets tired of that shit. But Jesus Christ man, that doesn't mean you blow up the country. That's just insane."

"No Captain, insanity is doing the same old things that have never worked, and somehow expecting them to work this time. The reality is that those who are in control are not going to give up that control, and they will never do anything that will allow their control to be threatened. The only choice we have is to change things ourselves. I met some other people who believe the same thing, and together we decided that we would do just that. Crazy? Perhaps captain. But insane? No."

The only response was the hum of the engines as the leader watched the two bridges move into the distance behind them.

"Captain, I realize I will never convince you of the value of our mission. But I just wanted to assure you that it is not just the act of a broken mind. That is why we have gone to every measure to see that no one needs to be harmed; no one other than those who have caused more harm than our little journey here could ever create."

Several minutes of hum-filled silence as both men stared out of pilothouse windows; one forward, and one aft.

The Captain glanced at the leader and then back to the window.

"So tell me, when does this little mission of yours officially begin? I mean, what do we do first?"

The leader smiled as he looked back down river, "But Captain, it has already begun. The first two devices are already in their place and ready to do their work."

The Captain had a tough time finding a breath as he looked back at the Crescent City Connection, now filled with morning traffic just 150 feet above the surface of the water. His hand shook just a bit as he drank from his coffee cup, trying to stop the sensation that he really needed to throw up.

Chapter 10

The morning passed just as it was supposed to pass, with everything looking like it was just business as usual. As the boat made its way under the span of the Huey P. Long Bridge, the morning rush traffic on Rt. 310 had ended, and traffic on the Hale Boggs was lighter than usual for late morning, so the Captain found it was a bit easier to keep breathing as he imagined seeing the two canisters slowly burying themselves in the murk below the bridges.

Just before noon, Frank came back to the pilothouse for the afternoon watch. "Hey Captain, where's your buddy?"

"Yeah, right. Did you get some sleep?"

"Yeah, some. Enough. I'll be fine. So, what's going on?"

"Well, they actually did it. The sons a bitches actually dropped a couple of those things under the bridges; three of them so far."

Frank looked out the aft window, "Holy shit, they really did it?"

"Fuck yeah, or at least that's what he said. You couldn't tell a thing from up here, but my guess is they are doing exactly what they say they are doing."

"Shit Charlie, we can't just sit here and let them use our boat like this, we've got to do something."

"Yeah, I know. But I'll tell you something. I don't think these guys are as crazy as I thought they were at first."

"You're not buying their crap are you?"

"Fuck no, nothing like that. But at first I figured they were a bunch of, I don't know, terrorists, or just lunatics out to make a name for themselves. Those kinds of people make mistakes we could probably take advantage of. But these guys, fuck, I'm not so sure they're the kind that make many mistakes; they might be crazy, but they're not stupid."

"Yeah. Where are we now anyway?"

"Just below Reserve. Got new orders to pick up another load at Mile 138. Still lots of big boats around here; I'm glad it's nice and wide."

Both men were quiet as they looked out the windows at the busy river traffic. Nothing was said as Charlie stepped from the chair and Frank took the controls for his six-hour watch. The two men had worked together for almost fifteen years on one boat or another, so they could run through a string of shifts without ever saying a word. As he watched Frank handle the controls to pick up the new load, he remembered the first trip they ran together, when "Deckhand" Frank first mentioned his dream of someday becoming "Captain" Frank. Charlie remembered when he had said those words and had decided to take it upon himself to see that the young man got his shot. There had been good times, and times he had to kick Frank's ass a bit to get a point across, but it had clearly all paid off in the end. Charlie couldn't help but let a smile creep onto his face.

"What the hell are you grinning at?" Frank said.

"Aw, I was just..."

The pilothouse door opened and the leader walked in as he put his cell phone in his pocket.

"Frank, I'm glad to see you here. I'd like to borrow the Captain for a few minutes."

"You're the boss apparently," Frank said as he looked out the front window.

The Captain grinned at Frank's bit of attitude, and said, "Ok Frank, let's see if you can keep her between those trees out there...that's where the water stops."

The two friends glanced at each other and shared a weak smile. They'd been through tough times before.

Chapter 11

"Captain, I thought you might like to see just how our little operation is working; I imagine you may be curious?"

The Captain moved to the open door and walked down the steps to the main deck. The leader followed, looking at a message on his phone.

The gangways on a towboat are just wide enough for one person at a time. If you needed to pass someone, one of you had to press your back against the side of the boat to make room for the other. At one point as the leader passed the Captain, Charlie thought about how he could just give a little nudge and watch the asshole fall to the water two decks below; if it just wasn't for those damn bracelets. The leader paused and offered a friendly smile.

There was no one in the galley as they entered. "Captain, we will only be able to make a brief visit to the doctor's workspace I'm afraid. As I mentioned before, we have taken every precaution with the radiation, but it makes no sense to press our luck and overstay our welcome if you know what I mean. The doctor and his team are prepared to deal with the risks, but I'm afraid you and I don't have all of the same protections they have."

The Captain hesitated.

"Oh, no Captain, it is perfectly safe for a brief visit. We could actually stay much longer, but again, we have no desire to risk anyone being harmed, so we're just being extra careful. Please, come with me."

The leader stepped from the galley door and walked to the stern of the boat where there was a door to a small storage room. The doctor's team had turned that space into their temporary laboratory, for assembling their little devices.

"The doctor and his team have made good use of the space, don't you think Captain?"

"Where are the things that were in there? We may need..."

"Have no worry Captain, everything has been temporarily moved to where it can be gotten to if needed, nothing has been lost. And, when we are finished, everything will be put back just as we found it. Here, I'm sure you are curious just how everything works."

The leader motioned for the Captain to follow him into the room. The Captain hesitated again and then entered.

To the right of the door was a small table with a silver case sitting on it next to a few simple tools, and to the left was a small stack of three empty boxes. There were some metal panels placed against the inner wall, but other than that, it was just an empty, cleaned out storeroom.

"Welcome to our little laboratory, Captain, please come in." The doctor was smiling as he nodded toward the visitors. "I imagine you were expecting something a bit more elaborate?"

The Captain stood and looked around the room, and the doctor continued. "Allow me to show you just what we are doing here, so you can be assured that there is no risk to you or your crew. In fact, you can see the extra lead shielding we have placed against the walls to make sure your crew is fully protected."

The doctor stepped to the middle of the room with a look on his face like the new daddy standing next to the hospital nursery window. "As I believe our friend has told you, we do not keep all of our supplies here on the boat with us; that would create too many risks. So, we don't need a very large space, or many other tools, just a few things to do a final assembly of our devices. Would you like to see one of them, Captain?"

"See one of the devices? You mean one of them is here, now?"

"Certainly Captain." The doctor added a small grin to his face. "In fact, you are standing next to as we speak."

The Captain turned to the table beside him and looked more closely at the silver container sitting on it. It was so plain he hadn't paid it any mind when he entered; a small silver case that looked like an old water softener you have at home, except for the fact that a water softener doesn't contain a high explosive that will fill the house with radioactive shit if the thing blows up. The look on his face and his sudden movement were noticed.

"Relax Captain," the doctor said. "The device is completely assembled and ready for deployment, so there is little danger from any radiation now that it is sealed. Besides, it has not yet been armed."

The Captain smiled and tried very hard to appear calm and in control, though his eyes didn't match that thought.

"Captain," the leader said, "the barges we picked up this morning held the pieces for the first three devices. Those were for the three bridges near downtown New Orleans. That last barge you picked up near Reserve held the materials for this device, number four, which is to be placed under the Gramercy Bridge that is just ahead of us now. We will pick up another new barge up near Romeville, as I'm sure you have seen in your new orders, and it will hold the materials for device number five."

The Captain was trying to take in the information in a way that would make sense in his mind.

"You see Captain, by not holding materials on our boat, we reduce any risks to ourselves, plus, we reduce the risk of drawing the attention of any monitoring device; as you said earlier, there are many of those around. Once the devices sink into the deep mud of the river bottom, they are fully safe from detection, but until that time we must be careful. That is why I said the first steps through New Orleans were the most challenging of our entire mission. With all of the monitoring around large cities, as well as the harbor shipping, we needed to be very careful to not do anything that might draw the attention; and it appears that we have been successful."

The leader turned to the doctor and his team.

"And now Captain," the doctor stepped toward the table, "we are approaching our next location, so we must make our preparations. Why don't you stay and see just how the process works."

One man picked up a piece of thin line from the corner. It had a small hook on one end that he connected to a ring on the end of the device. They slowly carried the device out the door and sat it gently on the deck. After checking the hook and ring, one of the men lowered the device into the water, handling the line carefully to see that it slid behind the boat away from the prop wash, and did not become caught in the wash and pulled into the props themselves. As they had done three times already, they played out the line to pull the device behind the boat, until the stern deck fells into the shadow of the Gramercy Bridge sliding past one hundred sixty feet above them. With a jerk, the rope disengaged the hook from the eye, and the device gently settled into the river beneath the bridge."

"We have some time before we will have our next supplies, so why don't we all take a bit of a rest?" The doctor sounded very pleased with their work. "And Captain, thank you so much for joining us."

The group headed toward the cool of the galley for some refreshment. The Captain glanced back down river at the bridge fading into the distance, where device number four gently settled in the river currents, coming to rest on the bow of a battered old rake barge, sunk in the river a decade ago after striking the bridge piling during hurricane Katrina.

Chapter 12

"Caught anything?"

It's what you shout at anyone sitting in a flatboat containing fishing poles. The shouter was standing on a dredge anchored just above the IC Rail Marine Terminal south of Romeville, and the fishing boat was going past on its way upstream. The boat carried two people with the poles, a couple of tackle boxes and a cooler, either for the day's catch or for the drinking that would make up for a poor showing.

"Just getting started, but we've got enough booze that it doesn't really matter."

And then, they were invisible again; just another boatload of guys fishing; doing business as usual.

Just a mile or so above the terminal they pulled to the shore into a quiet spot just below a set of barges. The spot might be a good place to find fish, but it didn't matter. While one fisherman tied the boat to the stern of the first barge, the second pulled a large bag out of the cooler. He lifted it up to the deck of the barge and followed it, then reached back to grab the second bag his partner had pulled from under the seat. He carefully lowered the bags into one of the barge's loose tank covers. He tightened the lid, jumped back into the skiff, and untied it from the barge.

They drifted back downriver in silence as they went through the plans for the next stop below Baton Rouge.

Chapter 13

It was the first time the Captain saw the entire group at one time. There were seven all together. The leader and his three goons, and the doctor with two others helping him. What struck him was how this group of murderers was sitting around the room, telling stories and laughing; more like a bowling team in the bar between games than people who had just sunk four dirty bombs into the Mississippi river. The Captain had a long list of questions he wanted to ask and was just opening his mouth to do so when he realized one of the guys with the doctor was a woman.

"Ah, I see you are surprised to see Susan here Captain," the leader smiled. "Doctor, why don't you introduce the Captain to your team, we have no further need for secrecy now that the mission is underway."

"Certainly, I will be most happy to. My work would be impossible if not for them." He turned to the man sitting on his left. "This is Lawrence, Captain. Lawrence is responsible for designing the casing for our devices, and for doing the final assembly here on our boat."

Lawrence nodded, smiled and reached a hand across the table to the Captain, who forced his own hand to respond.

"It is very nice to meet you, Captain. I am sorry for the inconvenience we have caused you, but I assure you it will be worth the trouble when we are finished."

"And this is Susan," the doctor nodded to the young woman sitting next to Lawrence. "Susan is our specialist in nuclear science, and is responsible for the, uh, dirty side of our mission."

Everyone in the group smiled and chuckled at the doctor's little bit of humor; everyone except the Captain.

"Susan was one of my graduate assistants at the university, and greatly impressed me with her abilities. When it came time to create our team, it was obvious to me that she was the best for the role. Her Navy training has proved to be invaluable."

"Navy?" the Captain heard himself ask.

"I was helping with cleanup after Desert Storm," Susan looked at the Captain with steel gray eyes, "I spent my time in places that no one else wanted to go."

"The doctor has several other members of his team, as you might expect," the leader smiled. "They are in different places, each doing their part in preparing our supplies for the mission. And you have met Bradley, Thomas, and Bear, my three colleagues." The leader nodded toward each of the men standing around the room as he mentioned their names.

"Yes, we've met," the Captain's said through clenched teeth. They simply returned the stare, but with an apparent lack of any feeling whatsoever; just business as usual.

"They are doing their part to collect the supplies as they arrive, and being here to help me in any ways that might be necessary as we go."

The Captain looked around the room at the group, "I'm just curious, you all seem to be fairly normal people." Everyone in the room smiled at each other and laughed, though the Captain hadn't intended it as a joke. "How did you end up here, as a part of this, this, this...'mission'?"

"I'll go first," Susan said. "As doc said, I was in the Navy, doing nuke work. I went into it with my eyes open; I knew very well that I might pay the price in twenty years or so, as exposure to the radioactivity began to mess with me. But I also knew that the Navy would take care of me. Then, as expected, about three years ago I started having symptoms; liver function, skin cancers...several things. But what I didn't expect was that the help I had been promised wasn't there. I spent months going from office to office, visits to different VA hospitals, each one of them saying my problems weren't from radiation. My medical bills broke me, and my parents. Then I started hearing from others I had served with. They were having exactly the same experiences. At first, I couldn't believe it and assumed there was some screw-up somewhere. But I began to realize there was no screw-up; there was just too much risk in revealing some of the things that had gone on, the things that really caused the problems we were having. So, the risk to the military was bigger than our risk; which meant we lost. I watched friends die, some of them horrendously, and it just made me furious. I had gone back to school to keep my mind busy, and that's when I started working with Dr. Shallenger, heard about the mission, and joined up. Something just had to be done."

Over the next several minutes, the Captain heard similar stories from the others; serious illnesses and deaths that might have been prevented, family members losing jobs, businesses, homes, because of decisions and actions made by others far away who never even noticed. As he listened, the Captain couldn't help but think about his recurring back problems and how the insurance company would not let the doctor perform the surgery that would actually fix them. But he sat in silence. They didn't sound like terrorists or murderers. But he knew that somehow, at some point, they had to be stopped.

The Captain walked back to the pilothouse to sit and stare out the window with Frank. The next bridge was the Sunshine Bridge, about twenty-five miles upriver. The leader said they would pick up the pieces for the device about five miles below the bridge; so that gave them a few hours.

"I'm going to try and sack out for a while," Charlie looked out the bow window as he spoke, "you ok here for now?"

Frank looked at him and shrugged his shoulders, "Sure, Cap, everything is just business as usual here. Go get you some sleep."

Charlie walked down the gangway to his cabin, picked up a book as he laid down, hoping that the latest western he had brought on board might distract him from the wild west show that has taken over his boat. Once again, sleep came quickly.

Chapter 14

She was certain she had turned it off, but there it was, her cell phone playing Sweet Home Alabama at full volume, and every face in the room turning to her with that smile that said, "Hah, you screwed up!" Emily tried to put her hand over the phone's speaker as she moved between the chairs to get to the door, where she stuck the phone next to her ear and yelled, "WHAT?"

"We've got a hot one. You need to get in here." It was Lennie Ryan; Special Agent in Charge of the New Orleans Field Office, and her boss.

"What? I'm off today. What is it?" she asked with only slightly less irritation.

"Gramercy Bridge, about 30 miles west of here. The NRC has called us in."

"A bridge? C'mon Lennie, they call every time one of those portable hospital trucks triggers a sensor. You don't need me for that. Call somebody else; it's my night off," as she started back toward the door to her weekly fitness club meeting.

The bridge sensors were one of the better-kept secrets spanning all the way back to the cold war. They had been installed to sound off anytime someone might be crazy enough to travel around with some kind of radioactive stuff in their vehicle. There were actually two sensors on each bridge, one at each end. That way they could look at the order in which they were triggered and identify the direction the stuff was traveling. They worked pretty well at first; back when radioactive stuff was a rare commodity. But today, with just the medical uses of radiation in mobile radiotherapy vehicles, those sensors were being triggered several times a day and had become just another piece of the routine. A hot sensor was certainly not a valid reason to give up a perfectly good evening off.

"It's not a bridge sensor. I don't know all of the details, but I do know that they've called in one of their tactical search and secure teams...so whatever it is...it's got them fired up. They've escalated it and want us there."

"They've called in tactical?"

"Yeah, apparently they think they've found something with Cobalt-60 in it. You need to get over there."

She stopped with one hand on the door. She really didn't need to go back into the weight-loss meeting. She didn't even need to be there at all. She didn't need to lose weight. She was in great shape. She just liked the process of counting the calories and the structure it gave. It was the one part of her life that she had any real control of right now. That's what she didn't want to miss tonight.

The presentation about the various acceptable substitutions for sugar was just getting underway as she turned from the door and walked down the hall where she could hear. And think.

"Cobalt-60? You guys better not be messing with me here, or I swear..."

"They're pretty sure." Lennie had the sound in his voice that said even though he was Emily's boss, he was very aware of the cost to be paid if anyone was dumb enough to yank her chain on her day off. She was the only person in the office that would dare talk back to him like that, and that's one of the reasons he liked having her around. "They found it three hours ago, and the NRC team did their routine first response. Now it's escalated."

"Ok, do we know of any loads of Cobalt-60 moving through that area today, anything from the military, or agriculture?"

Among other common uses, Cobalt-60 is one component in the equipment to kill bacteria in food processing, and in lots of other industries that need to have high powered sterilization take place. In other words, there is a lot of it moving around out there.

"Nothing."

"Ok, you said about three hours ago; which way was it moving?"

"Well, that's the thing, it wasn't the bridge sensors that caught it, so we don't know for sure that it was moving across the bridge. They think it is in the water under the bridge."

"Under the bridge? You mean, whatever it is...it's still there?"

"Apparently so. That's why Search & Secure was called in."

The hallway was silent as Emily stared at her shoes. She took a deep breath and looked at the bulletin board next to the parking lot door. She took the time to read a few old notices to keep herself from saying things she might regret later.

"So, are there any other little details I need to know about?"

"No, that's it. As soon as they realized something unusual was going on, they closed the bridge to traffic and called us in."

Emily looked at the time on her cell phone, began moving toward the door, "Whose team is on call?"

"It's Elliot's team."

"Ok, good. You might give them a heads-up that something might be coming their way tonight. And let the NRC guys know I'm on my way. With traffic, I should be there in about an hour," as she stepped out the door.

"They're at the Gramercy bridge, or just west of it. They said they would meet you there. There's a little road that goes up over the levee just about a half mile north of the bridge. They said to drive over the levee, and you'll see their boat."

"Boat?"

"I told you it wasn't a normal bridge alarm."

"Yeah, right."

She stuffed the phone in her pocket as she walked to her car.

Chapter 15

Driving across town, Emily had the feeling that this might be one of those days that explained why she went into this line of work in the first place. There were a lot of bad things being carried on the roads, right next to parents taking their kids to ball practice and ballet rehearsal, but fortunately, most people just didn't know about them. If they did, they would probably never leave their driveway. Some of the things sounded a lot worse than they were. Uranium was one of the first things people thought of when you mentioned radiation, and while it was certainly something to be careful with, you could sometimes buy it on eBay. But Cobalt-60 was a different thing altogether. For many uses, it was packaged into long rods that were inserted into the machines that use the radiation to kill germs and sterilize things. There were thousands of those rods being used in more than forty sterilization centers around the U.S. and over one hundred twenty around the world. When used correctly, it's not a high risk. But if you weren't very, very careful, someone getting too close to an unshielded Cobalt-60 rod for less than a minute would be dead within a week. And it was not a friendly week.

As she pulled south off of I-10 onto 641, she was pleased with how well she could find her way around. When the opening had come up in New Orleans, it was too good to pass up. Since she was a kid, she had been fascinated by the intrigue and mystery of the FBI. She sometimes wished she could go back and explain to young Emily that the intrigue and mystery were far more rare than the paperwork and boredom, but overall, she was happy with the path she chose. And growing up in a family living and working on the river, she knew that would always be in her blood, so when the New Orleans position appeared, it was a no-brainer. Her father had been a Captain on boats on the upper rivers for over forty years before he retired, and all of her uncles and cousins had taken the same path. So wherever and whatever she did, she knew it would always involve some kind of river.

Her mind followed that thread to create images of her dad now, sitting in a cognitive care unit she found for him in the city. Whatever he used to be, he was now a changing mix of things; sometimes a boat captain, sometimes a retired boat captain, and sometimes an angry old man sitting on the side of his bed staring at his shoes. He had always been difficult. In fact, Emily was probably the only person he ever spent time with without feeling the need to be The Captain.

She refocused her thinking as she approached the blockade, and after being waved through, found the gravel road leading up the side of the levee. A woman in an NRC Response Team jacket stepped toward her.

"I'm Doctor Karla Renshaw with the NRC. Thanks for coming."

"Just call me Emily. So it sounds like you have something interesting here?"

The woman got into the passenger seat.

"It's interesting, yeah. And it must hot if the sensor caught it in the water. Just follow this road to the other side of the levee. They're waiting for us."

"I was just told there was something under the bridge. How'd you find it?"

"One of our harbor boats was heading downstream after having some repairs done this morning. One of the mobile sensors had been acting up, so they dropped it in the water to make sure it wasn't leaking, and the thing went off."

"You're kidding me. They weren't actually looking for anything then?"

"Nope, what are the odds, right? They were headed to do routine scanning of cargo that came in last night below town."

"So just what is this thing they found?"

"Don't know yet. We've called for the ID and Secure team to take a look. They'll check it out and do what they need to do to make it secure."

The dirt path led down the river side of the levee and disappeared into a tangle of weeds and driftwood. Emily parked the car and followed the doctor through the mud. The small NRC harbor boat was tied up at the muddy riverbank, with a half-dozen people in NRC jackets standing around.

"Skipper, the FBI is here."

He had a blue life jacket over his windbreaker and a very serious look on his face. Emily stepped forward extending a hand.

"Agent Emily Graham. It sounds like you have an interesting one here."

"Pete Goodwin. Yeah, has Agent Renshaw filled you in?"

"She told me you found something and you've called in another team to check it out."

"Yeah, we really don't know what the hell is yet. We were just dragging the sensor about three feet underwater testing the seals when it pinged. There's over eight feet of water right there, so whatever is down there must be pretty nasty."

"Big?"

"Well, it's not the size that concerns us. With radiation, two feet of water works the same as an inch of solid lead. Since we're assuming the thing is on the bottom, that means the sensor pinged it through the equivalent of at least three inches of lead. That shouldn't happen."

"And you say its Cobalt-60?"

"That's the thing. That is one of the traces from the sensor, and we got that when we went back and dropped it deeper just to double-check things. But the initial trigger came from Caesium-137, and then we ended up with three or four other things. Hell, it's like a chemistry lab down there."

"You sure that sensor is working correctly?"

"Yeah, that was our first thought too. We've gone back with two others, and get the same results."

"So, what's your gut at this point?"

"Worse case? Somebody threw something off the bridge that was filled with some kind of a mix of dirty stuff. It was either not watertight, or it cracked when it hit the water, and now it's leaking. Caesium-137 is water soluble. Sealed inside a container it would pretty much be invisible, but the fact that we found it means it must be loose in the water; it and whatever else is making its way down the river. We'll know for sure once the team gets here."

Emily let herself enjoy the cool breeze sweeping across the water carrying the aromas of the river flowing by. She watched as the barges of a boat silently approached from under the bridge making its way upstream. As the barges drifted by, she thought again about her father.

The contrast in her mind was hard for her to comprehend. He had spent forty-five years driving these monster machines up and down rivers, knowing every curve, every sandbar, and being in control of his crew in a way that gained him the respect of all that knew him. But today, he sat in his room. Instead of remembering river curves and sandbars, he struggled to remember what town he was in, and how to get back to his room from the nurse's station. This morning he hadn't recognized her when she entered the room and seemed rather pleased to learn that he had a daughter living nearby; there in Chicago.

The sound of the waves hitting the shore at her feet brought her back, and she began creating her mental list of things to do. Call Lennie and fill him in. Tell him to activate Elliot's team and get them down here asap. And yeah, call the Corps of Engineers and tell them to shut down this river.

Chapter 16

While Emily made her plans, the boat was slowing to make a turn just fifteen miles upriver, just south of Welcome, Louisiana; a village of nine hundred people. It was just across the river from a steel mill and grain elevator, so it was a good place to tie barges waiting to be loaded or unloaded. At any one time, there might be a hundred barges unattended along the shore.

Charlie eased the rudder controls to allow the current to drift the boat down and toward the shore, and then come up under the small barge at the south end of the stack. It was nearing dusk, but things were busy here twenty-four hours a day so no one would notice as they collected their barge. And even if they were noticed, it looked like they were going about business as usual.

Charlie had sometimes thought about the thousands of barges like these parked all along the river, but it had never really bothered him; not until today. He held the boat steady against the barge as he watched his deckhand handle the line, throwing one end over the barge's timber head and connecting the other to the ratchet. The deckhand slid the long pipe over the handle of the ratchet to give him more leverage and tightened the line, pulling the barge fast against the tow. Charlie enjoyed watching a good deckhand at work. They knew what needed to be done, knew their tools and how to use them, and wasted no time getting things done. The good ones were always keeping eyes open for problems as well, knowing full well how quickly things could go bad out on the deck. Charlie's eyes lost focus as he remembered another deckhand just like this one, who was not quite as cautious, and overtightened a cable enough that it snapped, hurling hundreds of strands of hard, cold steel in two directions. One end gouged a hole in the barge, and the other went toward the ratchet and the deckhand. The poor rookie never even saw what hit him.

His eyes came back into focus as he saw two other men step onto the barge, both moving far too fast and carelessly to be deckhands. He watched as the men walked to the far side of the barge and stopped at a wing tank cover, the round hatch that opened into the storage tank along the side of the barge. They stooped to open it, and pulled out a canvas bag and carried it back to the boat, where he lost sight of them.

When his deckhand waved the all clear, Charlie eased the boat back into the channel and felt the twin screws bite into the water. He got a really miserable feeling in his stomach as the boat cleared the right turn of the curve and he saw the cars on highway 70 crossing the river on the Sunshine Bridge just ahead.

As the boat passed one hundred and seventy feet beneath the bridge, Charlie walked onto the gangway outside the pilot house and lost his dinner into the churning water below.

Chapter 17

While there were always bad reasons for it happening, Emily felt excitement and satisfaction as she watched the FBI response teams go into action during a crisis like this. It was partly the extensive training, and partly the commitment and work ethic of every member of the team; but when the call came in, things happened.

Elliot's Joint Terrorism Task Force team was in their trucks headed to the river. Emily had talked with the Coast Guard, the U.S. Department of Transportation, the local port authority, and was now on hold with the U.S. Corps of Engineers, going through the long list of steps to shut down one of the busiest commercial waterways in the country. Even with all of the simulations and well-practiced interagency communication plans, this was not something done easily.

Emily felt her phone vibrate with a second call coming in. She glanced at the number.

She closed her eyes, "Not now! Please, not now."

She hit the 'End call and answer' button.

"Hello Emily, this is Linda at Torchwood. I'm sorry to bother you, but we could use your help with your dad if you have a minute."

"Ok, what's up this time?" Emily gritted her teeth.

"He thinks he's on the boat, and he's mad at us because we won't let him go up to the pilothouse. He's been really confused today. When I came on duty, I found him sitting in my chair at the nurses' station, in his underwear, talking on the phone. He was ordering a pizza, but had somehow called Chicago."

"Aw jeez, I'm sorry Linda."

"Oh no, it's ok. That's really pretty calm compared some of the stuff around here. But after we got him back to his room he started getting upset again, saying it was time for his watch and he needed to go relieve the pilot. Could you talk with him a minute and see if you can calm him down? Sometimes your voice seems to calm him when he's like this."

"Sure, I can try."

"Ok. One sec."

Emily took a deep breath and slowly exhaled, forcing her voice to sound calm and friendly.

"Hey, these sons a bitches won't let me run my boat. You better tell them to follow orders, or I'm going to start taking names and kicking asses around here."

It had worked before, so Emily decided it was worth trying again. That was one of the perks of his having no short term memory anymore.

"Now dad, don't you remember? You told me you were breaking in that new pilot and wanted to see how he could handle the watch on his own this time. You warned him that you wouldn't be around to bail him out tonight. How's he been doing anyway?"

"What? Oh, yeah, I guess I forgot about that. Shit, I guess after being stuck on these boats for this many years I'm lucky to remember my own ass."

"You've had a lot on your mind lately, but it's ok. By the way, do you have any of those ice cream bars left that I brought you the other day?"

"No. I ran out of those yesterday; the guys here really like those. You need to bring some more."

"I'll do that dad."

"Well, thanks for calling; I've gotta go down to the dining room and see if they have any coffee left. It's not worth a shit, but I've already called the home office and told them not to put this cook on one of my boats again. I told them to find me someone who can at least make a decent pot of coffee."

"Ok dad, I'll bring more ice cream bars the next..."

He hung up, and Emily was back at the river.

She had learned a long time ago to never ask "What next?"

Chapter 18

He sat near the window, a cup of unsweetened black tea in front of him. The barista was still shaking her head from the dumb joke he told her, the kind she had come to expect during his daily visits. He looked to be in his 60's, though he could be older, he dressed and carried himself well.

"Grandpa! How you doing?"

The thirty-something walked to the table as the joke teller got up, receiving a hug.

"Ronnie, it's so good to see you. How's the kids?"

"Doing well grandpa, busy as usual. I can't tell you how great it was to get your message; we've not had a good visit for ages."

The older man watched the younger one intently as if they were the only two in the place.

"Yes, it has been far too long Ronnie. I'm happy you could make the time to come."

"Absolutely grandpa, no one could keep me away! You said you wanted to talk with me about something important; is everything ok? Are you alright?"

The old man waved the comment away with his hand, "Oh, of course, I'm sorry if I worried you. I'm doing just fine."

"Whew, that's a relief. When you said, it was important I..."

"It is Ronnie, very important. In fact, I've been thinking about this conversation since those Saturdays we used to go fishing together. Do you remember those?"

"Remember? Of course, I remember. You came to my rescue every Saturday, giving me an excuse to get out of the house for a while and away from the fighting."

The old man smiled sadly and nodded his head as Ronnie continued.

"I actually think I understood what you were doing even then, but didn't know how to say thank you for it. I really think you were the reason I got through all of that stuff with mom and dad. It was crazy."

"Yes, your parents tried to do what they could, but they had their own demons to battle with. I couldn't do much, but..."

"The fishing was enough...even with all of your stories."

"Hah, yes. But let's not talk about the past. I want to talk with you about what lies ahead. Go order something to drink; here, my card will get you a free one; then we'll talk."

The younger man walked to the counter as the old man watched, and listened. He thought about the boy he once was, the man he had become, and the man he might yet be.

"Thanks, grandpa, I need some caffeine right now. Now, what's this talk about what lies ahead?"

"Ronnie, do you think you are making a difference?"

The young man's mind stopped abruptly.

"Making a difference? What do you mean? With my job, or my family? I don't understand."

"No, no, of course, you are making a difference with your family, and I'm sure with your job as well. But I'm just wondering if you have ever felt that you would like to do more, you know, be able to have more impact on things around you. Bigger things."

He saw the confusion and hesitation in his grandson's eyes.

"Ronnie, I want you to think about something. If I told you that you have the opportunity to be more involved, and have more impact on what happens around you than you've ever imagined, would you be interested?"

"I don't.."

"Don't answer now. But what if it were possible that you could have an influence that reached into every corner of the world; would that interest you? And before you answer, you must know that you would also have the ability to see and understand things that will be terrifying, and sometimes horrible and unimaginably cruel. But you would know for a fact that you were doing things that mattered, things

56

that protected your family and others, things that would influence history."

"Grandpa, I don't understand. I don't know what to say. Tell me what you are talking about. Are you ok?"

"I'm fine Ronnie, and I understand how confusing this all sounds. I'm asking that if I were to offer you something that could change your life, give you and your family all that you ever dreamed of having and more, and put you in a position to do things for others that few others could do, would you be interested? Don't answer now. Go home, or back to work, and think about that one question. If you decide that you do want to accept that opportunity, meet me back here tomorrow morning. If you aren't interested, I fully understand, and it will make no difference at all. Nothing will change between us, and we will never speak of it again."

The young man sat, staring at his grandfather who now seemed to be someone far different from the man he thought he knew.

"Ok, grandpa. I'll think about it. I'll talk with Carol tonight and..."

"No! You must not speak with anyone about this; now or ever. And if you choose to accept it, you must always keep it to yourself."

The young man leaned back in his chair.

"Ronnie, I understand that I am asking you to keep a secret from the one's you love the most. And I understand just how difficult that will be for you to do. That is one of the reasons we are having this conversation; because that is the level of love and dedication required to follow the path I am talking about. But I assure you, accepting this role will never harm that love and dedication. In fact, it will only make it stronger and more meaningful. "

"But you..."

"Take time to think. If you decide this is something you want, meet me here tomorrow morning. If not, we will go on as if we never had this conversation; I'll tell you some more of those old fishing stories."

The old man's mouth smiled, but his eyes were far more serious looking. He stood, paused to say something to the barista that resulted in a groan, and walked out the door.

Chapter 19

Elliot and his team made good time getting to the river. Emily and the NRC agent met their truck at the levee.

"Hi Em. Looks like we have an interesting one."

Elliot was one of the few people who dared call Emily 'Em'. Others had tried it but quickly found that such a level of informality was something that had to be earned.

"Yeah. This is Karla with the NRC. And Karla, this is Elliot, lead of the JTTF."

They filled Elliot in with what they knew. He had already detailed one group to review the videos from bridge traffic, a second group to secure all land traffic around the area, and a third to begin evacuation of anyone near the bridge. Another group was back at their office computers digging through records to identify anyone who might be transporting radioactive materials through the area, and another was arguing with the various agencies responsible for stopping the multi-billion-dollar flow of goods up and down the river. Ultimately, they could have just said, 'The river is closed!', but the collaborative way was always the best option...when it is an option at all.

The NRC Search & Secure team was on-site; half of them in a van parked below the levee and half on a boat under the bridge. The boat group was hooking up a submersible robot to locate and identify the object to find out just what the hell they were up against. The darkness was taken care of with bright spotlights, but the current was an issue along with the murky water itself. Locating this thing would not be difficult. Seeing it might be the problem.

Emily, Elliot and the rest of the NRC team were standing on the shore above the bridge, waiting for their teams to do their jobs.

There wasn't anything you would call romantic between Emily and Elliot, but there was some kind of connection. It was partly because they were both so invested in their roles that they couldn't help but respect each other...they were too much alike. One night when they had been out drinking, someone asked if they were a couple. They both stopped cold and stared at each other in a way that clearly said neither of them had even considered that possibility. They decided that it wasn't because they couldn't be with each other, but that neither of them had any interest in being a part of a couple with anyone right now. Work was first, and second, and third. Emily had to put her father in that list somewhere as well. They spent time together but talking about work, or football, or telling stories they didn't feel they could tell anyone else. It was like being a couple, just without actually being a couple. It didn't make sense to them either, so they just didn't talk about it. As far as each of them was concerned, what they had was better than romance.

It is Elliot's phone that rang. He listened for a few minutes and then came back to the group.

"The bridge video shows a truck stopped on the bridge around three o'clock this afternoon. It was a rented panel truck stopped near the north end of the bridge for just about one full minute. The driver got out of the cab, walked around to the back of the truck and opened one of the doors. It was parked at a point where the cameras couldn't see behind it, so they couldn't see just what he was doing, but he then closed the door, got back in the cab and drove on across the bridge. It's like the driver knew exactly where to stop to avoid being seen. They were able to screengrab the license number and traced it to a rental agency in Thibodaux."

Emily made the call to Lennie to begin the search. It was just a search at this point. No one was to stop or approach the truck if it was found. Whatever they had dropped in the river may have made the truck just as hot. The stopping and searching part would be left to the experts.

The next sound was the NRC radio informing them that the boat had eyes on the object. It was a cylindrical container with a ring on one end. It was lying on top of a sunken barge, slowly rocking back and forth in the current. The device had apparently been damaged when it hit the barge, and one end of it was cracked and split open, revealing wires inside. The sensors confirmed traces of both Cobalt-60 and Cesium-137.

Unfortunately, the sensors also reported pings from about a half-dozen other elements, each one of them nasty.

"It looks like someone wants to get our attention," the NRC leader said.

Emily looked at him for a moment. "It worked."

Chapter 20

It would be about five hours before the boat reached the bridges at Baton Rouge. Charlie thought that if the river was as narrow here as it was up North, this would be one hell of a mess. Just above the Sunshine Bridge, the river turned completely back on itself before bending west again. As he steered the boat around the final curve, Charlie saw a small cabin boat approaching. The pilothouse door opened and the leader and Frank entered.

"How's it going captain?" the leader asked with a smile.

"Business as usual, I guess."

"Excellent. I just wanted to let you know that we have some new crew members coming aboard. I thought you might want to come down and see what was going on so you could, you know, update your crew, so they understand."

"New crew? What the hell's going on now?"

"I'll be happy to explain it all captain, come with me. Frank here can take over for a while."

"You alright with that Frank?" Charlie asked.

"Yeah, no problem Cap. You go check out the party, and I'll take care of things here."

Frank filled the big chair as Charlie walked to the door with the leader and stepped outside.

"You know Captain, this is my first time on one of these tug boats, but I can see how you could fall in love with it. Between the river itself, and the power of the boat, and being on your own and traveling, there is something really special about it for sure."

"It's a tow boat, not a fucking tug boat. And yeah, one man's paradise is another man's hellhole. Now, what did you want to show me."

They walked the rest of the way to the galley in silence.

There were three strangers standing in the galley unpacking a pile of boxes that made the small room feel even smaller.

"Don't worry captain; we will be moving this equipment into the room next door we cleared out earlier. Your galley will be back to normal soon."

The leader pointed to the boxes.

"This is the equipment that makes our mission foolproof."

Charlie glanced at him with a slight grin on his face.

"I know captain; nothing is really foolproof. But I think you'll see that we've come as close to that as possible. The centerpiece of our equipment here is that computer they are setting up now. It is able to communicate with the devices we're putting in the river. It links them all together."

Charlie's grin had gone away, "So you can push one button to blow them up."

"Well, yes, it could do that of course, but for now, it checks to make sure all of the devices are secure, so nothing happens before we are able to warn everyone to move to safety."

The leader turned to the man with the laptop, "How long before we're functional?"

"Should be just about an hour, then we'll get the GPS-synch running."

"Good, we're on schedule."

The leader turned back to Charlie, "There's more to this of course. But for now, I'll just say that this equipment also provides us with a few extra pieces of, well, protection as we finish our work here."

He smiled.

"Once this is turned on, there is nothing anyone can do to stop us or our boat. Now, why don't you go back upstairs and relieve Frank so he can get some rest before his next shift."

Charlie saw no option but to nod, head back to the pilot house and try to make sense of something that had begun to wander around in his mind. It was the tone of voice when the leader said that nothing can stop them, or the boat. Charlie really hadn't thought about what might happen when people figure out what was going on out here, and what steps they might take to stop them. Or to just stop the boat.

Charlie paused at the foot of the stairway leading to the pilothouse.

"Well, shit!"

Chapter 21

One positive thing about finding the object was that it made it a much simpler task to get river traffic closed. The problem of figuring out what to do with a few hundred ships and boats was in the hands of the Corps of Engineers, while Emily, Elliot and the others focused on removing the device, and finding out who the hell put it there. The NRC boat was sitting in the middle of the river, with the crew staring at small screens as the submersible robot sent images. Their immediate concern was the rocking. The device was already cracked, but nothing appeared to have leaked out; at least nothing visible. The first goal was to stop it from rocking in the current to avoid having it roll off the barge and bury itself in the six feet of mud at the bottom of the river.

The NRC agent's radio came alive, "We're going to lower a couple of sandbags and try to put them on each side of the thing. That ought to secure it enough for us to take a closer look at containing it. Then we have to find out just how much radiation is getting out, and where it's going."

A second NRC boat had pulled to the shore. There were now five NRC boats, a half-dozen state and local law enforcement agency boats, a collection of harbor patrol craft, and a growing number of boats carrying reporters. Only two media helicopters had arrived, but crowd control was becoming as much of an issue as dealing with the device. Emily spoke with the various agencies to begin forming a secure perimeter. The FAA was called and asked to temporarily designate the area as a no-fly zone. It would raise the hackles of the media, and they would raise seven kinds of hell about it. But, until they had this thing contained, Emily would deal with the PR crap later.

An agent from the new boat walked over and asked if they would like to come onboard to watch the video stream from the submersible. It was a small space, but everyone crowded around the monitors to see the dull gray-green light showing nothing more than specks of mud and gunk floating past the camera. Then, a shape began to form, and the curve of what appeared to be the end of a metal cylinder filled the screen. There was the small ring on the end, and a dark gap, where the end of the device had partially separated from the rest of the body. The camera took a position just above the device, and then a robotic arm appeared, placing a small sandbag on one side of the device, near but not actually touching the cylinder. The device gently rolled in the other direction, and then settled back against the sandbag. The arm returned with a second bag, placed it on the other side of the device, gently nudged it against the canister, avoiding the opened area so it could be more closely examined.

"Device secured," the NRC radio chirped.

Everyone watching the video exhaled a deep breath, immediately following it with a sheepish look as they realized that this was probably the simplest part of the entire task, and it was far too early for anyone to start relaxing.

The device stopped rocking. As the device stopped moving, the camera did not show the vial inside release the acid that ate through the insulating materials, arming the detonation circuitry. The camera did not tell them that all devices were now fully armed and ready to fulfill their mission.

Chapter 22

"Captain, you need to get downstairs!" the deckhand stuck his head in the pilothouse door. "I don't know what the hell is going on, but those guys are yelling at each other, and it sounds like there's trouble."

"Go get Frank and tell him I need him. Wait! You ever drive a boat?"

"What? Me? Drive a boat? Fuck no Captain. I mean, no sir, never done that."

"Well get over here, and pay attention. It's straight for a while here so if you just keep it pointed in that direction you'll be fine."

The deckhand moved closer but kept one foot outside the door.

"Look, Virgil; you can do this. Hell, you've been telling me that you want to be a pilot someday, so this is as good a time as any to get started. Now get over here."

The young man stood by the chair as the captain quickly explained the basics of keeping ten thousand horses moving in the right direction.

"Hell, the boat pretty much steers itself here, so you just need to keep your eyes open for anything that might get in the way, and just go around it."

The Captain gave Virgil a fatherly smile of encouragement, knowing full well the process is more involved than just going around something. Virgil returned a much weaker smile as Charlie moved away. The young man took a deep breath as he crawled into the seat, put a hand on the primary rudder control, and turned to give the captain a reassuring nod. But the captain was already halfway down the ladder to the main deck, trying to understand the shouts he heard coming from the galley.

The leader was standing in the middle of the room with his hands moving up and down. He was apparently trying to calm the doctor down, standing in front of him with a red face, perspiration on his forehead, shouting with a voice about three octaves above normal.

"But you don't understand!" the doctor shouted. "Now they will come for us! We have to act now, or it will be too late, and all of our work will be wasted."

"Yes, they found a device," the Leader said, "but they do not know how it got there, or even what it is. They know nothing at all about us, or our mission. You must relax."

"But they will find out. They are not fools. They will find out that it came from a boat and they will track us down, and they will..."

"We always knew this was going to happen. But doctor, by the time they do track us down, our system will be fully functional in a few minutes, and then, even if they do find us there is nothing they can do to us."

The Leader saw Charlie in the doorway.

"Ah Captain, we must apologize for this disruption. But as you can see, my team is highly committed to our mission, and are concerned about having it interrupted. But as I have told the doctor, everything has been taken into consideration and has been planned for."

Charlie stepped into the room.

"What happened? Did you say someone found one of the devices?"

"Yes, one has been found. Apparently, the device placed under the Grammercy bridge landed on an old sunken barge. Can you believe that? And by some totally random chance, a passing boat was testing one of their sensors and found the canister. It's almost like a bad movie, who could imagine such a thing?"

"Landed on a barge?"

"Yes. And it was cracked open a bit, allowing radiation to trigger the sensor."

"Wait, how did you find out about it? I've had the radio on and haven't..."

"We have our ways captain, as I have told you. Those of us here on the boat are a small part of the mission and have many friends who are involved in helping us be successful."

Another man entered the galley.

"OK, the GPS-synch is active. Our system is fully operational."

The leader paused, looked to the floor, then slowly walked to the door looking out to the river before turning to the technician.

"How many devices do we have online?"

"Six devices are reporting."

"All six? Excellent."

The leader turned to the others.

"Now gentlemen, our mission is unstoppable. Doctor, put your concerns aside and return to your work. Even if our work is discovered and we are found, no one can touch us. They have no choice but to watch as we complete our work. Our mission will now succeed; it is just a matter of time."

"But wait," the leader turned again to the technician, "are all devices fully armed? All of them?"

"Yes, all six are reporting as armed and ready for use."

Another brief pause.

"Captain, again, I am sorry we have disturbed you here, and I assure you that everything is under control. I'm sure you have other things you need to be doing."

Virgil! For the first time since leaving the pilothouse, Charlie remembered he had left the boat in the hands of an untrained deckhand. Taking steps three at a time he ran to the pilothouse where he found the young man leaning back in the chair, feet up on the console, looking like an old pro. Best of all, the boat was right where it ought to be. Charlie made a mental note that when this mess is over, he has a man to begin whipping into shape for his pilot's exam.

Chapter 23

With the device now secured, Emily returned to the phone to update everyone and to check on the progress of the various groups at work. Mid-call with her boss, her phone vibrated with the option to 'End call and answer.'

"Hello, Emily? This is Linda at Torchwood. I'm sorry to bother you again, but is there any way you could come in and help us with your dad? I thought we had him calmed down after you talked with him, but things have gotten a bit more difficult."

"Hi, Linda. It's, really tough to get away right now. What's going on?" She noticed a different sound in Linda's voice this time.

"Well, he went down to the dining room for a while and was doing just fine, but then he started getting upset again; we're not sure what triggered it. But we had to call security to come and help us get him back to his room. He ended up hitting one of them."

"He hit one of the security guys?"

"Yeah, he may be older, but he's still pretty strong. The guys are both pretty big, but it took both of them to get him back to the bed. He was yelling at them and throwing things at them. He's always gotten along well with Darnell, one of the guards, they talk and joke a lot. But when Darnell tried to talk with him, your dad punched him. And now he's just sitting there getting all worked up and really making himself more upset. Is there any way you could come in and help us?"

Dirty bomb; father. Which one was the most dangerous over the next hour or so?

"Sure, um, ok, I'll be there as quick as I can."

As she ended the call, Elliott walked up.

"Sounds like trouble. You need to go over there and see if you can help. I'll call if anything changes."

They made eye contact just to confirm they both understood this is how friends do things.

"By the way Em, state police just located the truck over in Donaldsonville. They're keeping an eye on it until tactical can get there. It will be quiet for a while, so go help your dad."

Emily walked to her car and headed to Torchwood.

Chapter 24

Joey Santiago sat in a booth near the door, enjoying his burrito dinner. He had skipped lunch, so although it might not be as good as what his wife made, he had no complaints. In fact, he came through Vacherie just so he could stop here, rather than going straight down 3213. He had earned these burritos, so it was worth the extra miles. With all of the delays, Joey wasn't sure just how late it would be before he finally got home tonight, and decided to call his wife to let her know.

Mr. Santiago also did not know about the state police watching him finish his meal as they sat in the alley across the street. He didn't notice them as they followed him out of the parking lot, and then down Highway 20 headed toward South Vacherie, on his way home to Thibodaux.

He was not aware that his rented truck had been identified, and that those following him knew he rented it four days ago, in Thibodaux, and was scheduled to return it there tomorrow morning.

He was not aware of the five vans filled with members of tactical groups from the FBI, the State Police and Homeland Security, all with the one goal of making sure that Joey and his truck did not make it back to Thibodaux.

All that Joey really knew is that he hadn't felt this tired in a long time. He had spent the past three days helping his friend move up to Ponchatoula, from one upstairs apartment to another upstairs apartment, meaning that every box and every piece of furniture was carried down and up three or four dozen steps, around narrow corners and through doors that were not built to carry things through. It hadn't helped that he spent a couple of days helping them pack everything before the move. So overall, while the food had been good, the sleep had been lousy. And why was it that every time you got a rental truck you got one that had problems. The steering on this one was so loose you had to constantly fight it to stay on the road. Between the packing and the carrying and the driving, his arms were dead weights. And just to add to the misery, that lousy dolly kept breaking free from the tie straps, ending up rolling around the back of the truck. To avoid paying extra for any damage, he has had to stop three times and get in the back to tie the thing down again. One of those times was in traffic, right in the middle of a bridge. He fixed it as quickly as he could, but everyone yelled and honked at him, and the people right behind him said some really nasty things. It wasn't his fault he had a lousy rental. It was almost enough to make a good man swear.

He tried hard to focus on the road ahead, shaking his head as he wondered just how this whole trip could possibly get any worse.

Chapter 25

Normal procedure after securing an unknown device was to take steps to identify what the device had been designed to do, and how it intended to do it. Since it was unwise to mess with an unknown device directly, a common step was to send a robot to X-ray the device. The NRC boat followed protocols as they prepared the robot to send back down to get those X-rays.

As before, those watching the monitors on the second boat saw the gray-green water slowly reveal the lines and curves of the device, now resting comfortably between two sandbags. There was no visible movement. As the submersible moved closer, one arm came into view holding a small X-ray unit that could be carefully moved along the length of the device. They completed a full test sweep, to check the currents and make sure there were no surprises that might interfere with full control of the robot. The submersible moved back to the end of the device and positioned itself. Then the video screen went white.

There wasn't time for anyone to ask. Before the surprise registered on their faces, they heard the loud muffled roar. They looked toward the bridge and saw the plume of water being lifted into the sky. As it cascaded back down, it covered them with water, mud, pieces of wood, metal and who knows what else. Water was still falling when the waves hit their boat, tipping it far enough to one side that the river rushed onto the deck, sweeping one crewman into the river. Those on the shore were hit by the mini-tsunami as well, which knocked some to the ground. Windshields shattered from the impact of falling debris.

After the initial shock, and as the mist and smoke subsided, the first thing everyone noticed was that the boat controlling the submersible was no longer there. When the mental haze cleared, other boats began a search and rescue for the men who had been on that boat, ignoring the water, falling debris and possible risk of released radiation.

There were no rescues to be carried out.

It was at times like this that the hours and hours of training paid off. As a group, everyone began to realize that the entire situation had just changed. The threat of a potentially dangerous radiation dispersal device had become a fully involved detonation of an RDD. The threat had become a reality and had taken the lives of three NRC agents. Both the NRC and FBI now had new protocols to implement; protocols that would bring in many more people and organizations. While team members continued their search & rescue, their leaders got to work.

Pete Goodwin, NRC lead, called to Karla, "Where is Agent Graham?"

"She had to deal with a family emergency. We thought she had time."

"Who's next in line there? Where's the head of their joint team?"

"That's Elliott Masterson. I'll get him."

"Yeah, tell him we have a team meeting in five and get Graham back here. Now!"

"Yes, sir."

Karla walked through the mud to where the task force team has set up their temporary base. The group of agents was standing and talking.

"Hey guys, I need Elliott. You know where I can find him? The Chief needs him for a meeting in five."

"I'll take that meeting ma'am; I'm agent Bleyers. I am temporary team lead."

"Where is Agent Masterson? Chief wants him there."

"I understand ma'am," Bleyers said more forcefully than he intended. "But I will handle the meeting. Elliot, uh, Agent Masterson was, on the boat."

Groups like the Joint Terrorism Task Force work hard to build a comradery that created the level of trust needed for group members to put their lives in each other's' hands. Losing a member of that team was fully unacceptable to them, leader or not. The fact that Elliot was more like a father to most of them than a boss made it that much more unacceptable. They knew when the next teams arrived they would be relieved to deal with their loss, but right now they had work to do. Agent Bleyers followed Karla back to the boat where they explained the command change to the chief.

In the darkness up river, the leader was enjoying a cup of warm coffee when the tech guy ran into the galley.

"We just lost number five!"

The leader nodded, took another sip of coffee, and waited for the call that would explain things. He had been through too much to panic so easily.

As the search and rescue came to a close, the survey began to determine how much damage the explosion had done, and most importantly, how much radiation was released. Another group began collecting pieces from the explosion, hoping to learn something that might help make sense of what had just happened.

The Chief started making his phone calls to notify offices that he had just lost three of his NRC agents, along with an FBI agent by the name of Elliott Masterson.

Chapter 26

Highway 20 travels down from Vacheri, eventually getting to Thibodaux. It is a narrow, two-lane road, lined with villages and other small collections of houses and buildings. There is a three-mile stretch just below South Vacherie where the road is surrounded by nothing but mother nature and her critters. A boat ramp with a graveled parking area was where the tactical group decided to carry out their activity. In one more mile, the road came back to civilization, so this was an ideal intercept location.

Joey Santiago had sung every song he knew, and since the truck radio wasn't working, had tried to recall poems his mother used to recite when he was a kid. His arms were numb from fighting the wheel, and his eyes were tired. He was curious why he hadn't seen any traffic coming toward him since South Vacherie but was thankful since he didn't have to work as hard to keep the truck from drifting across the center line.

It was dark and eerie enough that he wished he would pass a house showing some signs of life. He thought about how nice it would be if he was sitting at home, watching television with his family, instead of driving this rented demon through the darkness.

He blinked and rubbed his eyes. It had gotten so bad that now the lights up ahead were flickering, and turning lots of different colors. He glanced at the dark floor for a second to rest his eyes, then looked back to the highway. The bright lights were still blinking and getting much brighter. And now lights appeared in the darkness behind him. He shook his head, opened the window a bit wider and began singing Cielito Lindo at the top of his voice, another of his mother's favorites.

Joey hit the brakes as soon as his brain shouted at him. The truck was surrounded by bright light, and he saw what looked like men walking toward him. But these creatures were clothed in some kind of white suits, and their heads and faces were covered with masks. He remembered the stories his grandmother used to tell him about the abductions in the desert back home. He never paid much attention to them, but they were about spaceships, and about being kidnapped by spacemen in spacesuits; Joey's heart began racing, and it was getting hard to breathe.

Fortunately, this group of aliens spoke English, so Joey was able to dump the idea of alien abduction. Unfortunately, they didn't sound friendly, and he noticed several of them were carrying guns. They yelled at him, telling him not to move, and to turn off the engine. He did.

Some of the suits were carrying equipment, waving it around, under, and up and down the sides of the truck. After a few minutes, one of them yelled, "Clear!", and a bunch of people began moving toward his truck.

Joey Santiago was told to get out, and as he was led to a trailer sitting in the parking area, he saw them opening the doors on the back of his truck.

Over the next three hours, Joey Santiago told and retold his story to many different people. They asked lots of questions, and it felt like they didn't believe him. Finally, he noticed that everyone around looked disappointed, and one of them walked him back to his truck, said they were sorry for any inconvenience, and told him he could go on home.

Joey was glad he had called his wife about being a bit late getting home.

Chapter 27

It was quiet as Emily stepped from the elevator, and she felt a bit of relief. She turned the corner and saw two guys leaning against the wall. They were not the physical specimens she expected, but their uniforms said they were security guys. She swallowed her grin as she thought how they looked like an alternate Laurel and Hardy; one of them short and thin and the other taller and carrying enough weight to be an NFL linemen.

"I'm really sorry you guys," she said. "He really hit one of you?"

They both laughed out loud, and the short guy pointed to the big guy, "Really nailed him too!"

The big guy smiled, "I'll tell you, he's a strong old guy. It took both of us to hold him back and get him to stop throwing things. And just when I thought we had him calmed down, POW, he got me."

"Throwing things?"

"He threw his shoes at me when I wouldn't get out of the room," Linda said, "so that's when I had to call security. I'm really sorry we had to do that."

"Oh no, don't apologize for that. I'm just sorry you had to deal with this."

"Hey, it's fine." the guards said, "It made it an interesting night; things were getting pretty boring around here. I can't wait to get back downstairs and tell everyone how Darnell almost got decked by an 87-year-old."

"Well, thanks for being here guys. What's going on right now? Has he calmed down?"

Linda and Emily moved to her father's door.

"We're going back downstairs. Give us a call if you need us." The two guards engaged in more laughter and backslapping as they headed down the hall.

"I think he realizes he went too far this time," Linda said. "He finally quieted down and had been sitting on his bed. I can't get him to lie down, but I don't want to aggravate him again, so I figure he'll lie down when he gets tired enough. As long as he behaves, we're just fine."

"I'm really sorry; you guys shouldn't have to deal with this."

"Don't worry about it. Most of the time he is a sweetie; teasing and telling stories. I'll bet when the guys come back later he'll be their best buddy; probably won't even remember what happened."

"Ok, well thanks anyway. I guess I'll go in and see what happens."

"Just call if you need me."

Emily took a breath and stepped into the room.

"Hi, dad."

No response from the shape on the side of the bed, staring at its shoes.

"What's going on?" she asked.

The shape turned its head toward her, gave her a 'That's a dumbass question!' look, then turned back to the shoes.

"What's wrong dad?"

"I'll tell you what's wrong. Those sons a bitches stole my shoes...the ones that cost me three hundred dollars."

It wasn't the time to explain again that the orthopedic shoes only cost seventy dollars, so she tried more of a reality approach.

"Nobody stole your shoes, dad. You threw them at someone."

He turned to face her, "Who the hell told you that?"

"You threw your shoes at Linda, so she had to call security, and you ended up hitting one of them."

"That's a god damn lie!" His fists clenched, his eyes focused on her in a way that she couldn't help but step back a bit. "They took my shoes just like they took my billfold, and I even caught one of them stealing my TV set: he thought I was asleep."

"TV set?"

"Yeah, he came in with a ladder and took the damn thing off the wall. I'll bet it's the same son of a bitch that took my shoes."

Emily glanced up at the TV hanging on the wall.

"They're a bunch of god damned liars. Who are they saying I hit?"

"One of the security guys who was..."

"Well, I should have hit the son of a bitch. They came in here to try and throw me off of my own boat goddamn it. They're lucky I didn't throw their asses in the river. What are you doing all the way up here anyway? I thought you were still down in New Orleans."

Her phone vibrated in her pocket, and felt a bit guilty thinking that it gives her an excuse to get away for a few minutes."

"I'll be right back dad. I have to go talk to someone."

"Ok, no problem. Would you hand me that control thing there? I can't hear my program on the TV."

She heard the Bonanza rerun all the way in the hallway. "This is Graham."

"Em, uh, we have a problem."

It was Lennie's voice, but strange.

"Ok, what's up?"

"There's been trouble down at the bridge; at the river."

"They found something else?"

"No, there was, um, an explosion. They were trying to X-Ray the device, and it detonated."

"Detonated? Was anyone hurt? Is everyone ok?"

"Well, the explosion hit the boat...the one with the submersible. There were three NRC guys on it."

"Come on Lennie, are they ok? What's going on?"

"No. they didn't make it. The boat was right over the device when it went."

"Oh man, that's horrible. What about radiation...did the explosion spread a lot of radiation."

"We don't know yet. But Em, there's more."

"More? Ok, what? C'mon Lennie..."

"Em, Elliot was on the boat too."

She realized that Lennie was still talking, but what he said was being sucked into the echo of all of the other sounds around her as the hallway began spinning and swirling around her head, turning everything into a meaningless roar. She had no idea how long it lasted before she felt Linda tapping her shoulder.

"Emily, I think you can go now. He has calmed down again and doesn't even remember what happened. It looks like you've rescued us again! Are you ok?"

The 'Ok' seemed to register, followed by recognizing Linda, the hallway, and finally the phone in her hand.

"I'm fine, yeah. Just, um, yeah, I'm fine."

"Why don't you go on then. We can take care of things here now."

Seconds pass before her brain got her legs to start moving.

As she passed her father's room, she saw the two security guys had come back to check on things. They were sitting in chairs next to the bed laughing. Her dad was telling one of his stories, as they all ate the ice cream bars the guards had brought from the cafeteria. She was at the elevator when she put the phone back to her ear.

"I'm on the way back there now."

The phone went back into her pocket as the doors closed.

Chapter 28

Charlie was thinking about cheeseburgers as he guided the boat into the sharp bend in the river above White Castle, Louisiana. It was a nice break from the other thoughts that had been haunting his mind over the past four hours. As he watched the radar screen to stay in the middle of the channel around Bayou Goula Towhead, the pilothouse door opened. In walked his entire crew.

"Cap', can we talk?"

Smitty had apparently been appointed to speak for the group, most likely because he was Charlie's cousin, but also because he was easy to put in situations others didn't want to be in themselves. He was an outstanding engineer, but had trouble with most everything else in life; because of the booze.

"Well, hell, it looks like we're going to whether I say its ok or not. What's on your minds?"

Smitty glanced at the six men standing behind him, then looked at the floor.

"Well, Cap, we want to know when we're, uh, when the hell we're going to do something...about these assholes on our boat?"

There were nods and grunts of agreement from the others, which gave Smitty a bit more courage to stand up straighter and almost look Charlie in the eye.

"Do something? And just what did you guys have in mind?"

"Shit captain, we've been talking, and we can't just sit here and let these guys blow things up."

It was another crewman, Roosevelt Phelps, born and raised in bayou country.

"Ok, Mr., Phelps, just what do you suggest that we do?", the Captain looked him in the eyes.

The deckhand shuffled his feet, "Hell captain, I don't know. But we just gotta do something here, ya'll know that."

"I'll tell you what I'm by god gonna do." It was Ricky Pratt, a seven-year deckhand from the diamond country of Arkansas. "I'm gonna go out and cut this fucking bracelet thing off my arm and throw the son of a bitch in the river. I feel like some kind of fucking prisoner wearing this thing."

The group started slapping backs and saying other things they were going to do to end this mess on their boat. One voice was heard to say, 'with or without your help!' They became quiet as that voice echoed through the pilothouse. The Captain was not a man you dare to threaten, even lightly; ever. Most boats on the river carried someone who could tell stories of what happened when they had challenged Captain Charlie Graff. None of those stories were pretty.

As the group braced for the explosion, Charlie looked each man in the eye, slowly reached into his shirt pocket and pulled out the photo, held it in front of them and said, "And what about this?"

Every man unconsciously moved their hand over the pocket that held their photo.

"Look, do you think I don't want to stop this bullshit? You think I'm sitting up here pretending it's not happening? Fuck. This is my goddamned boat they're on, going to blow up my god damn river."

Charlie looked out the front window to make sure the boat was still in the channel and then turned back.

"We'll stop the sons a bitches. Nobody climbs on a boat filled with a bunch of hard-assed, good for nothing river-rats like us and gets away with it. That shit just isn't going to happen."

A few nods and smiles appeared.

"But listen, and listen carefully. We have to be smart. These guys are not stupid. We can't just run out there and make some half-assed move."

He paused.

"But we've got time. They plan to drop these things under every bridge on the river before blowing any of them up. I don't know if they're headed to Cincinnati or Minneapolis, but hell, you know as well as I do it's going to take almost two weeks to get this boat to either of those. So get your heads out of your asses. We will do something. I don't know what yet, but we'll figure it out."

It worked. The group was holding photos in their hands and nodding their agreement. Once again, the Captain had demonstrated he had the balls for this job.

"Now get the hell out of my pilothouse. Get back to work or get back in the sack...whatever. But use the brains that God gave you and do your jobs. As long as we're moving this boat up river, we've got time. All we have to do is find the right opportunity. But for now, just do your jobs."

The group moved toward the door as Charlie said, "Smitty, hang around a second."

Each man gave Smitty a look as they left him behind, feeling guilty for setting him up to be the fall guy like this. But the Captain seemed to be in a decent mood, so maybe Smitty would be ok.

"Charlie, I'm sorry, I didn't mean to cause any..."

"Smitty, god damn it, man. When are you going to remember to use your head?"

"I know."

"You can't let those guys set you up like that. How many times has that happened? That's how you got yourself thrown off of your last two boats, remember?"

"Yeah, I know. I don't know Charlie, I just..."

"And I'm not always going to be around to save your ass. I was able to get you hired on here by telling them I'd keep an eye on you. I tell you, Smitty, that booze has fucked up your brain."

Silence. Smitty was a great guy, with a great heart, and worked harder than any three other men. But Charlie understood that something was broken inside. He didn't know what started it, but he knew that the past thirty years of alcohol had done the damage. Even if he hadn't been a cousin, he was the kind of guy Charlie just couldn't help but want to take care of.

"Listen, Smitty, you meant well, I get that. We both want to do something to stop these bastards. But like I told the others, we have to be smart about this, and we can't just start raising hell. Understand?"

"Yeah, I understand."

"Tell me something, when did you have your last drink?"

Smitty looked him in the eyes, "I had a couple the night before coming back on the boat."

"Nothing since?"

"Hell no Charlie, you know I wouldn't bring nothing on the boats. I wouldn't do that."

"I know, I know."

Both men looked briefly out the window.

"I'll tell you one thing you can do for me, Smitty."

Smitty nodded his head.

"You know this boat better than any man on it. I want you to think about something."

"Ok, Charlie."

"At some point, if I ask you to stop this boat, I mean really stop it so that they can't get it running again, I want you to think about how you might go about doing that."

Smitty nodded and smiled.

"Don't blow it up, or sink it, nothing like that. But if we want to just put things out of commission for at least a few weeks, think about how you might do that."

"I'll do that Charlie, I really will. You want something that's really fast?"

"Yeah, Something they won't have time to stop if we do it."

"Roger skipper, I can do it."

"I know Smitty. Now go on back to bed, and we'll talk more in the morning."

"Night skipper."

Smitty walked from the pilothouse like a man with a purpose. Charlie hoped he did enough to stop any more thoughts that might get them, or their families, blown all to hell.

He had long forgotten about cheeseburgers.

Chapter 29

As an FBI agent, Emily had been in many situations you would call dangerous, but none of them had been as high risk as her drive back to the river tonight. Later, she would remember nothing between hanging up the phone on Lennie and arriving at the blockade. She would apologize for hanging up on him. She knew he was going to tell her to go home. He understood that Elliott's death would make this thing personal, and that was something the Bureau frowned on. Personal emotions could interfere with an agent's focus, so when personal and professional lives intersected, questions arose. So after saying she was on her way, she gave Lennie no time for discussion, but she knew it would come. She also knew there was no way anyone is going to take her off of this case regardless of any bureau policy. One way or the other, she was going to do her job and track these assholes down to see that they paid for what they had done.

Chapter 30

Things had clearly changed at the river. Emily found the new barricade at the intersection a mile from the river. She saw the long lines of traffic heading north as the people within that mile were under forced evacuation orders. She wondered if this was just precautionary, or if the radiation was really loose.

After showing her badge, she followed a sheriff's deputy through the emptying streets of Gramercy to the new incident command center in the parking lot of an old factory, about a half mile from the bridge and outside of the mandatory 500-meter secure range. Another time she might have been concerned about the various industrial contaminants that were most likely covering the ground here, but tonight, it didn't even cross her mind.

She joined the group from the second boat now gathered in a big van. Everyone was staring at screens, re-watching the video from the submersible, looking for a clue as to just what had happened. As they restarted it once again, there was no evidence that the submersible had touched the device. Data showed no magnetic fields, radio waves or other sensors the robot may have triggered.

There were others here too, including a new team from the NRC response group who specialized in deconstructing events like this. They usually referred to it as conducting an event post-mortem, but the first time one of them had used that term tonight it was made very clear the term would not be used again. They hadn't meant to sound insensitive to the loss of life, but their responsibility was to figure out what the hell had just happened to make sure that more lives aren't lost. It wasn't that they didn't care that men had died. It was that they cared so much that their focus was intentionally very narrow; to find the exact steps that led to the detonation.

The group turned away from the screens and pulled their chairs together into a little circle.

"Ok, what do we know at this point?"

Tracy Daniels was the head of the decon group. It was her job to pull the best ideas out of the entire group and help them find their best answer. She was smart and knew how to dig in muddy and messy situations and find gold.

"This is a good one. It's like they built this thing to do its job, but also to make sure that if anyone found it first, they would never get a chance to take a good look at it."

"Yeah, and that took some effort. This wasn't put together in somebody's garage." Will Bracken was lead of one of the decon teams.

The conversation began peeling back the layers of the onion they were dealing with, and Tracy kept pulling them back to the primary question for the moment; why did the thing detonate?"

The final hypothesis was that since the detonation appeared to have taken place at the moment the X-ray device was turned on, it must have been the X-rays themselves that triggered the explosion. This was unique and would have taken some time and effort. Whatever this device was designed to do, it was also designed to protect itself very well, and if it felt threatened, to destroy itself and the chance of someone getting a close look at it.

"I think we agree that the main thing we need to stress," Tracy began wrapping up, "is that whoever designed and built this thing has some serious expertise. We'll learn more if we can find enough pieces to model it, but like Will said, this is not somebody's garage or basement project."

"What are you suggesting agent Daniels?"

Pete Goodwin was still the lead NRC agent in charge of the incident, though everyone knew that was about to change.

Tracy Daniels stood and turned to him, "I think it is safe to say a few things, sir. First, that this is not the work of some loner wanting to make a point or get attention. There are too many areas of expertise involved. Second, to have that level of expertise requires several people with advanced understanding and skills in some rather unique fields, and you don't find a lot of those people around. Third, considering the extreme steps they took to keep the devices from being inspected; we have to ask why someone would take such extreme measures to keep that a secret."

"Unless..."

It was Will again.

"Unless what?" Both Pete Goodwin and Tracy Daniels turned to face the young man still sitting in the circle.

"Unless it's not the only one."

He had everyone's attention. Emily found herself pushing toward the circle.

"Unless they wanted to make sure we didn't get lucky and disarm this one, so we could then find out how to disarm others. I mean, that's how I would do it."

Pete Goodwin's phone interrupted the silence. He listened to the report from the tactical team that stopped Joey Santiago, stuck the phone back in his pocket and rubbed his forehead.

"It wasn't the truck. The device didn't come from the truck."

Several conversations began at once. Agent Goodwin raised a hand in the air and quieted things down.

"So, let's see if I understand this," Goodwin said. "We have a device; one that had to be created by very special people with very special skills, and who want to keep us from getting a good look at it, because they may have more of these things out there somewhere. And this one didn't come from the truck that we thought dropped it. So, we still don't know where the hell the thing came from. Is that what I'm hearing?"

He wasn't really looking for an answer, so no one offered one.

"Sir," Goodwin's number two asked, "earlier we put teams on call to scan under a couple of other bridges, like Hale Boggs and Huey Long, do you want us to send them in now, just to make sure..."

"No, no, not now. We only found this one because it was cracked. And we can't send teams in there if these things are set to blow up if they're found. We need to know more first. Tell those teams to hold for now. Ok people, it's time to escalate. Renshaw, get Washington on the line. Agent Graham, you need to notify your people that the FBI is now in charge of this investigation. Good luck."

Chapter 31

Frank went on watch as the boat passed the Plaquimine Ferry Landing, or the Sunshine Ferry landing, depending on which side of the river you were on. The ferry didn't run between seven in the evening and eight in the morning, so the only thing he had to keep an eye on was the stack of barges tied up on the eastern side of the river. Frank smiled as he guided the boat, thinking of the reasons he wanted to be a pilot in the first place. Not just anybody could do this. If you missed a step, even for a second or two, you could end up knocking the barges loose from the shore, or let your tow drift from the channel and end up ass deep in the mud, or you could really screw the pooch and hit that other boat, leading to phone calls and lawyers really messing up your night. Every pilot made a mistake now and then, but the really good ones avoided the mistakes that left too many dents and bruises.

While Frank drove the boat, the activity at Grammercy Bridge staging area continued. After making the necessary calls, Colonel Goodwin, Agent Renshaw, and Emily Graham headed home for a few hours of sleep. Their people knew how to do their jobs, so they took the time needed to get ready for what was sure to be a long morning. Sleep did not come easily. They each lay in their beds running the images from the video screen through their heads, and hearing the same words over and over again, 'Unless it's not the only one.'

As Emily finally drifted into sleep, Frank was keeping one eye on the small cabin cruiser approaching from the western bank near the Union Petro plant. He stepped out onto the gangway to watch it pull near enough to transfer the two devices to the doctor's crew. As he stepped back inside, the radar was just revealing the echo of the I-10 Horace Wilkinson Bridge at Baton Rouge.

At the Grammercy staging area, the teams were reviewing the initial reports from those investigating the impact of the explosion. It was far better news than anyone had anticipated. There was no visible structural damage to the bridge or its supports. The river channel had been messed up a bit, but the Corps of Engineers would be able to bring in a dredge and clean that up. But the best news came as NRC Agent O'Donnel described the early results of the radiation studies.

"We haven't found anything more than the small traces we saw before the explosion. It has spread out a lot more of course with the blast, but the levels are actually lower because of being spread out like that. Apparently, the detonation was a lot weaker than it was supposed to be, probably because of the damage we saw to the device before the detonation. Instead of being powerful enough to rupture the canisters containing the radioactive materials, it just distributed those canisters intact, not dispersing radiation. We have found two of those canisters, one underwater near the blast, and one on the side of the levee. From the size of the device, we are guessing there may be two or three more canisters still out there somewhere. But again, none of them appear to have dispersed their contents, so it appears that we have reasonable containment at this time."

The smile on Emily's face was not because of the good news at the meeting but was from the waves lapping against her toes as she sat on the beach, holding a cold margarita and staring at the sunset. It was a recurring dream, and one she never regretted. Normally, as the sun lowered itself into the water, she looked up at the stars and listened to Jimmy Buffett singing Margaritaville as he stood next to her there in the sand. But tonight, instead of singing Margaritaville, Jimmy was playing some stupid instrument that was making some really irritating buzzing sound, ruining the entire mood. As she turned to ask him what the hell he was doing, the light from the phone hit her optic nerve, and her brain began yelling, 'PHONE!'. She raised it to see the caller ID displaying Torchwood. The clock on the phone said three o'clock as she swiped the button.

"Hello." She said halfheartedly.

"Hey Emmy, it's dad."

What struck her first was that it actually sounded like her father.

"Dad?"

"Hey, I'm really sorry about earlier, I know you were just trying to help. I just don't know what happened. They said I hit someone; is that true?"

"Yeah, I guess so dad. That's what they told me."

"Shit. I honestly don't remember any of that at all. I just don't know what the hell is going on anymore; I just don't know."

"It's ok dad, they all understand. Before I left you were all in there telling stories and eating ice cream, so it's not a problem."

The fog continued to lift from her mind as she focused on the first real conversation with him in weeks.

"I know, it's not a problem for them, yeah, ok. But I just don't know how much more of this I can take. I just don't know what's going to happen..."

His voice trailed off, then returned.

"You know, I sit here and think a lot. Think about the things I've done and if it really accomplished anything."

"Now dad,"

"Well dammit, I do. I mean, I spent most of my time sitting on those damn boats going up and down the river, and what did it get me. I mean, look!"

"Dad, you were always there when we needed you, and..."

"Not as much as I wanted to be. You did most things without me. Sometimes it felt like no one ever really needed me. I mean, I drove those boats back and forth, going right through the middle of towns and cities and no one even noticed us going by. It was like I was invisible or something. Hundreds of cities and no one ever cared. What difference did it make? Hell, I could have done more for you if I had stayed home and sold cars."

These were the hard conversations. Honestly, his failing memory sometimes made things easier because he didn't carry all of these regrets around with him. No matter how much reassurance she gave, it didn't take his pain away. He did miss a lot of birthdays, and holidays, and plays and concerts. But Emily always realized that was just a part of the deal. Would she have rather had him there? Of course. But there was a good side to it as well. When he was home from the boat, he was completely home for thirty days, and sometimes more. There was no nine-to-five schedule, so sometimes when he came home, they just loaded up the camper and took off, coming back home in time for him to catch the next boat. Those were magic times and almost made up for all the rest of it.

"You know dad, I was thinking last night and remembering that trip we took to Cape Hatteras. Remember that?"

"Yeah, that was a good trip. But it sure has changed a lot. I was out there last week and couldn't even find that little campground we stayed in."

And that quickly, he was gone. The conversation turned to how hard it was to find a good pizza place anywhere near the hotel there in Chicago before he told her he needed to go take Duke out for a walk. Emily thought about Duke, the Labrador Retriever they had back around 1975, and as he hung up, she told him she hoped they had a great walk.

As she put her phone back on the table, an agent discovered a third container from the Grammercy Bridge device, about a hundred yards up the side of the levee, and Frank watched the city lights of Baton Rouge go by as the I-10 bridge moved silently over his head.

Chapter 32

"Emily, it's Lennie. Sorry to call so early, but we need you at a meeting. How quick can you get back to the river?"

She looked at her phone. Her dad's call ended just after three, and now the numbers looked something like a four.

"Uh, I can be there in, um, about an hour; I really need a shower."

"Make it 45 minutes. You can jump in the river if you need it that bad."

"You're a funny man this early in the morning."

He didn't laugh.

"See you in forty-five," and the line goes dead.

Thirty-seven minutes later Emily got out of her car at the staging area. Lennie was standing outside a van that hadn't been there earlier, along with a half-dozen other trucks and trailers that had brought a hundred new people to play.

"Em, thanks for rushing it." Lennie risked the "Em" part, and she let it slide.

"You need to know that there's probably going to be some noise to pull you from the case. I mean, with your, uh, with, you know...Elliot."

"Yeah, we'll see about..."

"But we need you here right now. And I'll do my best to keep you here if that's what you want. If you think you can handle it?"

"Thanks, Lennie. I'm fine."

The van was an incident response command vehicle, filled with technology, lots of people, and a full-size conference room. Lennie and Emily took the two empty chairs as she looked around at the others. Since the FBI currently controlled the investigation, Lennie did the brief introductions. Emily recognized the two NRC agents from earlier and heard names of the new people from the NRC, Homeland Security, the New Orleans District of the Corps of Engineers, the Louisiana Department of Transportation (LaDOT), and several local law enforcement and emergency response agencies.

"I need to introduce one other person who is still on his way here."

Emily hadn't noticed the speaker in the center of the table.

"Agent Arturo Dasilva is on his way from D.C. and will be assuming command of the FBI side of the activity."

"Thank you all for coming on such short notice," Dasilva said through the speaker. "Agent Ryan will brief you on the basics of what we're dealing with, recognizing that we have already lost four very good people here."

Agent Dasilva mentioned the names of those lost, and brief words of support were spoken around the circle.

Now Emily understood Lennie's comment about being pushed from the case. She didn't know Dasilva well, but remembered him from previous meetings and knew that he was one of those agents who likes the book, and had a way of getting what he wants. That's how he got to D.C. in the first place. Lennie seemed to know where her mind was going and his elbow brought her back to the table.

"I arrive in New Orleans at eight o'clock," Dasilva said, "and will be coming directly to the staging area. We will have a full briefing meeting at nine o'clock sharp. I expect to have more details before I get there. Now let's get to work."

Lennie opened the laptop in front of him.

"But before I go," Dasilva said, "did I hear Agents Goodwin, Renshaw and Graham being introduced?"

"Yes sir, they are here."

"I want to say how sorry I was to hear of the loss of members of your teams. That is something we absolutely want to avoid, and something that we will not lose sight of as we move forward. However, I will remind you that policies are very clear at this point. We will make every effort to keep you informed about progress in this situation, but you need to have the time to deal with the personal impact of what has happened. With that in mind, you are formally relieved from any further involvement in this situation as of now. Again, we appreciate the work you have done thus far. Thank you."

They heard Dasilva disconnect from the line.

Lennie stared at the laptop screen. Others in the circle glanced around the group with a mix of understanding, surprise, concern, while Agents Goodwin, Renshaw and Graham looked at each other knowing that their involvement in this situation had not changed. They stayed in their seats as Lennie began the summary.

After reviewing the basics of what had taken place over the past eighteen hours, Lennie began cutting new ground.

"The NRC has an update for us on the radiation risk. Agent Goodwin, fill us in."

"Thank you. Fortunately, our current analysis supports the survey conducted immediately following the explosion. There were multiple containers inside the device that hold the radioactive materials. However, it appears that the containers were not damaged in the blast, and there is no evidence of any release of radiation."

Nods and relief all around the table.

"At least three of those canisters have been located, and based on their size, and the size of the device itself, we believe there may be two or three additional containers still missing. But again, there is no sign that any of those containers have dispersed any radiation. "

Lennie attempted a smile, "Thank you, Agent Goodwin; we can use some good news like that this morning."

"Do we know why the containers did not disperse the materials?" A local law enforcement member asked. "They aren't on some kind of delay or something, are they?"

Lennie nodded to Goodwin to respond, "No, we believe it's because the device was damaged when it landed on the barge. Devices like this are usually designed to direct the force of a detonation in a very specific way, creating enough force to shatter the canisters and disperse their contents. We believe the damage reduced the direct force of the explosion and ended up just scattering the canisters rather than shattering them."

Everyone seemed satisfied, so Lennie continued.

"Ok, as Agent Goodwin said, the first report from the technical team is in agreement with the conclusions of the NRC agents last night.

This was not a simple device and would have required several people with some very specific skills in some highly-sophisticated areas. A behavioral investigation team is preparing profiles of the types of individuals who might be involved, and where they might come from. We hope to have an initial report from them by midday."

The behavioral teams were made up of a mix of psychologists, sociologists and others who had some unique understanding of human thinking and behavior. Rather than focusing on the device, they asked questions like:

What might someone be trying to do with a device like this? What kind of person might think like that? What kind of person had the ability to create this? Where might that kind of person spend their time? Who might that person associate with? Where might that person be right now, and where might they be going? Might that person be sane and just angry, meaning we might be able to use reasoning with them, or might that person be someone well beyond reason?

It was part science, part intuition, part hunch, and involved a lot of 'mights.' But this type of behavioral analysis had repeatedly proved to be an invaluable asset in cases like the Unabomber.

Lennie continued, "The behavioral team also agrees with the idea that there may be other devices involved. They rank the possibility of other devices at a ninety percent level."

There were mumbles and shaking heads around the table as Goodwin joined in.

"Last night we made the decision to not attempt to search other bridges for devices at that time, but, based on this information, we are going ahead and taking that step. The plan is to use fully passive search methods, which is how we accidentally found the first device. It may be that we only found it because of the leaks from the damage, but we believe it is worth the attempt. We currently have NRC boats in route to the Hale Boggs Bridge, downriver from here, as well upriver to the Sunshine Bridge. We should have reports from them by the nine o'clock meeting."

"Do they actually believe someone was able to transport these devices across that much territory?" The question was from the Department of Transportation. "We have radiation sensors at multiple locations throughout the city and metropolitan area. I think it's quite a stretch to think..."

Lennie smiled politely, recognizing the possibility of bruising the ego of a powerful organization. "We don't know what to believe yet. We found the first device because it was damaged. Otherwise, the NRC sensors would most likely have passed right over it. It is possible we are dealing with people who have designed something far better than our current technology is prepared for. At this point, we need to see what we can learn."

"I have a question, if I may." One of the local law enforcement officers raised a hand.

"Certainly."

"We are getting pressured to release something to the media. The explosion last night, the evacuation, and now this massive response, do we have information to release at this point to kind of soothe the hounds? Can we tell them that a device was found, but that there doesn't appear to be any real danger at this point?"

Everyone smiled at the image of the hounds.

"No. There is to be no mention of a device. That will just spark more questions. Trust me; we've been down this path before."

"We need to say something, don't we?"

"Yes. For now, we are saying that there was an incident in the river near the Grammercy Bridge that was fully limited to that area. There was no damage to the bridge and no damage to anything around the bridge. The river will remain temporarily closed while the channel is rebuilt, and to avoid congestion so the work can be completed more quickly the immediate neighborhood will remain under mandatory evacuation. That won't satisfy them for long but should hold them until we know more. Does everyone understand?"

As the group talked among themselves, Emily glanced at Lennie. Sometimes she forgot how capable he was in tough situations. When you spend so much time doing the mundane stuff, you can forget just who everyone really is.

"Alright then, I think that covers it for now. I'd like everyone to prepare an update from your teams for the next meeting. I'll see all of you back here at nine o'clock."

Emily gave him a grin as she stood up, "Yes you most certainly will."

Chapter 33

Frank had become used to taking abuse for his morning cup of tea. Everyone else drank the strong dark coffee from the never-empty pot, as he put green tea leaves and honey into the fresh hot water. Some in the galley were, like him, getting off shift and heading for bed, while others were going to work. Every morning he sat with his cup, talking and taking abuse, until he was the last one in the galley, finishing a few more sips before heading to his cabin.

He stared at the leaves in the bottom of the cup and wondered what they might be saying about him this morning. The door opened, and the leader walked in with the doctor and Lawrence; the guy who designed the devices.

"But why didn't it disperse as it was supposed to? That's what I need to know. Oh, hello Frank, finished with your watch?"

Frank looked up, nodded, and returned to his tea, as the leader continued.

"Frank, we were just discussing something you might be interested in. We just learned that one of our devices was detonated late last night; the one that landed on the barge at Grammercy Bridge."

Frank looked up from his tea.

"And unfortunately, it appears that four people were killed, which as you know is not at all what we wanted to happen."

If Frank was supposed to offer a comment, he didn't.

"But it also appears that the device did not work as planned, and did not disperse the materials inside. Since that is the entire point of the devices, we need to figure out why."

The leader looked at the doctor and his helper. Lawrence was the one to speak.

"I believe I can answer your question. The message we received said the canister had been damaged when it landed on the barge."

"But they said there was just a small crack." The leader shook his head.

"Yes, but even a small crack might do it. The explosion has to focus enough force in one direction to fracture the individual containers inside, to release the materials. That requires a specific form, and if that form is altered, the force is reduced. It is not a simple design, and that doesn't even include the need for the heat reduction..."

"Never mind about that now Lawrence," the doctor interrupted, "that has no impact on our question here...it is not important now."

"What about heat reduction?" the leader asked.

"Nothing to deal with at this point, I assure you." the doctor said. "We don't want things melting before they are able to do what they need to do; that is all. But I believe Lawrence is correct in his analysis, and we have nothing to be concerned about with the other devices."

The leader looked at the two men, as the doctor continued.

"If there is nothing else, I need Lawrence to help me in the workroom."

The leader nodded and turned to Frank.

"Frank, you look pensive this morning."

Frank stared into his cup.

"Did you have a good watch?"

Silence. The leader stood by the open door.

"Things are moving ahead on our end. We passed the Audubon Bridge a while ago, but of course, you know that."

Silence. The leader looked out the door.

"I see we're just passing the old St. Francisville Ferry landing. They shut that down a few years ago when they opened the bridge. Maybe after we complete our mission, they'll have to rebuild that old dock and start using those old ferries again."

Silence.

"Probably not here, though, its too close to the bridge. Maybe down closer to Baton Rouge. I guess we'll see. But wherever they put it, things are going to move a lot slower than they do now. That will shake things up pretty good, don't you think?"

Silence.

Frank got up from his seat, walked to the small kitchen to rinse his cup and put it on the shelf.

"Frank, I'm trying to be polite here."

Frank walked across the galley to the door and turned to the leader.

"You son of a bitch."

"Frank, what the hell is wrong with you?"

"I'll tell you what's wrong with me. I've had it with your crap, and I've had it with this fucking mission of yours."

"Frank, you need to calm down."

"Calm down? Fuck your calming down! You promised me that no one was going to get hurt. You fucking lied to me. This whole thing is one big fucking lie. You used me."

"Frank, no one is using you. And I didn't lie to you. I told you that we didn't want anyone to be hurt and I meant it. Nothing has changed since we first talked."

"Four people are dead. And what about Danny?"

"Ah, I see. Yes, Danny."

"Yeah, Danny. What about him? That wasn't part of the deal."

"Frank, what you don't realize is that Danny was part of the team, just like us."

Frank's eyes narrowed.

"Frank, what did you know about Danny?"

"Well, not too much, this was his first trip with us. He didn't talk much, but he was one hell of a worker. Too good to waste like that. That boy had a future on the boats."

"Frank, he was more of a worker than you know. Danny is a tragic story, but not for the reasons you are thinking of. He was a wonderful young man; an eagle scout, great athlete, the kind of kid who would do anything to help anyone. His plan was to go into medicine; maybe become a doctor. That's what led him to the military, and what got him into special services and that stretch in Iraq. He spent his time taking care of people in the hot zones; treating chemical and radiation victims. And that's where things went bad."

The leader's eyes moved to the open door.

"After getting out, and after the leukemia had started up, he went to the VA for help. Just like Susan found, they ran him around in circles until it was too late to do anything at all. He went back to school, more to keep busy than anything else, and that's where he met Susan; our Susan. Unfortunately, his illness progressed a lot faster than hers, and it became more difficult for him to continue at school. One day they were talking, and he told her he wanted to commit suicide and end the pain, but it felt too much like giving up; like losing. That's when she introduced him to the doctor. It was clear there was nothing that could be done to cure him, so they came up with a way that he could end his pain, and do something meaningful at the same time. The young man had no future on the boats, or anywhere else for that matter."

"So, his being shot..."

"Was all part of the plan, yes. We got him on the boats so he could learn what he needed to get the job here. You said he didn't socialize much. After working his watch, he had to go to bed to deal with the pain; his leukemia had become more difficult over the past two months. For a while, we were concerned that he wouldn't be able to make this trip, but he insisted. This was his way to do one more thing he hoped would help someone."

"I had no idea."

"I know Frank. None of us know everything that is going on here; that's how it has to be done. Now go get some sleep. We need you at your best. Remember, business as usual."

"Yeah, business as usual."

They shook hands as Frank stepped from the galley.

Chapter 34

"You knew I would be here, didn't you?" He smiled as he pulled out the chair and sat at the table. "You knew I couldn't resist finding out just what the heck you were talking about yesterday."

His grandfather smiled and took a long sip from what looked to be some kind of coffee and chocolate thing.

"I'm glad you're here."

"So, what is this big mystery you want to talk about?"

The older man's eyes narrowed, "First, go get yourself something to drink. I told my friend up there to fix you up one of my special drinks; here, use my card."

His eyes never left his grandson as he watched him walk to the counter and return with his mug. He was certainly the right man for the role, but was it really the right thing to do? And was this the right time? He knew the boy would grow into this man, and at some point, he would assume the role. But was this the time?

"I'm not sure just what this is, but it looks good," the grandson slid back into his seat as he took a first sip. "Oh yeah, excellent. You know your coffee like you know your fish."

"Ronnie, are you sure about this?" He was clearly not asking about the coffee.

"Well, yeah. I am. I mean, if there is a way I can do something to make more of a difference; you know, to do things that might have real meaning; then yeah, I want to know more about it."

"I know Ronnie. But this is not like something you read from a book, like the seven steps to making a difference. It's not something you learn and then bring it out and use when you need to. Honestly, it will change everything in your life. You need to be sure you want that."

"You said it would not hurt my family."

"Yes, this will have no direct impact on them or anyone else for that matter. The changes will be in you."

The younger man's eyes narrowed.

"I know what you are thinking. I remember having this conversation myself with my grandfather, and I began to wonder if the old man had lost his mind. But as he talked, I began to think that if he had done this, then it was something I wanted to do as well."

Silence as they both examined the froth on their coffee.

"So, you've been doing this, this role?"

"For some 60 years now, yes."

"Well then, that's good enough for me."

"Just one more thing Ronnie. As I said, everything will change, including our relationship."

The old man looked into his grandson's eyes.

"We will share things that no one around us will ever share; think and feel things that no one around us will ever think or feel. To others, nothing will change. But for us, there will be things that only you and I will know about and understand. And Ronnie, some of those will be hard things, difficult and sometimes painful things. We will live with them and will carry them with us, and no one around us will know. But we will have each other, and you will find that is more than enough."

"And we will make a difference?"

"More than you have ever imagined."

"I'm ready."

"One last thing before you agree. If you take this step, you must understand that you can never turn back from it; never give up the role once you have learned of it. No matter how difficult it might become, you cannot walk away from it."

"Grandpa, is this illegal?"

The old man showed a broad and satisfied smile.

"There now, that is the Ronnie I was counting on. That is the question that should be asked; excellent. No, there are no laws against anything you will do in this role. Do you have any other questions?"

"Just one. You decided to accept the role when your grandfather offered it to you. Looking at it today, did you make the right choice?"

The smile remained.

"Ronnie, I'll admit there have been times it has been difficult, but yes, I know I made the right choice."

"Then it is my choice too."

They stood, the grandfather embraced his grandson and looked into his eyes once again.

"Then it shall begin."

The grandfather turned, walked to the door and was gone. Ronnie reached for his mug and saw the note on the napkin.

"Tomorrow, 7:00am, here."

Chapter 35

Some FBI agents have a look that makes them ideal candidates for undercover work; a natural look that can blend into a crowd, unnoticed and at ease. Agent Arturo Dasilva was not that kind. He was one of those agents who could walk into a room stark naked, yet everyone would say, "There's a cop."

And Agent Dasilva had no problem with that. It went along with his commitment to the book; to following orders and making every effort to see that others did the same. Since entering the academy, he had excelled at most everything presented to him. When he met another agent who showed the right level of ability and commitment, Dasilva would do everything in his power to support and guide that agent. But when his path crossed an agent he saw as less than able or committed, he took it as his responsibility to remove that blight from his agency.

To Agent Arturo Dasilva, Emily Graham fell somewhere between those two positions. She seemed capable, and to have a commitment to the agency, but there was something wrong. They had entered the academy at the same time, but now he was in a big office in the D.C. headquarters, and she was in a regional office, certainly not a hotbed of criminal activity. He had been puzzled when he heard she had requested that placement. Whatever the problem was, he had already taken the steps to avoid having to deal with Agent Graham during this trip.

Even with his poker skills, Agent Dasilva had to focus to avoid showing his reaction as he entered the conference room and saw her at the table. He made the necessary introductions, until he came to Lennie, with Agent Graham at his side.

"Special Agent Ryan, it's good to see you again. The last time was Chicago if I recall." Dasilva shook Lennie's hand.

"Agent Dasilva," Lennie said. "I hope you had a good flight."

Dasilva's eyes had already left this conversation and were focused on Emily. The eyes narrowed and the smile on his mouth mutated to something different.

"And Agent Graham I believe. How nice to see you."

The handshake was more of a grip that did not end.

"Please accept my condolences for the loss to your team. Agent Masterson was a very good man."

It was partly the unending grip, partly the tone of voice, and partly the look in his eyes that caused Emily to grit her teeth.

"Thank you."

"But I am somewhat confused. I believe I was quite clear about following regulations in this situation. You do recall the agency's policy regarding proper response to personal loss?"

"Yes sir, I understand the regulations."

"Ah good." He released her hand and turned his gaze to the rest of the room as if she had suddenly disappeared. "Then we won't keep you."

Moments later, He looked back from the group and saw her still there.

"Is there a problem Agent Graham?"

"I asked Emily to remain in the meeting this morning," Lennie said. "We both understand the regulations fully, sir, but Agent Graham is one of the few people who has been involved in this situation since it began, and may provide important details. I believe regulations allow for this type of exception when circumstances warrant it."

Dasilva smiled.

"Of course. If Agent Graham should have something meaningful to offer, we certainly want to give her that opportunity."

Dasilva turned away. Emily punched Lennie on the shoulder as they exchanged smiles.

"Thanks."

"No problem. I meant what I said. But after this meeting, you really do need to get away for a while. Ok?"

"Sure Lennie; whatever you say."

Lennie knew better.

As he found his seat at the table, Agent Dasilva took a moment to make brief eye contact with each person and began.

"Good morning everyone. Thank you for being on time."

Good mornings echoed all around the table.

"We have a lot to cover here, so let's get to it. But first I want to explain that, even though regulations are quite clear about the matter, I have asked Agent Graham to participate in our meeting this morning. She has been involved in things since soon after they began, so she may have some insight to offer. I am happy to see Agents Goodwin and Renshaw here from the NRC as well since they bring that same overall perspective."

He paused and looked at papers in his hand.

"I was just given an update from the NRC regarding the canisters that have been recovered containing the radioactive elements. As you know, those types of elements have what are called signatures, which can be used to identify where the elements are from."

Everyone around the table knew at least as much about radioactive signatures as Agent Dasilva; most of them far more.

"Unfortunately, in our case, there appear to be numerous signatures identified, suggesting that we actually have a diverse mix of elements being used in these devices."

"We sometimes refer to that as a casserole." Agent Goodwin said.

"Yes, thank you, Agent, uh, Goodwin. What is important is that it means it will take longer to trace these signatures. So, we'll have to wait to see what we might learn there."

"But why would someone use this casserole approach? Is there an advantage to it?" The question came from a local agency member looking directly at Agent Goodwin. Goodwin turned to Agent Dasilva.

Dasilva nodded, "Go right ahead Agent Goodwin, this is in your area, not mine."

"There's not necessarily an advantage to it. It probably just means these people collected whatever radioactive materials they could find and put them together to make the devices. It is difficult to collect enough material to create this type of device, which is the primary reason we've not seen more of this kind of thing. It's not technically difficult to build an RDD, hell, the instructions are on the Internet. The problem is finding enough stuff to put in them."

A buzzing sound was heard. This time Lennie forgot to turn off his cell phone. He nodded at the grins around the table. Even Dasilva smiled; sort of. Lennie got up from the table, listened, then sat back down.

"They've found another device; this one under Hale Boggs."

Silence; then everyone spoke at once.

"A second device?" Agent Dasilva said.

"Yes. They're ninety percent sure. It's buried three or four feet in the mud, but there are traces of the same kinds of radiation as the first device. It's a lot weaker, which could be the mud, or could be because this one isn't damaged." Lennie reviewed the stream of messages hitting his phone, and now hitting everyone else's as well.

"I'm being told another team believes they may have something up at Sunshine as well." Agent Goodwin said.

"What the fuck..." Someone said it. Everyone thought it.

"Their sensors show something in the mud, about the right size, but it's deeper and better covered. It's actually kind of funny."

All eyes turned to Agent Goodwin.

"Excuse me?" Dasilva said. "Please help me understand the humor in this situation Agent Goodwin."

"Well, maybe funny isn't the right word. But, we found the first canister by accident while we were testing one of the sensors, right? Well, this time, they were pulling the sensor under the Sunshine Bridge when the coupling came loose, so the sensor came loose and fell to the bottom, partly burying itself in the mud. That's when it pinged the radiation. If it hadn't broken loose, we wouldn't have gotten the ping. Maybe not funny, but quite a coincidence."

Silence.

"Ok people, let's get on top of this." Agent Dasilva said. "This makes two known devices and a third possible."

"Probable." Agent Renshaw said.

"A third probable, yes. So, I think it's clear that we need to take this to the next level. Agent Goodwin, do your people have the resources available to fully identify and secure these new devices, and do a full search of more bridges?"

"No sir, not under these circumstances. Our normal task is to scan materials in the harbor, onboard ships, on the docks, not under fifteen feet of water and another six feet of mud. As I said, our role so far has been a coincidence."

"Then who does?"

Goodwin and Renshaw put their heads together, joined by three or four others.

Goodwin finally turned back to the table, "Sir, under these conditions, we believe the best option is to ask the NNSA to send an ARG Initial Response Team. No one else has their resources and experience with this kind of thing."

Heads nodded all around the table.

"For those who aren't familiar," Goodwin looked around the table, "the Accident Response Group is a team from the National Nuclear Security Administration that is ready to respond to any accident or significant incident involving nuclear weapons, providing three phases of action. Phase one is the initial response, which involves sending a six-person team to find the weapons and conduct an initial risk assessment. Phase two, the recovery operation, usually involves thirty-eight people with the ability to conduct a twelve-hour operation to safely recover the weapons. Phase three, or follow-on response, involves thirty-four people who expand the previous phases to fully remove and dispose of the nuclear weapon."

Goodwin paused.

"That seems pretty extreme Agent Goodwin," said Dasilva. "Are you sure we need to take that kind of step at this point?"

"Sir, as we speak, we have one detonation that requires cleanup, and may have two devices sitting under two major bridges in the New Orleans metropolitan area, each filled with casseroles of radioactive materials, fully capable of blowing themselves up and spreading those elements over a large part of the river, and the shore around it. Those need to be secured. And let's be blunt, we've only looked at three bridges so far, and all three had devices. There are three more bridges even closer to the city that we've not looked under. And even if we could find these things ourselves, we have no idea what to do with them. The best approach we tried so far has cost us three lives. Yes, I believe the situation is extreme enough now."

Agent Dasilva paused.

"Then that's what we do."

The table erupted again in side conversations and instant messaging, as Dasilva continued.

"Ok, that addresses the next step for the devices. There is another issue we need to pursue, and that is what we do to find out who is creating these devices and just how they are getting them into the water. Agent Ryan, where do we stand on that?"

Dasilva knew exactly where things currently stood. He had read the reports on the plane. He knew that the one solid lead had turned out to be some guy moving furniture and that no other key evidence had been uncovered. But this provided an opportunity to repay Lennie for his action with Agent Graham.

Lennie described the work that had been done, including Mr. Joey Santiago. He described the directions being taken in the investigation, and the expertise of all those involved.

"So, if I understand you correctly," Agent Dasilva said, "eighteen hours after beginning this investigation, we still don't actually know anything about what is going on, who is behind it and why. Is that correct?"

"I wouldn't put it that way, but..."

"I mean no disrespect Agent Ryan, I know the capabilities of the agency and am fully confident that you are doing everything you have been trained to do in a situation like this. And I also realize that while the FBI has control of this investigation, it is only one of the groups attempting to solve this puzzle."

Dasilva paused to look around the table.

"I just don't understand why nothing has been found yet, not one substantial clue. Its not like these people, whoever they are, are invisible or something."

A synapse sparked somewhere in the depths of Emily's brain. All she noticed was the desire to squirm in her seat as her heart rate increased and her muscles tensed. She blamed it on the comments being made by Agent Arturo Dasilva.

"With all of the videos available, all of the ability to monitor the transportation of radioactive materials, with all of the resources we have available to us, it is difficult to see how someone could just stroll right through a major city, putting bombs under our bridges, without anyone even seeing them."

Emily's eyes widened as the neuron chain reached her consciousness. Just like her heart rate and tension, she heard herself automatically saying, "It's a boat."

Only Lennie heard it, and he turned to her, "What did you say?"

Agent Dasilva paused to recognize Lennie's unprofessional interruption.

"Lennie, it's a boat. It's a goddamn boat. That's how they're doing it."

"Are you sure? How do you know?"

"I know. Its a boat."

"Excuse me, Agents," Dasilva said. "Is there something you want to share with the rest of us here?"

"It's a boat. That's how they're doing it. A boat." Emily's eyes were wide.

"A boat." Dasilva once again smiled, but Emily was rolling to fast to see it.

"It's a boat. Like you said, they're just moving up the river like everyone else, with no one paying any attention to them. No one notices, and no one cares. Yes...they are as good as invisible." It all comes out fast and clear, just like she's hearing it from her mind. She smiles because she can actually see the thing slowly passing through the city, doing what every other boat does; almost.

"Ok, let's assume it could be a boat," Dasilva said. "Do you realize how many boats go up and down the river every day, or even each hour?"

"No!" Emily wasn't talking to Agent Arturo any longer. She was putting pieces together and throwing them out there for anyone listening.

"Think about it. Just for a minute, think about it. If you wanted to put these things under bridges, why would you use the roads? Like you said, we monitor transportation of that stuff, doing it that way would be way too tough."

The transportation people nodded and smiled at the compliment.

"So why not just use the river? And if you don't want to be seen, you don't want to use one of the big ships. The NRC people are likely to stop them and do a mandatory scan. No, that won't work."

Now the NRC people were onboard.

"So what would you do? You'd find the kind of boat that everyone sees every day, but that isn't part of the normal security process."

"A tugboat!". Someone across the table said.

"Well, a towboat. A tugboat usually works in a limited area and if it went further someone would notice. But a towboat is different. It goes anywhere, hell, everywhere, and nobody pays any attention. Our friends out there are using a towboat."

Whatever Agent Dasilva may have wanted to do about this idea, the group around the table had already run with it.

"Ok then, it's an idea worth pursuing," Dasilva said. "Those of you with the Corp of Engineers, what's the best way to start looking at boat traffic at those bridges; see if anything jumps out?"

"It's underway right now." Arthur Nichols, head of emergency management for the New Orleans District said as he stood, put his phone to his ear and left the room.

"We'll pull more videos from the bridges;" someone from transportation said. "This time we'll look at the river instead of the bridges themselves."

Lennie turned to Emily, "Sorry Em, that time off is going to have to wait. You stirred this hornet's nest, so I suggest that you get to work and keep it going." He turned back to the table, "Don't you agree Agent Dasilva?"

"What, oh yes, no question about it. I'll handle any questions about regulations." Agent Dasilva paused a moment to understand what he had just heard himself say.

Agent Dasilva looked around as conversations and phone calls erupted throughout the room, "Ok, that should do it for now. We'll meet here again at five this afternoon; sharp." He rapped his knuckle on the table for his own satisfaction.

Emily leaned back in her seat, exhausted. She looked at the floor and whispered, "Thanks pop!".

Chapter 36

"Agent Graham, may I have a moment?" Dasilva said as they moved from the table.

"Of course."

"I have to say that I am impressed, and more than a bit surprised."

"Sir?"

"From your record, you appeared to be a very capable agent, but one who hasn't shown the initiative, or the drive, to jump into the deep end of the pool; if you understand what I mean."

"The deep end...?"

"I mean, look, you excelled in training, but when it was time for placements, you had your pick of some of the hottest locations where you could really make a difference for the agency. But instead, you picked this place."

"And what's wrong with...?"

"Don't get me wrong. New Orleans is a great city, and there is certainly work to be done here, but there were other places that would have given you the opportunity to be more in the mix of things and build the kind of reputation that really gets you somewhere. I've just assumed you didn't have that kind of drive. But this morning you showed me that you can play the game when you need too."

"Play the game? Sir, I don't think that..."

"Agent Graham, please. I'm not criticizing your behavior this morning; just the opposite. I like to see initiative in a colleague. But, in the future, when you intend to..."

"Agent Dasilva?" Arthur Nichols of the Corps of Engineers walked up.

"Excuse me, can we talk for a moment, about the boat?"

"Agent Graham is the person to talk with about that." Dasilva looked Emily, "We'll talk more later. Keep me in the loop."

"Of course sir." Emily said, followed by a deep breath, "Arthur, how are we doing?"

"I thought you might need rescuing there Emily. Our new leader seems to have it in for you."

"You know me, Art. I always seem to bring out the best in people. But, thanks. So, what do you think about the boat?"

"Hell of an idea, that's for sure. But it makes sense. They go up and down the river, hauling who knows what, and nobody pays much attention to them. We're probably talking about one of the long haul boats, right?"

"Yeah, I think we start there. I mean, so far they've put these things under two or three bridges here, but who knows what the real plan is? I mean, what if they plan to hit every bridge from here to Cincinnati, or Minneapolis?"

"Do you really think someone would be able to have that many of those devices?"

"I don't know Art, but I think we start with the worst case in mind and hope we've overestimated. So yeah, we're looking for the kind of long-haul boat that runs the full length of the rivers. How many of those would you say there are anyway?"

"Oh, it's not bad; probably only a hundred or so."

"Ok, then we start by looking for any that stand out somehow; and we just narrow it down."

"We're on it. It's just ten right now. How soon do you want an update?"

"How about ten-fifteen?"

"Right, there's no reason to rush things is there?"

"Agent Graham, another minute please?" Dasilva returned.

"Certainly sir."

"Plans are in place to find that boat?"

"Yessir, we're underway."

"Good. Look, Graham, it's your show. Your boss and I are going to be tied up dealing with media for a while. This thing is creating a feeding frenzy, and we're getting yelled at by pretty much everyone. I just got a call from a senator demanding that we reopen the waterway to avoid crippling the entire southern part of the country. He accused us of creating another Katrina."

"With radiation."

"That doesn't seem to register with him. But I imagine his phone hasn't stopped ringing, so he's just passing the yelling along to us."

"Aren't we lucky."

"We're going to be dealing with that for a while, so you're the point person on this for now."

"Thank you, sir."

"Don't thank me; it just makes sense. You also have the personal background with boats, so that might help. Besides, it looks like you're going to be around anyway, so you might as well show us what you can do."

Emily was trying to decide if that was a compliment, a challenge, or a threat.

"Just one thing Agent Graham."

"Sir?"

"No more surprises. If you get any more of those out-of-the-box ideas, you bring them to me first. Understand?"

"Understood." Emily knew that understanding something did not necessarily mean that you were agreeing to do it.

Emily smiled as she watched Dasilva walk toward the crowd of media, brushing the dust from his jacket, adjusting his tie and smoothing his hair.

She felt the vibration and reached into her pocket for her phone. She looked at the caller ID, took a breath, and hit the button.

"Emily? This is Linda at Torchwood. Do you have a minute?"

Chapter 37

Since Torchwood was on the way to the office, Emily did the math and figured she could spend fifteen minutes and still get to the meeting with the behavioral team. Linda said her father had something important he needed to talk to her about, and they had to talk today.

He was sitting in a wheelchair; dozing. She touched his shoulder. He raised his head, and a smile appeared on his face.

"Hi, hun. Its good to see you."

"Hi, dad. Getting a quick nap?"

"Hey, I need you to bring me some more ice cream. You know, the bars with the peanuts? Not those other things...don't bring those. Nobody likes them."

"I thought you liked those sandwich things."

"Yeah, but nobody else does. They all like the peanut things, so bring more of those."

"Ok, dad. I'll bring some the next time I come in. The nurse said there was something important you wanted to talk with me about."

"Yeah, I need that ice cream. The boys will be coming around tonight, and I'm out."

"That's what you needed to talk about?"

"Yeah, well, there is one other thing. You need to call the home office and tell them they need to get off their asses and get me a cook that knows how to make coffee. I've not had one decent cup on this entire trip. You tell them they'll find this cook standing on the next lock wall we come to, and there had better be a new cook ready to get onboard; one who knows how to make a goddamn cup of coffee!"

And that quickly, again, he was gone.

"I'll get your ice cream dad, but I'm not sure I can get back here today."

"What ice cream? Where's my shoes?"

She gave him a hug and stepped into the hall.

"Thanks for coming Emily, he wouldn't tell me anything but said it was important."

"Yeah, he needs ice cream."

"You're kidding. I'm sorry you came all the way for that. I didn't know."

"Nah, it's ok. It's probably going to be the most sane moment of my day."

Twenty minutes later she and Lennie stepped into the conference room the behavioral team had commandeered as their workspace.

"Ok, everyone," Lennie said, "as I said earlier, Agent Graham here will be the point person for the investigation. From here on, you report directly to her. I suggest you bring her up to speed with what you have so far."

Lennie pointed Emily to the chair at the head of the table and kept talking.

"Emily, you know Carrie Williamson, the team lead."

"Carrie, why don't you bring Emily up to date."

Carrie nodded and glanced at her notes as Lennie left the room.

"I'll give you the key points, and then we can try to answer any questions you might have for us, or you can fill us in if we're missing things."

"Sounds good."

"First, we agree there are probably more devices out there. With the effort involved in the design and placement, and the lack of a clear payoff yet, it suggests something bigger than what we've seen so far. So, we do believe there are more devices; maybe a lot more."

"Let me ask you something here," Emily said. "We were just talking about the possibility of a towboat being used to place the devices. If that's true, a towboat could run the entire length of the river. How does that idea fit with your thinking?"

"It is one very possible scenario. As I said, there must be some payoff for all this work, and it must be something big enough to merit the amount of effort involved. Nothing should be ruled out at this point."

"Ok, got it. What next?"

"The people behind this. The scale of this is significant, even with just the bridges involved so far. From designing the device, to securing the radioactive materials inside them, to transporting the devices to the river and placing them under the bridges; this would take a lot of people with a lot of knowledge, and some very specific levels of expertise. Someone had the engineering skills needed to design the devices. Someone had the expertise with radioactive materials to use it without getting killed in the process. Someone knew how to find the materials from a wide range of sources and then knew how to get them to the device builders. Finally, someone came up with the plan for placing the devices in some very public areas without being noticed."

"So, its potentially a large group."

"Absolutely." Another member of the team spoke. "If the method of placement is a towboat, it is unlikely that they have all of the devices on the boat at one time; the risk of being harmed or caught because of the radiation is just too high. That means there must be others who are getting the devices to the boat as they are needed, which involves moving a lot of devices over a lot of territory."

"This is a group of very smart people," Carrie said. "And it's a project that has been in the works for a long time."

Emily looked up from her notes. "How long?"

"Years. Just collecting this much radioactive material would take that long. There is a lot of it out there, but it's usually in small amounts. That's the primary reason we've not seen more of this type of thing before."

"That also explains the whole casserole idea." It was the other voice at the table again. "They collected what elements they could find, and just put them together to make the amounts needed for each device. We can also be secure in thinking that some of the material, if not most, came from outside the country."

"You're saying this could be more than a domestic act?" Emily felt the tingle on the back of her neck.

"It can't be anything else. While the people leading it may well be domestic, which we don't know yet, the overall event reaches well outside the country."

A few seconds of silence before Emily spoke.

"Ok then, do we know anything yet about any of these people? Who they might be and so forth?"

"We began with the person with nuclear expertise," Carrie said, "since that is such a unique field. We have narrowed it down to five individuals we believe have the ability to be involved in something like this. They all have a background in academics and are involved in nuclear research projects, here and abroad. Arthur is leading the group following those leads." Carrie nodded to a young man at the other side of the table.

"We should have more on them by afternoon." Arthur looked back to his laptop.

"Second is the engineer who designed the container, which also calls for some very specific expertise in this situation. We have eleven individuals on the short list there, eight of whom are in academics and three in government work. Lesele is leading that search."

"We just narrowed it to nine," Lesele said. "All in academics. The others don't have the mix of skills needed here."

"Excellent." Carrie smiled. "Hopefully that will get even narrower this afternoon."

"Just how do you narrow the search down from here?" Emily asked.

"There are several things we look at. First, as I said, are basic skills. Does the individual have real expertise in the specific areas required for this event? Then we look at where the individual is, and in this case, where they have been for that past few years, and of course, where they are right now. We look at their personal backgrounds and history. Everything from their financial status, political status, their mental and emotional status, anything that might help create the picture of who the person really is, and what they might be capable of. And, we look for any connections with others, especially others on our short lists. That is key, and can raise someone to the top of our list very quickly."

"Amazing."

"It's what we do. The group here is a mix of experts from a range of fields, from psychology to biology, to philosophy and religion, and even a couple of folks with interest in parapsychology."

"You mean ESP and that kind of thing?" Emily asked.

"Not that we necessarily accept them as having the same credibility as other scientific practices, but yes, we consider things like ESP and even things like witchcraft and Voodoo. Whether they are valid practices or not, they are belief structures that are common in the types of people we deal with. If we ignore them, we may miss information that leads directly to the person we need to find."

"That may explain why some people look at what you do as being a bit, uh, strange?"

"Agent Dasilva, you mean?"

"Hah, not necessarily him, but I do recall seeing a slight grin when he mentioned your involvement this morning."

"Yes, we are used to it, though. The important thing is that we use whatever resources we can use to get into the head of the person we are looking for. If we can understand them, even if a part of their thinking is complete fantasy, then we can find them and help you guys stop them."

"That works for me. So where do we go from here?"

"We'll continue narrowing the lists, and will have an update for you this afternoon. If we find anything significant, I'll be in touch immediately."

"I'll do the same."

Emily and Carrie stood and shook hands, while the rest of the group went back to their various conversations and list-narrowing.

"Before I go, can I ask you a question?" Emily glanced at the floor as she asked. "It's kind of strange, but it sounds like that might be right up your alley."

"Sure, what is it?"

"Well, it's my dad." Emily gave Carrie the brief history, ending with the visit just before this meeting.

"That has to be difficult to deal with, especially with everything else going on." Carrie focused on the human side of things.

"Yeah, it's a challenge. But what I'm wondering is, the whole idea of the group using a towboat came from something dad said to me when we talked when he was in one of his rare lucid moments. He's still in there somewhere. I'm wondering if I ought to tell him more about this whole thing and see if, you know, if he has any ideas or something. I doubt he'll even understand, but I was just wondering."

"Well, what have you got to lose? Some of the research on dementia is really fascinating, especially in patients who still have their clear moments. It seems that as the brain begins to lose connections in places, it actually creates new connections between things that hadn't been connected before."

"Like when he talks about a dog he had but mixes up the time and place he had it."

"Exactly. One theory is that memories are still there, but the roadmap has been changed, and one idea leads to one that was completely unrelated before. You might not learn anything at all, but I can't see that it would hurt anything if you told him about this."

Emily smiled, "Thanks, Carrie."

"No problem. But hey, remember, I'm also the one who just told you that we pay attention to witchcraft and voodoo too, you know?"

Emily laughed the first good laugh of the day. "That might actually be just what he needs at this point."

Lennie was standing in the hall as Emily left the conference room.

"Hey, we need to head back to the river."

"What? I mean, yeah, What's up?"

"The ARG people are going to be on-site in about thirty minutes. They'd like to meet with us. Plus, I think we just need to see how these guys do what they do."

Emily nodded.

"Our next meeting is at five back at the staging area anyway. I'll meet you there."

Chapter 38

As Emily arrived at the staging area, what grabbed her attention was the truck with its roof filled with antennae of every shape and size imaginable. Lennie was standing by the door with a man in a uniform. They spoke briefly before the man stepped forward.

"Agent Graham, welcome to ARG Central Command. I'm Lance Reyes, On-Site Commander."

Emily caught her breath. Though Reyes was older, his demeanor reminded her of Elliott. She knew she was probably reading too much into it, but she already decided that he was serious about what he was doing, was here to do a job, and didn't intend to leave without that job being done. It was a different look than Dasiliva's. She was sure Reyes wanted to maintain an image, but he intended to do that through results, rather than game playing. She liked this guy.

"Thank you, Commander."

"Special Agent Ryan informed me that you are lead investigator for this incident, so if you would like to step inside, I'll fill you in on ARG operations."

"Yes Commander, thank you."

Emily had seen this type of mobile command facility during joint training activities. It reminded her of something she saw during a family vacation to Epcot a long time ago; the walls filled with screens, rows of desks with technology and people who know how to use it. There is a constant hum of activity, yet it was calm enough for you to hold a simple conversation. These were the people you called when everything else had left you needing more.

"Please, let me explain how we do what we do."

They moved to a large screen displaying a live satellite image of the area. Glowing figures were moving around on it, some across the levee at Grammercy Bridge, some moving south on the river and some moving north.

"This is our communications center. We track every ARG asset from here. We know where everyone is at all times, so we can respond to whatever we might find. Right now, you can see our follow-on team at the Grammercy Bridge. They usually do their work to avoid a detonation, but in this case, they are tasked with finding any remaining artifacts, and ensuring the location is radiation-safe."

Emily watched the glowing images move; one on each bank and two apparently in a boat in the middle of the river. The screen changed.

"And here you can see our initial response team, half of them heading to the Hale Boggs Bridge and half to the Sunshine Bridge. They are tasked with confirming the presence of the devices there. Normally, if they find something they would conduct an initial risk assessment, but since the risk here has already been demonstrated, they will target the devices and prepare them for the recovery operations."

"It looks like you have things well under control." Emily watched the moving images.

"This is just half of the current operations, focusing on confirming and securing these devices. Because of the unique conditions of this situation, we have a larger theater of operations for this incident."

"Larger theater?"

"Our people are in full agreement with your office that there may be more of these devices out there. Because of that, in addition to the work being done here, we have activated multiple AMS units from Nellis Air Force Base, as well as Joint Base Andrews."

"AMS? That's the..."

"I'm sorry; the Aerial Measuring System. We have so many acronyms and tend to forget that not everyone is familiar with them. AMS provide specialized airborne radiation detection. They can cover a lot of ground very quickly, and their equipment is the best there is. They can find things no one else can find. The plan is to have a fixed-wing fly down the Ohio river from Cincinnati, through Evansville, down to the Mississippi. He'll be underway in about an hour. Another fixed-wing has already left for Minneapolis to travel down the Mississippi to the same spot. If there is anything up there under any bridges, they'll find it."

"Excellent."

"For the lower river, we're bringing in the helicopters. They can get down closer to the river and do a more robust search. It's slower, but it gives the best results. Plus, they will come in handy if we find anything interesting along the way."

Emily watched the screen, which had changed to a larger view showing the locations of the various members of the AMS forces at work.

"You can see the two fixed-wing birds, and one of the helicopters almost at its go station above Natchez."

Emily shook her head, "This is impressive Commander."

"All in a day's work ma'am. If there are more of those devices out there, our birds will find them."

"And then?"

"If one is found, we send a recovery team to secure the device and neutralize it if possible. Then a follow-on team goes in to package it and transport it so we can fully neutralize it. The entire process should take about thirty-six hours; normally."

"But I'm thinking this is not a normal type of situation?", Emily said.

"No ma'am, this does not look like a normal situation for several reasons. The number of devices, and the sophistication of the design; it presents some unique challenges. We're not sure just how unique it is yet, but we're hoping your people can help answer that question."

"In what way?"

"The main question we have right now, even if these three or four devices are the only ones out there, is if they are actually three or four individual devices or if they are somehow connected, behaving more like one, very large device. We'll know more once we get a good look at one of them, and we're hoping your behavioral teams will be able to give us insight into the thinking behind them as well."

"Yes, in fact, I just came from meeting with them. And yes, we are confident that more devices exist. Plus, there has to be a large number of people behind it, some domestic and some other, and they've spent a lot of time putting it all together."

"Do we have any intel on who is actually behind it yet, or what they are hoping to achieve?"

"We have two of the key roles narrowed down to a shortlist, and should have more on that later this afternoon. Once we can target one of them, pieces should begin to fall into place more quickly."

"That is what we need ma'am. One more thing, what's the level of confidence in the idea that they are using a boat to place the devices? How solid is that?"

"If someone has other options to put on the table I'll be happy to listen. But at this point, I am convinced it's one of the long-haul boats that can move the entire length of the river and never be noticed. If I were going to do something like this, I'd use a boat."

"Understood. I'll notify our birds to pay special attention to any boats along the way."

Emily began to speak, but Reye's continued.

"Not close enough to spook anyone ma'am. They'll take their time at the bridges, but as they fly down river, they'll side-scan any boats they pass. They don't get close and don't slow down, so it looks like they're paying no attention to them at all. But they'll get a clear sounding if there is dirty stuff onboard."

"Good, as you say, we don't want to spook anyone. That could get messy."

"Yes, ma'am. No worries about that. Our birds know how to stay out of trouble."

Commander Reyes turned from the screen and began moving toward the door.

"You'll have to excuse me Agent Graham, but I need to meet with my Grammercy follow-on team before we start getting data from all of the others. Things tend to get a bit busy when we have this many teams on the field at one time."

"Absolutely Commander. I need to check-in with my teams as well. I'll be in touch when we have more intel for you."

"I'll do the same ma'am."

As Emily stepped from the trailer, "Agent Graham, one more thing ma'am."

"Yes?"

"Ma'am, I knew Agent Masterson. Elliot and I were in basic together a long time ago. We went in different directions, but kept in touch, at least the holidays and such, you know?"

Emily felt herself nodding.

"I was sorry to hear the news ma'am. He was a good agent, and a good man."

"Yes. Thank you. He was."

"We'll find these guys, ma'am."

"Yes commander, we'll find them."

Chapter 39

Emily felt the phone vibrate as she walked across the staging area lot for the five o'clock meeting. With that recurring sense of dread, she pulled it from her pocket. She relaxed a bit as she saw the caller ID was not Torchwood.

"Graham."

"Agent Graham, it's Carrie Williamson, with behavioral."

"Carrie, do you have anything new for me?"

"Actually, we do. The team had a couple of lucky breaks, and I believe we have identified our nuclear expert. Our list is down to two, but I think we know which one is our guy."

"That is excellent. Tell me more."

"Both guys have been working at major universities involved in high-level nuclear projects. They both have the backgrounds and the access, and at some point, they have both crossed our radar in previous investigations for one reason or another."

"Really?"

"Yeah, but nothing ever came of it. But this time they both made the cut. As our investigation proceeded, we found one key thing that brought one of them to the top of the list."

"And that is?"

"The first guy is still known to be at his university; in fact, he is leading a three-day seminar there this week. If he was involved, he's not right now."

"And the second guy?"

"Hasn't been seen for the past three months. He's supposedly on a sabbatical doing research in Europe, but we've learned that he came back to the U.S. over a month ago, and didn't tell anyone. We don't know where he's been, and more importantly, we don't know where he is right now. For all we know, he's on your boat."

"Tell your team I appreciate their hard work. What do we know about our invisible guy so far?"

"His name is Doctor Peter Shallenger. He's originally from Austria, but has been a U.S. citizen since coming to the states twenty years ago."

"Ok."

"You name a high-profile school, and this guy has either studied there or been involved in some research with them. For the past eight years, he has been teaching at two schools and leads a half-dozen research teams at both schools. You want to guess what his primary focus is in that research?"

"What?"

"One of his grad students recently published an article entitled, 'Evaluating the Effectiveness of Particle Distribution Patterns in Radiological Dispersion Devices.' Does that tell you enough? He credited Shallenger as being, and I quote, 'the inspiration and guiding visionary behind his research."

"Damn."

"Exactly. Oh, and one more interesting little detail?"

"Yes?"

"One of the names on our short list for the engineer who built the devices...is one of Shallenger's grad students."

"Bingo! I think you're on the right path."

"We do too. We've not located that guy yet either, so it's possible we now know two of the people we're after."

"I'll pass the news along. Let me know as you learn more."

"Will do. And just so you know, we've now built a short list of people with the skills needed to deal with the radioactive materials themselves. This person has to have some real skill in the safe handling of the stuff, and the best place to develop those skills is the military. After a quick look at Shallenger's grad students with military experienced, we have four strong possibles. We're looking for them right now, so I'll update you shortly."

"I'll tell you what, witchcraft or voodoo or whatever, you guys are good!"

"Thanks, Emily. Later."

"Bye."

"Agent Graham, over here!"

Dasilva was calling to her from a trailer across the parking lot. She walked in that direction as she slid her phone back into her pocket.

"We'll have the five o'clock briefing in here. There aren't as many involved, so we don't need the large conference room."

She followed him into the trailer and found a seat at the table.

"This will be brief people," Dasilva began, "I know you are all busy. First, as you may know, Agent Graham is now the lead on this investigation. We need to go around the group and bring her up to date on everything. I've asked Colonel Nichols from the Corps of Engineers to update us on the search for the boat and asked Commander Goodwin to update us on what the NRC has found about the radiation. I'll give a brief update on the communications and media side of things. Colonel Nichols?"

"Thank you, Agent Dasilva, and hello everyone. As you know the Corps is actively working with NRC, the Port of New Orleans, local and state transportation people, the Coast Guard, and several local law enforcement agencies. While ARG is conducting the direct search, we're looking at everything we have here locally, attempting to identify the boat that placed our devices. It's more difficult since we are not certain just when the devices were placed, so we have tried to narrow the window of opportunity."

"How have you done that Colonel?" Dasilva asked.

"We can thank Colonel Goodwin and his NRC people for that." he turned to Goodwin who explains.

"Looking at the videos of the first device, based on the amount of silt around the device, we estimate that it was in the water no more than three or four hours. If it had been there longer, it would have shown more sediment build up."

"We narrowed our initial investigation to that window." Nichols continued. "Narrowing it further by only selecting those long haul towboats, as Agent Graham suggests, the list comes out to some thirty-four boats."

Someone whistled, while others shook their heads.

Colonel Nichols continued, "So now we're working to identify each of those boats and look at the data to see where they were, and where they are now. Fortunately, we track a lot of data on boats. Those that ever carry hazardous materials are monitored by Homeland Security's Vessel Tracking Service, and if we're lucky, most of the others subscribe to a system like MRTIS. If so, we can..."

"MRTIS?" Dasilva asked.

"Sorry, Mississippi River Traffic Information Service. It's a system for everything from weather information, to fleet management."

"It sounds like we have lots of data available," Dasilva said.

"Yes, sir. However, as smart as these appear to be, I'm sure they have taken that into consideration. So we also have teams taking the approach of just sitting and looking at video footage too, just in case."

"Thank you, Colonel. We'll look for another update at our nine o'clock meeting. Colonel Goodwin, what do you have for us?"

"Thank you, Agent Dasilva. As you all are aware, ARG is now in control of the ongoing investigation of the Grammercy Bridge device. They are much better equipped to handle what needs to be done there. So, we have focused our investigation on the radioactive materials from the first device."

"The so-called casserole," Dasilva said.

"Yes, the casserole. While we still have work to do, we have confirmed that we have quite a mix of materials, from a wide range of sources. We have identified signatures of at least seven different elements, and in some instances, the same type of elements originating from multiple sources."

Dasilva raised a finger, "So what does that mean for us?"

"First, it means they did not have access to large amounts of any one material, which is what we would anticipate. So they had to collect materials from a lot of sources; basically get whatever they could find to put in the devices."

"Do we know where they found it?" Emily asked.

"Some of it, yes we do. For example, the signature of one element was traced to a handheld nuclear gauge stolen from the back of a pickup truck in Virginia earlier this year."

"A handheld gauge?" Dasilva asked.

"Yes, they're pretty common. They are used to measure things like soil density; in this case, for road construction. In fact, this is one of those instances of the same type of element coming from more than one source. We have the signature of the same type of cesium, but traced to a device stolen in Connecticut back in 2010."

"Really?", came from someone at the table.

"And that leads to the next point of our findings. To collect this much material, these people have been working at this for a long time, maybe since 2010, but perhaps even longer. That's honestly why we don't see more of this type of attack taking place; its just too damn hard to collect enough material to create a big enough device."

"But apparently these people did," Emily said.

"Yes ma'am, it looks that way," Goodwin answered.

Brief silence before Goodwin continued, "The one bit of good news I can offer is that the latest tests from the ARG confirmed our finding that there was no release of radiation from the detonation at Grammercy Bridge."

"Thank you, Colonel," Dasilva said. "Keep us informed. Agent Graham, what do you have?"

"Thank you. I've just met with our behavioral investigative team, and we believe we have identified one, perhaps two of the people involved here."

"That's good news!" Dasilva said.

"We are still awaiting solid confirmation, but we believe the primary person behind the incident is a Doctor Peter Shallenger, an academic, and a man with the specific expertise required. His location is currently unknown."

"We don't know where he is now?" Dasilva asked?

"No, sir. He is supposed to be on sabbatical outside the country, but returned stateside a month ago, without any contact with anyone. But there is more."

"Please Continue."

"He appears to have a cadre of graduate students who have worked with him, one of whom is also a top-level engineer with the expertise required to design our devices. His location is also unknown at this time. We are looking closely at other grad students and colleagues of Dr. Shallenger, especially for those with a military background that could have provided the expertise required to handle the radioactive materials."

"Yes, the military would be the connection to look for," Agent Goodwin said, "especially anyone with in-theater experience."

"We have a short list in place, and we should have another update later this evening."

"Thank you, Agent Graham," Dasilva said. "People, it sounds like we are making progress. Let's keep our eyes on the ball and push things as hard as we can, without letting something slip through the cracks.

"Excuse me Agent Dasilva," Emily said, "I have additional from the ARG. "

"Of course, go ahead."

Emily gave everyone a brief summary of what she saw and heard while looking at the big screen with the glowing objects. As she ended, Colonel Goodwin spoke, "I'll tell you one thing, those birds they fly have hardware that can find anything someone might hide. Even sitting under three feet of mud and eight feet of water, those helicopters will fly right down on the deck and show us what's there."

"Hopefully, nothing at all," Dasilva said. "Ok everyone, we'll meet again at..." Dasilva stopped as Colonel Goodwin's phone interrupted. Goodwin answered, and then spoke.

"The ARG follow-on team has just found another container at the Grammercy Bridge; apparently another canister from inside the device."

"How much radiation?" Emily asked.

"That's the thing; there is no radiation other than some residual from being near the other containers. This canister is actually designed differently than the others we have found. Very differently. They are looking at it now to figure out just what it is."

"Don't anyone ask 'what's next.' Just don't do it." Emily shook her head and walked to the door.

Chapter 40

The helicopter moved inches above the water as it turned for another pass under the Highway 84 bridge at Natchez. The river was wide here, so it took a total of five passes before it began the journey downriver toward the Audubon Bridge north of Baton Rouge. It would have normally made a direct line south to the bridge, but their orders were to stay on the river and side-scan any towboats it found along the way. It was not as effective as a full-bore, direct scan, but it would do the job, and the boats would never know they were even noticed. They passed three boats before coming to the curve at Natchez Island, where they saw another four or five boats ahead.

Focusing on the boats, the helicopter crew didn't see the fishermen backing their aluminum flatboat into the water on the western bank across the levee from Morville. The fishermen loaded the large cooler into the boat and then stopped to watch the sleek helicopter pass by.

"Sure is quiet, ain't it?" one fisherman said.

"Yeah, think they're looking for us?"

"Well, not us yet, no. But they're starting to figure things out. I guess I'd better make a call."

They put the big bag in the boat and slid it under the seat, fired up the outboard, and slowly pulled out into the current. The man in front began stringing a rod and reel, just so things looked right, while the man running the motor punched numbers on his satellite phone to let them know there was a bird in the air and it was coming their way.

"Hell of a nice night, though, isn't it?" he said after putting his phone away.

"Beautiful. Sure is getting dark earlier now, too. Hard to believe it's only six thirty."

"Yeah, won't be long until we get snow back home."

Chapter 41

The leader and doctor stood in the galley door watching the helicopter pass by in the growing darkness. The leader smiled as he thought about the side scan, and how cocky the ARG people were about being sneaky.

"What do we do now?" the doctor asked.

"What do you mean? We just keep going. It's all been accounted for doctor; nothing has changed."

They went back inside.

Charlie watched the lights of the helicopter hug the shoreline as he guided the boat out of the curve above Natchez Island. Frank stood looking out the pilothouse stern window. Neither man had spoken since they watched the small fishing boat deliver the last device about fifteen minutes ago.

"Frank, I decided to surprise our guys with something a little special tonight."

"Do you mean what I think you mean?"

"Absafuckinglootly. We may have to put up with these assholes, but that doesn't mean we can't eat good. I radioed up ahead and ordered us a shit load of Bar-B-Q from Lamar's."

"Natchez's finest."

"Yep, it would be a sin to go by without it. They should be meeting us up here shortly before the bridge. In fact, that looks like them coming out now."

The small cabin boat pulled alongside, and seconds later began moving back toward the shore. It was only a matter of time before someone would walk in the door with a bucket filled with ribs, pulled pork, and pieces of Lamar's honey cornbread.

"I guess that's why you are the captain Charlie, hell, you're so damn smart."

As they watched the Highway 84 bridge pass over their heads. The thought of the device being lowered into the water was almost overshadowed by the thought of the Bar-B-Q. They both turned as they heard the pilothouse door open.

It wasn't ribs.

"Captain, you're needed down below. They're about to throw Smitty in the river."

"Well, shit, why the fuck not." Charlie nodded to Frank to take the helm and headed down the stairs to the stern of his boat.

As he came around the corner, he saw Smitty in the dim stern lights, hanging over the foam churned from the boat's massive propellers, his feet just touching the water, his eyes as wide as he's ever seen them, his neck firmly in the grip of Bear, the biggest of the bad guys.

"What the fuck is going on here?" Charlie asked as only a Captain can ask.

"Bear! Put him down." The Leader walked up, "Here, on the deck. Put him down. Now!"

"He tried to send a message, so Bear stopped him." The doctor was standing in the door to his workspace, watching the event with what appeared to be calm satisfaction.

"I don't care what the fuck he did," Charlie said, "you put his ass back on this deck right now. Do you hear me?"

Bear looked at the leader, then slowly turned and lowered Smitty until his feet found their place on the deck. Smitty looked at the Captain, "I'm sorry Charlie" squeaked out of his throat.

"Ok, now what the fuck is going on here?" Charlie asked.

"Yes, doctor, please explain what this all about." The leader said.

"Certainly. That boat came out to deliver the food the captain ordered. While Bear and the others were unloading it, this man came out to help and tried to slip a note to one of the people in the boat telling them about us. Bear found out about it, and that led to what you saw here."

Charlie started to ask Smitty if it was true but got the answer simply by looking at his eyes.

The leader sighed, "Captain, I suggest that you ask your crew to join us in the galley for a conversation. Let's say in about twenty minutes?"

"What for?"

"I believe I can resolve this little situation and can give you some information that should make everyone feel much better about our mission at this point. Twenty minutes, ok?"

"Well shit. Fine, twenty minutes."

Everyone went back to their work, leaving Charlie and Smitty standing on the tail deck.

"Charlie, I'm really sorry."

"Smitty, what did I just tell you last night? What the fuck did I just tell you?"

"But, I just..."

"Smitty, one more word. Just one more word and I'll throw your ass in the river myself."

Smitty tucked his head and walked round the corner toward the galley.

Charlie walked to the pilothouse to relieve Frank and eased back into his chair. As the boat slid under the twin spans of the Natchez highway 84 bridge, he reached for the bottle of chalky stuff to try and calm his ulcer. The ribs would have to wait.

Chapter 42

Emily grabbed a burger on her way back to the staging area and the nine o'clock briefing. She really wanted a Gyro, but it looked like a long night ahead, and she didn't need to spend it arguing with her stomach. After all, you can't really enjoy a Gyro without the Tzatziki sauce and onions, now can you? Just to make it more disappointing, her fries were soggy.

Hoping to avoid a call later, she stopped by to check on her dad. Maybe a few minutes now would help him settle in for the night. Besides, she had something she wanted to ask him; if he was actually there.

He was sitting in his wheelchair in front of the nurse's station, unshaven and uncombed, but seemed to be in a pretty good state of mind.

"Hi, dad."

"Well, looky at what the cat dragged in. What brings you out to the poor side of town?"

"I just wanted..."

"And did you bring my ice cream?"

Fortunately, she had gotten three boxes when she stopped for gas. "You bet."

"Well stick 'em in my fridge in there; they don't like 'em when they're soft you know."

She walked into his room and put the boxes in the small freezer compartment of his mini-fridge, which was empty except for four candy bar wrappers. He wheeled in behind her.

"Is that all that's left of the candy?"

"Well hell, a man's gotta eat, doesn't he? They don't feed you enough around here to keep a bird alive."

Nurse Linda smiled from the doorway. "Now Captain, you left food on your plate tonight."

He spun his chair toward the door, "Couldn't finish that crap; nobody could. I don't know how anyone can do that to a chicken."

He turned to Emily, smiled the smile she knew so well, "You gotta keep them in their place, you know. It really wasn't all that bad, but don't tell her that."

"Ok, you're the captain," Linda said. "Emily, if you need anything I'll be at the desk."

"Thanks, Linda, I'm sure we'll be fine." Emily moved the stack of papers from the chair and sat down, as dad rolled his wheelchair to the middle of the room facing away from the television and stared at his shoes.

"Dad, I have a question for you."

"Always use protection. That's the best answer I've got."

"Ok dad, thanks for that. But I've got a boat question for you, about..."

At the mention of the word boat, his head popped up, "Them sons a bitchen boats. I don't know why I ever got started with those..."

"Wait dad, hang on a second. I really need your advice on something. Its about work."

"Work? You don't work on boats."

"No, I know that. But I'm just curious. If someone on a boat wanted to sneak something onboard with no one knowing, how might they do that?"

"What do you mean nobody knows? If it's my boat I'm going to know about it, that's for goddamn sure. What is it they're supposed to be sneaking onboard?"

"Let's say it's like a box. Small enough to carry, but too large to hide in your suitcase or something like that."

"What's in it?"

"That doesn't matter. How could they sneak it on?"

"It sure the hell matters to me! Nobody sneaks a big box onto my boat, and I'm going to know what the hell is in it, and that's for goddamn sure!"

And with that, he was gone.

141

"That's the whole problem with this damn boat I'm on now; none of these assholes follow the rules, and the home office won't do anything about it. If I had my way, I'd throw every one of their asses off at the next lock and make the home office send me some people who know how to follow orders!"

Emily stood for a moment and watched her father disappear into this imaginary world once again. She thought of all the times he had been the one to have the answer for her problems and realized tonight wasn't going to be one of them. She leaned over and gave him a hug, which he didn't seem to notice. "I'll see you tomorrow dad. I love you."

He stared at his shoes.

"Well, you tried," Linda smiled as Emily came out of the room.

"Hopefully I didn't stir him all up for you."

"Nah, he'll be asleep in a few minutes and probably go through the night."

"Ok, good. Call me if..."

"We will. He'll be fine. You go get some rest; it looks like you need it."

Emily smiled a weak smile and walked to her car. It was time for another meeting.

Chapter 43

A crew on a towboat works and eats in shifts, so the galley is not large enough to hold the entire group at one time; like this one was trying to do tonight. Half of the group was unhappy about being dragged out of their sleep, while the other half was almost relieved to get a break from their work on deck. As they gathered, they were all thinking about the first meeting in here when Danny was shot. The mood was tense.

"Thank you all for being here so promptly." the leader said.

There were a few grunts.

"And I am sorry for having to wake some of you from your rest. I'm just sorry that Frank is not here to share it with us, but someone must keep the boat moving. I will not keep you long, and I do believe you will be pleased with what I have to say to you."

No one appeared to be willing to be pleased about anything at this point.

"First, I know you are concerned about your Smitty, and his, well, shall we say, unfortunate attempt to become a hero."

More grunts and grumbles.

"I'm sure you recall the conversation we had when we began our mission, and you remember the simple rules we agreed to follow at that time."

"Agreed?" the Captain said.

"I'm sorry, the rules that we put in place at that time. Is that more to your liking Captain?"

"You mean these bracelets?" one of the crewmen asked.

"Yes, the bracelets were a part of that, of course. Well, I am pleased to inform you that the rules have changed as of now."

One of the leader's men stepped forward.

"Thomas here will pass around a pair of scissors, and you are welcome to remove those bracelets if you would like. You'll notice that we have already removed ours."

A mix of "It's about time," and "Now we can..." echoed around the room.

"But before anyone misunderstands, this does not mean that you now have the option of throwing us off the boat. All it means is that we no longer need to worry about you trying to inform anyone of our mission."

"You mean you're finally giving up?" the Captain asked.

"Oh my no, Captain, not at all. It means that we now have things in place to protect our mission completely, regardless of what you or anyone else might try to do. And because of that, I'm sure you will be happy to hear that your families are no longer of concern to us as well, so our people watching them have moved on to other activities."

Lots of nods, and looks of relief.

"As for Smitty, he apparently did not believe me when I said that we had taken every precaution to protect our mission. When he handed his note to the person on the boat with the food, the person he handed it to was one of our people. We are very familiar with your routines gentlemen, even ordering Bar-B-Q."

"Just what are you going to do to him?" the Captain asked.

"Nothing at all. As I said, the rules have changed. Smitty is free to go about his duties as usual, though I do suggest he not make any further foolish moves. He can't possibly stop us, but if he becomes too much of an annoyance we will have to do something to, well, avoid the distraction."

"Then what's to keep us from leaving?" the Captain asked, "or letting everyone know what you are doing here?"

"Oh, we will be found; that is unavoidable. We knew it from the beginning. In fact, I'm sure you will soon learn that we have already been located. But, it makes no difference now."

"Located, when?" a crewman asked.

"It honestly doesn't matter. It changes nothing. Let me explain. As you know, we now have devices placed under every bridge from New Orleans to Natchez. One has unfortunately been removed, but that actually provided us with the opportunity to demonstrate the potential of the rest. What you are not aware of is that all of these devices are linked together, monitored by a computer in the room behind you there." He nodded to the group leaning against the wall.

"So you can tell it to blow the things up?" the Captain said.

"Well, yes, Captain, that would be possible. But the computer is actually there to make sure we can complete our mission; to protect us from anyone attempting to stop us before we are finished. I won't concern you with the details right now, but just understand that if anything happens to us, or to this boat, the results will be immediate. We need to do nothing at all. But on the positive side gentlemen; you can be sure that no one will do anything to threaten the safety of your boat or anyone on it. Not now. So, why not get back to work, or back to bed, and enjoy the rest of your evening."

From the look on their faces, it appeared that everyone in the room felt screwed.

Chapter 44

Agent Dasilva looked at his watch for the third time. The group was gathered around the conference table, except for two members. One was Colonel Nichols of the Corps of Engineers, and the other was Agent Emily Graham. The book was very clear about promptness, and Dasilva made a mental note to raise that issue with her later.

"We might as well get started," Dasilva said. "I appreciate you altering your schedules to be here at ten o'clock, rather than nine as originally planned. Agent Graham said it was important for us to reschedule. Unfortunately, it now appears that she has..."

There was commotion behind Dasilva as the door opened and Emily entered along with Lennie, Colonel Nichols, and Commander Reyes from the ARG.

"I'm glad you are able to join us," was what Dasilva was beginning to say, but Emily spoke first, "I apologize for the delay everyone, but I believe we have just obtained information you will all want to hear. I have asked Commander Reyes to join us to explain."

She and Nichols found their seats and Emily pulled a chair to the table for Reyes.

"First," Emily said, "we have our boat. Colonel Nichols can give us the details, and Commander Reyes and I will join in."

"Thank you, Agent Graham," Nichols said. "In our last meeting, I explained that because of the work of the NRC we had been able to narrow our search window significantly. Based on that, we reduced our list to three possible targets that fit the profile we were looking for. We began looking more closely at those boats until news we just received from the ARG helped us even more. We believe our boat is the Francis B., a boat owned by Arbel Fleet Services out of Louisville. She is the type of long haul boat we are looking for, and fits our travel profile perfectly."

"And it gets better," Emily said as she looked at Commander Reyes.

"Yes, it does. She's hot." Reyes said.

The room was silent enough to hear the ceiling fan running.

"What I mean is, one of our AMS helicopters scanning the bridges was also tasked to side-scan any long haul boats it passed as it moved downriver. It passed the Francis B. just below Natchez and got a reading."

Side conversations arose around the table, then fell to hear more.

"They had just completed a full scan of the Natchez bridge with negative results. After hearing of the hit on the Francis B., we sent the bird back upriver to Natchez after the boat had passed there. This time, the scan was positive. In other words, there was nothing under the bridge before the boat passed, and was something there after the boat passed."

"Son of a bitch." came from somewhere around the table.

"So at this point," Emily continued, "we believe the Francis B. is our target. We are currently finding out as much as we can about the boat and company. And I can also tell you that we now have full confidence in the identification of Dr. Peter Shallenger as the nuclear expert, and a Lawrence Abbot, one of Shallenger's students, as the individual who designed the devices. We also are looking at a Susan Handling, another grad student, who has the experience from three rounds of in-theater Navy service in nuclear activities. We believe they may all currently be aboard the Francis B."

Conversations continued all around the table.

"This is good work everyone," Dasilva said. "It sounds like we are making some real progress. I was going to give an update on the media circus taking place out there, but let me just say that we seem to have things under control for the moment. With that in mind, I want to stress that this latest information regarding the boat and personnel is to remain in this room, and is not to make its way to the public yet. Is that understood?"

Nods all around.

"If these guys learn that we know who they are, well, we don't want to spook them into doing something drastic."

Dasilva paused a minute.

"For now, we need to come up with ideas for what to do about that boat. Get your teams working on it, and we'll meet again here at eight o'clock tomorrow morning."

As Emily collected her things, her boss leaned over, "Em, we need to talk before you leave."

"Agent Graham," Colonel Reyes stepped up, "we need to speak with you about one more item before you go."

"Certainly."

"Go ahead and take care of them, and I'll be outside when you're finished," Lennie said as he leaves the room.

The room was empty except for Emily, Commander Reyes and Colonel Goodwin of the NRC.

Goodwin began, "I'm afraid there is more, and it may mean that we have even a larger problem on our hands. We thought we should speak with you about it before bringing it to the full group."

"Ok, what's going on?" Emily asked, looking at Commander Reyes.

"You'll remember that our Grammercy Follow-on team had located another canister from that device, and this canister appeared to be designed differently than the others."

"There was no radiation from that canister if I recall," Emily said.

"Correct. And the design was different from the other canisters. As it was examined further, we discovered that this canister was also constructed from a different type of material than the others."

"Is that why the radiation was not seen?"

"No, ma'am. There is no radiation with this canister; I'm afraid it may be worse."

"Worse?" Emily almost laughed.

"Yes, ma'am. This canister is built from material that is specifically used to insulate things from heat; to protect something from being destroyed by very high temperatures."

"Like from an explosion." Agent Goodwin said.

"Yes, like heat from an explosion."

"And we're certain of this?" Emily asked as her eyes have narrowed, and she leaned against her chair.

"Yes, ma'am. Ma'am, I'm afraid this device wasn't designed for radiation. This is the type of canister that is designed specifically to hold and protect materials that would be destroyed by heat; such as biologicals."

Emily heard her heartbeat and felt it throbbing in her ears.

"It is now our belief, ma'am, that this container contains some form of biological materials."

"A biological weapon?"

"Yes ma'am," Goodwin said. "we believe that is a very real possibility."

"The canister is en route to a secure bio facility where it can be fully examined." Commander Reyes glanced at his watch. "We should know more within the hour."

"So, you are telling me that in addition to holding several canisters of radioactive materials that can be blown all over the place, these things may also have one or more canisters that are biological weapons as well? Is that what I'm hearing?"

"Ma'am," Reyes said, "we believe that is correct ma'am. We will update you as soon as we hear more, ma'am."

"Ok," Emily said. "And, by the way, let's keep this on the QT until we know exactly what we've got, ok?"

"Yes, ma'am. No problem."

Reyes and Goodwin left Agent Graham alone in the room, leaning against her chair, trying to follow her mind going in about eight directions at once; not one of which was a good one. After a few seconds, she took a deep breath, shook her head to clear it, and stepped out the door. Lennie was waiting.

"What do we know about this Arbel Fleet Services company?" he asked.

"We're looking at it now. The CEO is a Gilbert Arbel, the son of the founder. He goes by 'Gil,' and he looks clean so far. We don't think he is involved in this, at least not directly."

"And what about the crew on the boat?"

"We're looking there too. At some point we need to talk with someone at the company about that, probably start with Arbel himself, once we make sure he is clean."

"Good. Let me know what you find out."

Lennie began walking to his car. He stopped and turned back.

"Em, how long will it take you to pack?"

"Pack?"

"I think you're right about needing to talk with Arbel directly. You need to get to Louisville and see if you can learn anything useful. I'll have a plane waiting for you at four o'clock. I suggest you go get a bit of sleep. But first, see what else you can find out about this Arbel guy, so we're not going in blind."

Lennie walked to his car and drove away. Emily stood still, staring at nothing in particular.

Chapter 45

It was almost twelve hours between bridges at Natchez and Vicksburg, and it had been quiet since the meeting in the galley. Frank opened the pilothouse door so the fresh air could help keep him awake. It was quiet. Really quiet. Quiet enough to think about what the hell he was doing on this damn boat.

Down South, Emily handed her bag to the man standing beside the small jet and climbed up the stairway. Lennie was already on board.

"Good morning Agent Graham. I trust you slept well."

Emily took a seat as the engines began to spool-up.

"Well, this is a surprise. What's the matter? Didn't think I could handle it myself?"

"No, of course not. It's still your show. I just thought an extra pair of ears might be useful."

They exchanged glances to show that they both understood how serious this whole thing was.

"I'm glad you're here," Emily said. "I always enjoy having a chauffeur."

"Yes, ma'am. Always happy to be of assistance."

As the jet leveled off for the brief flight to Louisville, Lennie started the work conversation.

"So, what have you found about Arbel?"

"He looks clean. If there are people involved inside the company, I don't think he's one of them."

"Do you think he knows what is going on?"

"Hard to say, but I doubt it. This company is his baby. Took it over when his father died, and he's built it into one of the strongest companies in the business; small in size but with quite a reputation. I just can't see him doing something that would risk that."

"So, if the company is that small, do you really think he doesn't know what's going on with one of his boats?"

"If he knows, I'm guessing he just found out and is trying to figure out what the hell to do about it; just like we are. I think it's worth talking with him to see."

"Ok, then. That's what..."

The vibration reminded her that she hadn't turned off her phone. She pulled it out and saw 'Torchwood.'

"Go ahead and take it," Lennie said. She hit the button.

"Hello?"

"Em, it's dad."

"Hi, dad, what are you doing up at this hour?"

"I was thinking about that thing you asked me; you know, about someone sneaking stuff on to a boat?"

"Yeah?"

"Well, I just remembered that did happen to me one time; some asshole sneaking booze onboard, but I caught him and threw his ass off my boat. He was a sneaky bastard, but he had his wife helping him."

"What do you mean, dad?"

"Well, she used to get the stuff, wrap it all up in burlap sacks, and stick them on a barge tied up there at Peoria. You know there's always barges tied there below town. I never did find out how the hell she knew which barges to put the shit on. So, we'd pick up the barge and when no one was watching he'd just go out and get the stuff. But I saw him one night. I didn't say anything, but when we got to the next lock, I told him the lock master had radioed and said he had a phone call up at the lock wall. He got off the boat to answer the call, and I just kept the boat moving."

"Oh, dad."

"A few minutes later I got a call from the lock master saying, 'Hey captain, you left a man here.' I told him to watch real close, and he'll see the guy's suitcase floating down that way in just a few minutes. What's that noise I hear?"

"I'm on a plane dad."

"A plane? What the hell are you doing on a plane? And when are you going to bring me my ice cream?"

"I brought that last night dad, remember?"

"Oh. Well, thanks for calling. Give me a call the next time you come to Chicago; we'll get a drink."

She put the phone away and saw that Lennie was leaning back in his seat with his eyes closed. This probably wasn't the best time to tell him about the biological weapons issue, which was fine with her. She leaned back, closed her eyes, and saw a beautiful beach; with people carrying ice cream cones with radiation labels on them, some woman burying burlap bags in the sand, and some guy selling biological weapons. Jimmy Buffett was standing there shaking his head.

Chapter 46

"Red sky at morning; sailor take warning. Isn't that how it goes?" the man in the back of the boat said as he saw the orange glow rising over the trees to the East.

The man in the front nodded his head, "I think so. I can never get that straight. It's red sky at night, and, um,"

"Sailor's delight."

"Yeah. So, I guess the weather guy was right; it's supposed to rain later."

"For once. Ya know, that's a job I think I'd like; they can be completely wrong and still don't get fired."

"Yeah, and you get to...shit! Watch that log! Cut er' hard left."

The guy in back jerked the tiller to miss the big piece of driftwood, tilting the small aluminum boat almost enough for water to spill over the side. Both men leaned to balance the boat, and as it tipped back, they almost rolled it over in the other direction. "Damn. We'd better pay more attention here...is everything ok?"

The man in front checked the bag under his seat, then opened the cooler. "Yeah, we're fine."

"Ok, good. Keep an eye open; it's not light enough for me to see anything yet. Hey, here comes the boat."

The Francis B. came out of the left-hand bend about eight miles below Vicksburg. This time the fishermen were taking their materials straight to the boat since this wasn't an area where barges sat along the bank. As the Francis B. got closer, the two men forgot about sunshine and weathermen and stayed focused on the task at hand. A sixteen-foot aluminum fishing boat was no match for a five-hundred-ton towboat. The massive screws from the Francis B. churned up the water behind it enough to capsize anything that got within fifty feet. And if they ended up in the water, the suction from the props would pull them under and treat them much like two pieces of asparagus dropped into a food processor. So, as they pulled alongside, they were fully focused. Neither man relaxed until both packages were handed off and they were headed back toward the shore.

"I hope we don't have to do that again," the man in front said.

"Not until Memphis. And that's going to be something like two o'clock in the morning; pitch dark."

It was quiet as the men watched the early orange sky. It stayed quiet as they loaded the boat back on the trailer and pulled it to the top of the levee.

As the fishermen took the levee road toward Quimby, another truck pulled into a parking space at Riverview Park just north of the Vicksburg Bridge. The passenger got out, carrying what looked like a small portable television with two joysticks on it. The driver opened the truck tailgate and lifted out a radio-controlled airplane, checked the various connections, moved a few switches, and then gently tossed the plane into the air.

"Is that a drone?" a young boy with a fishing pole asked as he walked up.

"Yep," the driver said. "Sure is."

"Cool! Whatcha doing with it?"

"Just flying around a bit; doing some testing."

The boy sat his fishing pole down and stayed to ask a few dozen questions as they watched the drone fly around.

"Checking to see how high it will go?" the boy asked. He was an observant lad. As the Francis B. approached the bridge, the drone increased altitude until it was invisible unless you knew exactly where to look. It flew down below the bridge and followed the boat as it passed the small group in the park.

"Yep," the driver said, "it did pretty good too, didn't it?"

"Sure did. That was awesome!"

There was more conversation as the men packed up the airplane until the boy remembered his fishing pole and headed down to the riverbank.

"Did you see anything?" the driver asked.

"Yeah, I think we got what we need." the pilot said.

"Let's get that sent right away."

"Just sent it. Let's go get some breakfast while we wait for orders."

Chapter 47

Grandpa was in his seat as Ronnie walked in the door. The old man waved him over to the table.

"Hi grandpa, let me get a drink; do you want something?"

"Let's wait a minute to order. Sit down, let's talk."

Ronnie realized his caffeine fix would have to wait a few more minutes, and sat down.

"So, what's the rush? Are you finally going to let me in on this little secret thing you've been hinting at?"

The old man smiled, but if there was such a thing as a sad smile, this was it.

"Not quite yet, Ronnie, I need to make sure you are really ready to take that step."

The younger man looked down and shook his head. "Grandpa, come on. I told you yesterday that I want to do this. I don't know what else to say?"

"I know, I know. But what I do need you to understand right now is that if you take this step, everything begins to change. As your grandfather, I've kind of been this magical kind of person, taking you fishing and telling stories, and..."

"Sometimes really dumb stories."

"Yes, that's true. But listen, this is important. If you do this, that magic is going to change. Up to this point, I've been in a position to try and make your life easier; to help you work through hard times, and to, you know, just be a positive thing in your life."

"Are you saying you won't be there for me anymore?"

"I will still be here, but if you take this step, we will be doing things together, no longer as grandfather and grandson, but as two equals, each doing our role."

"Ok."

"And Ronnie, you will learn things about me that no one else knows or understands. And some of those things may be very difficult to accept at first. And you will see that sometimes I may do things that seem wrong, even cruel at times; until you come to understand why those things are done."

"Now you're scaring me a bit."

"That's good. That's what I'm trying to do. And just to make it even scarier, there will be times that you will have to do things that will feel wrong or cruel, and will cause you to lie awake at night thinking about them."

"But you said my family would be safe."

"Yes, absolutely, of course. This has nothing to do with your family. This will be about you, and the questions you will ask yourself over and over, until..."

"Until I fully understand."

"Exactly; which will just take some time."

"But it's worth it?"

"Nothing will ever be worth more."

"Then I'm in."

The old man looked into his grandson's eyes. Seconds passed. It felt like one of those long moments standing at the airport gate having run out of words to say to the person leaving you, but you're not ready to let them go climb into the plane.

"Ok, then," Grandpa said. "I'll get us a couple of drinks, and we'll talk."

Ronnie watched as his grandfather ordered the drinks, pausing long enough to tell one of his stories. He wondered which story it was until he saw the barista throw his head back in laughter and shout, "It was the peanut!". That was one of Ronnie's favorites. Really dumb, but a good one. As he walked back to the table, grandpa glanced at the receipt stuck on the side of his glass, placed a cup in front of his grandson, and sat down.

"Iced mocha, right? That's what you like?"

"Absolutely! Looks great grandpa."

They enjoyed a sip or two as the older man's eyes focused on his grandson.

158

"Ronnie, what I am about to tell you must never be repeated; until the day you will choose the one person you have decided will be your learner. Do you understand?"

"Sure grandpa. Is that what I am? Your learner? What is that...like an apprentice or something?"

"Something like that, yes. One of our responsibilities is to ensure the continuance of the roles; and to do that, we must find someone who is capable of continuing the work when we are no longer able to do so."

"So you are stopping doing this?"

"Oh no, nothing like that, at least for a while. It will take some time for you to learn what you need to learn, but my hope is that when I do step aside, you will be ready to take my place. Nothing could make me happier, or prouder."

"I'll do my best."

"I know you will, and that's why I selected you. Tell me, what do you know about the existence of secret organizations throughout history?"

"Secret? You mean like the, uh, Illuminati? Things like that? Is that it? Are you in the Illuminati?"

The old man grinned.

"Illuminati? Ah yes, ok, well, that's the general idea. But no, I'm not talking about them. I'm talking about something quite different; something real."

"Ok, well what's that group at the schools? The Skull and Bones, and things like the Masons, though they aren't really secret, I guess."

"Ok, you have the view that most people have. That's what I would expect. But no, I'm not talking about any of those groups or a group that operates like that type of group, real or imaginary."

"What's the name of this group, let's see if I've heard about it."

"You see Ronnie, that's part of the difference. There is no name."

"Then...?"

"You went to Sunday School. Do you remember that story of the time Moses met God, and Moses asked what God's name was?"

"Yeah, kind of."

"Moses was told that God didn't have a name, but that Moses could just refer to him by some letters. Did you ever wonder why God did that?"

"Um, I don't think so."

"When you know someone's name, you have a certain amount of control over them. Like in here even, if I know that the barista's name is 'Bob,' I could yell, 'Hey Bob!', and he would probably look up from what he is doing to see who was calling him. I have some control over him, even though it's just a little bit."

"Yeah."

"God wasn't going to allow Moses or anyone else to have any control. The whole idea of being God is that God is in control. If Moses knew God's name, well, that was a problem."

"Then we're talking about god?"

"No, we're talking about control. If our group had a name, and someone knew that name, they would have some level of control over us. They would have the ability to identify us as a group. And the most important thing about our group is that no one controls us, no one even knows that we exist unless we select them as a learner. We do not exist. But, we are here."

"Ok, but..."

"Hang on. You mentioned the Illuminati and a few others. Just the fact that you know their names limits what they are able to be and do. It gives you the ability to ask me if I am a member, which means I risk being found out, which means the entire group risks being uncovered. If there is a name, there must be a thing. If there is no name, there may or may not be a thing."

"Well, then why did all of those, so called secret organizations, create names for themselves?"

"Because we wanted them to be seen, and talked about."

"You? You named them?"

"We created them to be distractions, so yes, we named them so they would be found."

"Distractions?"

"Ronnie, that's what we do. Our role as a group is to create distractions and disruptions when they need to be created. That was how we started a long time ago, and its what we've done ever since."

160

Silence.

"I can see I've lost you. If I recall sitting and listening to this when I became a learner for my grandfather, this is the point where I was finally convinced the old guy had lost his mind. It wasn't a secret group he was asking me to join; it was senility. Is that about right?"

"Well, the thought had crossed my mind to be quite honest. I mean..."

"Believe me, I understand. Well, I'm as sane as I've ever been. Which your grandmother always thought was questionable anyway."

Smiles and laughter.

"Ok, then what..."

"Hold on, you'll have lots of questions, and we'll take as much time as we need to see that they are all answered."

"It's just a lot to understand. I am joining a group that has been around for a long time, but that isn't real."

"Oh Ronnie, we are very real. We just don't exist. For now, just remember this, we are here to create distraction and disruption; nothing more and nothing less. We create those two things to keep any one person or group from becoming so powerful that they become a threat to the existence of humanity as a whole. We have no allegiance to any one group, or nation, or religion or thought, other than to our role. Our responsibility is to humanity: to every man, woman or child of every race, ethnicity, creed and country, who deserves the opportunity to live a life free of hunger and persecution. It may sound flowery and fanciful, but we are the only group who has that role; who carries that burden. And because of that, we cannot allow anyone to interfere with our work. And as I said earlier, sometimes that work means we have to do some very difficult things; things that, in the short view, may appear to be terrible. But they are necessary for us to succeed in the long term. For humanity to survive, we must succeed, and we must remain invisible and unknown. Do you understand?"

"I understand."

"Are you still willing to accept the role and the secrecy?"

"Yes, I've told you..."

"Good, let me get us one more drink and then we'll call it a day. We can talk more tomorrow."

"Thanks, grandpa, but I think I've had enough. If I have more caffeine, I'll be wired all day."

"Just one more, that's all. A small one." The older man walked to the counter, told another story, and returned with two small cups.

"Drink." It came out more as an order than a suggestion.

"Before we go, can I ask one more question?" the grandson asked.

"Of course."

"How has it been kept secret? Over all this time, hasn't anyone ever, you know, told others about the group? Especially if it gets as hard as you said it might."

"It has happened. But since we are very careful in selecting our learners, it has been quite rare."

"But what happens? How do you keep from being found?"

"Finish your drink; all of it. Drink it right down now." He reached across the table, picked up the cup and put it in his grandson's hand.

"Ok, ok. I'll drink."

"As I said, our relationship has changed. You now carry a secret that must be protected. Since you are my learner, I carry the responsibility to ensure that you understand, and follow the role."

"Yes, but..."

"Listen. We have learned that the time of greatest risk is when a learner is first told about the group. On occasion, the group member has misjudged their learner, and after he or she learns the truth, they decide they cannot continue. As a result, they carry the secret of the group without also carrying the commitment to the group. That is a risk that we cannot take."

It felt as though someone had just poured ice water down his back, "There was something in my drink wasn't there? That's why you made me drink it. That's why...grandpa, what's in this drink?"

"The second drink is the antidote; you can relax."

"Antidote?" He sat up in his chair, feeling his fists clench. "What did you do to me?"

"Ronnie, I told you our relationship would be changed. We have to be certain that a potential learner does not refuse the role after learning the story; the risk is far too great. So, the first drink included a

162

simple compound, untraceable, that is designed to become active within three hours if the antidote is not given."

"What would have happened without the antidote? What would have happened to me?"

"It would have been painless. It would have been diagnosed as a simple stroke. You should not have suffered any physical injury, only a disruption of your cognitive processes relating to short term memory. You would still be you. You would lead a life much like before. There would simply be a gap. A hole that consisted of the past hour of our conversation. Only in a few very rare instances has it resulted in anything more serious."

"What more serious? Death?" the younger man asked.

"Rarely. I'll see you in the morning." The older man touched his grandson's shoulder as he passed on his way to the door.

The young man sat staring into his now-empty cup, thinking about the man who had helped him survive his childhood, who had helped create his philosophy of life, who made him laugh and shake his head at dumb stories, and who had now almost murdered him.

Chapter 48

"All right people, somebody has been talking," Dasilva was not happy. The morning briefing was small, as Dasilva had excused all but the leaders of the various groups. "The media knows that Grammercy was some kind of dirty bomb. They also somehow know about the devices under the other bridges around New Orleans. They don't seem to know anything about how they got there, or that there may be more, yet. But somebody is clearly talking, and I want to know who it is."

The eyes around the table gave him two messages at the same time. The first was that no one around this table had violated confidentiality. The second message was that none of them liked being accused of that kind of behavior.

"I can tell you it sure as hell didn't come from any of my team!" Said by everyone around the table.

"Well, it's coming from somewhere, and it has to be stopped," Dasilva said.

It was quiet for a few minutes.

"Ok, look, I'm sorry." Dasilva started over. "I know none of you did this, and you know your teams better than I do. But this has really stirred things up. We were already under massive pressure to reopen the river and bridges, and while this helps explain why we haven't done that, it has created an entirely new bunch of problems. I mean, we just found out which boat is involved, and somebody told the media. This has brought out the crazies who want to see things for themselves. We've got crowds gathering all along the river to watch the boat go by. People are out in their fishing boats trying to get close and follow them. We even caught three guys in scuba gear trying to get to the device under the Sunshine Bridge to get pictures of themselves swimming next to the thing. We've had to call in the National Guard to try and keep things under control."

"We've tightened NRC security as well," Colonel Goodwin said, "I think we have it under control for now."

"The Corps has done the same thing," Colonel Nichols said.

"Good," Dasilva nodded. "We have more Guard standing by if you need them."

Dasilva looked at his notes, then at the group.

"Please just talk with your people again, and remind them of how important it is to keep things quiet right now. And I'm going to have to stop us there for now. I have to go meet with some media people to see if we can keep the lid from coming off any further."

"Agent Dasilva," Reyes from the ARG said, "could I have a moment before you go, sir?"

"I'm sorry Commander, I really don't have time right now. It will have to wait till later." Dasilva said as he walked from the room.

"Yes sir," Reyes said as he closed the video file on his tablet.

Chapter 49

"We'd probably better get going; he should be there by now." Emily looked out the window as she put her phone in her pocket. The flight had been quick, and Loren was waiting to meet them with the car. Loren Erickson was Special Agent in Charge of the Louisville office. Lennie had contacted her, partly out of professional courtesy, and partly because they really didn't know what they were walking into, and in those situations sometimes three could be better than two. Plus, if there was follow-on work to be done, it was wiser to leave that to the people who knew the area.

It was early when they reached the East Market District, so Loren suggested a little coffee and tea shop a block away from the Arbel offices. They had spent the time filling Agent Erickson in on the basics of the situation and getting more details from her about Arbel. He was well-known in the city, and Loren agreed with Emily's belief that he was most likely not involved in what is happening; at least not willingly.

Morning traffic was picking up, so they decided to leave the car where it was and walk to the meeting. It was not a fancy building. It sat in the middle of flat, square factories and warehouses. It had a certain charm about it, though, with two stories of dark painted brick, awnings over each window, and a windowed, wooden doorway straight from the eighteen-hundreds. It might not be fancy, but as Emily walked in, she was even more convinced that this Arbel guy did take personal pride in his company and wasn't likely going to take chances of throwing it away.

Emily told the receptionist they would like to see Mr. Arbel. The young woman showed a professional smile and asked if they had an appointment. Emily offered her business card and the well-rehearsed smile changed to something unrehearsed. She stepped from the room saying something about finding out if Mr. Arbel was available.

He was.

As the three entered his office, Arbel was standing behind his desk holding Emily's card. "How may I help you folks? It's not every morning I get a visit from the FBI, let alone three of them." His smile seemed to be genuine.

Emily made introductions.

"New Orleans!" Arbel said. "Now I really am surprised. What can I do for you? And, please, sit down."

"Thank you. Mr. Arbel, we need to ask you about one of your boats, to see what..."

"A boat? Which boat? Is there a problem?"

"That's what we're here to find out Mr. Arbel. The boat is the Francis B."

"The Francis B? Yes, that's one of our boats. And please, call me Gil; everyone does."

"Thank you, sir. What we need to know is if there has been anything unusual about the actions of the Francis B. over the past few days. Anything you might be able to tell us could be helpful."

"Unusual? About the Francis B? Not that I know of. I'm sure I would have been told if...besides, I look at the fleet reports the first and last thing every day, so if there was anything, uh, unusual as you say, I would know about it."

"Yes, sir. But if you could..."

"Just what is this about anyway?" Arbel leaned back in his chair.

"Mr. Arbel, Gil, are you familiar with the incident this week at the Grammercy Bridge near New Orleans?"

"Yes, the explosion? Just what I've heard from the news. And I'm familiar enough to know that shutting the river is costing us money. What about it?"

"Sir, we have reason to believe that the Francis B. may be involved in that incident. In fact, we believe..."

"Nonsense. There must be some kind of mistake. How could my boat be involved in an explosion? Are you suggesting it struck a line or something? Is that what this is about?"

"No sir, that's not why we are here. And I'm afraid..."

"I think you need to speak with my attorney if..."

Emily glanced at Lennie, who nodded his head.

"Mr. Arbel, this is not about a lawsuit. Sir, what I am going to tell you must stay in this office. You must tell no one about this information, do you understand?"

"Ok, yes, I understand."

Over the next five minutes, Emily and Lennie explained the reality behind the media's story of the explosion, and the fact that similar devices had now been confirmed under every bridge from New Orleans to Natchez.

"My God, is this for real?"

"Yes sir, I'm afraid it is very real."

"But I don't understand. What does the Francis B. have to do with this? We don't carry..."

Emily explained the tracking that had taken place, and the latest appearance of the device at Natchez tied directly to the Francis B.

Gil Arbel was silent for several seconds.

"So, you are suggesting that my men, on my boat, are involved in this thing? Listen, I know my people, and I know for a fact that none of them would..." Arbel clearly took this situation personally.

"Sir," Emily said as calmly as she can, "we're not suggesting anything about your people. All we know is that the Francis B. appears to be how these devices are being placed. Somehow it is being used..."

"All right, let's put an end to this." Arbel slapped the button on his intercom, "Debbie, send Alma in here, and have her bring the traffic sheets for the Francis B. with her, for the past week."

"I'm sorry sir," she responded, "Alma hasn't come in yet this morning. But I can get those reports for you if you'd like."

"Uh, ok, yes. For the past week, please." Arbel had a puzzled look on his face.

"Is there a problem sir?", Emily asked.

"No, or I don't think so. It's just strange. Alma is in here by four o'clock each morning. She handles the fleet traffic reports and has those ready for our staff meeting at nine. It's not like her to be late; and strange she didn't tell anyone. I hope she's ok."

"Yes, sir. Alma handles all of the traffic?" Emily glanced at Lennie.

"Yes, she's done it for a few years now. Her husband was port captain with us for many years. After he died, Alma seemed kind of lost, so I offered her the role, temporarily, just to give her something to do. She did such a great job we kept her. In fact, she helped setup the new system a couple of years ago. Honestly, she's probably the only person here who really understands the damn thing; other than Alex."

"Alex?" Lennie asked.

"Alex Mantelle. Every company has to have their techie guy nowadays, and Alex is ours. He works with Alma on the traffic system but does lots of other things as well. He's kind of our jack-of-all-trades around here for anything technical."

"I see. Is Alex..."

The door opened, and Debbie handed Arbel a folder. He opened it and flipped through a handful of papers.

"Yeah, it's like I said," Arbel said without looking up, "everything looks just fine here. A pretty typical run."

"May we take a look, sir?" Emily asked as she extended a hand.

"Sure, but I'm not sure that you'll..." he stopped as he saw Lennie pull papers from his pocket, hand them to Emily, and lean over to look at the two sets with her.

"What are you doing?" Arbel asked.

A few moments of silence as Emily and Lennie looked at the paperwork. They finally looked up, and Emily turned back to Arbel.

"Sir, I need you to look at something. Before coming in this morning, we pulled the MRTIS traffic reports for the Francis B. for the past week. You're familiar with the..."

"The river traffic service, sure. But what..."

"Sir, here, please take a look at the two reports; the MRTIS report and your internal traffic report." Emily handed him the papers.

Arbel scanned the documents.

"But, this can't be possible. There must be some kind of mistake here. You say these are both from..."

"The same time period, yes sir."

"But, how? Something must be screwed up with the MRTIS system. This shows the Francis B. turning around the other night and going back, even below New Orleans. That's not possible. Our records show it kept moving upriver. Besides, our boats never go below New Orleans. There has to be a problem with MRTIS."

"We had them confirm the data Mr. Arbel. And, we have images from bridge and traffic cameras showing the Francis B. all the way down to Algiers, below New Orleans."

"Photos? This makes absolutely no sense at all." He slapped the intercom again, "Debbie, tell Alex I need to see him. I need to see him now."

"Sir, Alex hasn't come in yet this morning either. There must be something going around. Do you want me to try and call him? Sir? Sir?"

"No. No thank you' Debbie. Not right now." His voice sounded like all the air has been let out of the balloon. Arbel leaned back in his chair and finally moved his eyes from the intercom to Agent Graham.

"I don't...I just don't...there must be some explanation for this...I mean..."

"Yes, sir."

"I, uh, I'm sorry, but I do need to go to our morning staff meeting. Our other boats, you know." Arbel was speaking but not to anyone in particular.

"Of course, sir," Emily said. "We have things we need to take care of right away as well. Why don't we come back in an hour; will that be enough time?"

Arbel nodded.

Gil Arbel was a big man. He looked like someone who spent time as a deckhand, worked his way up the ladder and built the physique that comes with that kind of hard work. It felt strange seeing him sitting here now with his head in his hands.

Chapter 50

"Look," Lennie said as they walked back toward the coffee and tea shop, "I need to head back and help deal with the media crap going on. I guess our Agent Dasilva needs help after all."

"Ok, I think we're good here," Emily said. "I want to go through my messages and then go back to Arbel in an hour. But, I have a question for both of you first."

They stopped walking.

"Does it seem strange to either of you that the two people involved in the traffic reporting both didn't show up for work this morning?"

"I was wondering the same thing," Agent Erikson said.

"Yeah, and it surprised Arbel too," Lennie added.

"Loren, why don't you go see what you can find about our two missing players. The big question is why they're both gone today, and where they are right now. Then we'll go from there."

"Sure thing. I'll get my team on it right away and let you know. Agent Ryan, can I give you a lift to the airport first?"

"Nah, you get going on the Arbel people; I'll grab a cab. Thanks."

Agent Erikson walked across the street to the car, while Lennie stood at the corner watching for a cab. Emily walked across Main Street, ordered a cup of black tea, and found a seat in a quiet corner. When she heard her name called, she walked to the counter, got her tea, and returned to her table. Someone had taken a seat at a nearby table, and he nodded as she walked by. Emily was not in the mood for conversation with a stranger but returned a polite nod, and then focused her eyes on the screen of her tablet.

After reviewing the routine messages, and deleting the usual collection of junk mail, she noticed the message with the video attachment. She saw that it was sent by Colonel Reyes at 6:45 this morning. She made sure the volume was down on her tablet to avoid disturbing anyone else and started the video. The image flickered briefly, and then displayed a perfect, birds-eye view of a towboat. As the view passed the boat, she saw the name Francis B. painted on the side. Emily sat up in her chair. The image moved to the stern of the boat where it stayed, following the boat as it moved upriver toward a bridge. After a few minutes, two men appeared on the back of the boat, carrying a large object. A third man was holding a rope. As she watched, the men lowered the object into the water and dragged it behind them with the rope. As the Francis B. passed under the bridge, the man jerked the rope, and the object disappeared into the murky water.

Emily replayed the video. And again. The images weren't sharp enough for her to make out any faces, but it was very clear what was going on. The object on the rope was the same size as the device found at Grammercy. And it was indeed the Francis B.

Emily's pulse was racing, and she wanted to stand up on her chair and yell something, like, "We got 'em!", but she knew that was not an option. Instead, she leaned back in her chair, turned off the video and allowed her eyes to move from the screen to the rest of the room.

The man at the nearby table also looked up and nodded a second time. Emily politely did the same, and immediately looked back to her screen. The man got up from his table and walked toward the door, but not before stopping to offer one more smile and nod. This time, Emily ignored it and began planning her second conversation with Mr. Gil Arbel.

Chapter 51

"Agent Graham, come in please." Gil Arbel saw her standing in the office doorway.

"Thank you, sir," Emily said. "I hope your staff meeting went well."

"Yes, just fine, thanks. Though I am even more puzzled than I was earlier; about Alma not being here."

"Sir?"

"She apparently did come in this morning as usual. She prepared the traffic reports, but left before the meeting; she told someone she was not feeling well and was going home."

"I'm sorry to hear that."

"Yeah, I worry about her sometimes. Like I said, her husband was our port captain but ended up with some type of cancer. It was a really hard time for both of them. I've tried to help Alma out as much as I can, but sometimes she still seems to be having a tough time of it. I'm just hoping she hasn't ended up with something like Harvey had."

"Yes, I understand. We actually have someone checking on her this morning, so maybe we can help ease your mind on that."

"Checking on her? What do you mean? You're not suggesting..."

"Mr. Arbel, I assure you, it's just routine. With her role in creating the traffic reports, we need to make sure we have all the information we need; especially with the discrepancies with the MRTIS reports."

"I still can't believe our people would be involved in something like this. I mean, even with those photos, it doesn't prove that the Francis B. is connected with these device things you are talking about."

Emily got up from her chair and walked to Arbel's desk.

"I need to show you something we just got this morning." She placed the tablet on the desk and started the video.

"Yes, that's the Francis B.," Arbel said, "and that looks like the Vicksburg bridge. But wait, who are those people on the stern tail? Those aren't our guys."

"How can you tell sir? I mean, are you sure?"

"Of course I'm sure. Our guys wouldn't be out there without wearing a vest; they know better."

"A vest?"

"A life jacket. Every towboater knows stories of what happens if you fall in the river without a vest. It's one of the biggest risks of the job. Our guys wear a vest anytime they're outside, 'cause they know I'll fire their ass if they don't. No, those aren't our guys. Who are they?"

"That's what we need to find out, sir. We're working on facial recognition now."

"I need to call my boat."

"Sir, wait. Please."

"I need to know if my people are ok out there. I need to know who these people are and what the hell they are doing on my boat."

"Yes sir, we want the same thing. But we don't want to spook them if you know what I mean. Right now, they don't appear to know we have tracked them down, so whatever they are doing, it seems to be safe for your crew. But if we spook them; well, we don't know what they might do."

"Yeah, OK. Alright. I understand. So just what can we do? I just can't sit here."

"No sir, we're not going to do that. Let's start by having you..." She felt the vibration in her pocket. "Excuse me a minute Mr. Arbel, I need to take this."

"Sure."

"Graham." She said as she raised the phone.

"Emily, it's Loren Erikson. We found Alma Hendricks; she's at home."

"That's good news. She told someone here that's where she was going."

"We've just confirmed she is here, but haven't talked with her yet. What do you want us to do?"

"I'll tell you what; have your people keep an eye on her, and you pick me up at Arbel's in thirty minutes; we'll both talk with her."

"Got it. See you then."

"You found Alma?" Arbel asked. "Is she alright?"

"She is at home, but we've not talked with her yet; you heard my side of the conversation."

"But she's OK?"

"As far as we know, yes."

Gil Arbel smiled, leaned back in his chair. His eyes closed for a few seconds and then opened to focus on Emily.

"I'm sorry Agent Graham, but these folks are like family to me; especially Alma, after all she's been through."

"I understand sir."

Arbel's eyes showed a question. "I'm curious. There was a captain I knew named Graham, any chance you know him? Jim Graham."

"He's my father, yes sir."

"You're Jim Graham's daughter? Well, I'll be damned. That means I saw pictures of you back when you must have been three or four years old; Jim showed those things to everybody. Where is your dad now; how is he?"

"He's in New Orleans, where I live. He's fine physically, but he's having cognition problems...you know, memory issues. A few months ago I had to move him to a new place; someplace they're trained to deal with that kind of thing. He can be kind of challenging to handle sometimes."

"That's Jim for ya. He was one of the old-school guys out there. He knew the river better than anybody I ever met, but he never quite figured out how to handle people; no offense, I mean."

"No, none taken. It sounds like you knew him pretty well."

"We rode together for several years up on the Illinois. He's the main reason I got my pilot's license; I don't think I could have done it without his foot on my rear end."

"Yeah, that's his approach."

"When I got off the river and took over the company, I tried to convince him to come with me."

"Really?"

"I thought he would make one hell of a port captain; he knew how everything worked, and knew how to sort through all the crap you have to deal with. But he wouldn't do it; said he was sick and tired of the boats, but wasn't about to trade them for a desk. I guess he stayed out there until he retired?"

"Yes, sir."

"Jim Graham's girl. I'll be damned. But I'm sure you want to talk about other things right now. Maybe when this is all over, we can have you out to dinner sometime; tell some stories about your dad?"

"I'd like that sir, but yes, we do need to talk about the Francis B. What can you tell me about the crew out there right now?"

"They're a good bunch. Charlie Graff is the captain. He's a lot like your dad; one of the guys who's been out there since high school. Charlie was working for my dad before I came in the office. Like your dad, he doesn't put up with any nonsense on his boat, so whatever is going on out there, I know Charlie isn't a part of it. If I know him, he's just waiting for the right opportunity to throw the guys into the river."

"And the others?"

"The pilot is Frank Maddox. He came here five or six years ago, and he's one of the guys Charlie has kind of taken under his wing. He'll be running his own boat in a few more months. He's smart, and has a good way of dealing with his crew. Tough, but fair; the guys like working for him."

"Do they both have families?"

"Yeah. Charlie's kids are grown and on their own, so it's just him and his wife now. Good kids, too. Frank has two kids, both in college. He lost his wife two years ago; some kind of infection that got out of control. They tried all kinds of things to stop it, but nothing worked. The kids were in high school then, so we gave him some time off to be with them and take care of things. I actually tried to get him to move here to the office. I thought they could move here to town, and he could work here so he could be home at night with the kids. He had a tough time of it for a while; I don't know all the details, but I guess there were some messy things with insurance. I even called our provider and threatened to change companies if they didn't step up and fix things, so they finally did take care of most of the issues."

"Yes, sir."

"The chief engineer is Smitty Reynolds; that's not his real first name, but its the only one he uses. He's Charlie Graff's cousin, which honestly, is probably the only reason he's still got a job."

"Sir?"

"Smitty is what you call, one of those colorful characters. He's a damned good engineer, but he's had a serious problem with alcohol."

"I see."

"And I mean serious. He starts drinking the day he gets off a boat, and he doesn't stop until he gets on the next one thirty days later. That kind of serious. I'll tell you his wife is a saint; I'm just amazed she hasn't shot him yet."

"Has the drinking caused any problems?"

"At work? Only once or twice; but that was quite a while ago. And mostly just stupid stuff that Charlie was able to clear up with a few phone calls to friends. Now he only rides with Charlie; they have kind of a family agreement. Smitty knows if he gets caught drinking on the boat, Charlie isn't going to make any more phone calls. Without the booze, Smitty is a great guy. Hell of an engineer, and hell of a friend; will do anything for you and works harder than any three men on the river. It's a sickness..."

"I understand. Who else is on the Francis B. right now?"

Gil Arbel described Roosevelt Phelps, the oiler, or second engineer, a man from the Louisiana bayou country.

"Goes out there and catches those big snapping turtles bare-handed. I'll tell you; the man isn't afraid of anything."

He listed the four deckhands: Clovis Landry and Virgil Amedee, two young men from Mississippi who came to the boats as their way of getting out into the world. Ricky Pratt, fresh from high school in Arkansas, with dreams of one day having his own boat. Danny Romero from Georgia, the newest crew member, just learning the deckhand role. "Charlie tells me he's a hard worker but doesn't seem to mix well with the rest of the crew; kind of keeps to himself a bit too much. But if anyone can bring him out of it, Charlie's the guy."

And finally, the most important crew member on any boat; the cook, Dorian Dufries. "We always put Dorian out there with Charlie. She's the only cook we've got who knows how to make coffee the way Charlie likes it. If we give Charlie anyone but Dorian, I get calls; I mean lots of calls from Charlie threatening to throw them off his boat. So, that's the crew."

"I know this is a difficult question, but are there any of those people that you would have any concerns at all about; I mean, any of them who might..."

"Might be involved in something like this? Absolutely not!"

"Alright. One last thing for now. You've told me a bit about Alma, and I'll talk with her later, but what can you tell me about Alex; the tech guy?"

"Alex? He's one of those nerdy, tech guys I guess. Smart as a whip, and a hard worker. I don't understand about half of what he says, but he's done a good job for us."

"How long has he been here?"

"Alex came a couple of years ago, as we were talking about doing the system update for Alma's work. We did a search and Alex was the top of the list; came from out East I believe, around Baltimore. He's quiet, but has brought us into the twenty-first century."

"That sounds good, thanks. Is there anything else you can think of that I ought to know right now? Anything at all?"

"No, I don't think so. Other than I know that whoever those other people are on my boat, my people aren't involved with them; not willingly anyway."

Emily got up and started toward the door.

"Mr. Arbel, I want to remind you to not say anything about our conversation to anyone else; here at work or anyplace. Until we understand just what is going on here, we don't know who might be involved, and what these guys might do if they know we are coming."

"I understand. Just take care of my people, alright?"

"Yes sir, we'll do our best."

Emily walked from the office and stood in the shade of a small tree as she sorted through the events of the past seventy-two hours and waited for her ride.

Chapter 52

"Do we know anything about this Alex guy yet?", Emily asked as Loren drove east on Brownsboro Road.

"Nothing yet," Loren said. "When we found Alma, I put more of the team on him, so hopefully we'll hear something soon."

"Good move. How did you find Alma?"

"We started at the house and saw her standing on the patio; just got lucky."

"We'll take that when we can get it. She didn't notice anything?"

"We just drove by, so I don't think so. We've got two cars watching the place, but from a distance. There's one of them now."

Loren turned onto Hite Avenue, pulled alongside a sedan parked against the curb.

"Anything going on?" Loren asked the man in the parked car.

"Nope. Quiet as can be."

"Ok, we're going in. Stay put for now."

The man nodded as Loren drove up the road and turned into the curved driveway leading to the small patio.

"I'll follow your lead," Loren said to Emily as they walked up the neatly trimmed brick sidewalk. Emily knocked on the door, and after a few moments, they heard footsteps inside.

"Yes?" As Alma Hendricks opened the door, Emily immediately thought of Aunt Bee from the Andy Griffith show she used to watch as a kid. Though probably quicker and smarter than Opie's aunt, Alma had the appearance of someone more likely to be working out a new chocolate chip cookie recipe than falsifying business documents.

"Alma Hendricks?" Emily asked.

"Yes, I'm Alma Hendricks." She smiled weakly and looked at the two women. "Come in. I imagine you are from the police? I've been expecting you."

Emily and Loren glanced at each other.

"We're with the FBI Mrs. Hendricks. We'd like to ask you a few questions if you don't mind." Emily followed Alma through the small kitchen to a very tidy living room.

"The FBI? Oh, my. I had no idea." Alma pointed to chairs and slowly found one for herself.

"Yes, ma'am. I am Agent Graham, and this is Agent Erickson. Are you willing to speak with us for a few minutes?"

"Yes, of course. As I said, I was expecting someone from the police. Where should we begin?"

It was rare that Emily had felt so welcomed by someone she was investigating.

"Well, first all, are you feeling well enough to talk right now? I understand you came home from work because you were not well."

"Oh my, no, I'm fine. When Alex came in this morning and told me someone was coming about the reports, I just thought it was better if I got today's reports finished and came home. I didn't want to create a problem for Gil, Mr. Arbel, there at the office you know."

"Alex told you we were coming this morning?" Emily asked.

"Well, not that you specifically were coming; not the FBI. He just said that things had changed. Someone had found out about the reports and would be coming in."

"Did he say how he knew someone was coming this morning?"

"Oh no." Alma waved a hand in the air, "he never explained things like that to me. He always seemed to know more than he told me, and that was fine with me. I really didn't want to get involved in any of that stuff; whatever he was doing."

Loren took notes as Emily continued.

"Do you know where Alex is now, Mrs. Hendricks?"

"Why no. Isn't he at the office?"

"No, ma'am. Apparently, he left before anyone was there as well."

"My goodness. Maybe he felt like I did and just went home. I don't think either of us wanted to embarrass Gil."

"Yes, ma'am. We're checking his home too. Why don't you help us out by explaining just what it was that you did; what it is that might be embarrassing at the office?"

"Certainly. Well, I guess it started shortly after Alex came to work with us. He was responsible for the new computer system for fleet traffic you know. Before that, we had to do it all by hand, one page..."

"Yes, ma'am. What happened when Alex joined the company?"

"Well, that was about the same time I was having more problems with my health. Everyone at the office thinks that Alex is kind of, you know, cold or unfriendly, but he has always been very sweet to me, always asking how I am doing, he is really a very nice boy."

"Yes, ma'am."

"Well, as I said, it was when I was having some problems. My husband, Harvey, had gotten this rare form of cancer. We tried everything we could, but nothing helped. There were other treatments, but the insurance company wouldn't let us try them. They said they were too experimental. Then, when Harvey died, I had all kinds of troubles getting the insurance company to pay the bills they had said they would approve. They threatened to sue me; even take away our house, the one we had lived in for forty years. If Gil hadn't gotten involved, I'm afraid that they might have really done that. At work, Alex always listened to me talk on and on about all of it. He was a real comfort for me. Not that the others weren't too; Alex just always seemed to go out of his way to check on me, you know?"

"Yes ma'am, that must have been a big help."

"Oh, it certainly was. Especially as things got worse."

"Ma'am?"

"Well, just after we finally got things worked out with the insurance, I went for my annual checkup for the company, and I was diagnosed with the same kind of cancer that Harvey had."

"I'm so sorry."

"Oh, thank you. But you know, honestly, I think I was more worried about having to go through all of the insurance problems again than I was about the cancer itself. Isn't that silly? But it's true."

"Yes, ma'am."

"And that's why when Alex talked with me about his idea for teaching the insurance company a lesson I thought it sounded like a good idea. We both felt that no one else should have to go through what I had gone through. At first, I wasn't sure. I mean, I didn't want to do anything that might hurt Gil, after all he had done for Harvey and me. But the more I thought about it, if we could get the insurance company to change, then Gil wouldn't have to deal with them again for any of his other people. So I agreed to help Alex."

"And change the traffic reports?"

"Well, not at first. When we started, he just wanted copies of the reports so he could look at them."

"For the Francis B.?"

"Oh no, for all of the boats. It was about a month later that he talked to me about the Francis B. He showed me a report he had made up himself, and he asked me to look at it and see if I saw anything wrong with it. I made a few suggestions, and he seemed happy."

"What happened next?"

"Well, nothing happened for a long time. In fact, we didn't even talk about again it until last week. He came in early and asked me to take another look at a report to see if anything had changed, and then said that we were going to start our little lesson for the insurance company. We actually started it three days ago. Since then, every morning I ran the normal traffic reports for all the boats, but for the Francis B. I substituted Alex's pretend report for the real one."

"Three days ago."

"Yes, that's right. I still don't understand how that little report is going to teach the insurance company anything, but Alex and his friends seemed to know what they are doing."

"His friends? There are others involved?"

"Oh, I don't know who they are, or where they are, but sometimes he mentioned that he had talked with others who were helping with his plan. I don't think any of them were around here, though."

Emily and Loren had a brief side conversation.

Alma looked to the floor, shaking her head, "I know Gil will be so disappointed in us. I just hope he understands that we were trying to make things better for everyone, especially for him. I hope he understands. He's a good man."

"Yes, ma'am."

"So, what do we do now? Do I have to pay a fine or something? Has Gil said anything about my job? I hope changing that one report hasn't created too much confusion at the office. It was just the one boat."

"Before we go, ma'am, how are you doing? You mentioned the results of your checkup earlier."

"Yes, well, I'm afraid it's not good. I had tests yesterday, and it seems the cancer has spread. After seeing everything Harvey went through, I've decided to not do all of those expensive treatments and fight more with the insurance. The doctor tried to get me to change my mind, but no, I just don't want to do that. He says I have another month or two before things start getting bad, so I'm going to make the best of it. I'd like to travel; maybe go to New Orleans. I hear its wonderful down there."

"Yes, ma'am, it is. Alma, Agent Erickson will be back in touch with you this afternoon. I'm going to ask that you stay here until she comes back, ok?"

"Why certainly, if you need me too. Oh my, am I under arrest or something?"

"No, ma'am. But we do need you to stay here until we sort things out. Until Agent Erikson comes back, there will be another agent outside, just for security."

"Security? I don't understand."

"Yes ma'am, but until we can get everything sorted out, this is standard procedure. We need you to stay here. Ok?"

"Yes, of course."

As Loren pulled out of the driveway, "Do we take her in?"

"Not right now. I don't think she's going anywhere. Plus, I think we probably know as much as she can tell us anyway, at least until we find this Alex character. And until we find him, I think she's safer with someone watching her right here."

"Safer than in our office?"

"I don't know. There's something going on here that I don't like."

"You mean these other people with Alex?"

"Well, maybe. Somebody told him we were coming this morning. And who knew that? Lennie and I knew it, the jet pilot knew it, and you knew it. How the hell did Alex find out?"

"This is getting weird."

"Weird is the right word. We've got a bunch of guys on a boat, with devices that anyone would say would be impossible to build, somehow bypassing all existing security measures for that kind of thing, and now we've got some other group of people who seem to be involved here, and to top it off, somebody in there seems to know what we're doing before we even do it. Yeah, I'm going with weird for that."

"Do we have a mole?"

"Somebody talked. Right now that looks like either me, or Lennie, or the pilot, or you."

"Or..."

"Or, there's somebody else in here that we don't know about."

It was quiet as they drove past the Arbel building on the way to the interstate.

"Where do you want me to take you? You look like you could use some rest."

"Yeah, it was a short night for sure. Where's the nearest decent hotel?"

"There's a Hampton, or a bunch of others at the airport."

"Nah, let's stay close and make it easier. The Hampton is fine."

"Ok. Then I'll get an update from my team looking for Alex, and head back to talk more with Alma. You still OK with letting her stay at home?"

"For now, yeah. Unless you find something that changes things. At this point, I think she's more of an innocent victim in all this. But if you find otherwise, it's your call."

Emily got out of the car and checked in at the Hampton downtown. She put her bag on the table and stretched out on the bed to rest her eyes. In ten seconds, she was back on the beach. There was a boat floating offshore with three guys throwing nukes in the surf, and some woman in the chair next to her, editing a spreadsheet and baking cookies. Jimmy Buffett was nowhere in sight.

Chapter 53

"Hey boss, how's the media circus going?". Emily had seen the little sign about the complimentary buffet and wine bar when she checked-in, so after her two-hour nap, she decided to go down and call it dinner. While munching on the free food, and enjoying a rather nice local red wine, she called Lennie.

"You ever see those videos of a bunch of sharks eating something? That's about how it's going. Somehow, they are getting information we've not released yet, so we're mostly running around playing catch-up and stopping rumors." Lennie sounded tired.

"That's something we need to talk about. Who knew that we were coming to Louisville today?"

"I'm not sure, why?"

"Well, the reason those two Arbel people weren't at work today is because they knew we were coming."

"How'd they know?"

"That's what I'm saying we need to figure out. Who besides you, me, Loren and the pilot knew about our trip? I didn't tell anyone other than dad, and I doubt he remembered."

"Geez Em, let me think. The only people I talked to about it were Dasilva and Reyes. Of course, our guys at the office knew, and our pilot, like you said."

"Neither Dasilva or Reyes seem to be the type that talks."

"Unless there's a microphone in front of him." Lennie said, "Oh, did I say that out-loud?"

"Ha, having fun with Mr. Super-agent there Lennie?"

"Nah, we're alright. He just really likes polishing his image. I guess there's nothing wrong with that; its just not my style."

"Good thing; otherwise I'd have to shoot you."

"Yeah, thanks. Ok then, until we find out what's going on, I think you and I had better keep a tight lid on things."

"Do we tell Reyes and Dasilva?"

"Em, at this point I trust two people; you and me."

"Sounds like a plan. By the way, it sounds like you need to get some rest."

"Yeah, got a bit of sleep on the plane, but otherwise I've been going since yesterday. I'm heading home now to try and stretch out for a while."

"Good. I'm at the hotel here, going through notes from the interviews today catching up on messages from Reyes and others."

"Right. Let's talk in the morning."

"Yep."

Emily put the phone on the table and sipped her wine. Lennie was a nice guy. He was a bit older, but not that much. He had got a nice sense of humor, which was one of the things on Emily's list. He was in good shape, and was serious about his work. Her mind screeched to a halt; she looked out the window and shook her head to clear the haze. What was she thinking? It was Lennie. He was her boss, which created all kinds of issues if they were to...to...besides, they're both full-time career people. Maybe she needed more sleep, or maybe it was the wine, but it kind of surprised her when she realized she had never thought about Lennie like that before.

As she came out of the haze, she became aware of the man standing next to her table. He was older, decently dressed, and had a smile on his face; a cross between a college professor and a traveling salesman.

"You look lost in thought. May I join you?", the smiling man asked.

"Oh, yeah, I guess I was." Emily glanced at the folder on the table. "But honestly, I have a lot of work to do here. I don't mean to sound rude, but I really don't think..."

"Agent Graham, just a few minutes, please," he pulled up a chair and sat down, still smiling.

"How do you know my name?" Emily made eye contact and felt her body become tense. "Who are you?"

"I'm Steve. That will do for now."

Emily sized him up. He appeared calm and at ease, like someone experienced in introducing himself to women at hotel buffets. His hands were on the table, so there was no immediate threat there. His smile was well practiced; good enough to pass for real. Maybe he's a regular here, someone at the desk told him her name, and she was next in line to enjoy his hospitality. So, maybe this was an opportunity to put the jerk in his place. Emily smiled.

"Steve. Ok Steve, just what can I do for you?"

"Agent Graham, we need you to give us time. It's important that you don't act too quickly."

Emily had responses for most every pick-up line, but this was the strangest one she'd ever heard.

"I'm not sure what you mean. Act too quickly; about what?"

"The Francis B., Agent Graham. We need more time before you do anything about it."

Emily paused.

"What about the Francis B.? Who are..."

"We're on the same team here, Agent Graham, I assure you. And I'm asking you to..."

"Same team? What are you; CIA, Homeland Security, something like that?"

"I'll let you get back to your work there," he nodded at the folder on the table. "You're doing a fine job, by the way. Perhaps this will help you with one part of your journey." The smile was still there as he handed her a business card, stood up, put the chair back where he got it, walked out of the lobby, and out the front door.

Emily saw that it was not a business card at all, but just a piece of paper with a handwritten note on it: Shippingport Drive, 1.3 miles. She ran to the parking lot that had cars but no Steve, then remembered her folder. She walked back to the table and called Loren, telling her about the note.

"That's a road on Shippingport Island, west of town by the locks," Loren said. "We'll check it out."

Emily grabbed her folder and bag of popcorn and headed back to her room. As she pushed the elevator button, she realized that Steve was the guy at the coffee shop this morning. How had she missed that?

Although it violated a rule she never broke, as she stepped into the elevator she heard herself say, "What next?"

Forty-five minutes later her phone rang. "Agent Graham, it's Loren. We're at the address on the note, and I think you need come out her. A car will pick you up in ten minutes."

And that's why Emily never violated her rule.

Chapter 54

The barge they were picking up was tied up to the east side of the river, alongside a bunch of other barges carrying rock to rebuild the shore. The river made a wide, sweeping turn near Chatham, and the currents were constantly eating soil away from the shore and redepositing it as sandbars on the south side of the bend. The rock slowed it down, but it was just part of the ever-changing river that made a boat pilot pay attention. It was another twelve miles to the bridge at Greenville.

Four hundred and fifty miles to the northeast, if you were a crow, Emily's car crossed the McAlpine Locks Bridge and turned onto a road with a large security gate. The gate was open. Signs said to stop, and keep out; all of the normal messages that accompanied a government area surrounded by a tall fence with barbed wire on top. But the gate was open. From the looks of the massive equipment, Emily decided it was a construction site for the locks and the hydroelectric dam nearby.

"It's just another mile." her driver said.

Their conversation had been limited. Apparently, the driver had been instructed to stay focused on making it a quick trip. When Emily first got into the car, she asked what this was about. The driver said, "I'm not sure. Agent Erikson will fill you in when we get there."

After passing the construction buildings, the road was one lane of gravel, with trees on the left, and the Louisville and Portland Canal on the right. Emily saw a railroad bridge above the road ahead, but before going that far, the car slowed and turned into a muddy gap in the trees. About fifty feet in, the path opened into a clearing, strewn with weeds, and three cars. Emily saw Loren walking toward them as they parked.

"I thought you would want to see this for yourself," Loren said.

Emily saw that two of the cars were agent's cars. The third was a small sedan; looked like a Toyota, probably just a year or two old and in pristine shape. The plates were local, the windows and doors were closed except for the front passenger door. As she walked closer, she noticed that the inside of the car was as clean and neat as the outside, and there was a body stretched across the front seat. It appeared to be male, probably in its twenties, and hadn't been here more than a few hours."

"Let me guess," Emily said.

"Emily, meet Alex," Loren replied.

Eight dozen questions went through Emily's mind at one time, about half related to Alex and how he got here, and the other half about this guy named Steve, and how he knew.

"It looks like a suicide," Loren said. There's no sign of a wound or a weapon, so I assume it was some type of poison or something. The coroner will tell us."

"We're sure it happened here?" Emily asked, "or could he have been dumped here?"

"There's no sign of any tracks or anything, so it looks like he drove himself and did the deed. But there is a camera at that front gate, and we'll look at the video from that."

"That gate is always open?"

"Usually, at least during the day."

"And we know this is our Alex?"

"He has ID on him. I stopped everything and called you as soon as we found that. We've not done anything else yet; I thought you might want to get a fresh look."

"Yeah, thanks. Go ahead and start again; I'll watch along."

The crime scene team went back into action, carefully examining every inch of the car, and of Alex. As they finished their initial search, one of the investigators walked over.

"Not much more than fingerprints. It's like a new car. Nothing in the glove box, nothing under the seats. The trunk looks like it's never been opened. The car was registered to him two years ago, but he sure couldn't have used it much."

"Ok, Phil. Let's see what we find after you take it in."

Loren turned to Emily. "Anything else you want to see here?"

"Not now. Is the coroner here yet?"

"Yeah, she's waiting over by your car."

Emily walked over to the young woman in the jacket with 'Coroner' on the back.

"Hi, I'm Agent Graham with the FBI, are you our coroner?"

"Yes, ma'am. Jolene Morgan, Chief Medical Examiner for Jefferson County. We were told you had something that needed special attention."

"Yes, excellent. Agent Erikson will fill you in with the details, but yeah, we need to know as much about this guy as you can learn."

"Cause of death, existing or past trauma or health issues, things like that?" Chief Examiner Morgan asked.

"Exactly. Now that we have his ID, we'll do a full background, but anything you can add to that will be extremely important. How soon will you do this?"

"When you say it's time to start, we'll take him in and get right on it. I can get you preliminary findings later tonight, and we'll push the rest as hard as we can."

"Thanks. He's all yours."

Emily and Loren walked back to Emily's car.

"One more thing for now," Emily said, handing Loren a plastic bag. "Here's the note card from our new friend Steve. See if you can pull any prints off it; other than mine."

"I'll let you know," Loren said as she took the bag. "You going back to the hotel?"

"I think so. It looks like tomorrow's going to be a long one. By the way, did you notice the marks on Alex's hand?"

"You mean the bruising? Yeah, what do you make of that?"

"Let's see what the examiner says, but they look a lot like bruises on my dad's hand from his IV's."

"So, you think he had an IV recently?"

"They're the kind of marks you get from having a lot of IV's; like for some type of ongoing treatment for something. But let's see what they find. Call me if you find anything else, uh, interesting."

Emily got back into the car and had a quiet ride back to her hotel. The beach was waiting for her; and tonight Jimmy Buffett was back, sitting on the hood of a car singing a new tune about IV tubes, cheap red wine, and somebody named Steve.

Chapter 55

For the first time in two days, Charlie found himself smiling as he passed under a bridge; this one just below Greenville, Mississippi. The idea had come to him after the incident with Smitty, and the conversation in the galley when the leader said that he knew the authorities would find them, but it wouldn't make any difference. What bothered Charlie the most was how confident he was that nothing could be done. That was the moment Charlie decided that he had to come up with a plan; no one ever tells a riverboat guy that he can't do something, especially on his own boat. He had spent his watch-time thinking about it, and when he was off-watch, he studied the navigation maps, hunting for the place. It all came together this afternoon, and it was time to get his crew ready for action. They would strike in three hours.

"You want to see me?" Frank asked as he stepped into the pilothouse.

"It's time to put an end to this. Listen, I've got it worked out. I need you to get the crew up here, quietly, so the crazies down there don't know what's going on. Smitty tells me the assholes are all down in the galley talking right now, so if we're quick, I think we can pull it off. You need to kind of spread 'em out a bit, don't have them all come up at one time...but see if we can get everybody here in about ten minutes. Ok?"

"I'll do my best Cap." Frank smiled as he stepped back out in the darkness.

Over the next several minutes, the pilothouse filled with the crew; one at a time.

"Is everybody here?" Charlie looked around the group, "Good. Now listen up. I have a plan for stopping these sons a bitches, but it will only work if we're all together; all doing our part."

Lots of nods around the room, along with "It's about time!" and "Fuckin A Cap!".

"Hang on. Before we get any farther, this ain't the movies here, and things could go bad real quick. These guys have got real guns down there."

"Captain," Clovis Landry's deep Mississippi drawl broke the silence, "ya'll know we just gotta do something here man. I mean, shit, we can't just let them keep droppin' these things in the river like this; not from our boat."

"That's right," fellow Mississippian and future-pilot Virgil Amadee said, "we gotta do something, and if you got a plan then I think it's what we do."

After a minute or two, every voice was heard, and while the accents varied, the sentiment was the same.

"Ok then, listen up, and listen close; we don't have much time here. I've been looking at the maps, and I think I found a place that's far enough away from things; a place that if anything does go wrong, it's not gonna be a problem for a lot of people."

Every eye was focused on Charlie.

"You all know the sandbar just below Monterey Bend; there below Beulah?"

Nods all around.

"We're gonna park this boat right on top of that bar, and park it deep enough that it ain't coming back off on its own."

More nodes and side conversations.

"But captain," Frank said, "what about the bridges?"

"Hang on Frank. But you're right. This will keep them from getting to any more bridges but doesn't do anything about the one's they've already hit. There's two parts to this plan, and the first is to hit that sandbar. Smitty, you ready to do something here?"

Smitty poked his head out from the back of the group, "Sure Charlie. What do you need?"

"When it's time to do this, I want those engines running full tilt to push us clear up on top of that bar. And as soon as we hit it, its the time for you to shut them down; and I mean really shut 'em down. Do you know what I mean?"

"You bet Cap'n."

"Ok then; now for the tricky part. We've got to get to that computer in the storeroom by the galley; that's how they control the other devices. We've got to make sure they can't use it to set those things off."

"How you want us to do that Cap'n?" Virgil Amadee asked.

"There's usually just that one guy in there, so if a couple of you big Mississippi boys could take care of him, the rest of us can deal with the others. They've got guns, so..."

"I swing a pretty mean ratchet when I need to." one of the deckhands said.

"There ya go. These guys are mean, but they've never tangled with a bunch of pissed off river rats before, so let's show them what that means."

"When do we get there Cap'n? How much time we got to get ready?"

"We'll be at the sandbar in about three hours. Now get the hell out of here before somebody sees us. Frank will get with everybody to work out the details."

They started to leave, one-by-one.

"Frank, think you can handle this?" Charlie asked.

"Hell yeah skipper, I'll take care of things." Frank smiled as he stepped out the door.

Chapter 56

"Hullo," Emily grunted into the phone. Her eyes wouldn't focus, but she thought it showed eleven-thirty.

"Hey, you need to come and pick me up," her father said, "I'm getting the hell off this goddamn boat. Come and get me."

Her focus returned.

"Dad, what's going on?"

"I told you what's going on; you need to come and pick me up."

Emily wondered if she should try reality, or join the battle.

"Dad..."

"I've had it with these people. They don't know how to run a boat, and they won't let me do my job, so I'm outta here."

"Dad..."

"Look, I'm getting off at the LaGrange Lock, so you need to come and get me."

"Dad, I can't come right now, I'm in Louisville."

"Louisville? What the hell you doing down there?"

"I'm working dad."

"So you won't come and get me?"

"Dad, I can't leave right now. I'm stuck here for another day or two, at least."

It was quiet for a few moments.

"Dad, do you think you can put up with them for another couple of days? Then I can come and pick you up." It was a gamble, but Emily was betting that he wouldn't remember any of this by morning.

"Well shit, yeah, ok. I guess. But I'm not putting up with any more of their crap."

"Ok, thanks, dad, I understand."

"I'm off watch now," he said, "so I'm going back to bed. Thanks for calling." And the line went dead.

Emily lay back down in bed and thought about the times she had been truly excited to get a call for her and her mother to come and pick him up somewhere. Those surprise visits were always fun. And they always took them to some interesting places; a lock, or a coal or grain dock in the middle of nowhere. And it was always in the middle of the night for some reason. He would hop off the boat as it approached their hometown, then they'd drive down to let him get back on after the boat had gone passed. Short, but nice.

The phone interrupted her memories.

"Yes?" she said a bit more forcefully than she intended.

"Agent Graham? This is Jolene Morgan, from the Medical Examiner's office. I'm sorry if I've called too late, but I thought you might want an update."

"Of course, Jolene," Emily sat up. "I'm sorry; I do appreciate you calling."

"I have some preliminary results. The full report won't be back for a day or two, but I think I have some information you'll find interesting."

"Yes?"

"Direct cause of death was poisoning. It looks like a cyanide base, but it appears to be something quite unique."

"Unique? What do you mean?"

"Well, cyanide has a wide range of formulations, and there are different ways it's used to design this type of kill-pill, as its sometimes called. How familiar are you with this type of thing?"

"Fair, I guess. But please educate me."

"Sure. Cyanide is used because it is quick, it's easy to conceal, and not difficult to get."

"It's a quick and painless way to go, huh?"

"Oh no, that's the myth about it. It can be relatively quick, sure, but it's not painless. Most every fast-acting poison still has other effects before the individual dies. There can be severe pain, muscle spasms, gastro problems like vomiting and diarrhea, breathing difficulties; it's not as clean as the movies make it look."

"But it didn't look like Alex..."

"That's the thing. What he ingested was a combination of things; the cyanide was just one part. There were other drugs that would have knocked him out almost immediately, so he wouldn't have experienced the usual discomforts of the cyanide; not consciously anyway. And there were still other drugs to minimize the gastro issues, which is probably why we didn't see the results of that at the scene. That's why I say this is unique. Your friend Alex took a pill created by someone who really knew what they were doing."

"Have you seen these before?"

"Not personally, no, but I've read about them in the research. This type of thing is usually found in the really out-there cases."

"Like spies and things like that?"

"Well, we usually don't even see it there. Those folks usually don't care if the victim suffers a bit before he goes. But, there's more that you ought to know. Even without the pill, this Alex guy would have been gone within a month. He was already a dead man walking."

"What do you mean?"

"He was full of cancer. It looks like it was stage four pancreatic, but it had metastasized and was throughout his abdomen. There were signs of several surgeries, and indications he had undergone a range of chemo treatments."

"The IV scars on his arm."

"Exactly. But not for a few months. He must have decided to just stop and let things happen."

"So, just let me make sure I understand what I'm hearing. This guy was going to die within a month anyway. Oh, do you think he knew that?"

"There's no way he didn't know. And normally, that would lead me to think that he had just decided to take control of things and kill himself. But that doesn't explain where he got this really strange pill."

"Yeah, for sure. Anything else right now?"

"Nothing important. I'll give you a call when the next results come in."

"Yeah, thanks, Jolene."

Emily closed her eyes and watched the surf roll against the beach. Under a palm tree next to her was a table where a woman was performing an autopsy, and just behind her, a guy in a lab coat was mixing up the contents of a giant poison pill. Jimmy Buffett was standing in the surf, wearing his flip-flops, and shaking his head.

Chapter 57

Charlie watched the radar as the boat passed the large Choctaw Bar Island, and pictured in his mind what was going to happen in two hours at the smaller sandbar upstream. The door opened and the leader stepped inside.

"Evening Captain; about ready to call it a night?"

"Yeah, another thirty minutes and Frank can have it." Charlie decided to be graceful to the poor guy who was about to become fish food. "What brings you up here at this hour?"

"Well, I'll tell you. I was laying there and couldn't sleep. I realized that I hadn't really explained everything to you after that night with your guy Smitty, and I thought I ought to do that."

"I think I understand things..."

"Well, I want to make sure. You see, you and your crew are an important part of our mission here, and I'd hate to have anything, you know, create a problem just because of a misunderstanding."

He had Charlie's attention.

"You see Captain, I told you that we had things under control, and there was nothing to worry about even after the authorities found out what we were doing. But I didn't explain just why you shouldn't worry."

Charlie felt something stir in his gut; it felt like worry.

"I think I left you with the impression that what makes us secure is that little computer downstairs; the one I said was monitoring the devices? Well, that is not quite accurate. The computer only monitors the devices, and has no real control over them."

"So..." Charlie's gut churned.

"No, wait, let me explain. As we planned the mission, it occurred to us that if the computer was the key to the devices, then all anyone had to do was to somehow get that computer away from us. That would never do. That's why we came up with a much better way to control the devices; a bigger and safer way."

"What could..."

"The boat is the key, Charlie, your boat controls the devices now."

"But how..."

"I thought you might find that interesting. Actually, it's pretty simple. First, you're familiar with GPS of course; you use it all the time. Well, we have a computer out there, somewhere; that's the beauty of the cloud today isn't it Charlie; you can be anywhere and still be connected. Well, this computer is following the movement of our boat using its GPS signal. If, for any reason, we stop and do not move for more than one hour, the signal is sent to start timers on every device out there."

Charlie's gut-worry turned to nausea.

"Timers?"

"They're set for twelve hours, like I said before, to give people time to get away from them. So, if this boat stops for more than one hour, every device blows twelve hours later, and nobody can stop them."

Moments of silence as Charlie worked to lower the acid in his stomach and work out his next move.

"Well, I feel so much better," the leader smiled. "I think I can sleep now; now that you understand how things work. It would have been horrible if something might have happened to you or your crew, or our boat, simply because you did not understand things properly. Good night Captain."

The leader walked out one pilothouse door as Charlie stepped out the other to allow the nausea to do its thing. As he eased back into his chair, he felt a moment of relief as he thinks how lucky it was to find all this out before they got to the sandbar. But another thought came into his mind. What if this hadn't been luck? What if it was the leader's warped way of saying he knew what was being planned, and was giving Charlie the opportunity to stop it? But how did he know? Was the pilothouse bugged? Or, what if, God help them, someone in his little group of crew members talked? And if so, who might it have been?

As Frank came in to relieve Charlie for his midnight watch, Charlie looked at him, told him to let everyone know the plan was off, and walked to his cabin. He picked up one of the navigational maps from his table and threw it against the wall.

Chapter 58

"Don't worry, it's just coffee." He saw the question in his grandson's eyes.

"Ok, yeah. I have to admit I was wondering", the younger man grinned as he took his first sip.

"You can relax. There will be no more surprises; not like that anyway."

"So no more risk of having my brain fried or something like that?"

The older man looked down at the table as he took a drink.

"What?", his grandson asked.

"Ronnie, there are no more tests like I said. But, you do need to understand something about the compound in that first drink. The antidote neutralized it, as I told you, so there is nothing to be concerned about. However, that compound is also designed to have a very specific impact on the human immune system."

"What?"

"That compound causes the immune system to develop a sensitivity to a second substance; a specifically designed compound that has very little chance of being introduced into the body through any normal activities."

"Ok."

"But if a learner or role keeper were to take any steps that might be a threat..."

The sentence finished itself as the two men looked at each other.

"But how? I mean, does that mean someone is going to be following me around listening to everything I say, and reading what I write? What about in my own home? Have I given up privacy completely?"

"Ronnie, what people don't understand is that there is no such thing as privacy; not here, not at home, not anywhere. Like we said before, everything is connected to everything else; the only thing that truly separates them is time."

"Because of technology."

"It has always been true, technology has simply reduced the amount of time involved. Something that once might have been safely secreted for decades now becomes revealed in hours or minutes. But it's not about technology, it's about the fact that if you are willing to wait, to allow time to create the connections needed, you can accomplish things that, in the short-term, appear impossible."

"Ok, so the idea is that if I were to change my mind about what we are doing, and say something to someone about our work, somebody would eventually find out and give me the stuff that would trigger my immune system to stop me. Is that the idea?"

"Well, there's more to it than that, but yes, that would be one way to describe it. But again, there is absolutely nothing to be concerned about as long as we fulfill our role. "

"Ok, and about that; our role, I still don't understand what it is that we actually do. You said we create disruptions and distractions; but what does that mean, really?"

"It means that sometimes we need to take steps to influence how things go in the world. We see things unfolding in a way that could be dangerous if allowed to continue, so we take steps to somehow distract people, disrupt the process and stop the dangerous thing."

"Like by starting a war? Or killing someone? Is that part of it? Something like a World War, or Kennedy, or the Trade Center? That wasn't because of our group, was it?"

"No, no, nothing that direct. Doing something like that would put us at too great of risk of being discovered. Besides, wars and things like assassinations and random terrorist attacks are short-term attempts at solving problems. They are carried out by people who are seeking immediate results and aren't willing to do the things necessary to bring about real change. They are usually people who are serving some personal agenda; attempting to establish some narrow religious or political philosophy, or get revenge on some other group. They're short-term acts, and most always have short-term results. We always think long-term."

Grandpa stopped to sip from his cup.

"Now, it is true that sometimes the distractions we create can result in someone attempting to carry out a direct act somewhere in the world. That's why it might appear that we are involved in those types of horrible things. And sometimes, we must end up creating distractions for those as well. In fact, tomorrow I'll tell you about something we are dealing with like that right now. But right now I need to go and take care of something."

"Something about the group?"

"What group Ronnie?" He smiled at his grandson as he walked toward the door.

Chapter 59

"Good morning Agent Graham," the caller ID was blank, "I hope you had a good night's rest?"

Emily connected the voice.

"Just fine thanks, now, just who are you?"

"It's Steve. You remember; we met yesterday. Did things work out with Alex?"

"Work out? Well, we found him at the address you gave me, but I guess you already know that. What is this all about and..."

"Good, yes, I'm glad I was able to help you with that. You have a lot to do yet, and I'll do my best to help you out when I can."

"Look, Steve, you need to..."

"Agent Graham, please, you're just going to have to be patient with me here. As I said, we are on the same team. And for now, we need to do things carefully, and right now that means keeping it simple. I just wanted to call this morning to talk about Alma."

"Alma Hendricks? What about her?"

"I wanted to assure you that Alma had nothing to do with anything more than she told you; helping Alex by changing those traffic reports."

"How do you know what she told us?"

"She is a dear lady, and has been through so much with her husband, and now her own health issues; I would hate to see her be put through any more difficulty. She knows nothing more."

"That's very nice of you, uh, Steve. But why should I believe what you say? How do I know you're not just trying to protect her for some reason?"

"Yes, that is exactly what you should be asking; very good. I'm glad to see you are keeping your head in all this; it's going to be important over the next few days."

"The next few days? What is..."

"Agent Graham, Emily, you can trust what I have told you about Alma. Alex was the key in the Arbel office; no one else there had any idea of what was going on. And at this point, there's nothing anyone there can do about what is happening."

"Then who...?

"I must go now. But before I do, I want to say two more things. First, as I told you yesterday at the hotel, we need more time to take care of this situation; at least another couple of days. It is important that you make sure that no one does anything to try and stop that boat, or even interfere with its movement up the river."

"I can't..."

"Agent Graham, trust me on this. If anything is done to that boat, the results may be immediate, and profound. You must see to it that the boat is not interfered with until I let you know we are ready."

"You're asking...?

"No. I'm not asking; I'm telling. You cannot let anyone do anything to the boat. And the other thing; it is no use for you to try and trace our calls, or try something like grabbing a voiceprint to find me. We have seen to it that such things would be a waste of time, and you do not have time to waste."

"So, let me get this straight. I'm supposed to leave Alma alone, and everyone else at the Arbel office. And I'm supposed to tell everyone to leave the boat alone too. So what do you expect us to do here; just sit back and let them keep putting those things in the water? You know I can't do that."

"What you need to do is focus on what is important right now. You have names: Shallenger and his grad students, the members of the boat crew, and now Alex. How are they connected? Why those people, on this boat? And I'll tell you what; I'll add one more name to your list: Dennis Bowers. I'll leave it to you to figure out where he fits."

"Bowers? Who is..."

"Enjoy your day, Agent Graham. We'll talk again soon."
Click.

Chapter 60

"When are you coming back to New Orleans?" Lennie asked as Emily connected to the nine o'clock conference call. The call replaced the usual morning briefing and included just the two of them, Commander Reyes, Colonel Goodwin from the NRC, and Carrie Williamson from Behavioral.

"It looks like I may be able to finish up here this morning. Why? What's up?"

"There's a lot going on right now. We'll fill you in."

"Ok, sure. I've got a couple of meetings and will head to the airport around noon."

"The plane will be waiting. We looked at the update you sent this morning Em, so unless anyone has any questions about that, Commander Reyes, why don't you begin."

"Sure thing. I have a couple of pieces of new information about the devices. First, the teams are still developing a temporary solution for securing the devices we've located, and any we find upriver. As we saw with the Grammercy device, these people have taken some pretty extreme measures to protect the devices, so we're cutting new ground here. We know the devices are sensitive to X-ray; that's what happened at Grammercy. We're also concerned that they react to movement. One thing we hadn't revealed yet was that we had a submersible drone in the water at Vicksburg as the boat passed there."

"You mean the drone that sent the video?" Lennie asked.

"No, that was in the air. We had a second one following the boat underwater; something we kept as our little secret until now. Since the water is so murky, it was listening rather than using visuals. When the device was dropped, the submersible stayed with it as it buried itself into the mud. And after a few minutes, there was a sound from the device."

"What kind of sound?" Emily asked.

"We were able to separate that sound from the other ambient noises in the water. It sounded like glass breaking."

"Glass?" Lennie said, "What the heck?"

"We believe it was the sound of a small glass container breaking, like something you would keep a liquid in. Like an acid."

"I don't like where this is going," Emily said.

"We believe it's possible that when the device sinks into the mud and stops moving, a vial releases an acid to eat through some insulating material to activate a movement sensor. We've seen it done before, and if it is true, any movement of the devices could set them off."

A moment of quiet on the line.

"So, what do we do?" Lennie asked.

"Ideally, we find a way to get our hands on one of these things before it gets put in the water, so we can look inside and really find out what's going on in there. But until then, we look for ways to secure the devices without moving them. Its not an approach we like to take, we would rather get them out of there, but it may be our only option for now."

"How would you do that?" Lennie asked.

"The goal would be to somehow see to it that, even if the devices blow, they can't do the kind of damage they can do right now. One option might be to do like the Soviets did at Chernobyl and build some kind of cover to drop over the devices, something strong enough to contain most or all of a detonation."

"We agree that is the best option at this point" Colonel Goodwin added. "Based on what we saw at Grammercy, a reinforced concrete container might do it. But we don't know the true potential of the explosion since the Grammercy device had been damaged. And as for how quickly we can do it; we have to build the things, transport them to the devices, and then be very careful to make sure that putting them in place doesn't cause the mud to shift. Our people are bringing in a prototype container now, and we're working with Commander Reyes and the ARG to setup a test site just below Grammercy. We hope to see how much space we need to leave to avoid creating any kind of movement for the device. We should have some results by tonight."

"You said you had a couple of things?" Lennie said.

"We have reports back on that third canister we found. It is, in fact, a bioweapon."

"Christ!" someone said.

"The reason it is designed to resist heat is that it contains Bacillus anthracis."

"Anthrax?" Emily asked?

"Yes. It's a Tier 1 agent and adds an entirely new dimension to what we are dealing with here. The CDC is sending in a team to deal with that side of things."

"So this is some kind of double attack then," Emily said, "both radiation and anthrax. Who are these people and what the hell are they trying to do?"

A brief silence before Reyes spoke, "Well, I guess that's what we're counting on you finding out for us Agent Graham, while we do our best to take their devices out of action."

"Thinking about that," Emily said, "who all knows about these two new pieces of information so far; the movement trigger and anthrax?"

"I guess just us right now." Lennie said, "I mean, some of our people know the bits they've been working on of course, but we're the only ones with all the pieces."

"I recommend we keep it that way for a while," Emily said,

"I've not even had time to brief Dasilva on this yet," Lennie said.

"Don't," Emily said, "not Dasilva, not anyone. There have been too many strange things going on over the past two days, which leads me to think we have a leak in here somewhere. And I don't think this is information we want to get out there yet."

"Ok then," Lennie said, "that's how we handle it for now. Everyone agree?"

"Yes," Goodwin said.

"Absolutely," Reyes said. "Any idea where this leak may be living?"

"Not yet, but it seems to be high enough to know things most people don't know. Everyone keep your eyes and ears open."

"Ok Em," Lennie said, "your gut is usually worth listening too."

"Where is Agent Dasilva anyway?" Emily asked. "Why isn't he here?"

"He left last night," Lennie said. "Told me he was called back to D.C. for some reason; wouldn't say why. That's why we're having this call instead of the full group meeting this morning. He said everyone should update him when he gets back."

"When does he get back?" Emily asked

"Don't know," Lennie said. "Haven't heard from him since last night. I'm not surprised, though. Things are getting pretty crazy with the media here, and the people in the big offices are starting to pay attention. My guess is that right now; Agent Dasilva is getting chewed on a bit."

"Pity," Emily said.

Chapter 61

The rivers up north could get pretty narrow and crowded which forced a pilot to stay focused. While the lower river has its surprises, it was wide enough to also give you time to sit back, enjoy the view, and daydream about what you might be doing if you weren't stuck on a boat for half of your life. Charlie was taking one of those moments when two crew members stepped into the pilot house: Clovis Landry and Virgil Amadee, the Mississippi boys.

"Cap'n can we talk with you a minute?"

"Sure, what's on your mind?"

"Well Cap'n," Clovis began, "we all been talkin', about last night ya' know?"

He glanced at Virgil.

"Yeah, Cap," Virgil said, "the guys wanted me and Clovis to come and find out what happened? Why we didn't go ahead and stop these assholes when we had the chance?"

"The guys sent you up here?"

"Well, yeah Cap'n, everyone's kinda upset, ya know, wonderin' why you let these people keep doing the stuff n' all."

Charlie looked at the two men as they shifted from leg to leg, glancing from the floor to the window and occasionally at him. He realized it is a fair question, but also didn't know if one of the group was a snitch.

"Well, I'll tell ya. You can go down and tell them that we didn't do it because I decided we weren't going to do it, ok? Last time I checked, I was still captain of this damn boat, and if I decide to not to do something that's the way it's going to be and I don't have to explain myself. Is that clear?"

"Yessir Cap'n," Clovis eked out, "we don't mean nothing here. It's just that some of the guys, well..."

"Some of the guys what?" Charlie asked in his captain's voice.

Clovis didn't have the nerve to continue and looked at Virgil, "Well, Cap, some of the guys wonder if maybe you might maybe kinda agree with these people a little bit, and you know, maybe are..."

The look on Charlie's face caused Virgil's vocal cords to stop functioning.

"Boys, let me tell you something, and let me make it goddamn clear so you both can understand it, ok?"

"Yessir." was barely heard.

"This is my goddamn boat. And nobody comes on my boat and tells me what I'm going to do and gets away with it. And nobody comes on my boat and uses it to put anything under no goddamn bridges and gets away with that either. I don't agree with those people, and I'm not letting them get away with anything. But as long as I'm captain here we'll do things the way I say they're going to be done, and I decided last night's plan was not the way to do things. End of story. Is that clear enough for you?"

"Yessir Cap'n, clear as shit," Clovis said. "We'll tell the guys to..."

"You tell them to get their asses back to work and do their jobs, and I'll keep doing mine. Got it?"

"Yessir Cap," Virgil said, "we'll tellum' just like you said."

The two men left the pilothouse faster than anyone had in months, as Frank walked in the other door.

"What was that all about?" Frank asked.

"Aw shit. They're all pissed that I stopped the thing last night. They think I'm letting these assholes get away with what they're doing on here."

"They'll calm down. It looks like you set 'em straight."

Moments passed as they watch the river drift by.

"Can I ask you something?" Frank asked.

"What?"

"Why did you decide to stop things last night?"

Charlie looked at Frank for a full minute before responding.

"What I'm going to tell you stays right here; understand?"

"Sure Charlie, I understand."

"Last night, after everybody came up and we talked, that Dennis guy came up here."

"What did he want?"

"He said he wanted to tell me more about their little mission, so I understood things better."

"Geez. What did he tell you?"

"That's not important. But the more he talked, I got this feeling that he knew something...he knew what we were planning to do, and he was trying to warn me to not do it."

"Shit. How would he have found out?"

"I dunno. Either they were listening in somehow, or somebody told him."

"You don't really think somebody in the crew is helping those guys out do you?"

"Shit Frank. I just don't know. I mean, I've worked with most of these guys for years, and I thought I knew 'em. I just...these are all good men. I just can't believe one of them would do that."

"Yeah, I know what you mean."

Minutes passed.

"Charlie, I need to ask you something, and it might make you mad."

Charlie turned to look him in the eyes.

"What is it?"

"Do you think it might be Smitty?"

"Smitty?" Charlie said, "what do you mean?"

"I'm sorry, I know he's your cousin an everything, but I just..."

"Look, Smitty may be a drunk, but he's the most loyal drunk you're gonna find anywhere. He's not going to..."

"I know Charlie, and I'm not suggesting that he went and told anybody anything; not intentionally anyway. But you know how he can get to talking, and how he sometimes says things he shouldn't be saying. So I just wonder if maybe they, you know, got him to say something about last night, that's all."

Charlie stared out the front window.

"I didn't mean anything Charlie, I'm sorry. I'm sure it wasn't Smitty."

"Shit Frank, like I said, I don't know what to think right now. Hell, for all I know, you might be the one who told them."

"Yeah, that sounds like something I'd do. I've worked for the past ten years to get my license, so hell, why not throw it all away by helping some lunatics sticking bombs under bridges, huh?"

They laughed and turned back to the window.

"I'm heading downstairs," Frank said, "you need anything?"

"You might see if there's any of that cake left and bring me a piece when you come back up."

"Sure thing Captain. I can handle that."

Chapter 62

"Mr. Arbel, I can tell you that we have no plans to take any further action with Alma Hendricks at this time."

Through the past hour of their meeting, Gil Arbel had spent most the time asking about his people to make sure that they were as safe as possible. Emily was doing her best to assure him that everything was being done to make that happen.

"Of course, this is an active investigation, but at this point, it appears that Alma had no idea of what was going on, and thought she was doing something that would be good for the company, and for you personally."

"She's a good person, Agent Graham," Arbel said. "In fact, I don't know of one person in this company that I wouldn't trust with my life. I don't understand what is behind all of this, but I simply don't believe any of my people are involved; not knowingly anyway."

"Yessir."

"Please just remember; boats can be rebuilt, or replaced. Not my people."

Arbel's eyes met hers, and Emily thought he looked exactly like her dad did that day he dropped her off at her dormitory at the beginning of her freshman year. She had given dad a big hug, but that didn't seem to be the thing do now.

"Yessir, I do understand. We'll do our best to keep them safe."

"Good, thank you. Is there anything else I can do for you this morning?"

"Well sir, I'm going to be leaving today, so Agent Erikson here will be leading the investigation here. She's going to need access to your records, especially for the Francis B."

"I'll tell everyone to give you whatever you need." Arbel looked at Lorene Erikson.

"Thank you, sir," Erikson said. "We'll try not to be too much of an interruption."

"Whatever you need. If there is any problem, just tell me."

"Before I go," Emily said, "there is one more thing I would like to ask you; something that may or may not have any connection with what is happening."

"Sure, I'll do my best, what is it?"

"One of the things we are trying to determine is just how they are getting these devices onto the boat. With this many, and with the possible radiation, it's unlikely they have them all onboard at one time, so they must be getting them somehow as they move up the river. One possibility is that someone is bringing them out to them, but I'm wondering about something else as well."

"Barges?"

"Uh, yessir, how did you know?"

Arbel smiled, "Because if I was going to do something like this, that's how I'd do it. You're talking about all of the barges parked along the river, right?"

Emily nodded.

"Yeah, it makes sense. Many of them are in places where no one watches them, they're easy to get to, and no one would pay any attention to a boat that stopped there; assuming it was just doing its job. I'll bet your dad said something about that, didn't he?"

"Well, in a way, yessir."

"We've thought about this for a long time, wondering when somebody might do something. But we really don't have other options if we're going to operate smoothly. You understand why we do it don't you?"

"I think so."

"Most people see our boats on the river and assume they just keep going back and forth, pushing barges from New Orleans to someplace up river. They don't realize that we actually have different rivers out there that are constantly changing. For a captain to learn and keep track of all of that, safely, is impossible. We have some captains that know the Lower River, some that know the Upper, some the Ohio

217

and some the Illinois or Tennessee. We route our traffic to keep those captains where they know things best. So, a boat might bring barges up from New Orleans, and tie them off below Cairo; then another boat picks them up to take them up whichever river they need to go next. We're always needing to leave barges somewhere to wait for another boat. The elevators and normal docks need to stay clear to do business, so we find other places."

"I understand."

"You're wondering if these people might be putting their things on barges along the river, and the Francis B. is picking them up as they go by?"

"Yessir, that's what I'm wondering."

"As I said, it's exactly what I would do. And, I may be able to help even further with that. Right now I believe the Francis B. Is just below Helena, Arkansas. If it were me, I'd probably use a barge tied up somewhere down by Friar's Point. There are a couple of docks there, and it's a spot everyone uses, so I could get in and out, and no one would pay any attention. It's about ten miles below the Helena Bridge, so I wouldn't have to keep that radioactive stuff around all that long."

"Friar's Point," Emily said as she wrote, "yessir, thank you."

"Are you going back to New Orleans today?" Arbel asked?

"Yessir, I am, I'll be flying back shortly."

"Do me a favor and say hello to your dad for me, will you? Tell him I miss arguing with him."

"Yessir, I'll do that. Thank you."

Emily and Lorene Erikson left the Arbel offices and found a table at the coffee and tea shop they visited yesterday morning. As Lorene got the drinks, Emily called Lennie.

"Hey, boss. Just wanted to let you know I'll be heading back there in about an hour. We've finished with Arbel and need to talk with Agent Erikson, then I'll head to the plane. Should be in Orleans in a couple of hours. Where will you be? We've got some things to talk about."

"We've got a change of plans Em. When you're done there, we need you over in Memphis."

"Memphis? What's going on?"

"Well, I'll give you the short list and can fill you in later. First, it seems our Dr. Shallenger did some of his latest work at the University there, and the two grad students on the boat with him were with him there as well. Plus, this thing is really getting out of control, media-wise. By the time they get to Memphis tomorrow, I'm afraid we may have a major circus taking place. You need to see what you can do to help local authorities deal with that. We've got the National Guard on standby if you need them."

"Oh good, I was afraid it might be something difficult you were wanting me to do. Heck, I should have time to take in a visit to Graceland while I'm there."

"Funny. Did you find out anything more in your meeting this morning?"

"Yeah, Arbel confirmed something I've been thinking about. You need to talk to Reyes and see if they can send one of their drones down the river below Helena, to a place called Friar's Point."

"What's that about?"

"Arbel thinks they may be using barges tied up along the river to get the devices on the boat, and he says the best place to do that this time is Friar's Point. My guess is that they probably don't put them there too long before the boat arrives, to avoid someone finding them. If Reyes could get a drone up there looking for radiation in the next hour or so, we might get lucky."

"Ok, I'll let him know."

"Good deal."

Lorene came back to the table with drinks.

"I'll call again from the plane. Going to tie things up here and head out."

Emily put down the phone and took a sip from her drink.

"I called and have two people on the way to Arbel's office right now," Lorene said. "We'll go through everything and see what we can find."

"Yeah, good. See how far back Alma was altering things, and see if you can find if any other boats were involved."

"Ok. I'm thinking we should take a closer look at the crew members as well. I know Arbel thinks they are all clean, but..."

219

"Absolutely. Let's make that everyone at Arbel's, not just the crew. So far it looks like the only one involved was Alex, but we need to be sure."

"Got it."

"And let me know if you hear any more from the M.E., or anything about Alex at all, ok?"

"Absolutely."

"Ok," Emily drained her cup, "it looks like I'm on the way to Memphis."

"Give you a ride to the plane?"

"Nah, you get back to Arbel. I'll grab a cab."

Emily walked to the door, hesitated and came back.

"You did some good work here Lorene. You've built a good team."

"Thanks, Emily. We'll stay on top of things."

An hour later, Emily walked up the steps into the jet, took a seat, and thought about all of the other reasons for making a visit to Memphis. They all sounded better than this one.

Chapter 63

Frank relieved Charlie just before noon. After a few minutes of small talk, Charlie went to the galley where he found a big pot of Dorian's gumbo on the stove. Usually, Dorian Dufries' gumbo brought a big smile to Charlie's face, but today he wasn't sure how his stomach was going to react.

Dorian noticed his hesitation, "Ya'll not feeling well Cap'n? I thought my homemade gumbo might kinda cheer y'all up a bit, since y'alls been kinda dealin' with things, ya know?"

"It smells great Dorian. My stomach's just been kinda bothering me a bit this morning."

"Well, I can't imagine why it wouldn't be Cap'n. But I tell you what we's gonna do. I'll fix you up a glass of my special stomach relaxin' tea, and you'll be just fine. I tell you Cap'n, there ain't no ulcer around that can beat my tea. You'll drink it right down, and then you can enjoy yourself a big bowl of gumbo. You go sit yourself down, and I'll bring it out; go ahead now."

Charlie smiled as best he could, and sat at the table. The biggest thought in his mind was why the hell he hadn't retired last year. One more year added a few bucks to each month's pension check, but hell, that didn't feel like much as he sat here now, his stomach burning, trying to figure out how to get his boat back under control again.

"Well, shit," Charlie mumbled as he turned to look out the small window.

"What's wrong Captain?" Smitty asked as he walked in the door next to the table.

"Sit down a minute Smitty," Charlie nodded, "I need to ask you something."

"Sure enough Cap. What's on your mind."

Charlie paused a second to decide which path to take and settled on the straightforward one.

"Smitty, you remember what we talked about last night upstairs, with everybody up there?"

"Sure Charlie, that plan you had. I never did hear why you stopped that anyway. What happened?"

"Smitty, I need to ask you something, and I need you to be perfectly honest with me."

"Sure Charlie. I ain't gonna lie to you. What is it?"

"Smitty, did you talk to someone after coming downstairs last night? I mean, did you talk to any of those other guys on the boat here; about anything at all."

Smitty looked at the wall for a second, thinking.

"No Charlie, I didn't say nothing to nobody. Besides, I wouldn't have told anyone anything."

"Well, I don't mean you told them anything, but did you talk with anyone and maybe accidentally said something, you know, get to talking and maybe said something?"

"No Charlie. I didn't do that. After the meeting last night I went to bed. I didn't talk to nobody and didn't say nothing to nobody. If anyone says I did, they're a goddamn liar, and you need to tell me who it is so I can go kick his ass."

"No, no, no one accused you of anything. I'm just talking with everyone to see if I can find out...well, to make sure no one said anything."

"Is that what happened, Charlie? Did somebody tell those guys what we were going to do? Who did it?"

"No. I don't know Smitty. But somethings going on here, and I don't like it one goddamn bit."

"Here y'all go Cap'n," Dorian slid a glass of something thick and green in front of Charlie. "Y'all drink this right down while I fill y'all up a big bowl a my gumbo. That ol' ulcer ain't gonna give you no problems nohow 'tall.

Dorian was absolutely right.

Chapter 64

"Agent Graham? I am Carlos Rodriguez, from the Memphis Field Office, welcome to our city."

"Agent Rodriguez, it is good to meet you. I've been wanting to come up for quite a while and get a look at some of your community programs. Your Teen and Youth Academy, and Junior Special Agent program really sound exciting."

"Yes, thank you. We've had some good success with those. I'll be happy to introduce you to the agent in charge of those if you have the time."

"Thanks. If not this visit, then another time. Right now, I need to get to the University."

"Yes, that's why I'm here. Your boss briefed me on your plans, and I updated him on what we've been doing here. Our people are ready to help in any way that we can."

During the twenty-minute drive to the campus, Agent Rodriguez updated Emily on what they had been doing in the area.

"As usual," Rodriguez said, "this type of thing brings out the gawkers and crazies. They tell me the boat won't come through here until maybe three o'clock tomorrow morning, but I'll tell you, they started camping out down there yesterday afternoon as soon as the news broke. I guess we can expect it to get worse, based on what I hear from down South."

"There's a lot of people?"

"Last I heard there were probably a couple of thousand at the riverfront. But the bigger challenge is going to be the boats. I guess there's a regular flotilla building up down there to meet the boat. We're working on clearing that out now, but I think it's going to be a constant battle."

"The National Guard is on standby if you need them."

"Already called 'em in. Was hoping it wouldn't go that far. Here's the campus now. You wanted the Engineering people, right?"

"Yes, that's apparently where Shallenger spent his time."

They parked in a near-empty lot, walked inside the modern looking brick building, and found a young woman sitting at a reception desk.

"May I help you?"

"Yes," Emily said as she handed the woman a card. "I am Agent Graham with the FBI, and this is Agent Rodriguez, I am looking for the office of Dr. Shallenger."

"Dr. Shallenger?" the girl said with a confused look on her face. "Dr. Shallenger is in the Biomed Tech Special Projects section, but I'm afraid he's not here."

"Yes, I know."

"I mean, he's not been here for some time now. I believe he is working on a project in Switzerland, or Austria, or someplace like that. I don't know when he might be returning, or if he even is."

"Yes, I understand. Could you please tell me where his office is? Perhaps I could speak with someone there?"

"Certainly. Third floor; turn left from the elevator, and its the office at the end of the hall."

"Thank you very much," Emily said as she turned.

"But I'm afraid there's no one up there right now; they all left early today for a meeting, I'm not sure where."

"Oh?"

"But, I know they will be here tomorrow morning; they have a regular staff meeting at nine o'clock, and they never miss that. Engineers are kind of like that, you know?"

"Nine o'clock? Fine, thanks. We'll plan on coming back then."

"Shall I leave a message to let them know?"

"No thank you. We'll just stop by in the morning. Thanks again."

As Emily and Rodriguez walked toward the parking lot, Emily's phone began vibrating.

"Graham."

"Agent Graham? It's Jolene Morgan from the Louisville M.E. office."

"Yes Jolene, how can I help you?"

"Agent Erikson said I should probably call and update you. Is this a good time?"

"Absolutely. What's up?"

"We have more results back from the lab, and they confirm our earlier conclusions about the cause of death; the poison pill idea."

"Ok, that's good, isn't it?"

"Yes, but there is more. The lab says that the other compound in the pill; the stuff that would have made it so fast-acting, is apparently something quite rare. In fact, it's a combination they've never seen before; it's got them pretty stirred up, asking lots of questions. I told them they would have to contact you with those."

"Yes, thanks, Jolene. What do you make of all this?"

"Well, was this Alex guy some kind of chemist or something? Something this unusual had to be put together by somebody who really understood how things worked, and who had access to getting that stuff in their lab."

"In their lab." Emily paused, "You mean like a lab at a university or something?"

"Something like that, yeah. Either that or some genius with one heck of a fancy basement."

"Ok, thanks, Jolene. Anything else right now?"

"No, I'll let you know."

"Thanks." Emily stuffed her phone back in her pocket, looked at Rodriguez, and turned back to the building.

They walked back to the reception desk, and Emily asked, "Is there a chemistry lab somewhere around here?"

"Oh hi! Back again? Chemistry lab? Sure, there's several of them here in the building. Is there something specific you are looking for?"

"How about a lab connected to Dr. Shallenger's work; anything like that here?"

"That would be the Special Projects Lab, up on third. Off the elevator and turn right, the other end of the hall."

"Thanks," Emily said over her shoulder as she was already half way to the elevator.

The hall was like most hallways in university science buildings. A bit darker than most, clean, but clearly the home of people who don't

225

worry much about things like feng shui. Along the green walls were several large bulletin boards with notices that made sense only to other scientists; mostly presenting grant opportunities, or jobs in some lab somewhere, but occasionally also holding the legible notice about a bake sale, or mixer that took place several weeks or semesters ago. Emily smiled to herself as she remembered feeling like she was visiting some foreign country when she walked these halls in college. They found a sign reading "Special Projects Section," opened the door next to it, and walked in. A young woman looked up from a table.

"Can I help you? Are you authorized to be here?" she said in something other than a Memphis accent.

Emily held out her card, "Is there someone in charge I could speak to please?"

The young girl looked at the card, hesitated a moment, and then nodded. "I will get Dr. Saenz for you. Please, stay right there; you're not sterile."

She walked to the far side of the room, handed the card to an older man, and both returned to the door.

"Yes, I am Dr. Saenz, what can I do for you? But please, could we step into the hallway first; please."

They stepped back into the green hallway.

"Thank you. I don't mean to sound rude, but some of our projects involve very delicate materials, and any outside contamination can be problematic. That door should have been locked. But I'm sorry, please, how can I be of help to the FBI?"

"I'm sorry if we caused a problem, but we are looking for some information about some work done for Dr. Shallenger, and wanted to find out if it was handled in your lab here?"

"Of course. We work on many special projects with Dr. Shallenger. Which project are you interested in?"

"This project had to do with poison, and involved creating..."

"Please, say no more. Yes, I'm sure I know the project you are asking about. It was, I believe, about two years ago, if I recall correctly. But I'm not sure I will be able to give you much information about it, as it was part of a highly-classified project he was involved in. We signed several non-disclosure agreements and things like that."

"I understand. And I certainly don't want to get you into any kind of trouble here, Dr. Sanz..."

"Saenz."

"Yes, Saenz, I'm sorry. As I said, I don't want to get you into any trouble, but it is very important that we find out what we can about this project. If necessary, I can have agent Rodriguez here make a call to..."

"That will not be necessary Agent Graham. As I said, the project was at least two years ago, and I believe it would be ok for me to talk with you about them. What would you like to know?"

"Thank you. I appreciate your flexibility. Let's begin by just telling me what your part of the project was?"

"Certainly. It was actually quite a fascinating experiment. As you are most likely aware, Dr. Shallenger and his associates sometimes are called on to work with some highly dangerous elements."

"Radiation; things like that?" Emily asked.

"Well yes, radiation for one. But also some things in the biological world that can be extremely dangerous if not handled appropriately."

"Biological. Things like Anthrax?"

"Yes, of course, that is one of the things they work with. But there are many others. Well, as I was saying, those can be very dangerous if not handled appropriately, and if something were to happen with some of them, well, there is no treatment available for that situation. That, in fact, was usually the goal of his projects; to develop treatments for just those situations."

"I understand."

"However, the students doing that work were at very high risk, and Dr. Shallenger was very concerned about what would happen to one of his people should they experience an accident with one of those bio-agents. He came to me one evening and asked if we could work together to develop, what he referred to as a 'last resort' element; a compound that would cause an immediate and painless death for that person. I must admit, at first I was taken aback by his request; it seemed like a completely misguided thing to do. But then I began to realize the horrible experience that faced the poor victim if they were left to face the consequences of their accident. Some of those would have been quite painful, and drawn-out; something I finally agreed should be prevented if at all possible."

"So you created this kill pill for him?"

"Kill pill? What an interesting term. But yes, I guess that would describe the result of our work."

"Do you know if Dr. Shallenger's people ever had to use one of those pills?"

"No, I'm afraid I don't, and I pray that they did not. We, of course, never had the opportunity to test the compound on a human, so as confident as I was in its effectiveness, I must admit I held some concern. I did not want to cause more discomfort for someone already in such a grave situation."

"Do you still have the information about the project or the compound?"

"No, nothing at all. Dr. Shallenger asked for everything to be returned to him when we finished. Besides, I was happy to no longer have anything to do with it. Dr. Shallenger kept all of the materials from the project in the safe in his office with the records of all of his projects. He showed me the safe one day; I was amazed at some of the work he was doing. He has such ability; it is quite amazing."

"Yes, thank you, Dr. Saenz. Agent Rodriguez may be back to talk with you further, but thank you for your time, and cooperation."

"Certainly."

Emily and Agent Rodriguez began their second attempt to return to their car. Emily was quiet until they reached the parking lot.

"I'd like you to put somebody here watching the building tonight, just in case any of Shallenger's people come back in."

"Should we call you if they do?"

"Not unless you think something is going on. I'd just like to know if anyone comes back, to compare it with what we hear in the morning."

"Got it. Will do. Where to now?"

"Well, we have a conference call at four thirty, so we've got some time. Why don't you take me to my hotel so I can get settled and catch up my notes."

"No problem. We've got you downtown, so you'll be close to the office, and the river."

As they drove the thirty minutes to the hotel, "So, what's your take on all this so far; our Dr. Saenz?" Emily asked.

"The kill pill project? Just spooky to me. But I had no idea they were doing that kind of stuff here. I thought that kind of high-risk bio-stuff was only done in a few, really secure labs across the country; with stuff like anthrax and things like that I mean."

"It is, or supposedly is. I think Dr. Saenz may have let the cat out of the bag in our conversation there. It will be interesting to see if Shallenger's people tell the same story tomorrow morning."

They traveled a few blocks in silence.

"Tell you what," Emily said, "we've got some time before the call, and I'm starved. Is there someplace close we can get something to eat?"

"Memphis style, you mean?"

"Do we have time?"

"Agent Graham, there's always time for Memphis barbecue."

Chapter 65

The video image from the drone was exceptionally clear on Emily's laptop.

"You say this is from the drone flying at thirty-five hundred feet?" Emily asked.

"Yes, ma'am." Agent Reyes answered

"Tell us what we're seeing," Lennie said.

"Ok, sure." Agent Reyes said. "You see the bank of the river there, and the trees, and there on the right side you see the barges and buildings; that's the dock above Friar's Point Emily talked about."

"Got it," Lennie said.

"Now for the interesting stuff. Let me bring up a recording from about twenty minutes ago."

The computer screen flickered until a new video image appeared, showing the land east of the dock.

"Along with the video, the drone is tasked to do some basic scanning for radiation signature. It was a long shot, but we figured it was worth it. Well, we got lucky."

"Is that the dot I see there moving south?"

"Yes, that's it. It's a pickup truck pulling a small boat. We don't know where it came from, but we saw it when it pulled off of Route One. Route One is the one you see there going straight down to the town."

"Got it," Lennie said.

"So this truck went up on the levee road you see running straight along the river, pulled down this little road into the trees next to the river, where they put the boat in the water and headed south. That's what we've got on the live screen, here."

The screen flickered again to show the small boat moving downstream, glowing brightly.

"Notice when we zoom in," the video zoomed until the small boat filled the screen, "we see two glowing spots. The device must be in two pieces at this point; not put together until after they're picked up."

"That makes sense," Goodwin said. "One is probably the arming mechanism."

"That's our thought too, Pete."

They all watched silently as the boat began to slow.

"There, see that group of five barges on the east side of the river?" Reyes said, "That looks like their target."

As the fishing boat reached the barge, the two fishermen had no idea they were being watched, recorded and discussed by four people hundreds of miles away. They placed the two pieces into the barge and began the short trip back to the truck, talking about what they were going to have for dinner when they got to Memphis.

"So now we have a solid target at the barge, and the glow on the boat is weakening. It looks like you were right Agent Graham."

"Way to go Em!" Lennie said.

"How long can that drone stay up there, Agent Reyes?" Emily asked.

"Several hours yet. I've already got a second one on its way there."

"A second drone?" Lennie asked.

"Yeah, I thought it would be good to confirm that they actually do stop and pick this barge up, but I also want to keep an eye on that truck."

"That was my thought too. Let's stay with the truck for now." Emily said.

"With that in mind," Reyes continued, "Agent Goodwin and I have an idea to put on the table. It's a bit of a push, but we think it's worth talking about."

"What's that?" Lennie asked.

"It looks like, what, another hour before the boat actually gets up to Friar's Point, and if they leave that much time at all of the stops, we may have an opportunity here."

"Grab one of the devices?" Emily asked?

"Exactly. Go in there after they place it, get a good look at it, and get some pictures of it for the lab folks."

"I think is worth the shot," Emily said. Let's make sure the guys in the truck aren't sticking around to watch things; oh, never mind, I see they're already heading out. Excellent."

"It's possible they have someone else sitting in the trees there watching," Lennie said, "but I agree, it's worth the risk. The next bridge is Memphis, right? Let's follow the truck up there and see if we can pull this off. Who do we send out?"

"Goodwin and I have people in mind from his team and mine," Reyes said. "They're the best we got; if anyone can do this, it's these guys."

"Just make sure they leave it the way they found it," Lennie said. "We don't want them to know we've found one yet."

"No problem," Goodwin said. "These people know what they're doing."

Chapter 66

It was five o'clock as Frank guided the boat under the aging span of the Martin Luther King Jr. Bridge just below Helena, Arkansas. He shook his head as he saw the activity on the bridge. It was a mile or so away from town, but there was quite a crowd up there, stretching across to both sides of the river. A handful of small boats was running alongside the Francis B., with people waving and blowing horns. "What the hell?" Frank said out loud as the bridge drifted into the distance behind him.

The pickup truck was moving up Route sixty-one toward Memphis, just passing the big sign for the Tunica Arena and Expo Center.

"Hey, there's a rodeo!" one of the fishermen said.

"Looks like a big one, too." the other man said.

"Think we got time to stop?" the first asked, "We don't need to be up there 'til like two o'clock."

"Nah, probably better not. But sure looks like a good one."

"Hey, they got a hog roast too. You sure we ain't got time?"

Above them at four thousand feet, the drone kept watch as they passed the Expo Center and continued north on Route sixty-one.

About three hundred and twenty miles straight south, the crews were waiting to try the big experiment. The large reinforced concrete box looked like a coffin as it hung from the three cranes the Corps of Engineers had anchored in the middle of the river. When they got word, the cranes would slowly lower the coffin into the river. The hope was that the box would sink itself into the muck of the river bottom, safely encasing the sample electronic device they had placed there, without causing any movement to the device. If the mud around it shifted, the motion sensor inside the device would trigger, which in this case would just cause a little red light to glow. If it worked, they'd try it again downriver, where the motion sensors were connected to something a bit more dramatic.

The video flickered on Emily's laptop screen as the Francis B. slowly moved past Helena. "We're going to bring this drone home as soon as the new one is on-scene," Commander Reyes said, "so we'll cut the feed, for now, to save on battery for this one."

But they had seen what they needed to see; the next device placed in the river, and the truck. They talked briefly about their next steps when the pickup truck gets to Memphis, and agreed to connect again as soon as Reyes saw that happen. Emily closed her laptop, stood and stretched muscles that had been tight for the past thirty minutes; or three days. She decided to go downstairs and compare this hotel's free wine bar with the one in Louisville. She reached for her shoes and felt the vibration from her phone. The caller ID said 'Unknown.' A question raced very briefly through her mind about what it meant that she'd not heard from her dad for so long, but that thought vanished as she hit the button.

"Agent Graham, hello. It's Steve. How are you enjoying Memphis?"

Whoever this guy is, he was good. They had tried tracing the phone and the voice and tried a few more creative things, but they all lead to a dead end. It was the kind of situation that irritated field agents and got the techno-nerd folks really excited. As good as he was, Emily was confident they would eventually peel back the layers and find him. In the meantime, she would play along.

"Just fine, Steve, though I've not had much time to see it. We have this little situation here, you know."

"I like you, Agent Graham. I like your attitude. I knew we made the correct choice."

"Choice? What does that mean?"

"Never mind; it's not important now. First of all, I am calling to remind you that we still need more time to complete our work here; at least a few more days. You need to let your people know that, ok?"

"Listen, Steve, I've told you before, I can't just tell everyone to sit back and wait just because some guy named Steve keeps calling and telling me too. That's just not going to fly."

"Agent Graham, Emily, this is extremely important; I can't express just how important it is that we are able to complete our part of the work here."

"I still don't understand what part that is, Steve."

"My, I am so pleased that you are handling this as you are. Resolving this situation is going to take that kind of fight and energy, but I assure you, I am not the one you need to fight with; we are on the same team."

"Team? You've said that before, but I still don't..."

"Emily, do you know how to check your phone's contacts while you are on a call?"

"Yes, of course."

"If you do that now, you'll find a new contact there, one named Steve's Friend, do you see it there?"

"How did you...that's not possible. This is a secure phone."

"Yes. What I want you to do is to wait about thirty minutes and then call that number."

"But who..."

"Agent Graham, call the number in thirty minutes and simply tell them who you are. You can handle it from there. By the way, thank you for taking care of Alma; I appreciate that more than you know."

"Alma? Yes, of course."

"Have a nice evening Agent Graham. Remember; thirty minutes."

Click.

Chapter 67

Emily made a quick trip downstairs for a bag of popcorn and two plastic glasses of wine; one red and one white. She checked the time, sat on the end of her bed, raised her phone and touched the new contact on her list. She heard it ring.

"Hello."

"This is Agent Emily Graham of the FBI."

The silence lasted a bit longer than Emily was comfortable with.

"I said, this is..."

"Yes dear, how are you? How are the kids? Is everyone alright?"

Dear? Kids? Emily's brain searched for how the pieces fit.

"Who am I speaking with?" she asked.

"Yes dear, I'm just fine. I just started my watch here above Helena, Arkansas. We'll be in Memphis in a few hours."

Emily stood up, dropping the popcorn.

"Is this the captain of the Francis B.?" Emily asked.

"Yes dear, certainly; that's not a problem. I think that will be fine. You know me, good ol' Charlie."

Her mind was spinning as rapidly as the room.

"You're not able to talk now, is that correct?"

"Of course, dear. That's right; you tell the kids we'll do that when I get home."

"Captain, are you and your crew alright?"

"Alright? Why yes, dear, I think it is perfectly alright to do that if you want too."

"Captain, how many of the other people are there? How many on your boat?"

"Well, let me think a minute hon; I'd say maybe five or six, something like that, yeah, a half-dozen ought to do it. You know how we all like catfish."

"Captain, is there anything we can..."

"Listen, hon; I need to go right now. This bend here is a sharp one, and the current is making it a bit tough. I'll call you back later, and we can talk more, OK? Bye dear."

Click.

There was popcorn all over the floor, she hadn't even noticed spilling the red wine on the bedspread, and she was sweating; not perspiring, but sweating. She downed the glass of white in one gulp and sat back down on the bed. Her phone began to vibrate.

"Hello, Captain?"

"Agent Graham, its Agent Rodriguez, we have a problem."

Emily stared at the floor, then at the newly tie-dyed bedspread.

"Why doesn't anybody ever call me to tell me we have something good! I'm sorry Rodriguez, what is it?"

"We've had an explosion."

"Oh no, which bridge?"

"No, it's not a bridge; it's at the university."

"University?"

"I've sent a car for you. Apparently, there was an explosion in the Engineering building we visited this afternoon, on the third floor; a big one. They say there are casualties."

"I'll be there as soon as I can."

Emily put down the phone, crushed popcorn into the carpet as she collected her things and headed downstairs to meet her car. Fifteen minutes later, with the help of the flashing red light on the car and the driver showing his badge three or four times, they pulled up to the edge of the parking lot they had used earlier. Now, it held a collection of fire engines, rescue equipment, and other vehicles and tents, all crowded with people in various uniforms and heavy equipment. In the reserved parking area, there were three or four long black bags, about the size of a sleeping bag. Emily and Rodriguez walked up to a small group of people in the center of things and showed their credentials.

"FBI?" a man in a state police jacket said, "that was quick. What brings you here this evening?"

Emily gave the quick version of how her visit relates to the situation they were all aware of on the river, and the mood immediately changed. Any thought of departmental or territorial competition vanished in a puff of smoke like that still drifting from up where the third floor used to be.

The state police jacket began, "So far, we know that at least three people were killed, but there are as many as eight or nine reported missing."

"These are all from the third floor?" Emily asked.

"Yes ma'am." a fireman in a white hat said. "Fortunately, the explosion was fairly well contained to the third floor only."

"Where on the third floor?" Emily asked.

"That's something we are still investigating Agent Graham. My men report extensive damage throughout the third floor."

"Both ends?"

"Yes ma'am, we are looking into the possibility that there were two explosions; one at each end."

"That means it was not likely to be an accident."

"That is correct ma'am."

Emily looked up at the darkness where she had talked with Dr. Saenz, "What do we know about the people?"

"As I said, we have three fatalities at this point, none of them identified yet.

"Our office is working on that now, Agent Graham." A hand is extended, "I'm Dr. Cordelia Palma, from the Shelby County Medical Examiner's Office. "I assume you have someone you'll want working with us on this?"

"Yes, we will, thanks. Agent Rodriguez will have someone here shortly."

Rodriguez had already stepped away to make the call.

"How soon can we go up?" Emily asked the white hat.

"My people haven't finished securing things yet." the white hat said, "it may be a while."

"Chief?" Emily looked at the white hat.

"Thorn, ma'am, Dennis Thorn."

"Chief Thorn, could you ask your people to do something for me? It's rather important."

"Certainly, Agent Graham. What is it?"

"In the offices at one end of the hallway, to the left of the elevator, the east end I believe, there is supposed to be a safe containing information we would very much like to secure and take a look at."

"Say no more Agent Graham." He stepped away lifting his radio to his head.

"They're on the way," Rodriguez said as he returned "should be ten or fifteen minutes."

"Good. Dr. Palma, I realize you have a lot of things to accomplish, but it would be very helpful if we could put victim identification at the top of the list?"

"Absolutely, not a problem."

"Agent Graham," Chief Thorn said, "my team says we can go up now if you need to. It's not fully secure, but we believe it is safe enough for a brief visit."

"Excellent, let's do that."

Emily, Rodriguez and the Chief walked toward the entry and were stopped by someone holding a box.

"Here, you need to put these on. We've not been able to make a complete sweep for any chemicals that might have been dispersed up there." The man with the box handed each of them a rather awkward looking mask with a large cylindrical filter on the front. "We never know what might be in these places when a lab is involved."

Emily stopped, her feet cemented to the ground as she remembered the conversation with Dr. Saenz.

"Chief Thorn," she said as she pulled off her mask, "you need to get your people out of the building; immediately. Do you have a decontamination facility setup here?"

"Yes, we're doing that now. What's the problem, Agent Graham?"

"Chief, we're still investigating, but there is the possibility that one or both of the labs up there contained some very dangerous things; you need to get your people out of there until we can send in the people who can find out."

"Agent Graham, I assure you that my people are very good..."

"Chief, what experience do your people have with things like anthrax?"

Silence.

"Anth...son of a...." the Chief ripped off his mask, grabbed his radio and began shouting orders.

"Anthrax?" The question came from someone who's uniform was a jacket and tie. "Excuse me, I am Dr. Bellingham, head of the Special Projects Division, I can assure you there is nothing like that in our building."

Emily made eye contact, "Dr. Bellingham, I believe your Dr. Saenz may disagree with that, based on my conversation with him this afternoon."

"Well, with all respect, I'm afraid you are mistaken. I know my lab and my people. If there was something like Anthrax here, I would know that. You simply misunderstood."

Emily paused, tired of having to decide whether to be political or blunt. This time, blunt won.

"Dr. Bellingham, you are familiar with Dr. Shallenger in your department?"

"Yes, of course, but he's actually not with us right now, he's on a..."

"Dr. Bellingham, you're also familiar with the situation we have taking place right now on the river; with the devices under the bridges?"

"Why yes, I've seen the news; it's horrible. But I don't understand what..."

"Dr. Bellingham, what if I were to tell you that your Dr. Shallenger is on that boat right now? In fact, he is the person responsible for those devices, and he developed them right here, on the third floor of your building."

Bellingham took longer to find words.

"And sir, what if I told you that we believe those devices do, in fact, also carry a biological payload; specifically, anthrax. I'm afraid that is not public knowledge at this point, so I must insist you keep it to yourself or face rather serious charges."

Dr. Bellingham's face melted. Emily decided she would call Lennie later to let him know she may have let the cat out of the bag about the anthrax, but clearly, it had served its purpose here. A new group of fully suited people was slowly approaching the building, carrying an assortment of gadgets.

"We're not prepared to fully contain and remove something like anthrax," the M.E. said as she came back to the group, "but we should be able to safely determine if it's here. For now, everyone needs to go over to the decon tent and be processed. If there's anthrax in there, we're all too close to it."

It may have just been the stress, but for a quick second, Emily wished she had brought the bedspread with her. Maybe the decon people could get that stain out.

Chapter 68

Emily called Lennie after returning to her hotel.

"Officially, agent Graham," Lennie said, "I have to say that I am deeply concerned about your breach of confidence in this situation. The information about the biological component of the devices was not to be made public until we were ready. You may have now put us at risk of these people doing something drastic, which may end up creating more panic as people hear about it."

Emily was silent.

"But unofficially, Em, I hope I would have had the guts to do the same thing. You're sure these people won't talk?"

"I think I made things pretty clear of what happens if they do."

"Yeah, right. So, you're ok then; there are no problems after the decon?"

"I'm fine, and so far no one else has shown any symptoms of anything. The CDC is here, and they say that if there was actually any anthrax here, the heat from the explosion and fire should have taken care of it. That's the reason they went to all the trouble making that special canister."

"Right. Anything else?"

"I'm waiting for a call from Agent Rodriguez with the latest. I came back to the hotel to change."

"Ok, good. Colonel Reyes, anything from you at this point?"

"Just to let you know our team is on the way to Memphis; should be there within the hour. They're ready to do the grab when we give them the go ahead."

"What is the thinking on the location?"

"That's a bit tricky," Reyes said. "There are several places where barges are usually tied there, but most of them are closer to the bridge than at Helena. We're thinking they need that time to get the pieces of the devices assembled, so it makes those places doubtful. There are several docks and marinas further south, but those are all pretty built-up, making it risky for them to try and go through there. They seem to be smarter than that."

"Yeah."

"We're going to follow the truck, and do our best to keep our guys close enough to get in and out in time. Right now, our money is on a spot near the entrance to Lake McKellar. There are usually a few barges there, and it's across from a place called Dismal Point; it just seems appropriate."

"Colonel Reyes, have I ever told you that you people have a warped sense of humor?" Emily said.

"We do our best ma'am."

"I love it. Where is the truck now?"

"They're in Memphis ma'am. "At a motel on South Third Street."

"The boat should be up there about..." Lennie began.

"Should be at Dismal Point about two o'clock. I'll call you when we're moving."

"Sounds good Colonel. Good luck."

"Yes, sir."

"Anyone got anything else right now?" Lennie asked.

"Well, maybe. But I've not figured out what to make of it yet."

"What's that Em?"

"You know our guy Steve, the one that called me about finding Alex?"

"Yeah."

"He called again, and this time he somehow actually put a contact on my phone."

"A contact, what do you mean, a bug?"

"No, a contact, an entry in my contact list. He somehow added a new contact to my phone."

"I didn't know you could do that," Lennie said.

"Me either," Reyes added.

"Well he did, and he told me to wait thirty minutes and call it. So I did. You'll never guess who it was."

"C'mon Em." Lennie sounded tired.

"It was Charlie Graff, the captain on the Francis B."

"What the hell?", Reyes said.

"You have the phone number for the captain on the boat?" Lennie said. "What happened when you called him?"

"He's a smart guy," Emily said. "I introduced myself like Steve said, and after a second, Charlie started talking to me like I was his wife."

"There must have been someone there listening."

"Exactly, but he handled it well. Like I said, he's smart."

"Did you find out anything?"

"It sounds like the crew is ok right now, and that there are about a half dozen others on the boat, other than the crew."

"Half dozen, that's more than we've seen," Lennie said.

"Yeah," Reyes answered, "we'll take another look at the drone vids, and see if we can get some better ID on just how many we've seen."

"He had to end the call but said he would call me back when he could. I don't know when that might be."

All three were quiet for a moment.

"OK, just who is this Steve guy you're talking to Em?"

"I have no idea. Whoever he is, he keeps saying we're on the same team, and he keeps congratulating us for what we're doing. And...well, no, never mind."

"What?" Lennie asked.

"He said that he likes my attitude and that it's clear they made the right choice."

"Right choice of what?" Lennie asked.

"I don't know; it sounded like he meant me. What the hell is going on here Lennie; who is this guy?"

"I have no idea Em, but I guarantee you we'll find out."

"Yeah, I think...wait, I have another call coming in that I need to take."

"Steve?"

"No, it's the M.E. Talk with you later; gotta go."

She pushed the button.

"Hello, Graham here."

"Agent Graham, I'm glad I caught you, I have something you'll want to know."

"Yes?"

"They found a survivor in the building, from one of the labs. She was in a restroom changing clothes when the blast happened. She's pretty badly injured, but she's alive and on the way to Presley Trauma Center, our Tier one trauma center. I've got a car coming to pick you up."

"Yes, thank you. I'll be waiting downstairs. Do we know who this person is?"

"No ma'am, like I say, she is pretty badly injured. They don't expect her to last very long."

Chapter 69

Emily walked down the hall to the ER window, showed her badge and asked to see the patient brought in from the fire at the university. The woman behind the glass said she would have to get the nurse, and stepped into a hallway behind the station. Emily noted the security features around her. The wire mesh glass, reinforced doors with digital panels, a security guard leaning against the wall in the corner. She smiled as she remembers that hers was not the only occupation with its risks.

"Yes, can I help you?" The woman in the nurse's uniform looked like she might be a lot of fun and tell some really dirty stories when she was out of uniform, but right now, she was in it.

"Yes," Emily showed her badge, "I am Agent Graham with the FBI, I'd like to see the patient brought in from the university fire please."

"I'm sorry; Agent Graham, was it? That patient is not able to have visitors at this point. I'm afraid her condition is far too serious, and the doctors are working with her now."

"Nurse?"

"Drew."

"Nurse Drew, it is my understanding that it is highly unlikely that this person is going to survive her injuries for much longer."

"The doctors are doing everything they can to avoid that right now Agent Graham. I'm sure you understand."

"Certainly. What I need you to understand, is that this young lady may be the only person remaining who has information relating not just to the explosion and fire, but to the situation we are dealing with right now on the river. If you would please share that information with the doctor, I would certainly appreciate it. Just a few moments may save many more lives."

Nurse Drew paused, as Emily watched her face change from "How dare you!" to "Oh my!", and she stepped back into the hallway. She returned moments later.

"Please come this way, Agent Graham."

Emily followed her through the secure doorway, into a large room surrounded by numbered glass rooms. They walked into another smaller space, with just five glassed-in rooms, a handful of people at screens, and a far more serious and solemn feel. The nurse stopped in front of Room One.

"I must warn you, the young woman's injuries are quite severe. She is highly sedated, so she may not respond to you."

As she entered the room, Emily saw nurses rolling equipment out of the room and placing it back in the hallway. She was pretty sure it was not a good sign.

She would feel very guilty about it later, but as she walked up to the young woman on the gurney, Emily immediately thought back to those camping trips with her family, when she was making s'mores and left the marshmallows over the flame a bit too long. She blinked her eyes several times to force her mind to behave, and spoke."

"Hello, I am Emily Graham from the FBI. Are you able to hear me?"

Any natural movement was difficult to see, but Emily heard a faint hissing sound that she began to understand was a very faint "Yes."

As Emily thought of what to say next, the faint sound continued. With help from Nurse Drew, Emily understood the sound to be "We met this afternoon."

Emily felt the shudder begin in her ankles and quickly race up her entire body. The poor soul in the bed in front of her was the young woman who had met them at the door of the lab earlier today, with the assertiveness to question their very right to be there. Emily struggled to find air.

"I remember; yes."

Do I say how sorry I am? No. Do I ask how she feels? No. Do I reach out and give a comforting touch on the shoulder? No. While Emily continued the battle inside, the young woman's eyes focused, and the sound came again.

"Please...please..."

"Yes?" Emily leaned in closely to hear.

"Please...Susan. Please...is Susan alright? Is she...safe?"

"Susan?"

"Please...tell her I am sorry. Dr. Shallenger...he lied to her...to both of us...he lied...please...I am so sorry...tell Susan..."

Silence; nothing more.

Nothing at all.

Emily stood in the darkness of the parking lot breathing in the cool night air; more like gasping. Where is this going? First the Grammercy bridge, and Elliott. Then more bridges, and anthrax, and then Alex and Alma, and then Steve, and Charlie. This was the kind of night that she and Elliott would sit in a dark corner and nurse a drink while they told stories about what they were going to do when they really hit it big. Of course, they never really did anything to actually help them hit it big, but it was great conversation. And it helped nights like this make as much sense as they were capable of making. She took another deep breath and walked to the car.

"Rodriguez, where can a girl get a drink around here."

And as they drove out of the parking lot, "Tell me, have you ever thought about what you would do if you, you know, really made it big time?"

Chapter 70

It just wasn't the same. Not just because Rodriguez was married and had family waiting back home, but when you got down to it, he wasn't Elliott. Emily knew she would have to deal with that grief process everyone talks about, but she also knew it wasn't going to be right now. Right now, she needed to still somehow feel that he was out there somewhere, listening.

Emily decided that she'd have a good cry about all of this one of these days when she had the time, but right now she sat on the edge of the bed pushing popcorn around with her toes and imagining the designs she could see in that big red stain on the bedspread. She was waiting for the late, late news, hoping to hear that something positive had happened out there somewhere. She looked up as the lead story came on live from the Memphis riverfront; a place called Martyr Park.

"Fucking appropriate." she heard herself say.

It actually surprised her to hear it. Emily grew up in a towboat family, so she was familiar with all the terminology of towboat slang. She usually limited her language to the less forceful terms, and when the big ones came out, it was a sign that things were getting to her. Apparently, this was one of those times.

Emily watched as the camera showed the crowds gathered along the riverbank, stretching from below the I-55 bridge, there to Martyr Park, through Tom Lee Park, past Mud Island and the Hernando Desoto Bridge, all the way to up above Harbor Town; almost five miles of people. The National Guard was keeping other boats off the river, which had created an ongoing back and forth contest that added to the excitement. The crowd was a fascinating mix of ages, vendors with drinks and barbecue, scattered DJ's and live bands, random guys waving flags and beer cans, and girls lifting their tops to the cheers of the flag and beer can wavers.

For a moment Emily wondered if she should go down there to check on things but then decided there was nothing she could do anyway, and neither waving flags or lifting her top sounded better than lying down on her colorful bedspread and closing her eyes for a while. Two o'clock wasn't that far away.

The noise from the late, late news faded into the dull roar of the surf as it rolled against the beach, where Emily sat in her chair, wearing a funny looking mask with a big round cylinder on the front, and making s'mores.

Chapter 71

The video on her laptop screen was a bit harder to follow this time since the drone was using infrared technology to follow the pickup truck. Before Emily had joined the call, Reyes and Goodwin had watched the truck stop at a local rent-all storage facility, where it picked up the two glowing dots now riding in the boat behind the pickup. A team was on the way to that location now to search for clues, but it felt like a formality; these guys were too good to leave clues.

"Ok, here we go," Reyes said. "That's them moving along Mitchell Road there, the long straight one. Our people are shadowing them on those two roads above and below them. They'll have to get on the same road shortly, so they'll stay a ways behind them."

The glowing dots on the screen turned north, then west, then east again. They pulled off the main road, and passed the TVA plant, cutting onto a gravel road just before the water treatment plant.

"A lot of those roads are gated," Reyes said. "These guys have done their homework."

They ended up on the road running along the top of the levee, and a mile and a half later, drove down to a work area with a small boat ramp."

"Ok," Reyes said, "they're at the ramp behind the steel plant. That was one of the locations on our list, so the team will get into position to move in as soon as they drop the device and leave."

Moments passed with no movement from the truck. Then, the two men put their boat in the water and slowly moved across the small inlet toward the river. As they reached the river, they stopped again.

"Somethings wrong here," Reyes said.

From the bottom of the video screen, another large object came into view.

"Shit!" Reyes said. "It's the boat."

"What do you mean Reyes?" Lennie asked.

"They must be going to take it directly to the boat this time and not drop it on a barge to be picked up. I guess they agreed with us that there just wasn't a safe place to leave it that wasn't too close to the bridge."

"What now?"

"We'll call the teams back. Where's the next bridge?"

"Next one is at Carruthers, Missouri. But they won't get up there till around seven o'clock tonight." Goodwin said.

"Well damn." Reyes said, "We don't have a choice. We'll send the teams up there and try again."

The four people were quiet as they watched the glow from the small fishing boat move out into the river to meet the Francis B. and then slowly move back to the shore. Emily turned on the television and watched the live broadcast from the riverfront, now completely out of control as the Francis B. passed by. Emily was going to tell the group she was logging off to grab a couple more hours of sleep when her phone began to vibrate. Caller ID said 'Unknown.'

"Graham."

"Agent Graham? Emily Graham?"

"Yes, can I help you?"

"Are you there on the shore Agent Graham? Are you watching?"

"Excuse me?"

"Allow me to introduce myself. My name is Dennis Bowers. You may have heard of me?"

"Bowers?" The neurons were tired, but they fired, remembering the name Agent Erikson had had no luck tracking down. "Yes, of course, I have heard of you. But I'm afraid that's about all."

"Yes, Agent Graham, I understand of course. Well, I'll be happy to clarify things for you. My name is Dennis Wilson Bowers, originally from Cincinnati, Ohio, but currently, well, currently you might say I am mobile."

"Mobile?"

"I am on the Francis B. Agent Graham. In fact, I am currently borrowing the Francis B. for our little mission here; the one that has brought you to Memphis."

"What are you doing Mr. Bowers, how can we bring an end to..."

"Agent Graham, we can talk more later, and I'll be happy to answer any questions you might have. But I assumed you would be awake, watching us pass by, so I thought it was a good time to call and introduce myself. Oh, and to say that I understand you had a very nice conversation with our Captain earlier today. I must say that he is a very bright man, I can see why he is the captain. I was standing right beside him and had no idea it was you on the call. But, of course, we are prepared for such things here."

"Is the captain OK?"

"The captain? Oh my, of course. He and his crew are critical to our mission; I don't know what we would do without them. I don't mean that he is actually a part of our group here, I am truthfully sorry to say that is not the case. But we rely on his abilities with his boat to see that we reach the full completion of our goals."

"Just what are those goals? What are you trying to..."

"Later, Agent Graham, later. I just wanted to let you know that you no longer need to play cat and mouse games with the captain, or anyone else for that matter. You now have my number. In the future, as you have questions, you may call me directly. Not at the moment, of course. It's late, and we both need to get some rest."

"But..."

"I can't tell you how good it is to finally meet you, Agent Graham. I look forward to talking with you again."

Click.

Emily stared at her phone for a few seconds, then jumped to the table and the laptop. "Guys! Guys! Are you there?"

The three men had logged off to finish their plans and try to get a bit of sleep. Emily found the contact for Lorene Erikson and hit the text message icon.

She typed, "CK Dennis Wilson Bowers, Cincinnati Ohio, call me at 9 am."

She tossed the phone on the bed, briefly considered screaming, and finally chose to just lie down and go back to the beach.

Chapter 72

The alarm went off at six o'clock, and Em dragged herself into the shower. Just as she got the shampoo lathering, she heard the phone. Dripping water all over the floor, she saw the caller ID say 'Unknown.'

"Graham." She said as she wiped suds from one ear.

"Good morning Emily, it's Steve. I hope I've not caught you at a bad time?"

"Bad time? Nah," Emily lied, "just gimme a second."

She turned off the shower and stepped out of the tub, wrapped a towel around herself, swiped suds from her ears, "Ok, I'm here."

"I'm sorry to bother you so early, but it is important I talk to you before you speak with anyone else today."

"Why?"

"Emily, things are going to get difficult today."

"Difficult? DIFFICULT? Gee, as calm as things have been, I would hate for things to get..."

"Emily, I didn't mean that the way it sounded. I know how things have been for you. I understand far better than you know. But I'm afraid you are going to have to deal with things today that take this to a new level."

"What kinds of things?"

"What you need to know, is that you must make sure that nothing is done to interfere with that boat yet, we need more time."

"More time."

"Yes, we must..."

"Look, Steve whoever you are. You have been telling me that you need more time for what, three days now? And I have gone along and done what I needed to do to get you that time. But it's gone on long enough, and I can't do this anymore without knowing some real reason that we should let them keep dropping those things in the river."

"I understand your frustration..."

"Don't tell me you understand anything about me, Steve. I still don't know who the hell you are, or why I or anybody else should listen to anything you have to say any longer. We need to stop that boat."

A few seconds of silence.

"Ok," his voice is slow and calm "you're right. It's time I tell you a bit more to help you understand."

"You think?"

"But listen, Emily, what I am going to tell you must absolutely stay between you and me for now. You can tell no one else about this; not Lennie, no one. Do you understand?"

"If I can't tell Lennie, then..."

"No one Emily. Not even Lennie. You have a mole in your network, perhaps more than one. We don't know who they are yet, so we cannot take the chance of anyone hearing this. Do you understand?"

"Yes. Ok. Fine. How do you know...and just who is 'we'?"

"Good. Let me first say that there are still things I can't tell you because if you knew them, you would be at risk; you and everyone around you, including your father."

"My father?"

"Emily, I am just a path, a channel; a way for communication to get where it needs to go. I am a link between you and one of two groups that are, let's just say that are trying to accomplish different things. One group is attempting to do something they hope will destroy much of what makes us secure as a country, and the other group is doing everything they can to stop them. I am a part of that second group; I'm on your team."

"Two groups? So just who are these..."

"I can't tell you that. Besides, it doesn't matter. What matters is that we stop the group set on destruction; the group now in control of the Francis B. Do you understand?"

"Are you with the government?"

"No. And that is all I can tell you."

"So how do I know you're not playing me here? How do I know you're not with that group on the boat, just trying to get me to let you continue your, thing here?"

"Agent Graham; Emily, you're simply going to have to trust me here. We don't have the time to spend having this kind of debate right now. Are you ready to have me tell you about today?"

Trust. Her mind flashed images of Elliott, of the grad student in the emergency room, the glowing dots on the video from the drones, and finally her dad. Trust?

"Ok. Tell me."

"The pressure has become intense from the politicians to do something about what is going on. They aren't interested in who is involved or why it is happening; they just want it stopped. They have directed the military to step in and do whatever they need to do to bring an end to things."

"Military? But we already have..."

"I'm talking about hardcore military Emily. People that make Special Forces look calm and peaceful. These aren't your normal groups, in fact, these are people nobody ever talks about."

"When are they coming?"

"They will be at your meeting this morning. They need the rest of you to buy-in, to make sure none of you are in the way and somehow create problems for them. Emily, you have to get them to wait."

"But I'll need a good reason to..."

"Find one. Emily, the people behind this are prepared for anything. If the military goes in to take out that boat, we don't know what might happen next; or where. We need more time to find out so we can be prepared to stop it. If you don't stop them, well, what happens next will make everything so far look, look, well...Emily, you simply have to get us that time; do you understand?"

Silence.

"Emily?"

"Yes, Steve. I understand. How much more time do you need?"

"I don't know Emily; I honestly don't know."

Click

She stepped back into the tub and turned on the shower to rinse the dried shampoo out of her hair.

Chapter 73

"What brings you up here so early?" Charlie smiled as Smitty stepped inside the pilothouse. "Everything running Ok downstairs?"

"Running fine, Charlie. I just wanted to talk with you a minute if that's ok."

"Sure. What's on your mind?"

Smitty glanced back at the door, then stepped up next to Charlie's chair, "Is it true that you talked to the F.B.I? Did they really call you?"

"Where'd you hear that?"

"The guys are talking about it. Is it true?"

"Yeah, it's true."

Smitty's tired face broke into a smile, "Good, now we can take care of these assholes. Did they tell you what they are going to do? What do we need to do, cause we've got some ideas."

"They didn't tell me anything Smitty; we didn't have time. And when I do get a chance to talk with them again I'm going to tell em' not to do anything yet."

Smitty's eyes grew narrow as the smile disappeared.

"But..."

"No Smitty, we can't do anything at all right now. And before you start thinking I'm trying to help them again, let me tell you something."

Smitty looked at the floor.

"Smitty, look at me!"

Slowly, he raised his eyes.

"Smitty, if we stop this boat, or even slow it down, all of those things they put in the river are going to explode; every one of them at the same time. Do you understand?"

"How do you..."

"That's just how it is, Smitty, that's just fucking how it is. They've got everything somehow tied together, and if this boat stops moving up the river, twelve hours later shit happens. So for now, we just keep moving up the river."

Smitty's mouth was open, but nothing was coming out.

"So you tell the guys to just keep doing their jobs. That's all we can do right now, ok?"

"Ok Charlie, I'll tell 'em."

The two men stared out the window.

"Smitty?"

"Yeah Charlie?"

"I'm not saying we're giving up here, you know."

"I know Charlie."

"We're gonna stop these assholes somehow; I just don't know how yet."

"Yeah, we will."

They looked out the window.

"You know what I'd like right now Charlie?"

"A drink?"

"Yeah, maybe a couple."

"Me too Smitty; me too."

Chapter 74

"OK, here's what I don't understand." the young man said as he sat down with his iced mocha.

"And good morning to you as well," his grandfather smiled.

"I'm sorry, but I was lying awake last night trying to figure out how this works; this nameless thing that creates disruptions but is invisible, and never does anything directly."

"I didn't say we never do things directly. We communicate directly with each other all the time. That's the only way we can do our work."

"But how? Do you have scheduled meetings, or just pick up the phone and call someone when you need something? How does it work?"

The old man smiled.

"There are several ways we communicate; it all depends on the circumstances. I mean, I received a message while I was waiting for you to get here this morning."

"Here? Somebody called you here? Isn't that dangerous?"

"No, no one called. You're right; that would be far too risky. No, we have more subtle ways of communicating; remember, we've been doing this for a long time, so we've developed a number of options."

"For example; what happened this morning."

"OK, take a look at your cup there, what do you see?"

"My cup? Um, it's cardboard, got some flowers or something painted on it, with a plastic lid."

"What else?"

"Well, it's got a label stuck on it showing what I ordered, and..."

"What else is on the label?"

"The time I ordered, the date, and a bunch of numbers that probably mean something in their accounting system somewhere."

"Now, look at my cup, at my label; what do you see?"

"Same thing; your name, date and time, and a bunch of numbers."

"Anything different about the numbers?"

"Well, they're a bit different, but that makes sense, every purchase is recorded differently. And you've got one set of numbers there that's not on mine; must be because you have a card or something?"

"Or something, yes. That number tells me that I have to make a call later, to discuss a situation we have been, well, monitoring recently."

"Oh, come on. Are you saying that the coffee company here is part of the group too?"

"No Ronnie, they have no idea that they are providing us with this channel. Remember, we've been around for a long time, and have been able to influence a lot of things as they have been put in place. In this instance, several months ago, some programmer got a message from someone to add a few lines of code to a new merchandising program, so they added them. They didn't know what they were for and didn't really care. And now, those few lines of code allow us to use that program to send simple messages to each other."

"No one figured it out?"

"Of course not. There were many programmers adding lots of lines. And in this coffee company now, there are so many departments, each with their specific areas of expertise. When they look at those numbers, if they don't know what they're for, they assume some other department does."

"Ok, how did the program know to give you the numbers with the message, and not me?"

"Did you use your debit card to buy your drink?"

"Yeah, you mean you've hacked those too?"

"My understanding that the term hack means to break into a piece of software and do something to it. That's not how we did it. Like the label, we..."

"You had the card software written to do it."

"Exactly. It's far simpler that way, and invisible."

"So if I go up and use your card, I might get a message that was intended for you?"

"No. What else happens when you go up and order something?"

"I tell them what I want."

"What else?"

"Oh, well here they do that thing of asking you your name. It's a cheesy way to make things feel more personal, but I...wait. You're telling me that's part of it too?"

"Voice print technology, I think they call it. They're always updating things with these new features, and when we hear of a good one, we add it to our resources."

"This is crazy."

"Crazy? Ok, have you ever gotten one of those unsolicited telephone calls; you know, about student loans, or a car warranty or something?"

"I hate those things. I'm even on a no call list."

"I don't get those."

"Why not? I'd love to know your secret."

"When I say hello, it recognizes my voice and skips all the silly stuff and gives me the message. It's that simple."

"You're telling me that those calls are..."

"It's a quick and simple way to get word out when we need to."

"You realize this is starting to sound like some science fiction movie, don't you?"

"That's the general idea. Too foolish to believe; or to even consider believing."

They both paused to drink.

"I guess the main question I've got is why you've not been caught? Especially since you say that you do things all around the world. Do you realize how many agencies and things there are out there looking for things like this?"

"You mean like ISI in Pakistan, RAW in India, GRU in Russia, MI6 in Britain, or how about MSS in China or ASIS in Australia, you mean that kind of thing?"

"Ok, yeah."

"How long have each of those been around Ronnie?"

"I don't know, probably at least...ah, but not as long as you?"

"Each of those groups was built, and as they were built, we played our part. We saw to it that certain precautions were taken."

"To keep you invisible."

"It's far easier than you would think. People tend to see things they are looking for, and completely ignore the things they would never expect to see. Even those well-trained people. In fact, in many ways, they are easier to distract."

"But if..."

"Ronnie, I am sorry. I will answer all of your questions that I can, but right now I must go. I have to respond to..."

"The label..."

"Yes, the label. As I said, we have a situation we are monitoring rather closely; something we set into motion but has, unfortunately, been misdirected by someone who was not appropriately screened. I intended to tell you about it today, but it will have to wait until tomorrow. Please say hello to your family for me."

"I will grandpa, I will." the young man said as he watched his grandfather wave at the barista and walk out the door.

Chapter 75

"Good morning everyone. I wasn't sure I would be back in time for the meeting, but I was able to get away sooner than anticipated. Thank you all for coming in."

Agent Dasilva was in his chair at the table, surrounded by the full group of leaders from the groups focusing on the Francis B.

"I need to introduce three new members of our group this morning." Dasilva nodded to three men sitting together, two in khakis and one in a very busy military uniform. "This is Colonel Chambers, and Lieutenant's Massey and Chavez. They are here from D.C. to join in our activities."

Nods around the table.

"We will take a few minutes for any updates, and then Colonel Chambers will speak with us about their role and how it impacts what we are doing. Let's begin with Agent Graham who is following the situation upriver and is joining us from Memphis this morning; Agent Graham are you there?"

"Yes sir, I am." The speaker in the center of the table was crackly, but clear enough.

"We have all read the reports of the explosion, and Agent Reyes has updated us on your efforts with the boat and devices, is there anything else you need to bring to us here this morning?"

Well, there is this cyanide kill pill, the Steve guy, the phone call to the boat captain, and the one from Dennis Bowers.

"No sir, nothing more at this time," Emily said out loud.

"Ok then, Colonel Reyes, anything more from you that we haven't read in the paperwork?"

"No sir."

"Special Agent Ryan, how about you?"

"No sir, nothing to add," Lennie said.

"Then let's get right to Colonel Chambers. The meeting is yours, Colonel."

"Thank you, Agent Dasilva." Chambers stood, brushing his uniform to straighten his colorful collection of medals. "First, I want to congratulate each of you, and your teams, for the work you have done to address this situation so far. I assure you, your efforts will not be forgotten. However, I believe we can all agree that, at this point, the situation is still highly fluid and remains extremely dangerous. Because of that, we have been directed to join in the efforts to bring an end to the situation, using the particular resources we have at hand. Therefore, I need to inform you that I will be assuming command of operations at this time."

The silence around the table did not hide the frowns on most every face.

"As I said, your efforts have been admirable but stated quite simply; the Francis B. continues to place the devices under our bridges, putting thousands, if not millions of American citizens at risk."

Silent frowns.

"Agent Dasilva was involved in the meetings in Washington and heard the decision that I am announcing now. Based on that decision, I am directing those of you who are involved in activities relating directly to the Francis B. itself, to stand down; pull your people back and allow us to take control."

The silence was broken by mumbles, and side conversations.

"Of course, those involved in activities not directly relating to the Francis B. are to continue those activities; those of you securing the canisters, providing security and crowd control. But I say again, any of you engaged in any activity whatsoever that is related directly to the Francis B. are to stand your people down immediately. Is that understood?"

Seconds pass.

"May I ask," Colonel Goodwin began, "with all due respect sir, what branch or branches of the military do you represent that is taking charge? I'm not familiar with your uniform, sir."

"I'm afraid that is classified Colonel. But, I assure you, we are quite prepared to do the things that need to be done in this situation."

"Can you tell us what you intend to do Colonel Chambers; regarding the boat, I mean?", Lennie asked.

"Normally that would also be classified. However, because of the speed at which we must act, and the risk to anyone not moving out of the way quickly, I have been cleared to give you basic details of the actions we will be taking. Anything more than a cursory overview will not be possible. Lieutenant Massey and Chavez will give you those details. But first, I must stress again that the information you are about to receive is classified, and if it travels beyond the confines of this room, or this telephone call Agent Graham, the individual responsible will face very serious charges."

Chambers sat down as one of the two other men stood. "Thank you, Colonel. Our directive is to stop the Francis B. from placing more devices, as quickly as possible, using whatever means necessary. This comes from the highest levels of leadership, based on their concern for the immediate and long-term impacts of this situation. As Colonel Chambers said, exactly who we represent here this morning is classified, but I assure you that we are prepared to take the steps necessary to accomplish the task assigned to us. As to exactly how that will be done, Lieutenant Chavez will give you what details we can."

He sat as the third man stood.

"It is our intent to target the Francis B. with a highly focused NEMP, a nuclear, electromagnetic pulse."

Silence.

"This will allow us the level of narrow target discrimination that we need, and reduce the risk of significant collateral damage. We believe an NEMP of a proper frequency and strength should neutralize any electronic activity within the area of the boat, and accomplish that quickly enough to avert any possible signaling from the boat."

"Colonel Chavez," Reyes asked, "am I to understand that you intend to drop a nuclear weapon on this boat?"

"The nuclear aspects of this weapon are minimal, but yes Commander. We believe the effects of the nuclear action will create the immediacy that is required."

"Just how do you plan to deliver it?" Reyes asked.

"That is confidential at this time Commander. However, it is public knowledge that NEMPs have been delivered as payload from aircraft, carried by CHAMP missiles, as well as using drones. Again, the specific method we will use remains classified."

"When and where do you plan to do this?" Emily asked from the speaker.

"I remind you that this information remains within this group, but the current plan is to deliver the NEMP to its target as it slows to navigate a bend in the river just north of Tiptonville, Tennessee. Based on current movement of the target, that would establish a delivery time of zero-one-hundred hours tomorrow morning."

"Tomorrow morning?" Lennie asked, "isn't that a bit quick?"

"Based on our calculations," Chavez answered, "that location provides the best opportunity for a slow moving target, and Tiptonville is the nearest population center; about seven miles away which should be ample distance from the event. Any collateral damage should be minimized."

"Collateral damage?" Lennie asked, "Can't you use one of those electromagnetic things that can just take out the electronics without causing other damage?"

"In this instance, Agent Ryan," Colonel Chambers said as he leaned forward, "we believe it is important to take no chances. This device will include a small nuclear warhead that will maximize the effectiveness of the pulse."

"What does that mean for the people on the Francis B.?" Emily asked.

"I understand your concern Agent Graham," Colonel Chambers said, "however, I am afraid that we have no alternative, and that the odds of anyone aboard the Francis B. surviving the event are minimal. Unfortunately, it is the inconvenient and unavoidable outcome of this action."

"Inconvenient?" Emily said, borrowing her father's captain's voice.

"Agent Graham!" Dasilva interrupted, "I believe we all share your concern here, but we will need to save further discussion of this for a later time."

"But..."

"Later, Agent Graham." Dasilva turned back to Chambers, "Have you considered other options here Colonel? I mean, this seems..."

"We have examined every possible approach to this situation, Agent Dasilva, I assure you. And I must make one more thing very clear. We are not presenting this information to have a discussion about it here. We are informing you of what is going to happen, and to give you the time to get your people out of the way, is that understood?"

Silence.

Emily was pacing the floor of her room in Memphis, cursing Chambers, Massey, Chavez, and Dasilva. And Steve. Just how in the hell was she supposed to give him more time? As she listened to the conversation, she opened a map on her laptop to find this place called Tiptonville, Tennessee. As Chambers had said, just above Tiptonville, the river made a complete turn upon itself, forming a narrow loop that was bound to slow the Francis B. down for a while. Emily rubbed her forehead as she looked at the map; the headache was telling her that something was connecting in her mind. She looked at the map, and the river, and then she saw it. While Tiptonville was just seven miles to the south, if you went north instead, in eight miles you found another little town. Emily stared at the screen as her headache subsided and her clenched jaw slowly turned into a grin.

"Colonel Chambers," she said, "did you say that this NEMP would be used on the river seven miles north of Tiptonville, Tennessee?"

"Yes, Agent Graham, that is what I said."

"Emily," Dasilva began."

"So," Emily kept rolling, "what you are telling us is that you intend to detonate a small, nuclear device on the river, just eight miles south of New Madrid, Missouri, the location of one of the most active fault lines in the central United States? Do I understand that correctly?"

Silence.

More silence as Chambers looked at Massey, who looked at Chavez, who looked at Chambers.

"Or do I have that wrong?" Emily asked.

"No, uh, Agent Graham," Chambers said, "that, uh, does appear to be the situation and something that may not have been taken into consideration up to this point." The glare he offered to Massey and Chavez was brutal.

"Uh," Chambers continued, "I believe you have raised an issue that, uh, merits further study, so we will, uh, delay the implementation of our activities until, uh, that study is, uh, completed. In the meantime," Chambers regained his composure, "I will expect each of you to see that your people continue their efforts to resolve this situation using the resources you have available."

Chambers rose and marched from the room with Massey and Chavez following a safe distance behind. Everyone around the table was trying to understand what had just happened, but all felt that, whatever it was, it was good.

Emily was sitting and staring at her laptop, shaking.

"Agent Graham," Lennie said, "I guess you had better find yourself a car and start up the road toward Carruthersville. The Francis B. should be there around five o'clock or so. You heard the Colonel; go continue your efforts!"

Chapter 76

Emily was heading up Route 3 past Millington when the phone rang.

"Graham."

"Emily, it's Carrie Williamson, from Behavioral."

"Oh, hi Carrie, it's good to hear from you. What's up? "

"Well, I'm not sure I should be telling you this...it may be nothing at all."

"What is it, Carrie?"

"Well, you know that Agent Dasilva, from Washington?"

"Dasilva, of course? Is he causing you problems?"

"No, nothing like that. It's just that, wasn't he supposed to be in Washington or something?"

"Yeah, he was. In fact, he just flew back in time for a meeting this morning."

"Well, that's the thing. My husband and I went downtown last night, you know, down to this little place we like in the Quarter?"

"Yes."

"Well, I was sitting there, and I swore I saw Agent Dasilva come in the door."

"Really?"

"Yeah, he went up and sat at the bar next to some guy. I made the excuse to go to the little girls' room so I could get a closer look."

"And..."

"It was Dasilva, I'm sure of it. He wasn't in Washington last night at all."

"Did he see you?"

"I don't think so. We were sitting in the back where it was dark, and he stayed at the bar for about twenty minutes and then left."

"Ok. I wonder what is going on here?"

"I don't know Emily, but I thought you'd want to know."

"Yeah, absolutely. Thanks."

She put the phone down as it rang again.

"Graham."

"Agent Graham, doctor Cordelia Palmer, from the Memphis Medical Examiner's office."

"Doctor Palmer, yes ma'am."

"I have some additional information for you, is this a good time?"

"Yes, I'm on the road, but tell me what you have."

"Ok, we have identified five of the victims from the university last night, in addition to the young grad student you saw at the hospital, Sasha Gomez."

"Sasha? That was her name?"

"Yes. One of the other fatalities was a graduate student working with Dr. Saenz in his lab, and another was Dr. Saenz himself."

"Yes, and the others?"

"The others we have identified so far are all graduate students working with a Doctor Shallenger. They were found in the lab at the opposite end of the building. So far we have not found Dr. Shallenger."

"I don't believe you will Doctor Palmer. Have more bodies been found?"

"So far, it appears there have been thirteen fatalities in all, which fits with those reported missing. We are still working on identification of the remaining eight, but they were all found at the end of the building away from Dr. Saenz's lab."

"Thank you, Doctor Palmer."

"There's one more thing Agent Graham, something Chief Thorn asked me to pass along to you."

"Yes?"

"You had asked about a safe? He said they did find the remains of a safe in Dr. Shallenger's office, but that it was destroyed in the explosion. He said it looked like it was at the center of one of the explosions."

"They did determine there was more than one?"

"Oh, yes, I'm sorry, I thought you knew. There were at least two explosions; one in Dr. Saenz's lab, and one in Shallenger's office."

"Thank you, Doctor Palmer. Oh, did they say anything about the anthrax?"

"They didn't find any live spores of Anthrax. However, they did find equipment in Shallenger's lab that would be used for that type of research. I'm sorry I don't know more."

"That's enough Doctor Palmer, believe me; that's enough."

Emily drove past the Atoka Cinema and saw the feature of the 'Week of Classics' was Goldfinger, with Sean Connery. She shook her head, "Where the hell is James Bond when you need him?"

She shook her head as she thought back over the past four days. So many crazy things had taken place, including this Colonel Chambers and his secret army planning to drop a nuke on the most active fault line east of the Rockies. Could those people really be that stupid?

The thought pushed her back in her seat. Of course not. Emily jerked the car to the side of the road, reached for her phone and jabbed at the buttons.

"Colonel Reyes, Emily Graham. Listen, I can't explain right now, but I need you to dig me up a phone number."

Chapter 77

Two miles before she reached the river, Emily pulled onto Route 181. According to her GPS, the next turn should be less than a mile. She knew she couldn't explain it to anyone if they asked, but she wanted to see this bridge up close; before it became just another pin on their map. She turned onto Bungie Road and followed the slow curve to the south. Just before driving under the high span of the bridge, she turned onto a dry mud path, stopped her car, and walked to the riverbank. She heard the whine of the traffic crossing the bridge above her head. For someone growing up around the river, places like this just felt peaceful; for now.

She watched the muddy water slide under the bridge; imagining the invisible line down the middle that separated Tennessee, where she stood, and Missouri, where she was going next. Louisiana, Mississippi, Arkansas, Tennessee, and now Missouri; she wondered just how much further this adventure was going to take her.

She pulled the phone from her pocket and entered the number Reyes had texted her. It rang.

"Chambers."

"Colonel Chambers, Agent Emily Graham here. With all respect, Colonel, I just wanted to ask how far you were planning on letting that thing go this morning if someone hadn't asked you about New Madrid?"

Silence.

"Agent Graham, we need to talk."

"Yes sir, I think that would be a good idea. Just how..."

"Not like this, Graham. Where are you?"

"I'm standing under the Caruthersville Bridge at the moment Colonel."

"Good; here's what you do. Are you familiar with the casino at Caruthersville?"

"Casino? No sir, I'm not..."

"There is a little bar and grill there, a place we can look like a couple of gamblers and not be noticed. I'll meet you there in two hours."

"Are you in Caruthersville Sir?"

"I will be in two hours."

Click.

As she lowered her phone, she noticed that she had a missed call. She pressed the callback button.

"Dasilva."

"Agent Dasilva, I'm sorry I missed your call. Cell service has been in and out around here."

"Not a problem Agent Graham, thank you for calling me back." Dasilva sounded bright and bubbly, which made the hair stand up on her neck. "Do you have a moment?"

"Yes, sir."

"Good, I won't keep you long."

"No problem sir."

"Graham, I just wanted to say how impressed I was with how you handled that military thing this morning."

"Oh, well, thank you, sir." Just where the heck was this going?

"I have to say, and I mean no offense here Emily, but it is more than clear that I did misjudge you before."

"Yes sir." Emily said in place of "What a jerk!"

"Graham, when this thing is done, I think we should sit down and have a conversation. I believe you have a lot more to offer the agency, and I'd like to see if I can help open some doors for you."

"Well, thank you, sir, I appreciate that." She said as she picked up a small stone and threw it into the river, imagining Dasilva was out there.

"That's all I wanted to say for now, Emily. I'll let you get back to work."

"Thank you, sir. I appreciate the call."

The line went dead three seconds before she remembered the call from Carrie Williamson and missed the opportunity to ask him how he enjoyed the drinks in New Orleans. But what was all that buttering up about? It may have been honest, or it may have been an ego trying to share the little victory over Chambers. Or, maybe, just maybe, it was how a mole kept in contact with someone who had information worth collecting. Emily walked back to her car, got in, and sat. She needed to go find that casino, but part of her wanted to pull back out onto the interstate and see how far west she could get before someone found her. The Grand Canyon should be pretty this time of year.

The phone again.

"Graham."

"Well hi there, what are you up to no good today?" Dad sounded like he had ten years ago.

"Hi, dad. Not much, still working."

"Are you involved in that thing on the river; with the boat?"

"Yep, I am."

"I've been watching that on the TV, damnedest thing I've ever seen. It just ain't right you know."

"What do you mean dad?"

"I mean, it just ain't right. They've been saying they think the crew is involved; helping them, you know. That's bullshit. There ain't no real towboater would have anything to do with something like this. Especially that boat; the Francis B. That's one of Gil Arbel's boats and I can tell you for a fact that old Gil wouldn't put up with shit like that from his people."

"Oh yeah, you know him, don't you?"

"Know him? Hell, yes I know him. I ran boats for him for a while; got his ass out of some pretty tight jams sometimes too. He wanted me to come and work in the office too, but I told him that wasn't for me."

"He told me that."

"You met Gil? How is the son of a bitch anyway?"

"He's fine dad, and he told me to say 'hi' to you."

"He's a good man. That's why I know none of his people would be involved in this thing unless something was really screwed up."

"Screwed up...what do you mean?"

"Well shit, you know as well as I do that a real towboater has river water running through his veins; and they're not going to do anything to screw things up. Most of us wanted to be on the river since we was kids; that's why we put up with the things like having to be away from home so much. That's the only part that hurt, the only thing we cared about as much as the river was our family, and what being away from them was doing to us."

"I know dad."

"The only way anyone on that boat is helping with this is if they got real problems at home; something messing with their heads, you know? That's the only way. Who's the captain on there now?"

"Charlie Graff dad."

"Well hell, there you go. I helped Charlie get started. There's no way in hell he'd be involved in something like this. Who's the pilot?"

"Frank Maddox."

"Don't know him. He been around long?"

"He's been with Arbel for a few years."

"Yeah, well he may be OK. But I'll tell ya Em; you want to know about a river-rat, look at their family. If home is OK, we're good. If something's messed up at home, it eats at us twenty-four hours a day."

"Ok, dad."

"Gotta to get some lunch. You be careful."

"I will dad. Thanks for calling."

Click.

Emily's head was spinning as she drove into Caruthersville, following the signs to the Lady Luck Casino.

Chapter 78

Emily walked into the casino's bar and grill an hour before Chambers was to arrive, so she decided to have lunch. She selected the blackened chicken sandwich, sweet tea, and at the last minute threw in an order of fried green tomatoes. She started to count up the points but stopped. Emily knew she didn't need to go to a weight-watching group. She went because she liked the routine, the structure; keeping track of those points. In her job, in her entire life really, it helped to have some things that were just that simple.

She sipped her sweet tea and made the call to Agent Loren Erikson back in Louisville.

"Loren? Hi, Emily Graham. How are things going?"

"Oh, hi Emily. Nothing much here; I was going to send you an update later this evening."

"Excellent."

"We released Alma Hendricks from any further involvement. We also went through records at Arbel's office, and it does appear that the Francis B. was the only boat that was involved. As for Alex, we're still digging, but all the paths we've followed into his background have been dead ends so far."

"It sounds like you've been busy. As for Alex, I'm not surprised. My guess is that we're never going to find out much more about him. But yeah, keep looking. I have one other thing for you at this point."

"Yes?"

"We did brief backgrounds on the crew of the Francis B., but I'd like you to take that up a notch."

"Full backgrounds?"

"Yeah, as much as you can find, especially looking at their families."

"Families? Immediate families?"

"Yeah, start there. But let's take it a level or two beyond that; immediate relatives, things like that, you know?"

"Absolutely. Anything particular you're looking for?"

"Nothing specific, but just wanting to know if any of them have any situations back home that might be causing them undue stress, things like that."

"Got it. We'll get going on that now."

"Thanks, Loren.'

Click.

Emily put down the phone as a plate was put in front of her, filled with a sandwich large enough for three, and another bowl with what looked like a dozen tomato slices covered in batter. Emily smiled. These casinos knew how to keep people happy.

As she reached for a tomato, a shadow fell across the bowl.

"Agent Graham, it looks like you have things under control."

The voice was Colonel Chambers, but the look caused her to hesitate. The uniform had been replaced by a pair of jeans and an old St. Louis Rams sweatshirt.

"Colonel, you're early. I was just..."

"It looks good." He turned to the young waitress, "Bring us another of these, just like this; make it two."

"Two?" Emily said, "you must be hungry."

"I have someone with me; he's in the john." Chambers sat down. "Go ahead and start; it's no good cold."

"Thank you, Colonel. I hope you didn't..."

"Graham, if you think you embarrassed me this morning, you can put that out of your head. We were counting on you to call us on that plan."

"Me sir, and who is we, if I might ask?"

"Here he is now."

Emily turned, and the slice of tomato slipped from her finger.

"I believe you know Colonel Reyes?"

277

Chapter 79

Reyes smiled as he pulled out a chair and sat.

"Good afternoon Agent Graham. You dropped something."

"I already ordered for us Lance;" Chambers said. "Same thing she's having."

"Looks good to me." Reyes nodded.

Emily picked the slice from her lap, "OK, does one of you want to explain just what is going on here? Reyes, what are you doing..."

"Agent Graham, Emily if I may." Chambers said. "Colonel Reyes and I go way back; we were in Desert Storm together. Saved each other's asses more than once."

"That's for sure," Reyes said.

"So..." Emily began.

"Graham, I don't know if you've noticed it," Chambers interrupted, "but there are some really fucked up things going on with this project you're involved in; on many levels."

"You noticed that too?" she said.

"Lance has been keeping me in the loop since he's been involved, and when I was given orders to get involved, we knew something was going on. We haven't figured it out yet, but one thing we know for sure is that you've got a snake in the nest; somebody playing for the other team, and they're somebody up high."

"I know. I just don't know who it is."

"We need to find out." Chambers said. "Unfortunately, that's just a piece of it."

Two more glasses of sweet tea showed up, and Chambers took a drink.

"Emily," Reyes said "it's not unusual that Bill was called into this situation, but the problem is how it was done. It's understandable that we should consider military options if things end up forcing us in that direction."

"Sure, but..." Emily began.

"Yeah, but." Chambers said, "They didn't ask me to consider possible military options. They hauled me in before a pile of politicians and office-jockeys and instructed me to do what I said in the meeting this morning; to stop the boat immediately, and at whatever the cost."

"Why?" Emily asked.

"I started to ask the same thing as a responsible officer," Chambers said, "and was told point blank that my job was to follow orders or they would find someone else who would, and I would spend the rest of my career at Leavenworth."

"So Bill and I started thinking about how he could follow orders," Reyes said, "and still buy us time to find out what the hell is going on. That's when we thought of..."

"New Madrid," Emily said.

"Exactly." Chambers said. "It was a long shot, but Lance said there was no way in hell you wouldn't call us on it. I'm happy to see he was right."

Emily sat, staring at her tomatoes.

"What's wrong Emily?" Lance Reyes asked.

"I was just thinking," she said, "this is another situation when something happened, and then somebody told me they had planned it and knew how I was going to respond."

"Another?" Reyes asked, "What do you mean?"

"Ok, I've told you about this guy, Steve, who keeps calling me?"

Reyes nodded.

"He keeps saying how he knew they had made the right choice when they picked me. And then the guy on the boat, Dennis whatever, he said the exact same thing when he called me."

"Who's the they he's talking about?" Chambers asked.

"That's what I asked Steve. He said there are two groups, somewhere, and this whole thing is some kind of a fight between them. One of them wants to destroy things, and the other is trying to stop them. But he won't tell me who the hell they are."

"That confirms what we've been thinking Lance." Chambers said. "This isn't just another militant terrorist group or the work of some loner-outfit. This thing has been in the works for a long time and has legs that go in lots of direction."

"It's amazing they kept it hidden for so long," Emily said.

"That's because some of those directions go up." Chambers said. "We just don't know how high-up. Anyone got any ideas about this little mole of ours?"

"Nothing specific," Reyes said. "How about you Emily?"

"Well," she hesitated.

"What is it?" Chambers asked.

"I'm not sure. It's just that...well, Agent Dasilva."

"Dasilva?" Reyes asked.

"Yeah, I know," Emily said, "You know he spent the past couple of days back in D.C. for meetings?"

"Yeah," Reyes said.

"He said he just got back in time for the meeting this morning." Chambers said.

"Yeah. Well, I have it from a solid source that he was in a bar in the French Quarter last night, sitting and talking with someone."

"Last night? There could be a mistake; maybe it was someone who looked like Dasilva." Reyes said.

"It's from one of our agents," Emily said, "someone who specializes in behavioral studies; personal identification, recognition, things like that. If she says it was him, it was him."

"Well, that's certainly interesting." Chambers said.

A few moments of silence.

"Ok," Chambers continued, "here's what we're going to do for now. Reyes, your folks are doing this photo thing in a couple of hours, so you need to stay on that. I need to go listen to the suits yell at me for screwing up their mission, and hearing how lucky we were that Agent Graham saved us from disaster. Graham, why don't you spend some time and see if you can start pulling these pieces together and see if you have any ideas for just what the hell is actually going on here. And Graham, see if you can drum up anymore about Dasilva, and why he lied to us this morning."

"OK, I'll have Lennie do some digging as well." Emily said.

"Well," Chambers said, "that's another thing. I recommend that we not trust anyone, and I mean anyone. Somebody stinks in this thing, and we need to smell 'em out. We only bring people into our conversation when we are absolutely certain they're clean. Agreed?"

"Agreed." Emily and Reyes said.

"Graham, are you comfortable with Agent Ryan in this?" Chambers asked.

"Lennie?" Emily said. "You think Lennie might be our mole?"

"I'm not saying that." Chambers said. "But we need to be careful; that's all."

"Yeah," Emily said, "I think we're OK with Lennie. He's the least of my worries right now. But I understand, so I'll be careful."

"I do have one more thing before we go," Reyes said.

"Yes?" Chambers said.

"Tomorrow morning, the Francis B. reaches the place where the river goes in two directions; the Mississippi continues north, and the Ohio cuts to the east. If we're going to keep ahead of these people, we need to know which way they're going."

"That actually might be what I need to hold off more military action Reyes." Chambers said. "But yeah, we need to figure that out. Let's follow up this evening after you get those pictures."

The two men stood and moved toward the cashier. Emily paused, looked at her empty plate, and tried to remember tasting any of it. She hoped it was good.

Chapter 80

Bravo Team began tailing the pickup as it turned west out of Dyersburg. Alpha Team turned at Halls and was slowly moving up Route 181 waiting for guidance from Bravo. Delta Team was sitting on the Great River Road just north of the bridge, ready to move as needed. Echo Team was watching things from the Missouri side of the river at Cottonwood Point, just in case. Based on previous drops, the best guess was that the fishing boat would go in the water on the Tennessee side near Echo Team; a place called Mitchell Point where barges were frequently tied.

Emily sat in her car as she watched the video stream show the fishing boat pull away from a small dock west of RT. 181, leave their glowing objects on a barge tied across from Cottonwood Point and return to the dock. As Bravo Team followed the truck back to the highway, Alpha Team was in the water moving north from the Bunge Grain terminal to Mitchell Point.

"Center, this is Alpha Team, do you read?"

"Read you clear Alpha, go ahead," Reyes said.

"Eyes on the target. Permission to make contact."

"All teams report status," Reyes said.

"Bravo moving east and clear. Confirm go."

"Delta confirm go."

"Echo confirm go."

"Alpha, you are cleared for contact."

Emily watched as the small craft approached the barge, and a half-dozen men climbed aboard.

"Echo, maintain eyes to the south," Reyes said.

"Affirmative center."

"Echo Team is watching for the Francis B," Reyes said to the people at their laptops. "They are still downstream, but when they come around the bend there, they could spot us."

"Center, Alpha has contact. Two targets in hand. Video should be live now."

The screen flickered, and Emily was looking at the live feed from the barge showing the two pieces of the device. The men took them from their bags and began taking photographs of all sides.

"Center, Alpha has images."

"Confirmed Alpha," Reyes said.

"Center, it appears that the two pieces have covers held in place by screws. Permission to attempt to remove covers?"

A brief hesitation.

"Confirm Alpha; you are go for covers."

"Keep your fingers crossed people," Reyes said to those at their laptops. "It's a risk, but if we can get a look inside it might pay big dividends."

Emily leaned forward to watch as the first screw was removed, then the next, and finally the small round cover was removed."

"Center, Alpha. First cover is clear. Photos in progress."

"All teams report status," Reyes said.

"Bravo now westbound on I-five-five. Confirm go."

"Delta confirm go."

"Echo confirm go."

"Alpha Team, center. You are clear to continue. Bug out is ten minutes." Reyes said.

"It should be at least thirty minutes before the boat gets here," Reyes explained to the viewers, "but we need to get them out of there early enough to make sure they're not spotted."

"Center, Alpha. Cover one is secure, cover two is clear. Photos in progress."

"Confirmed Alpha."

"The image on Emily's screen flickered briefly and showed video from the drone following the Francis B. up the river. They were about one-half mile from the long curve leading to Mitchell Point."

"Alpha, Center. Status."

"Center, Alpha. Cover two is secure. Two pieces are in their bags and back in their nests. Alpha Team requesting permission to come home."

"Alpha, permission confirmed. All teams report status."

"Bravo north on eighty-four, entering Caruthersburg."

"Delta standing by."

"Echo standing by, river still clear."

Moments later.

"Center, Alpha Team is home."

"Confirmed Alpha. Congratulations."

"Bravo and Delta Teams, this is Center. Job complete. Report to base. Echo, maintain watch to confirm pickup."

"Bravo confirmed."

"Delta confirmed."

The laptop video continued to show the boat moving north, stopping briefly to secure a new barge and then moving on up the river.

"Center, Echo. Pickup confirmed."

"Pickup confirmed. Echo, you are clear to return to base."

"Echo confirmed to base."

"Congratulations Reyes, your teams did a good job," Lennie said.

"Absolutely!" Goodwin said.

"Thanks," Reyes said. "I'll pass that along. We'll get those photos and the video to the lab and see what they can learn."

"One more question Reyes," Emily said.

"What's that?"

"Is it OK if I breathe now?"

Chapter 81

Emily drove back to the muddy road under the bridge and watched as the Francis B. passed by. She saw the activity on the stern of the boat, and while it was too far to see clearly, it looked about the same as the videos from the other bridges. She pulled her phone from her pocket and pressed the button.

"Hello, Agent Graham."

"Hello Dennis, I see you are still moving ahead with your plans."

"Of course. Are you here? Where are you watching us from?"

"Look to your right, to the Tennessee side of the river, just below the bridge," Emily said as she raised an arm.

"Ah, yes. How nice of you to come and see us at work. I'm sorry we don't have a crowd this time."

"Well, this is a few miles from Caruthersville you know."

"Yes, and I see you have taken the steps of providing us with an escort now as well. That is fine. I expect we'll have quite a different reception as we move on up the river."

"You mean St. Louis?"

"Ah, not yet Agent Graham. It's too early to reveal our long-term plans. You will learn that sometime around noon tomorrow."

"Look, Dennis, whoever you are, you do realize this plan of yours is not going to work, don't you? You surely have to realize that we can never allow that to happen. We need to figure out how to bring this to an end before things get completely out of control. You need to know that the military may get involved."

"The military? Oh my, that would be most unfortunate."

"You don't understand..."

"No, Emily, it is you who does not understand. You say that our plan is not going to work, and I am telling you that it already is working;

it has worked. The reality is that there is nothing that you, the military, or anyone else can do to stop that plan; nothing at all. I am sure it is difficult to accept, Agent Graham, but all you can do is stand along the riverbank and watch as we pass by. As a wise man once said, it is finished."

"What if I told you they were talking about destroying your boat, and everyone on it?"

"And what if I told you that it wouldn't matter? Oh, a few of us would die, of course, along with the innocent crew of this boat. But it would not stop what is happening."

Silence.

"But enough of this talk," Dennis said. "I must go to the galley and have dinner. The cook is preparing ribeyes for us this evening; I've asked for medium-rare. As always, Agent Graham, I have enjoyed our conversation."

Click.

Emily stood until the Francis B. passed out of sight in the curve near Caruthersville. She looked at her watch and decided it was too early for a motel. She got into her car and headed up I-55 toward New Madrid.

Chapter 82

"Where did you say you were Emily?" Reyes asked.

"New Madrid. I know, but it seemed like the place to be."

"Graham," Chambers said, "I have to say, the more I get to know you, the more I like you."

"Thanks, Colonel. Listen, there's something I need to tell you before we get into anything else. I talked with Dennis again."

"On the boat?" Chambers asked.

"Yeah, I called him at the Caruthersville bridge."

"And?" Reyes asked.

"I tell you, there is something going on here I don't feel good about. I told him we need to figure out how to stop this, and that we could never allow them to succeed with their plan."

"Yeah?" Reyes said.

"I even hinted that the military might get involved."

"What did he say to that?" Chambers asked.

"It didn't faze him. He told me there was nothing that I, the military, or anyone else could do to stop their mission. But that's not what bothered me the most."

"What?" Reyes asked.

"He kept saying we couldn't stop their plan, but then a couple of times he made it sound like it was already done, he said the mission was already finished."

"Finished?" Chambers said, "but they're still dropping those things in the river."

"Exactly," Emily said. "He didn't mean they were finished with what they were doing, but that the outcome was finished; somehow, there was no way anyone could stop things from playing out the way they want them too."

Brief silence.

"So, what do you think?" Emily asked.

"Might just be over confident; trying to spook us." Chambers said.

"Maybe they've decided that what they've done is enough," Reyes said. "Even if they don't get all the way up the river, they figure they've created enough trouble to make it worthwhile. What do you think Em?"

"I'm not sure. First, have we learned anything about those devices; from the photos, I mean?"

"I just got the first briefing on that," Reyes said. "You know about the two parts; one of them holds the canisters with the radiation and bio-stuff, and the explosives in it, and the other holds the electronics to trigger everything. They probably wait to put them together to make them easier to carry."

"And to make sure they don't go off before they're ready." Chambers said.

"Yeah, right. And like we thought, it looks like there is a motion trigger involved; a glass vial that is broken when the device stops moving. it releases acid to eat through the insulation, arming the motion trigger. They say it's pretty well done."

"Anything else?" Chambers asked.

"Yeah, apparently there are two radios inside, maybe more. One looks like a receiver, and that might be what reacts to X-rays. The other is a transceiver, both sending and receiving signals."

"So, these things are listening to and talking to something else?" Emily said.

"Looks that way," Reyes said.

"Like to each other," Emily said.

"The good news is that while the triggers don't seem to do anything until they are armed," Reyes said, "the transceiver was already active. They were able to capture some of the signals, and they're working on those now. If we can read those, we might just figure out what is going on."

"You've gotten quiet Chambers," Reyes said, "something on your mind?"

"I'll say out loud what I'm guessing we're all thinking, especially putting this together with Dennis' attitude in Emily's call. My hunch is that these devices are all talking to each other, maybe taking attendance if you will. If anything happens to any one piece, boom."

"How does that fit with what happened at the Grammercy Bridge?" Reyes asked. "That device didn't trigger any others."

"It was also never fully armed, remember?" Emily said. "My guess is that the link with the others was never fully established."

"So if we take out a device, they all go." Chambers said.

"Looks that way," Emily said.

"Ok then," Reyes said, "anyone got any other good news for us tonight?"

"I have one thing." Chambers said. "I made a few calls to check on Emily's report of Dasilva being in town last night. The flight records show that he traveled from D.C. to New Orleans on an early bird flight this morning."

"That means..." Reyes said.

"Wait," Chambers continued, "a buddy of mine at the airport tells me Dasilva was not on that flight, even though the flight manifest says he was. So I made a couple more calls, and it seems our Agent Dasilva actually came back on a transport early yesterday afternoon. Let's just say that I know the pilot, and he tells me Dasilva took a nice long nap in a jump seat on that flight."

"So he was lying this morning," Reyes said.

"And someone has altered the flight manifests," Emily said.

"Then, the question is why." Chambers said.

After a few seconds of silence, "Ok guys," Emily said, "I'm heading up to Cairo, Illinois to see which way things go tomorrow. I'll have the phone on, so call if you hear anything more."

"You going to stick around New Madrid long enough to watch the boat go by?" Reyes asked?

"I'm going north. I've seen enough of that boat for today, thanks." Emily said.

Chapter 83

"Lennie, it's me," Emily said.

"Where the heck are you?"

"Still at New Madrid long enough to grab a sandwich, then I'm heading up to Cairo; figure that's the next place we need to be watching."

"Ok. Have you learned anything since they got the photos this afternoon?"

"No, it's been pretty quiet. I figured I might as well move on up North."

"Yeah, makes sense. You driving or flying?"

"Driving. I've still got the rental from Memphis; is that a problem?"

"No, no. Just didn't know if I needed to keep the plane handy for you."

"Nope, it's not much of a car, but it rides nice. It should be less than an hour up there, so I figure I'll find someplace around Cairo to crash and get a few hours of sleep."

"Don't know much about the place. Just be careful."

"I will; you know me."

"Yeah, and by the way, I never did congratulate you on how you handled that Colonel Chambers this morning."

"Oh, yeah, thanks."

"But be careful Em; those guys don't like to be made fools of. Have you heard anything from him yet?"

"From the Colonel? Um, no, nothing yet."

"Well, don't be surprised if you do. And it probably won't be friendly. Just watch your back."

"I will Lennie; no worries. He's the least of my problems right now."

"Ok Em; you be careful."

It felt bad lying to him. Lennie had been the one guy she had counted on since she came to New Orleans. He wasn't Elliott; it wasn't that kind of connection. Lennie was a part of her work life; it was actually after the first interview with him that she made up her mind to take the role. They could talk about anything, and secrets had never been a part of their relationship. It just felt wrong.

Emily was hungry, so she pulled into a convenience store for a slice of pizza and a drink large enough to last the hour up to Cairo. As she pulled onto I-55, she reached for the pizza and started thinking back through the day. It had just been twelve hours since her now-famous conversation with Colonel Chambers, and that time also included another bridge, a conversation with Dennis, the meeting with Chambers and Reyes, finding out about Dasilva's lie and a few other odds and ends. And now she had lied to Lennie.

As she took the eastbound exit onto I-57, she smiled at the billboard advertising Sikeston's throwed-rolls. She was there once as a kid with her mom and dad. It was on one of those unplanned trips when he got off a boat, packed the pickup camper, and just headed out. The throwed-rolls were on a trip to Houston, Texas that ended up stopping in San Antonio, partly because dad wanted to see the Alamo and see how well it matched the movie, and partly because they ran out of time to get all the way to Houston. They had spent that time stopping at places like the gas station with the dancing chickens; put a nickel in the slot, a door opened, and a chicken came out and danced for ten seconds. Now she realized it was Pavlov's conditioning turned commercial, but then it was magic. Tonight, as she drove through Wilson City, Missouri, it reminded her of that small town in Oklahoma just after the big sign announcing they had entered Indian Territory. They had stopped at a restaurant there, and Emily spent the entire meal waiting to see someone ride up on a horse, take a seat in a booth, and lay their feathered headdress on the seat beside them. She added that evening to the list of disappointments of being an adult. The next day, her father felt exactly the same way about the Alamo.

The highway had been banked on both sides by trees, creating a hypnotic-like view, so she was happy to see an opening in the trees as she crossed Highway 37. She reached for her still half-full drink, congratulating herself for skipping the caffeine-free version tonight. She turned the cup to find the straw...what's that?

The large dark van seemed to appear from nowhere. In the instant that passed, Emily seemed to realize there was no intersection there; just a little dirt path leading to the line of trees; there was no reason a van should be there. She realized that it was pulling right into her path and that it was far larger than her rental, and that...

Someone watching it happen might have noticed the van parked in the dark and might have watched it slowly pull up to the road before lurching into the eastbound lane. They might have seen the small car smash into the left rear of the van, and spin several times as it slid off the north side of the road where it overturned in a grass ditch. They might have seen the van slow, just briefly, and then continue driving up Highway 62. But no one was watching. There was no one there. Just the taillights of the van moving to the northeast, and the rental car lying in the dark.

Chapter 84

"You heard anything from Graham?" Chambers asked.

"Nope, you?" Reyes said.

"Nah, she must still be on the way up to Cairo. Cell service isn't good in some places up there."

"Yeah, well let's go ahead, and we'll fill her in when she gets settled. Have we learned anything more?"

"Yeah, they're still analyzing them, but they've had some luck with those radios. They determined the frequencies the transceiver is using and were able to monitor some of the traffic. They actually checked the other devices already out there, and it looks like they're all talking on the same frequencies."

"That means they are talking to each other?" Chambers asked.

"Looks that way."

"Damn."

"Yeah. And so far, they think the devices are also talking to two different servers, from the IP addresses or something like that; it's above my pay grade."

"Yeah, I hear ya'. Two servers?"

"They've traced one of them to Arizona, and the other to someplace in Eastern Europe."

"It's foreign?" Chambers asked.

"Well, not necessarily. It's talking to something there, but it could have been set up by anyone, and might just be a distraction. "

"Do we know what these things are talking about?"

"Not yet. And, they say there is a third connection somewhere; they see the traffic but haven't targeted it yet."

"What could that be?"

"Don't know yet," Reyes said. "Might be another server, might be someone's cell phone. Hell, who knows. You still not getting anything from Graham?"

"No, and I don't like it." Chambers said.

"She said she was heading up to Cairo; she had a car, didn't she?"

"Yeah, she's had more than enough time to get there."

"Have you tried calling her again?"

"Five or six times. Just get the recording."

"Maybe I'm getting old, but I'm going to send one of our drones up that way to take a look," Reyes said.

"I'm climbing into one of our birds now; can be up there in twenty minutes. Where are you; I'll pick you up."

Chapter 85

"Agent Dasilva?" the voice on the phone asked.

"Yes." Dasilva answers.

"I am calling to inform you that the first action is completed."

"Excellent. Were there any complications?"

"None."

"When can I expect to hear about the second action?"

"Within twenty-four hours."

"Good," Dasilva said as he put the phone back in his pocket.

He smiled as he thought about how well things were going. It never ceased to amaze him how these people would go to such lengths to protect themselves, yet leave the most simple and obvious paths open. Their training prepared them to always be on guard, but time in the field made them sloppy. As much as Dasilva hated that, he also knew that he was depending upon it. The smile weakened as he reminded himself of how little time he had to finish his work. With the first step completed, the pressure was eased, but he knew he couldn't rest until the second step was completed as well. Twenty-four more hours; barring any complications.

Miles to the north in Cairo, Illinois, Reyes and Chambers passed through sliding doors and moved down the brightly lit hallway, to a woman sitting behind a desk.

"May I help you?" she asked.

"Emily Graham, where can we find her?" Chambers asked in full Colonel voice.

"Yes, one second." They watched her press keys and stare at her computer screen until her polite smile changed. "I'm sorry sir, visitors are not allowed for that patient."

Two badges shined over the desk, "Which way to her room please?"

The woman automatically glanced to the hallway to the left, "I'm sorry sir. But she is not..."

Chambers and Reyes were already heading down the left hallway, hunting for someone who knew where they needed to go. A doctor stepped out of a room as they passed; badges were still in their hands.

"Excuse me, doctor," Chambers said, "we're looking for a patient by the name of Emily Graham; she was brought in earlier this evening."

The doctor's eyes focused on the badges, and then on the two very determined looking men holding them.

"Yes, I am doctor Greer. But I'm sorry..."

"Doctor, Greer is it?" The Colonel was tired, "please understand; I don't mean to create problems for you tonight doctor, but we have reason to believe that Agent Emily Graham experienced an attempt on her life this evening that led to her being brought to your facility. If that is indeed the case, and those responsible find out they failed; well, Doctor, these people will not hesitate to walk into your hospital here to finish the job. Now I ask you, Dr. Greer, are you prepared to deal with that situation when it occurs tonight?"

A very brief pause.

"She is in here." Dr. Greer said as he opened the door.

Emily was sitting up in bed, a small bandage on her forehead, and in the middle of an argument with a nurse attempting to do something next to the bed. Emily turned to the opening door.

"Would someone please tell this nurse-person to give me my damn cell phone!" Emily said to everyone in the room.

Chambers and Reyes stopped, looked at each other, and then back at Emily.

"I'm sorry ma'am," the nurse said, "but I've explained that cell phones aren't allowed because of the equipment."

"See what I've been putting up with here?" she said to Chambers and Reyes as they walked toward the bed.

"Are you OK?" Reyes asked.

"Other than not getting my cell phone, yeah, I'm fine. Just a bump on the head; they tell me I'll really feel things tomorrow, though."

"What happened?" Chambers asked as he glanced at the nurse and doctor in a way that suggested they find something to do someplace else for a while. They understood.

"Somebody ran me off the road. I was just driving along. There wasn't any traffic. Then I saw something moving by the right side of the road. Before I could do anything, it pulled right out in front of me, and I tagged the back of it; that's the last I remember for a bit. Apparently, I was there for ten or fifteen minutes before somebody drove by and saw me. Things are blurry, and I was hanging upside down there, but apparently I was lucky; that little rental car was a good one."

"Did the other car run a stop sign or something?" Chambers asked.

"No, there was no sign and no road there at all. They just pulled out."

"Like they were waiting for you." Chambers said. "Who all knew where you were going tonight?"

"Who? Well, you guys, and Lennie, and Dasilva."

"Dasilva knew?" Chambers asked.

"Yeah, I talked with him before I met you guys in Caruthersville. So, you think this was more than an accident, huh?" Emily asked.

"It's sounding that way," Reyes said.

"I'm glad to hear that." Emily said, "I didn't want to be the only one. When can I get out of here?"

Reyes walked to the door and invited the doctor and nurse back inside.

"So doc," Emily said, "where are my shoes? I have work to do."

"I'm sorry Agent Graham," the doctor said, "but you've had a head injury, and we need to keep an eye on it for at least twenty-four hours."

"Twenty-four...?' Emily began.

"Doctor," Chambers interrupted, "considering what we spoke about in the hallway, do you think it might be possible for Agent Graham to leave the hospital this evening, as long as we have one of our medical people keep a close eye on her? And at the first indication of a problem, they'll bring her right back. I'm just thinking of security here; for all of us."

Dr. Greer looked at his shoes, at the nurse, at Emily, at Ryes, his shoes again, and then at Chambers.

"I believe that would be acceptable; for security reasons, as you say."

The nurse looked at him; then at the floor.

"Good," Emily sat up and swung her feet off the side of the bed; and stopped. "Whoo!"

"Are you OK?" the nurse asked.

"Fine, just got up too fast. I'm fine."

"That's going to hurt for a while, so I'll give you something to keep it manageable." Doctor Greer said. "If it gets too bad, or you have double vision or have trouble focusing, you get back in here right away."

"Right doc. Will do," Emily said. "Now, where's my cell phone?"

"So, where are we going?" Emily asked as they walked outside.

"Right now we're finding you a room so you can get some rest," Chambers said, "and then we'll meet for breakfast and figure things out from there."

As the three walked across the parking lot to Chambers' car, Emily noticed several missed calls. She saw two messages. One was from Steve, and one was from Dennis. Both left essentially the same message: "I heard about your accident, and I want to assure you we had nothing to do with it."

Chapter 86

"You look tired," Ronnie said as his grandfather sat down with his cup, "didn't you sleep very well?"

"Does it show?" the older man said. "I slept in bits and pieces; this thing we have going on right now."

"Is that the thing you said you would tell me about this morning?"

"Yes, but I'm not sure it's the best way to introduce you to how things work."

"You said something had gone wrong; someone had misdirected things?"

"You do pay attention, don't you? That's good."

The old man took a long sip from his cup.

"You see Ronnie, as I said before, the most important task we have to carry out is to remain invisible; to never put ourselves in any position that might make us visible, or even give someone the idea that we might actually exist."

"Yeah, I remember."

"What that means is, as we decide that we must take steps to create some type of distraction, we do it by creating several layers of communication; we usually refer to them as channels, and we use those to guide how things take place."

"Has someone found out?"

"No, it's not that serious. But one of the risks of doing things this way is that we must put a lot of trust in the people we select as those channels; we give them a direction to move, but they have a lot of freedom in how they might do that."

"I'm not sure I understand."

"Ok, in this situation for example; but first, let me give you a little of the background."

He took another long sip.

"Over the past several years, we have become concerned about some of the things we have seen taking place among those with power; both political and economic."

"You mean in the states? I can understand that."

"Not just that, Ronnie, it's global. Remember, we are not responsible for any one individual nation; our focus must be far more encompassing. The things you see happening here are happening in countries all around the world; the consolidation of wealth and power in an increasingly smaller number of people; and the expansion of beliefs and actions that are harmful to those without wealth and power."

"You mean..."

"Please let me continue. Throughout history, this type of development has usually led to very dangerous times; but never on this scale. It has been limited to individual nations, or continents. However, technology has made the world so much smaller; and movements like this now have the ability to feed off of each other, and assume far more power than was possible before. That is why we decided we needed to create a distraction; to disrupt the momentum that was building with this mindset, and to frighten people enough to make them ask the very difficult questions. Something so frightening that those without wealth and power would unite and demand changes be made."

"Wait a minute, is this about what I've been seeing in the papers about that boat; the one with the dirty bombs? Is that what you did?"

"No Ronnie, or not directly anyway. Remember, our goal is to ensure a safe future for our world; not to do things that would destroy parts of it. But, yes, we took the steps to begin what you are referring to, but what you see is not at all what we intended."

"But did you intend to put bombs out there? With radiation?"

"Our intent was to place the devices, yes, including the radioactive materials. But, they were designed to never be used; they were built to malfunction if someone actually attempted to use one of them. Think about it Ronnie; there would never need to be an actual explosion to create the distraction. Simply learning that someone had placed these things in the middle of the country would create the same type of powerful human response we saw after Pearl Harbor, or Kennedy, or the Trade Center. Just the threat of such a thing would do that. Our devices were created to be highly secure containers of the elements; nothing more. Never something that could be put into use."

"What happened?"

"As I said, the problem with using channels is that one of them might take it upon themselves to change things. That is why we go through such pains in selecting those channels. The person selected to be channel number 1, this Dr. Shallenger, somehow his mental instability was not recognized. By the time we learned of how he had changed things, it was not possible to stop them; not directly anyway."

"You let him go ahead?"

"Ronnie, the first day we spoke I told you that there may be times that we have to make some very difficult decisions; choices that may look like horrendous and even evil choices. This is one of those times. If we took direct steps to stop him, it might have made it possible for an investigation to lead to us; or at least to the idea that someone like us might exist. And as I have said, we can never allow that to happen, even when faced with risks such as Dr. Shallenger."

"What have you done about him?"

"The same thing we always do; we looked for steps we could take to disrupt his plan, rather than attack it directly. As we understood what he was doing, we learned about the F.B.I. agent that was helping him. So, we began looking for connections to someone near that agent who could become involved in a natural way. We found that one of his colleagues actually had an understanding of those boats from her family background, so we built channels pointing to Agent Graham, whom you are reading about in the papers."

"So she knows about this?"

"No. Again, Ronnie, it's all about channels. When the decision was made to involve her, we put channels in place; I believe five, and only one of those channels has direct interaction with her. We named that channel Steve."

"But what if that Steve channel gets caught? Aren't you still vulnerable?"

"No. All that Steve knows is the name of the channel who communicates with him."

"And that channel only knows..."

"The one communicating with them, yes. And none of the channels know more than the specific message they are to communicate. None know anything about the overall distraction; other than what the media knows to tell them. And, Ronnie, we have channels involved there as well."

"Now you're telling me you control the media?"

"Not directly, no. But the media is competitive, and always looking for a scoop. All our channels need to do is occasionally offer them one; one that will guide them either toward or away from where we need them, and then let them do their jobs. The media is a great asset for creating blindness where we need it; they have such great ability to distract."

"What kept you up last night? Have things gone wrong again?"

"Some things have happened that are making it more difficult. When we make the decision to involve someone like Agent Graham in one of our actions, we feel a responsibility to do as much as we can to protect them from harm. This is one of those times that I am being reminded of just how corrupt a man can become. But, time is on our side, as always. If we select the right people to be involved, use the channels to provide them with the information they need, and give them time to act; they will be successful. Ronnie, all meaningful change takes time, Only the fool demands it happen right now."

A brief pause.

"Would you like me to get you a refill grandpa?" Ronnie said as he glanced at the empty cup.

"No thank you. I'm afraid I must go. I have things I must do." The old man stood.

"Is there anything I can do?"

The grandfather paused, looking at his grandson.

"Yes, there is; something that might help you better understand what I've been talking about. This morning, did the young woman ask you for your first name when she took your order?"

"Yeah, she always does. You said it was because..."

"Let's start with that. Let's assume that, before they did ask for names here, we decided that it would be very helpful if they started doing it, to help with our communications, like I told you yesterday."

"Ok."

"Your task is to find a way to get this company to start doing that. We already have the technology built into the system, so all we have to do is get them to use it by asking each customer for their first name. How would you get them to do that?"

"You mean who would I ask?"

"No, no, remember the channels. You will not communicate with anyone about it directly, and want to have at least four channels involved so the origin of the idea could never find its way back to you. None of your channels knows why they are doing what they are doing, but just have a simple message to communicate to someone else. How do you start that message, until some morning you walk in here, and the young lady asks you for your first name?"

"Well, maybe I could..."

"We have no use for maybe Ronnie. We must get the action taken, and we must ensure that we are never uncovered. Think about it, and I'll see you in the morning."

Ronnie was staring at his empty cup as the old man walked out the door.

Chapter 87

"How are you feeling this morning?" Reyes asked as she approached the table.

"They were right," Emily said. "I hurt in places I didn't know I had."

Reyes and Chambers watched as she eased herself into the chair, and noticed the various colors of bruises on her arms.

"You think that's something," she said, "you should see the rest of me. I'm pretty much one large bruise."

"Are the meds helping?" Chambers asked.

"Not using them. I need to keep my head clear."

"And how's the vision?" Reyes asked. "How many fingers am I holding up?"

"Look, I'm fine," Emily said, "let me get some coffee, and I'll be good to go. What's the plan today?"

"Before we do that," Chambers said, "let's talk about what happened last night. Did you get a good look at the thing that pulled out in front of you?"

"No, it was just dark."

"I mean," Chambers continued, "was it big, or small?"

"I really don't remember; it was just all so fast, I just saw a dark blur." Emily lied. For some reason, she wanted to keep the van a secret for a while. Maybe it was a result of the concussion.

"Ok," Chambers said, "maybe it will come back to you. But just one more thing. Who all did you say knew where you were going to be last night?"

Emily sipped her coffee. "Um, you two, Lennie and Dasilva; I think that's it. I had talked with Dasilva before we met in Caruthersville, and called Lennie just before I left New Madrid."

"Did this Steve guy, or Dennis know?" Reye's asked.

"Dennis," Chambers said, "he's the guy on the boat, right?"

"Yeah," Reyes said.

"I didn't tell them." Emily said, "But I guess they did know I had been following the boat up the river, so they might have figured it out. Do you still really think it was intentional?"

"We think that's the most likely scenario, yes," Reyes said.

"Ok," Chambers said, "we have to make some decisions here. We've got the meeting this morning, so just how much of all this are we going to tell everybody? I don't like hiding things, but it seems pretty obvious that somebody in there is screwing with us."

"Well," Reyes said, "they'll know about Emily's accident..."

"But just that it was an accident," Emily said.

"All but one anyway," Chambers said, "so I suggest we leave it at that; it was an accident. Right?"

"Right." Emily and Reyes said.

"And one more thing," Chamber said. "Graham did a fine job of stopping the New Madrid action, but all it really did was make them more determined than ever to get the boat. I'm getting new orders just before our meeting; I have no idea what they will be, but they're not going to make the same simple mistakes again."

"Any idea at all what they are going to do?" Emily asked.

"My guess is the same thing," Chambers said, "but in a more suitable location."

"Still nukes?"

"Like I said; they want that boat stopped."

They each sipped coffee.

"What about the devices?" Chambers asked. "Emily, we found out that it does look like the devices are talking to each other, so there's the risk that if we take one of them out, it might trigger the rest of them."

"And I got a call just before getting here," Reyes said, "they've determined that the other connection on the radios is actually on the boat."

Pause.

"So," Emily said, if anything happens to any of the devices, things go boom. Plus, if they're linked to the boat, messing with it might trigger things too?"

"Looks that way." Reye's said.

"Well," Emily said, "let's look at the bright side of things."

"And what might that be?" Reyes asked.

"Well, I think we just figured out how to stop them from nuking the boat."

Chapter 88

Emily listened to the conversations taking place around the table. The meeting was scheduled to begin five minutes ago, but Agent Dasilva was not there yet, and no one seemed willing to take his place at the moment.

"I'm sorry to keep you waiting," she heard Dasilva say as he approached the table. "Let's, uh, let's get to work here. I am afraid I need to cut this brief this morning. So we'll just ask for any critical updates, and go into more detail this afternoon."

"First, I'm sure everyone is wondering how you are doing this morning, Agent Graham? We heard about your accident."

"Yes, I'm doing fine, thanks. Just a few bruises."

"What happened up there?" Colonel Goodwin asked.

"Oh, I swerved to miss a deer...it was one of those narrow, two-lane roads with no shoulder, and I guess I overcompensated. Kind of foolish, I guess; considering."

"We're just glad to hear you are OK," Dasilva said. "Do you have anything for us this morning?"

"Nothing critical, no sir."

"Fine. Commander Reyes, how about you?"

"Yes sir, thank you," Reyes said. "As you all know, my team has been able to secure key data on the devices, and are in the process of analyzing it now. I hope to have a full report for you soon."

"Is that it?" Dasilva said.

"For now, yes sir. I have nothing to add at this time."

"OK then. Colonel Chambers, I understand you have an update on planned military activities?"

"Yes, Agent Dasilva, I just came from a briefing. I am here to report that no further military actions are planned at this time. We continue to monitor the situation, and will be prepared to take steps if and when the situation merits such action."

"I was told an intervention was planned." Dasilva began.

"Yes, sir. Those orders have changed, sir." Chambers said.

"Interesting," Dasilva said. "Colonel Goodwin, do you have anything to give us this morning?"

"Yes sir, thank you. I am here to report that, after multiple attempts to develop a functional prototype, the decision has been made that covering the devices with a secure, sarcophagus-like container is not feasible. We tried to create a container that could be lowered over the devices without causing any residual movement that would trigger the devices. Unfortunately, the floor of the river is simply too unstable. A device wide enough to avoid causing movement to the device would be far too wide to contain an explosion, making the effort meaningless."

"So, do we have an alternative solution in mind for securing the devices at this time?" Dasilva asked.

"Not at this time," Goodwin said, "no sir."

"OK then," Dasilva said, "does anyone else have anything to add right now?"

"Sir, I do have a question." Colonel Nichols from the Corps of Engineers said.

"We have heard that evidence has been found that these devices out there are somehow connected, perhaps with radios of some kind. Is this true? I'm sure you understand that my people out there are concerned about accidentally triggering one of those things, after seeing what happened at Grammercy."

"Yes Colonel," Dasilva said, "a fair question. Colonel Reyes do you have anything on that for us?"

"As I said," Reyes said, "my people are still studying the data from the devices. But I can say that we have not found any risk of detonating a device other than X-rays, or movement. And I assure you, Colonel Nichols, if that changes, we will notify you and your people immediately."

"Thank you, Colonel Reyes," Nichols said.

"All right then," Dasilva said, "we will schedule another meeting for a full update this afternoon. Thank you for your time."

Emily heard people standing and leaving the room.

"Graham," Dasilva said, "Chambers, and Reyes; please stay on the line for a moment, won't you?"

When the room has become quiet, "Graham; a deer?"

"Sir?"

"Graham, I'm not sure why you chose to be so creative this morning, but one of these days you'll have to make it a point to explain it to me."

"Yes, sir."

"And Chambers, Reyes, just where do you happen to be this morning, since I notice you are not at the table as usual."

"We were concerned about Agent Graham, sir," Chambers said, "so we came up to make sure she was all right."

"I commend your loyalty to a team member gentlemen," Dasilva said, "but that does not explain your being up there the day before her, uh, accident. And it does not explain why you made no mention of a few things in your update this morning; things such as the confirmed radio signals linking all devices with the boat, and a few other things like that."

"Sir, we felt that..." Chambers began.

"Listen, each of you," Dasilva said, "and listen good. I don't know what you believe you are going to accomplish, but let me remind you that withholding information during an investigation like this may be interpreted by some as an attempt to thwart that investigation, or perhaps an attempt to aid those committing the crime being investigated. As I said, I don't know what you think you are doing, but let me make it very clear that if I find you are withholding information, or if your actions interfere with this investigation in any way, I will see to it that you pay for that; do you understand me?"

"Yes sir." from three voices.

"Good. Now," Dasilva continued, pronouncing each word slowly and clearly, "is there anything else you want to update me about before we end our meeting this morning?"

"No sir." From three voices.

Click.

Chapter 89

It almost felt routine now as Emily watched the video of the fishing boat placing the glowing objects on the barge; this time south of Cairo, near the town of Wicklife, Kentucky. There were four glows on the screen; suggesting enough pieces for two devices. The question had been which way the boat would go as the river split into two channels; one turning east as the Ohio River, and the other continuing north as the Mississippi. Since there was just one bridge on the Ohio side and two on the other, she took it as a clue and began making plans for moving northward.

As at Caruthersville, Emily found a dried-mud road leading to the riverbank near the bridge on the Missouri side of the river. She walked out onto a pile of rocks sticking out into the river, and stood at the very end, enjoying the peacefulness. The Corps of Engineers built these barriers along the river where they wanted to control the currents; forcing the river to keep the main channel deep and clear of debris. The current slowed as it hits the barriers, causing the sediment in the water to fall to the bottom, creating man-made sandbars; homes for a range of critters and insects. Of course, controlling something like the Mississippi River was an ongoing battle; a slower version of what Emily was feeling as she waited for the Francis B. to come around the bend to her right. Her head was throbbing, and she couldn't decide how much of it was from the wreck last night, and how much was from the conversation with Dasilva this morning. She picked up a handful of rocks and aimed them at pieces of driftwood stuck in the sand.

She felt the vibration and reached for her phone.

"Em, how you doing?" Lennie asked.

"I'm fine; just a bit sore."

"I mean after the meeting this morning. I hear that Dasilva went off on you."

"Oh, that, yeah; I'm OK."

"I tell you Em; something is going on here. After he finished with you, he stormed out of there and went straight to his car; wouldn't talk to anyone. He almost looked like a crazy man."

"He sounded pretty upset, yeah."

"I'm worried about you Em. I mean, first, you got the thing with Chambers, and now Dasilva. What's Chambers really doing up there with you anyway? And Reyes? What's going on Em, are you really OK?"

"I'm fine Lennie, really. They came up to Caruthersville to do that thing with Reyes' team getting the photos, and when they heard about my accident, they were already on their way up to Cairo anyway, so they came by to check on me; it's no big deal."

"Just watch yourself. I have a bad feeling about this thing, and I don't want you getting caught in something here."

"Thanks, Lennie. I'm fine. I'll keep my eyes open."

"Ok Em, give me a call later, OK?"

"Sure will. Thanks."

She stared at her phone for a few minutes trying to figure out where to file this call in her head. She looked up as the Francis B. came into view, and smiled as it turned left into the Mississippi River channel. The river was narrower here, and since her sandbar extended about a third of the way out, Emily could feel the vibration as the boat came near. It was close enough for her to see the open pilothouse door and the two men standing on the gangway. She guessed that one of them was Captain Charlie Graff, and the other was Dennis Bowers. She found herself waving, simply because that's what she did anytime a boat passed by. The two men waved back.

She raised her phone to call Dennis but was distracted by the movement at the back of the boat. She watched the young woman step from a door and move to one side, as two men came out carrying the cylinder. A third man held a line that he attached to one end of the device, and then lowered it into the water. She watched him play out the line and saw the wake of the device as it dragged behind them. As the boat passed under the bridge, he jerked the line, and the device

311

disappeared. Emily then noticed the other guy with them; the really big guy, standing and watching as the others stepped back inside the door.

She jumped into her car and drove across the bridge, through Cairo, and past the hospital she had been in last night. She turned onto the Levee Road, followed it to where it went under the elevated ramp to the bridge and found the dried-mud road. She stood quietly as the boat passed by, adding the I-57 bridge to its list of accomplishments.

The vibration caused her to jump. The caller ID said: Torchwood.

"Hello, this is Emily."

"Emily, this is Linda, at Torchwood, do you have a minute?"

"Sure Linda, what's up?"

"Well, there's something I need to check with you about; about your dad's meds."

"Ok."

"Well, you know he does this thing of trying to make us think he takes his meds, but tries to hide them under his tongue, or stick them in a pocket, things like that?"

"Yeah, I've talked with him about that. Did he try it again?"

"Well, I'm not sure, but that's why I needed to call you. You do remember that you're supposed to clear it with us anytime you bring him some meds that aren't on his script list, right?"

"Sure. But I've not brought him anything in, why are you asking?"

"Well, I was in with him this morning, and I found a pill that it looks like he hid in a shirt pocket."

"Geez, I'm sorry. I'll talk with him when I..."

"No, that's ok. What concerns me is that the pill isn't on his list. In fact, I'm not sure just what this pill is; it's not labeled or anything. So I was wondering if you had brought him something off the shelf; I know how he is always asking you to do that."

"No, I've not brought him anything since...wait, its not labeled?"

"No, it's a capsule, a large one, like a laxative or something like that."

Emily's head began to throb again.

"Linda, listen to me. Where is the pill now; I mean right now?"

"I've got it right here in my hand, why?"

"Linda, put it down; put it down now! Now!"

"Ok Em, it's down. What's going on?"

"I can't say for sure, but listen; here's what I want you to do. Do you have a plastic bag handy; something you can seal airtight?"

"Sure, right here."

"OK, good. Do you have gloves on?"

"No."

"OK, if you don't have gloves, use a piece of paper or something and push the pill into the plastic bag, and seal it up tight. OK?"

"OK, just a sec."

Silence.

"OK, it's in the bag. Em, what is going..."

"OK, now put the bag someplace where no one can get to it, and make sure that no one opens it or even touches it, OK?"

"Sure Em. I have to say you're scaring me here."

"Good. Like I said, it may be nothing. But if it's what I think it is, you have a good reason to be scared. You held it in your bare hand, right?"

"Yes, I'll go wash them."

"NO! Don't put water on them. Do you have any hand cleaner, you know, a gel or foam, or something that isn't water?"

"Yeah, we've got that."

"Go clean your hands with that, maybe two or three times, and then wipe them off with paper towels and put them in the hazardous materials container, OK?"

"Geez Em, OK, but what the heck is going on?"

"Make sure the bag is someplace safe. I'll have someone come and pick it up from you shortly. Don't give that bag to anyone unless they prove to you they're from the F.B.I. office, OK?"

"OK Em. I understand. Am I going to be OK?"

"Just wash with the stuff like I said and stay away from that bag until someone gets there."

"I will. Someday will you tell me what this is all about?"

"Yeah, I will when I can."

"Thanks, Em."

"One more thing Linda, who has been in to visit with my dad recently; over the past couple of days?"

"I don't know that anyone has been here Em, at least not while I've been on duty. But I can ask around."

"Please do that Linda. And do you guys have video of the hallways there, I mean do you have cameras there?"

"Yeah we do, but I'm not sure how long they keep them. Do you want me to ask?"

"Yes please, and if they have them, tell them I need copies of any that show dad's hallway for the past four days. Tell them the F.B.I. is securing them as part of an investigation. OK?"

"Investigation? I will Em. Now you do have me scared."

She ended the call and punched the button on her phone.

"What's up Em?"

"Lennie, listen very carefully. Here's what I need you to do."

As Emily got into her car, she felt something in her stomach, growing and churning and taking on a life of its own. It was a feeling of rage that surpassed even what she had felt when Elliott was taken. If she was right, someone had just tried to kill her father; her daddy. If she had been angry about the van attempting to hurt her last night, it was nothing compared to what she was feeling now. Someone, whoever it was, had crossed the line. Whatever else they had done, or might do in the future, the biggest mistake they would ever make was this one. As Emily drove toward the highway, she had no idea how she would do it, but for the first time in five days, she was absolutely certain that these assholes were going to pay.

Chapter 90

There was a lot of water between Cairo and the next bridge at a place called Thebes, on the Illinois side of the river below Cape Girardeau, Missouri. It would be about seven hours before the boat got there. While the real crew members were either on watch or resting, the doctor's crew was hanging out in the galley, playing cards. Since Dennis was not a card player, he walked up the steps to the pilothouse where Frank guided the boat, and Charlie was stretched out on the padded bench along the back wall with a paperback in his hands.

"A quiet afternoon," Dennis said.

Silence.

"Wasn't so quiet back at Cairo," Frank said. "Did you see those crowds. This is insane; all those people out there, waving signs and yelling. People are nuts."

"Well, maybe not nuts, Frank. But they are hungry for something that will excite them and make them feel something good for a change."

"And that's you, I suppose?" Frank said.

"Well, not me, but what our mission stands for, yes. People are tired of having a few rich and powerful people controlling things and deciding who lives or dies. They want change."

"Yeah, I guess. But you really think this is the way to do it?"

"To bring about change? I'm afraid so Frank. Like I said earlier, we've tried other ways, but the people in control are too well protected. So people just give up and believe there is nothing they can do. We're reminding them that they can do something and can change how things work."

Silence.

"Captain," Dennis said, "you're quiet back there. I'm sure you have thoughts about this?"

Charlie raised his eyes from his book, "Bull shit!"

"What do you mean?" Dennis asked.

"I mean it's all bullshit; this little speech you just gave and your whole goddamned mission thing you're doing. It's nothing but bullshit; plain and simple."

"But you don't think..."

"You may be right that the rich people have too much power. And you may be right that insurance companies and things like that are nothing but sons a bitches. But what you are doing here is just as screwed-up, and just as wrong any of them are. You've got the fancy words and fancy speeches, but you're just the same as they are; nothing but a bunch of self-serving, piss-ant, bull shit artists, plain and simple."

"I'm sorry you feel that way Captain. I really am. I think that if..."

"If you really wanted to make the changes you are talking about; there are ways of doing it. It might take time, but that's how things work. You're just like those long hair hippie sons a bitches who want everything right now and aren't willing to do the hard work needed to get things done. And you don't care about those people out there. You don't care about a damn thing but yourself. It's bullshit; that's all it is."

Moments of quiet.

"Captain, I do understand how you feel."

"Bullshit" Charlie mumbled and stared at his book.

"No really, I think I do. And if I thought this mission was doing more harm than good, I assure you I would have nothing to do with it. In fact, I would do everything I could do to stop it."

Silence.

"And honestly," Dennis continued, "I have to admit it does bother me a bit. I mean, I'm not blind to what is happening. For example, the next place we're coming to is Thebes; a quiet little place in Illinois that's been there since 1835."

Charlie glanced up, then back to his book.

"Yes, like I said, I'm not blind to all this. It troubles me that we're going to change that little town with such a history. Did you know that the railroad bridge we're going to hit there was opened in 1905, and it's still in use? Did you know that Abe Lincoln practiced law in Thebes, and there is a story that Dred Scott was kept in one of the jail cells there? And we're going to turn that town into a place that no one will be able to visit for fifty years; do you think that doesn't bother me a bit?"

Dennis looked out the window as Frank steered the boat and Charlie looked at his book.

"All I think right now," Charlie said, "is that I think you need to get your ass out of my pilothouse. And that's something you don't need to spend any time thinking about."

Dennis looked at the Captain briefly, glanced at Frank, and stepped out the door and walked downstairs to watch the card game.

"Bull shit!" Charlie said.

Colonel Chambers and Commander Reyes were sitting in a helicopter passing over Scott City, Missouri on the way to Cape Girardeau. Lennie was in New Orleans, handing a sealed box containing a plastic bag to the pilot of an F.B.I. airplane ready to fly to Louisville. Agent Arturo Dasilva was on the phone hearing that action two had been completed. Agent Emily Graham was driving a new rental car, the same model as the last, up Route 3 on the way to Thebes, with the windows rolled down, singing Free Bird with Lynard Skynard on the radio.

Chapter 91

Dasilva was in his chair. It was ten minutes after four, and neither Agent Emily Graham, Colonel Chambers or Commander Reyes had joined the four o'clock meeting. Calls to each of them had gone unanswered. As he looked around the table, Dasilva also did not see Agent Lennie Ryan. The tension in his body was as noticeable as the strain in his voice, "Well, it appears some of our key members have chosen to not attend our meeting. Since they were to provide the updates we are waiting for, I see no reason to keep you from your work any further. This meeting is adjourned."

His jaw was set as he walked from the room. His tires threw gravel as he pulled out of the parking lot. Thirty minutes later he was sitting on a bar stool next to a man in a very nice suit.

"I've told you what I know," suit said. "She was on her way to Thebes; the last report said she was on Route 3 somewhere around Olive Branch."

"Somewhere near Olive Branch?" Dasilva said. "You mean you don't know where she is for sure. Is that what you're telling me?"

"Relax," suit said. "There isn't anyplace she could go; she's on Route 3. It's fine."

"Fine," Dasilva said. "Fine? After your screw-up with her last night, don't sit there and tell me its fine."

"About last night; we thought we..."

"Save it; I'm not interested. You were to do a job out there and so far it's not been done. And now you tell me you don't know where she is. Listen, if I need to find someone else to do this..."

"No, we'll take care of it. We'll take care of it."

"See that you do. Now, what about her father? What happened there?"

Suit stared at his drink before saying anything more.

Across town, Lennie was sitting at a small desk watching video recordings of a hallway. He had been at it for half an hour and stood to stretch his arms.

"There's about ninety-six hours of it all together." the guy sitting next to him said. "The nurse said you wanted the past four days."

"Yeah," Lennie said, "that ought to give us what we need. Have you looked at any of it yet?"

"Nope. I just pulled the tapes and put them out here. What are you looking for anyway?"

"Not sure; maybe someone going in this room right here," Lennie pointed to the door on the screen, "someone who visited the guy in that room."

"I guess you could put it on fast forward and watch for something. That might help."

"That could work," Lennie said. "But I've got people who can do this for me, and they have the ability to enhance things if they find someone we need to identify. Do you have copies of these?"

"Nope, those are the only ones."

"Ok, then, I'll take these with me and have the team go over them. If somebody went in that room, they'll find them."

"So you guys are the F.B.I. huh? For real?"

"For real, yeah."

"Cool."

"Yeah, sometimes. You got a bag for these?"

Chapter 92

The pickup spot was near Rock Springs. The fishing boat came from the Illinois side and met the Francis B. as she passed. Fifteen minutes later the device was settling itself into the mud below the historic Thebes Bridge. A hundred and fifty years ago or so, steamboats carrying Union Troops to the South passed under the span, but tonight the Francis B. was the only boat on the river. Dennis stood in the galley doorway, watching the sunset illuminate the old Thebes Courthouse. He had read that it was on the historical register, and he could almost see Lincoln standing on those old steps watching the boat pass by.

"Pity," Dennis said to himself.

"What was that?" Dr. Shallenger asked as he stepped outside followed by Bear; the big man.

"Oh nothing," Dennis said. "Just taking in the view."

Both men watched the shore pass for a moment.

"Doctor, do you ever have second thoughts about what we are doing; I mean about how we're doing it?"

"Second thoughts? Absolutely not." Shallenger waved a hand in the air. "What we are doing will bring about changes that must take place."

"Yes, I know. But I mean, the destruction; especially of something like this little town, it's just sad."

"A small price to pay."

"Yes, I know. At least it's just buildings and things; we're not doing anything that will harm people directly. Just things."

"Yes, my friend, just things."

Another moment watching the shore.

"Have a nice evening my friend," Shallenger said as he touched Dennis' shoulder and stepped back inside.

"You too," Dennis said as he turned and noticed Bear still standing inside the door.

"Purdy night," Bear said.

"It certainly is Bear." Every time Dennis looked at him, he was reminded of those big guys who played prize fighters in the old movies. He was huge, and strong, but seemed to be a bit awkward both physically and mentally. If he had to describe Bear, Dennis would say that he had a body and heart the size of a bear, and a brain the size of a child. Dennis had almost changed his mind about recruiting Bear for the role. Not that Dennis had lied to him, but he was certain that Bear didn't really understand what was going on. All Bear understood was that he had been asked to come on a boat ride, and do whatever he could do to protect his new friends. Loyalty and friendship were things that Bear understood.

"Whatcha doin' out here Dennis?" Bear asked. "There's skeeters out here."

"Just looking at the town there. Did you know that Abraham Lincoln was there once?"

"Ain't he the guy on the penny?"

"Yeah, that's him.

"Dennis, do you think they got any more ice cream tonight? That was good."

"I bet they do Bear." Dennis glanced at the shore and then at the smiling hulk beside him, "Let's go find out."

Chapter 93

While the crowds at Thebes had been small, Cape Girardeau made up for it. The first groups appeared just after they picked up the devices, lining the shore as the boat made its way around the bend below Marquette Island. Marquette Island was not large but was surrounded by sandbars that made it look much bigger. It was in the middle of the river, with the navigation channel going to the left, and a shallower channel to the right. As the Francis B. approached, Charlie saw that the right-hand channel was filled with pleasure boats of all shapes and sizes, all being kept out of the main river by Coast Guard cruisers. As he shined his bright arc spotlight in that direction, he heard the horns and cheers all the way out here in the middle of the river.

Dennis entered the pilothouse.

"Are you feeling better this evening Captain? I really didn't intend to upset you like I did this afternoon, and I want to apologize for that."

A brief pause.

"I'm fine," Charlie said in short words. "Don't worry about it."

"Hey, that F.B.I lady that called you; Agent Graham, I think you knew her father, a James Graham?"

Charlie turned to look at Dennis, then back to the river.

"Yeah. I knew him."

"Well?"

"Yeah, I knew him pretty well. He's the guy that trained me, so I probably know him as well as anybody did."

"I'll tell you what, I really feel bad about earlier. Would it help if you gave her a call and talked with her? You told her you would you know."

"That was because I couldn't talk then."

"I know, but why don't you call her. I'm sure she's up there by the bridge to watch us go by."

"Well, I don't know."

"Tell you what. Give her a call and just talk. The one rule; no talking about the mission, or the boat. OK?"

"OK." Charlie paused. "Thanks."

Charlie reached for his phone, found the number in the list of recent calls, and pushed the button.

"Graham."

"Agent Graham? This is Charlie Graff, Captain on the Francis B."

"Captain Graff, it's good to hear your voice. Is everything OK?"

"Fine Agent Graham, are you here at Cape?"

"Yes. I'm with the police on the bridge. I wanted to go down by the river, but the crowds are out of control."

"I see them from here; we're just coming around Marquette Island."

"Captain, do they know you are calling me? Is it safe?"

"Yes, they know. In fact, it was his idea that I call you."

"His? You mean Dennis? Why would he do that? Is there a problem?"

"Yeah him. But no, there's no problem. I think he believes it will make me feel better and that I'll be nicer to him or something."

Charlie glanced at Dennis.

"So, you're just calling to talk?"

"Yeah, I guess so. So, your dad is Jim Graham?"

"Yes, he's my dad. You know him?"

"He taught me most of what I know out here; he's the reason I got my ticket. He was a stubborn son of a bitch but he sure as hell knew his...oh, I didn't mean anything..."

"Don't worry Captain; it's not the first time he's been called that."

"Please call me Charlie. How is your dad now anyway? Where is he?"

"And I'm Emily. Well, he's in New Orleans now."

"New Orleans? That's great."

"Well, actually he's having some problems; not so much physically, but his mind. Some issues with dementia."

"Oh, I'm really sorry to hear that. Damn. How bad is it?"

"It comes and goes. Sometimes he knows where he is and who I am, and sometimes he has no idea."

"That's a shame. He deserves better. You say you're on the bridge up there?" Charlie asked as the boat approached the span.

"Almost in the middle. It might be too high, but I'll wave."

Charlie stepped outside the pilothouse door onto the gangway.

"I see you there. Not well enough to see if you inherited your dad's good looks, but I do hope you were spared that."

"Yeah, he says I look more like mom did."

"I was really sorry to hear when she passed. We met a few times when Jim had me over to the house to help get me ready for my pilot's exam. She made one hell of a pecan pie."

"Yes, she did Charlie."

A brief pause as Charlie stepped back into the pilothouse.

"Charlie, tell me, is there anything we can do to bring this thing to an end here?"

"Emily, I'm afraid that's something we can't talk about tonight," Charlie said as he glanced at Dennis.

"I understand."

"Well, it's been nice to visit with you. Say hello to your dad when you see him."

"I'll tell him, Charlie. You take care."

A brief pause.

"Charlie?"

"Yes, Emily?"

"Is Dennis there with you?"

"He's standing right here."

"Could I talk with him please?"

Charlie offered Dennis the phone, but he shook his head.

"He, um, can't do that right now Emily. I'm sorry."

"No problem Charlie. I understand. You take care of yourself, OK?"

"You do the same."

Emily stood on the high span of Cape Girardeau's Bill Emerson Bridge. She watched the stern of the Francis B. move away to the north and covered her ears to block the roar from the crowds lining both sides of the river.

"Feeling better?" Dennis asked Captain Charlie Graff.

"Yes," Charlie said. Then after a brief pause added. "But I still think you and your friends down there are full of bullshit, and if I can find a way to stop what you are doing I goddamn well guarantee you I'm going to do it."

"Good night Captain," Dennis said as he stepped from the pilothouse.

Chapter 94

It was an hour's drive from Cape Girardeau, Missouri to the next bridge at Chester, Illinois. Emily decided to get the drive out of the way tonight and sleep in before the boat passed there around five in the morning.

She was tired. She hadn't slept that well after the so-called accident. She was not taking the pain meds, so while her head was clear, it felt like someone was playing a bass drum inside. The noise at Cape Girardeau hadn't helped. She checked her phone when she got to Cape and saw a half-dozen missed calls; several of them from Dasilva. As she pulled onto I-55, she shook her head thinking there were still places in this country where you couldn't get a cell phone signal or decent music; you know, like they have back home. She decided she would return those missed calls tomorrow morning. After all, she reasoned, it was late, and she didn't want to bother anyone like Dasilva if she didn't have too.

She began punching buttons on the radio to find something worth listening too when she felt the vibration.

"Graham."

"Emily, it's Lennie, can you talk?"

"Yeah, I'm in the car heading to Chester, what's keeping you up at this hour?"

"I knew you would want to know; I just got a call from your Medical Examiner up in Louisville. She said the pill we sent her is the same as the other one. Do you know what she means by that?"

There was a brief pause as Emily focused on keeping the car on the road. Her head was spinning as she thought about what had almost happened, and that whoever was responsible was still out there running around somewhere.

"Em, are you there?"

"Yeah, I'm here. Sorry. And yeah, I know what she means."

"Is it important; anything I need to know about?"

"Not right now, no. I need to think a bit, and I'll let you know."

"Ok. You said you're driving again? Where the heck are you?"

"The boat gets to Chester around five in the morning, so I decided to drive on up there tonight. Figure I'll sleep late enough to get this head to stop aching."

"What is it, about two hours up there?"

"Nah, it just takes about an hour on I-55. It's an easy drive, and there's not much traffic. I just wish I could find something on the radio."

"Ok, well, you be careful. Hey, did you ever hear anything from Chambers or Dasilva yet?"

"Nope, no problems from either of them."

"Good. But keep your eyes open, OK?"

"Will do Lennie. Go get some sleep."

"Take care Em."

Just over an hour later, Emily parked her car at a Best Western motel, made her way to her room on the second floor, and closed the door behind her. As tired as she was, there was a smile on her face. She had no idea that the little town of Chester was known as the hometown of Popeye the Sailor Man. Popeye's creator was born and raised in Chester, and since she had seen the first sign on the highway, she had been wearing the same grin. Popeye was how dad had gotten her to eat spinach so many years ago. There was something about the stuff that just did not want to go down her throat, but when her dad bent his arms and did his little dance while singing the Popeye The Sailor song, she could gulp it right down. There were good times back there, and while they made her smile, they made her wish he could remember them too.

It had been a while since Emily had been to the beach, but after a quick shower, she crawled into the queen-size bed and closed her eyes. In a minute or two, she was watching the surf from her beach towel, trying to hear the waves as she watched her dad dodging the pill-shaped rocks someone was throwing at him from behind a palm tree. Jimmy Buffett was sitting in the sand with a bandage on his head, trying to get a signal on his cell phone.

Back in Cape Girardeau, Colonel Chambers woke to the sound of his phone.

"Chambers here."

"Colonel Chambers?"

"Yes, what is it?"

"Colonel, my name is Steve. I'm sorry to bother you at this hour, but I need to let you know that Agent Grahams' life is in danger."

"What? Steve? Are you the guy that's been calling her?"

"Colonel, please. There is time for that later. Right now you need to understand that Emily is in danger. Do you know where she is?"

"I believe she drove on up to Chester earlier, to be there for the boat tomorrow."

"Colonel, she is indeed in Chester, at the Best Western motel. I knew that, and now you know that. What is important is that there are others who know that as well."

"Who the hell are you?"

"As I've told Emily, we are on the same team, I assure you. But these other people are not. Do you understand?"

His phone was lying on the bed as he bolted out of the motel room door fastening his pants. He moved across the hall in one step and pounded on a door. "Reyes...Reyes...get your ass out here. We've got trouble."

Chapter 95

The alarm went off at four, which she figured would give her enough time to get ready for the boat. Emily rinsed her face, took care of her other usual morning things, picked up her bag, and opened the motel room door.

"Who the hell are you?" she asked the man sitting in the chair next to her door.

The man picked up his radio and mumbled something. "Just one second Agent Graham. I must ask you to please step back inside your room."

"What the..."

The man stood. His size and facial expression convinced her to do exactly as he said. The shiny badge and sidearm also helped. She went to the window and saw a half dozen black cars in the lot, with a group of people standing and looking at her car; from a distance. The only person near it was wearing something that looked like an overstuffed parka covering his entire body. She began putting the pieces together as the door opened and Chambers and Reyes stepped inside.

"Ok," Emily said, "would somebody like to tell me what is going on here? Where did you two come from; again."

"You can thank your friend Steve." Chambers said.

"He called you?"

"Yeah, around two o'clock or so, saying you were in danger."

"Danger?"

"The thing is, he knew exactly where you were, and said the other people knew too. So, Agent Graham, fill us in. What do you really know about this Steve, and who the hell are these other people?"

"I've already told you what I know. Really. He's the guy that gave me the address for that Alex guy at Arbel's in Louisville. He's called a couple more times. All he'll tell me is that we're on the same team and that this whole thing is about two groups who are fighting. But I've already told you all of that. What is going on now?"

"Now?" Reyes said, "oh not much. We've just got a guy out there trying to disarm some kind of bomb somebody stuck under your car last night; something like that...not much."

"Bomb? What the..." She looked for the right words as she noticed her body slowly lowering itself onto the edge of the bed. She didn't think she was fainting, she'd never been that type, but for some reason her body had decided to take a brief break to reflect on things, leaving her mind to fend for itself.

"From this point on, no more going off on your own, OK? Either one of us or someone from the team needs to be with you at all times. Are you OK with that?"

"What if I have to go to the bathroom?" she asked.

"We'll close our eyes," Reyes said. These are people who know when a bit of humor is the one defense to use.

"Ok, let's do this again," Chamber said, "who knew where you were going last night?"

"Well, the only people I talked with were you guys and Lennie. I guess maybe the boat Captain; I may have told him when we talked. And..."

"You talked with the Captain again? What about?"

"It was strange. He called me, and said that the Dennis guy told him to give me a call, just to talk."

"Talk? About what?"

"Apparently anything except what they are doing out there. We mostly talked about my dad; they worked together."

"Ok, he might have told the Dennis guy about your plans. Who else? Dasilva?"

"I don't think so. The last time we talked I didn't know I was coming up here tonight. In fact, I didn't even know where I was staying until I got up here, so how did they know what motel I was in?"

"They might have someone tailing you."

"Or you're bugged."

"Me?"

"Your car maybe. It's a shot."

"Well," Chambers said, "whatever it is, from here on you've got company; we're not giving them a third chance. What time is it? The boat gets here at five."

"Guys," Emily hesitated, "there's one more thing I think you need to know, under the circumstances."

"And that would be?" Reyes asked.

"Somebody tried to kill my father in New Orleans."

"What do you mean?"

"His nurse called yesterday after finding a pill in one of his pockets; he hides them there sometimes and just pretends to take them."

"OK," Reyes said.

"This pill they found was the same as the one that Alex used to kill himself in Louisville; one of those kill pills created by the guys helping Shallenger."

"You're sure about that?"

"Lennie got the call confirming it a few hours ago."

A long silence as everyone looked at their shoes. Emily noticed she was standing again.

"OK then, someone is doing their best to get you out of the picture here Graham." Chambers said. "They figure they can either take you out, or your dad, but either way you'll no longer be a problem. Somehow, we need to have a really good conversation with this Steve guy."

"If we're going to the river," Reyes said, "we'd better get started. I think we have enough people here to provide Agent Graham with protection.

Emily once again collected her stuff, and followed the two men from the room as she sang to herself, "Me, and my sha...dow". Humor; sometimes it was the only way.

Activity at the river was larger than Caruthersville but smaller than Cape Girardeau. Instead of watching from the riverbank, Emily was standing in the middle of a group of agents and other official looking people, all paying more attention to the crowd around them than to the boat. As the boat passed, Emily was still close enough to see the pilothouse door open, and a man step out onto the gangway. It looked like he was holding a phone.

She felt the vibration.

"Graham."

"Agent Graham, its Dennis. I want to apologize for being so rude earlier, and for not accepting your call. That was completely inappropriate of me. All I can say is that I had many things on my mind, and I truly want to apologize."

"It's not a problem. I was not offended."

Chambers gave her a very strange look.

"Agent Graham," Dennis said, "I would like to make it up to you, and offer you something that you may find to be very interesting and meaningful."

"Yes. And what might that be?"

"I would like to invite you to join us on the Francis B.; to come and see what we are doing, and give us the opportunity to explain things appropriately. Plus, I believe it might be helpful for you to see that the crew is perfectly safe, and has not been mistreated in any way."

"Come aboard the Francis B? Me?"

Both Chambers and Reyes stared, open-mouthed for a moment before both began shaking their heads.

"Yes, please. I assure you that you will be perfectly safe. Will you join us, please?"

"When? How?"

Heads were shaking more violently although both men's eyes showed that they knew she is going to go.

"I want to give you time to make arrangements. Are you familiar with the little town of Kimmswick? It's a very nice little place not far below St. Louis; lots of history there. I have a friend who will meet you at the little marina there. He will bring you out to the Francis B. so you can ride along as we go through St. Louis; it should be quite a ride. But please, just yourself; I'm afraid we won't be able to provide hospitality for any of your other colleagues at this time. Can I tell my friend you will meet him there?"

Emily knew she should have a discussion with Chambers and Reyes.

"Yes, I'll be there."

"Wonderful," Dennis said. "Agent Graham you have made my day."

"I'm glad to hear that," Emily said.

"One more thing before we go, Agent Graham?"

"Yes?"

"I want you to know that none of the things that have happened over the past twenty-four hours, things with you and your father; none of those things have been from us. None of them."

"How did you know about..."

"Until Kimmswick Agent Graham. And thank you once again."

Click.

Three hours later, Emily was in a helicopter heading for Kimmswick, Missouri, sitting between Colonel Chambers and Commander Reyes, neither of whom was convinced that what they were doing was a good idea. Even with the headsets, it was difficult to talk, so Emily allowed herself to drift off. She watched the surf gently lapping against the sand as she sat on her chair, watching the man underneath it trying to disarm the bomb someone had put there. Jimmy Buffett was standing down by the surf, completely surrounded by men in black suits and wearing sunglasses.

Chapter 96

"You look rested this morning," Ronnie said, "things must be getting better."

"No," the older man said. "If anything, it's even more challenging than before. But as I told you, we have time on our side, so we trust our people. But, the real question, have you come up with your action for our cashier up there this morning, to ask for your first name."

"I did," he said proudly. "In fact, I've got a couple of ways it could be done."

"Well, in that case, I'm afraid you have failed my little test."

"What do you mean? You've not even heard my ideas."

"I don't need to hear them; you've already told me that you don't have confidence in either one of them, so it would be a waste of my time to hear more."

"I don't understand. Are you telling me now that you can read minds?

"No, Ronnie, but if you tell me you have more than one way to do the task, it means that you don't have the confidence that either of them will do the job. If you had an action that you fully believed in, you wouldn't need another. Remember Ronnie, the risks are just too high, as we're seeing out there right now; we have to wait until we have the action that we know is the one best action to take. "

Brief silence.

"So, I guess I screwed up."

"Yes, but don't worry about it; I did the same thing. All it means is that you still have things to learn; and we already knew that, didn't we?"

The old man smiled.

"Ok, yeah. So, are you going to tell me how you actually did it; the asking for first name thing?"

"Sure, but I'm afraid it's not all that exciting. Let's start by asking if you wanted to change some behavior of someone like the cashier here, who would probably have the most clout to do that in the company."

"You mean the boss; the CEO?"

"Well, maybe, but they've got many other things on their plate; most of them looking a lot more important than this. Who else? Think about what the cashier does, and what they represent."

"Represent? Well, they're someone that deals with all the customers, so do you mean like they represent the company; something like that."

"They represent the face of the company; exactly. When people interact with the cashier, it's one of the few times they directly interact with the company. So its important that they do a good job, right? And who in the company probably spends a good deal of their time worrying about that kind of thing?"

"PR? Marketing?"

"There you go. So, if we could find a way to get the marketing people to believe it would improve the customer experience to call them by name..."

"They've got the clout to get it done. So, we talk with someone in marketing, and..."

"Channels Ronnie. At least four of them, more if possible."

"Ok, find someone who knows someone in marketing..."

"Better still. Where do marketing people get their ideas for how to improve things in the company?"

"Reading I guess. So you write a book."

"Keep thinking. Publishing is complicated. Where else?"

"Well, from talking with each other, maybe at conferences or something."

"Now you're catching on. If you had an idea you wanted to plant in someone's mind at a conference, how could you do that?"

"Have a speaker talk about it, or have a workshop."

"Ok. In this case, we began by digging through the marketing research databases and the libraries, until we found good information about the value of personalizing the customer transaction. We found good material on the role of using the customer's first name; we found someone's dissertation on that, and even a couple of small companies that were doing it and showing that it worked.

"Ok, so you contacted them?"

"No, always channels. We identified a few of the most popular marketing conferences, and the names of the people responsible for marketing and promoting those conferences. We saw to it that they received emails from people who may or may not have existed, asking if the conference was going to include speakers or presentations about this idea of customer first names, and mentioning an article or two they had read, or that dissertation. I think you can figure out the rest; that was the last we had to be involved."

"Then someone in marketing at this coffee company went to the conference and heard about it, and that's why they do it here now?"

"Yes."

"So they think they're just doing some neat little PR thing to make people feel cared about here, but they're really providing us with a way to communicate."

"Exactly; it's a positive thing for both of us."

They sipped from their cups as the young man glanced at the cashier.

"Ronnie." The old man was smiling.

"Yeah?"

"Do you realize that was the first time you have referred to our group using the term us?"

"I did?"

"Yes; but it's not the first time you've made me proud. I'll see you tomorrow morning."

Chapter 97

"Look, I can take care of this," suit said as he sat at the quiet end of the bar.

"Forget it," Dasilva said. "You had your chance, and you blew it; I've brought in someone else."

"But..."

"It's already done. You're out."

"You can't just push us out of this like that; you can't do that."

Dasilva sipped from his drink as he slowly turned to face the very expensive suit.

"Just what are you saying?"

"I'm saying that we had a deal, and if you back out on it now, I can't be responsible for what might happen."

Dasilva drained his glass and set it on the bar, never breaking eye contact with suit.

"You're threatening me; is that it? Is that what you're doing here?"

"Well, no, it's just that..."

"Ah, that's good to know." Dasilva waved to the bartender for a refill. "Because if you were doing that; threatening me, that would seriously change our relationship here, you know?"

"No, I wasn't trying to..."

"And with everything going on right now," Dasilva said as he watched his glass filling "I'm afraid I don't have time to be all political and, you know, spend time negotiating with threatening me. I would simply make a call and have someone take care of the situation for me. I'm sure you can understand."

"Of course." Suit seemed to have lost his voice. "Don't worry about it; I was just hoping to have another chance to prove that we could take care of things for you."

"No time for that now. As I said, I found someone else." Dasilva tipped his glass in a toast to Suit, drained in it one gulp, looked at the empty glass, and smiled. "So, I guess we're finished here, right?"

Dasilva walked slowly from the bar, got into his car, and pushed the button on his phone.

"It's Dasilva. I need you to get word out to everyone to cancel the nine o'clock briefing this morning. I know, but I've got things I have to take care of. Tell them we'll reschedule for later. I don't know when yet; I'll let you know."

He pulled into traffic and drove across town. Thirty minutes later he found a spot in the lot and walked up the sidewalk to the building. The sign carved into the arch over the door read: Federal Bureau of Investigation.

After showing his badge and other credentials, he followed someone along a row of cubicles, finally stopping in front of a closed door.

"This is it," the someone said as he turned and headed back to where Dasilva had found him.

Dasilva knocked.

"Come in," Lennie said.

Dasilva stepped into the room.

"Agent Ryan," Dasilva said, "do you have a few minutes?"

"Of course," Lennie said as he nodded toward one of the chairs in front of his desk.

"Thank you. Look, I realize that we've not gotten off on the best foot in all this here."

"Oh, no, it's fine."

"Let's be honest Lennie. I can come across as a real pain in the ass sometimes; a hardcore company-guy who acts like a real jerk. I have to admit that I know that, and honestly, it's intentional; it can sometimes get me what I need."

"Well..."

"And I know that I've treated you that way since I've been here; so I wanted you to know it wasn't personal, OK?"

"OK, sure."

"But look, we need to see if we can find a way to work together here; especially with things as they are with Agent Graham. I think we need to put our cards on the table and do what we need to do to make sure she's safe. What do you say?"

Lennie's mind was racing. He thought of at least five very good reasons to not trust this guy. Putting cards on the table meant risking giving away information that could create more problems, rather than fixing anything.

"Sure," Lennie said, "I think that's a good idea."

"Good. Why don't we get together for drinks tonight and go over things; compare notes and see it we can help each other fill in any gaps?"

"Sounds good to me," Lennie said. "I do need to make some calls now, but how about sometime after six?"

"I'll give you a call then," Dasilva said as he rose and moved toward the door.

"Thanks for your time Lennie." Dasilva smiled.

"Thanks for stopping by Arturo." Lennie smiled back.

Both smiles disappeared as soon as the office door closed.

Chapter 98

"Well, dammit, at least let us put a wire on you."

The discussion had been going on since landing in Kimmswick twenty minutes ago but had so far done nothing to help Chambers and Reyes feel better about what Emily was about to do.

"No," Emily said, "no wire. These guys aren't stupid."

"Emily, think about it a minute," Reyes said. "Why in hell would these guys invite you out there like this? It just doesn't make sense. It's never smart to go into a situation when you have no idea what you're going to find."

"And remember," Chambers said, "someone has tried to take you out of this twice now, and even targeted your dad. Who would benefit most from that? These guys, that's who. And now you're walking right into their hands."

"I know, I know," Emily said. "But Dennis assured me I would be perfectly safe."

"Said the fox to the rabbit," Chambers said.

"Ok, I get it. I do," Emily said. "But this will give me the chance to get a look at what's really going on out there; see how many are involved, make sure the crew is really OK. Hell, maybe even find a way we can do something to stop them. I think it's worth the risk."

Silence.

"Besides, I'm not totally helpless you know."

"That's not what we're saying here Emily," Chambers said, "it's just that..."

"No," Reyes said, "she's right. I don't like it any more than you do Bill, but she's right; she needs to get on the boat. We just need to make sure we're ready to move in if anything does go sour."

"I really don't think it will," Emily said. "But yeah, just in case."

"I still don't like it," Chambers said, "but OK. So, just how long are you supposed to be on the boat?"

"He said I could ride with them through St. Louis, so they'll probably let me off somewhere north of there." Emily paused, "And I think I know the place."

"What do you mean?" Reyes asked.

"The Chain of Rocks Lock is just north of St. Louis. They'll have to stop there for a while, so that would be the perfect place to let me off. That's how I'd do it if it was me."

"Chain of Rocks Lock?" Reyes said, "That's where they lift the boats up, right?"

Emily looked at him.

"Hey," Reyes said, "I'm from Arizona, and spent my military career in a desert. Give me a break."

"Ok, sorry," Emily said. "Yeah, there are places where the river is too shallow for a boat, and one of those is just above St. Louis. It's a bunch of rapids called the Chain of Rocks. They dug this canal to go around the rapids, and built the locks there to hold back the water to make it deep enough."

"So it's a dam," Reyes said.

"Well, kind of," Emily said. "It does block the water and make it deeper above the lock, yeah. But instead of just blocking the water, it's got gates that can open and close, and they're far enough apart to let a boat in between them. A boat can go inside the lock from either side, they close the gates and then either fill the lock or drain it to raise or lower level of the water to match which way the boat is going."

"How long does that take?" Reyes asked.

"It depends, but I think at least thirty to forty-five minutes."

"Then, you're telling us we're going to have the boat trapped inside a big box up there for maybe forty-five minutes?" Chambers said.

"That's one way of looking at it I guess," Emily said.

"Are you Emily Graham?" a man in jeans, a torn sweatshirt and a mud-stained St. Louis Cardinals ball cap approached the group.

"Yes, I'm Agent Graham," Emily said as Chambers and Reyes moved between her and the stranger.

"I'm supposed to give you a ride, ma'am. To meet the Francis B.,"he said as he removed his hat and folded it in his hands.

"You're sure about this?" Reyes asked.

"Yeah, I'm sure," Emily said as she turned to the stranger. "Let's go."

His boat was something like her grandfather's when she was a kid and went fishing with him. The man apologized for the scattered nets and poles, and Emily did her best to assure him it wasn't a problem. As they moved south along the shore, Emily couldn't hide her smile as she listened to the outboard motor and the constant slapping of the water hitting the bow of the boat.

"There she is," the man said, "won't be long now. You maybe want to hang on a bit; it can get a bit rough."

Emily felt her heart beating faster and her breath getting short. It wasn't the idea of being on the boat that bothered her; once she was on board she would be fine. The problem was getting onto the boat in the first place, especially when that boat was moving; and the Francis B. was showing no signs of stopping. The man pulled his small boat alongside the Francis B., staying about twenty feet away and matching the speed. Then he jerked the outboard and aimed directly for the side of the huge towboat, rocked up and down over the waves, and turned at the last minute until they were rubbing against the side of the big boat. Emily held the seat to steady herself as she stood in the rocking boat and suddenly saw her feet leave the floor as she felt herself float into the air. Seconds later she landed gently on the solid deck of the Francis B. and turned to see a very large man standing behind her.

"I hope I didn't hurt you or nuthin'." the large man said.

"This is Bear, Agent Graham," Dennis said. "Welcome aboard the Francis B."

Chapter 99

"I must apologize, Agent Graham," Dennis said as they stepped inside a door and moved down the narrow corridor.

"But there are some things I must help the others with for a few minutes here. I will come back as soon as I can so we can talk, but for now, let me take you to the pilothouse where you can talk with the Captain. He is not on duty right now but is there with Frank, his Pilot."

"You'll want to search me first, of course," Emily said as they began climbing the stairs.

"Search you?" Dennis said with a look of surprise, "why on earth would we want to do that? You are our guest here Agent Graham. Besides, as I have already explained, there is nothing you can do to stop our mission here, so we need not bother with such unfriendly things. Ah, here we are, just up those last steps and you'll find them there. Please forgive me, but I am needed below."

Dennis turned and walked back down the steps, leaving Emily on the small gangway. She glanced toward the shore where she saw Chambers and Reyes still watching her, walked up the stairs and opened the door.

"One of you gentlemen must be Captain Charlie Graff." she said with a smile.

"That's me, and you must be our Agent Graham. Frank, this here is Jim Graham's girl, you remember me talking about him?"

"Yeah," Frank said, turning in his seat, "nice to meet you."

"Charlie," Emily said, "I think we ought to talk."

Miles to the south, Dasilva moved through the cubicles until he reached the door and shoved it open without knocking.

"Lennie, have you heard the news?"

"Huh, about what? I'm kind of busy right now."

"She's on the boat. Emily is on the damn boat."

"What are you talking about?"

"Grab your stuff; I've got a jet waiting, we need to get to St. Louis."

As the plane lifted off the runway, neither man knew exactly what was going on, but both had long believed the principle that whenever you were in a really bad situation, it was always best to have your enemies close by you, so you could keep an eye on what the hell they might be up to."

Chambers and Reyes were back in their car heading up I-55. At this point, they had decided to skip the bridges along the way, and head straight for the Illinois side; and the Chain of Rocks Lock. They hadn't decided what they would do when they got there but were making calls to make sure they had the right people there to do whatever it was.

Emily and Charlie stood on the gangway as Frank picked up the barge tied across from Cave Creek Park. Over the next hour, they talked about the past six days. They each added their pieces of the puzzle and stopped talking only once; as they passed beneath the Jefferson Barracks Bridge.

"So Alex was the only one involved at the home office, huh?" Charlie asked. "You're sure about that?"

"Yeah, it looks that way."

"Good. I couldn't believe Gil would have had anything to do with it, or Alma either; any of them really."

"What do you know about this Dennis guy?" Emily asked. "We've not been able to find out much."

"Not a lot. He said something about losing a child, and that was why he got involved in the first place, but that's about it."

"Yeah, that's all we know. He was from Cincinnati but hasn't been seen there for a year or more, so we don't know what he's been up to."

"With the rest of these clowns, I guess."

"You two out here enjoying the view?" Dennis said as he climbed the stairs to the gangway.

Emily turned to look at the riverbank, almost covered with people; some waving signs or flags, some waving and cheering.

"This is crazy," Emily said.

344

"And we're still ten miles from downtown," Dennis said. "It looks like everything is going just as we planned."

"Do you honestly think this will change the things you want to change?" Emily asked.

"I'm sorry," Dennis said, "I just came up for a second to make sure you were doing OK. We're about to pick up a barge with all of the devices for the St. Louis bridges, and I'm afraid we're all going to be quite busy for a while. But I assure you, we'll have time to talk as soon as we're finished. Enjoy the view."

Dennis turned and walked back down the stairs and through a door.

"Do you know anything about this Doctor Shallenger?" Emily asked.

"Just that he's a real nut job. He really thinks he's doing something good here. He seems to be the real guiding force behind the whole thing."

"Not Dennis?"

"I don't think so. Dennis is the front man, taking care of things out here, but Shallenger is calling the shots; most of the group are his people. And you say somebody blew up his office at the university?"

"Office and two labs, along with about fifteen people."

"What about all the talk of no one getting hurt in this?" Charlie asked.

"Yeah, that's a question I'll ask the good doctor if I get the chance. Especially since you think he's the head guy."

"I think so, yeah, at least on the boat here. But they've got others involved; I've heard them talking on the phone. Don't know who they are, but there's more out there."

"We know about the ones getting the devices to the boat; we've been watching them," Emily said.

"Good. I'd appreciate getting about ten minutes with each of them when you catch them; in private if you don't mind."

"Yeah, me too."

"How long have you known Frank?" Emily asked.

"Frank? I guess he's been with me four or five years now. He came on as a deckhand; a damn hard worker. He showed interest and

345

potential, so I've tried to help him move up; like your dad did for me. Why?"

"Charlie, we've got a couple of moles on our team here; one in my group somewhere, and I believe one in yours as well."

"You think Frank is helping them? Nah, I can't believe that. He's not the type."

"I'm not saying he is Charlie, but somebody is, and it's somebody who is involved enough to know everything that's going on."

"Hell, I've known most of these boys since they learned to tie a line; know most of their families too."

"I know Charlie, I feel the same about my people. But somebody in here is dirty. We need to be careful until we find out who."

Silence as they watched the Poplar Street Bridge slide toward them. The river didn't really get any narrower as it ran through St. Louis, but the industries and docks along the shore made threading the needle through the eight bridges an interesting challenge.

"I'd better go back inside and see if Frank needs some help," Charlie said as he stepped back inside the pilothouse.

Emily stayed outside and watched the afternoon sunlight bounce off the Gateway Arch. The park beneath it was filled with people, with bands, vendors, and noise. Someone was attempting to raise a huge banner from one side of the arch, and park police were attempting to pull it back down. All she saw of the sign was a brief glance at the word Boom.

The two men worked together to guide the boat down the channel. On a normal day, there were hundreds of barges parked along the river here that need to be avoided. And today, the path held another twenty or thirty fully loaded towboats the Coast Guard had stopped to clear the way for the Francis B., each of them taking up that much more space. Just like along the shore, each boat was lined with crew members standing and watching as they passed; many blowing horns. Emily wasn't sure which side they were cheering for.

Chapter 100

After the Poplar Street Bridge came the Eads, then the Martin Luther King Bridge, then the modern towers and cables of the Stan Musial Memorial Bridge carrying I-70 across the river. As Emily looked ahead from the gangway, the only two remaining were the old McKinley Bridge and the Merchants Railroad Bridge.

"Agent Graham," Dennis called from the door below, "why don't you come with me?"

She walked down the stairs where Dennis was holding the door open.

"We're just about finished here, but it occurred to me that you might like to see how things work; how we actually place the devices. I assure you it is perfectly safe."

She followed him through the door, down a corridor and two more flights of stairs, before stepping out onto the open deck of the boat.

"This way," Dennis said. "Watch your step."

Emily walked along the narrow deck and turned the corner to the open platform at the rear of the boat. She recognized Bear standing to one side, and Dennis. She identified the man she believed was Shallenger, and the young woman who must be Susan; the one she carried a message for from the hospital. Another young man was doing something with the device that was leaning against still another man, while still another third held the end of a long piece of line.

"So these are them?" Emily said to herself.

"Agent Graham, please come closer. You see Lawrence here is fastening the line to the ring that will be used to lower the device and activate the arming mechanism. Lawrence one of Dr. Shallenger's students, and is responsible for the actual design of the devices. Quite a young man."

It occurred to Emily that Dennis sounded like a proud father, showing off his child's science project.

"And this is Bradley, holding the device, and Thomas, preparing the line. They will lower the device into the water."

The three men all nodded, and the one called Bradley actually waved.

"Are these people for real?" Emily thought.

"There, in the doorway," Dennis pointed, "is Susan, another of Dr. Shallenger's students, and the brains behind the radioactive components of the device. We couldn't have done this without her."

Susan nodded, and appeared to blush.

"Of course you know Bear, over there by the side, and this..."

Emily almost expected a drum roll.

"And this is Doctor Shallenger." Shallenger had ignored the conversation so far and continued to do so as he watched everything the others were doing. Dennis noticed Shallenger's lack of response.

"I'm afraid the doctor is focused on work right now. I am sure he will be happy to talk with you when we are finished."

Dennis and Emily stood silently as the group lowered the last two devices into the water, and she felt the boat make a slight turn as it left the main channel to enter the Chain of Rocks Canal. The lock was just another mile away. Emily knew that if she was going to learn anything important during her visit, time was running short.

Shallenger walked toward Emily, brushing something from his hands.

"We have another device for the lock," Shallenger said, "but it is all prepared and waiting. Won't you come and take a look?"

Emily followed him to the door and hesitated.

"No, no; it is perfectly safe, I assure you. Please come in."

Emily walked in and saw the shiny cylinder lying on the table, apparently all ready to go.

"I know that this must appear to you to be completely inappropriate," Shallenger said, "but if you could have seen how long and how hard we have worked, and could see the results that we will bring from our mission, I am quite certain you would understand things quite differently."

Emily looked at Shallenger, and his hand so gently stroking the side of the cylinder. She decided it was now or never.

"I appreciate that Doctor. But what I am still trying to understand is how you can continue to say that no one will be harmed by your mission..."

"Which is true..."

"When people have already been killed because of your actions."

"Please, Agent Graham..." Dennis began.

"No!" Shallenger said, "Dennis, it is a perfectly fair question. After all, Agent Graham is, of course, speaking about the loss of her dear friend when they attempted to retrieve our device at the Grammercy Bridge. Such an unfortunate accident."

She wasn't sure if it was the thought of Elliott or the smugness on Shallenger's face.

"I am speaking of Agent Masterson, yes Doctor," Emily said, "but I am also speaking of Alex and the thirteen people killed in the explosions at your laboratories, and the perhaps thousands who will die because of the biological elements of your little devices here."

Emily saw every face in the room frozen in confusion; all but one.

Dennis looked like someone had hit him in the face, "What are you talking about? Explosion? And there is no biological component, that's nonsense. Lawrence, isn't that right? And Susan?"

"Right," Lawrence said, "my device was built for radioactive modules only."

"Are you going to tell them, Doctor," Emily heard herself say, "or shall we open up that canister on the table and prove me wrong."

"This is nonsense," Shallenger said. "Can't you see that she is trying to confuse you? She is attempting her own form of disruption just to distract you. This is nonsense; I will not listen to more of this."

Dennis moved past Emily and stood in the doorway.

"Get out of my way Dennis," Shallenger said. "Don't be more of a fool than you already are."

The look on Shallenger's face immediately showed that he realized he had said something he knew he should not have said out loud.

"And what does that mean?" Dennis said, then turned to Emily, "What about this bio canister? What's inside it?"

"Anthrax."

"Impossible," Lawrence said. "My modules were designed for radiation. Something biological would never withstand the heat of the explosion."

"Someone designed another container," Emily said. "Isn't that correct Doctor Shallenger"

Shallenger's face was bright red, and veins were showing on his forehead and neck. He looked around the room, at the floor, then at each of them.

"Yes, all right, it is true," Shallenger spoke as if from a pulpit. "You fools. They came to me with an idea that I knew would never work; would never bring about the type of changes we really need. So yes, I changed things; I improved the plan. Radiation would create a certain level of fear in people, of course, but to accomplish our goals I knew it would take more; it would take them seeing bodies, every day, in the middle of their cities, in their own neighborhoods, in their own families...that is the only thing that would cause the level of anger that is needed to change the way things work. So yes, yes, it's true. And the explosions; we had to cover our tracks; it is unfortunate but a reality."

The words echoed around the small room and seemed to collect somewhere inside of Dennis Bowers. The others looked confused and shocked, but he took on an appearance of something quite different. He opened his mouth to speak but closed it again.

"And look at how far we have come," Shallenger continued, "all of our devices, each of them ready to create the type of world that we all want to live in. We have done so..."

The growl began somewhere deep down, and as it rose higher, Dennis began leaning, and then moved toward Dr. Shallenger. Shallenger saw him coming, dodged around Dennis' outstretched arms, and made a step toward the now-open doorway. Dennis spun and hurled himself in Shallenger's direction, got one arm around his neck and shoved him through the door onto the deck of the boat. Shallenger twisted to free himself and yelled to the two men standing nearby to help him. Before either could step forward, Dennis planted a foot against the deck and lunged once more, throwing them both off-balance toward the churning water. Bear was near enough to reach out a hand to his friend, but even with his bulk, he too was pulled off-balance by the force of the two men falling. Lawrence ran out the door to make sure that Susan was safe and one of Shallenger's flailing arms caught him by the collar. In the next moment, although all four men disappeared; the image that burned itself into Emily's memory was the look on Bear's face as he tried to understand why he was falling into the churning mass of water below him.

The propellers on the Francis B. were twelve feet in diameter and spun at eighteen hundred revolutions per minute, so the change in vibration was barely noticed before the slight, red stain appeared on the surface of the water. In fact, the only person who noticed the vibration at all was Charlie, as he walked around the corner of the stern deck.

"What the hell was that?" He said. "What'd we hit?"

Emily, Susan, and the two goons were standing on the deck as Charlie appeared. One of the men pulled out a revolver.

"All right. This isn't over yet." The man said as he stepped forward.

"One more step and I'll shoot you in the fucking ass!" Smitty said as he leaned around the corner holding a very shiny, chrome plated, three-fifty-seven magnum in his shaky hand.

The man with the gun looked behind him and lowered his. Emily stepped forward and took it from his hand, looking at Smitty the entire time.

"Smitty, where the hell did you get that?" Charlie asked.

"I'm sorry Charlie," Smitty glanced at his shoes, "I know the rules, but a man's gotta protect himself doesn't he?"

Charlie shook his head and tried not to smile.

"Remind me to write you up about this later, ok?"

"Sure Charlie."

"Somebody want to tie these two up?" Emily said.

"I've not had to tie a line for a while," Charlie said, "but I'll give it a shot."

Charlie found a small piece of line in the storage room, and tied each man's hands behind him, with a bit of coaching from Smitty.

"It ain't pretty," Charlie said, "but it ought to do the job."

"I'll stay here and watch them if you want." Smitty said.

Charlie looked at Emily, who nodded.

"Sure Smitty," Charlie said. "Just try not to shoot one of them." He smiled as he glanced at the two men being moved into the storeroom. "But if you do, try to hit 'em where it won't bleed too much. We've got enough mess to clean up around here."

"And what about you?" Emily said as she looked at Susan and cuffed her hands behind her.

"I, I, I don't know," Susan said. "I don't know what to do...I just want to go home."

"You come with us then," Emily said as she tied the young woman's hands behind her back.

Emily, Charlie, and Susan climbed back to the pilothouse, where Frank was slowly guiding the Francis B. between the narrow walls of the Chain of Rocks Lock.

"Where you people been?" Frank asked. "What's going on."

Charlie began to tell what he knew, as Emily felt the vibration from her phone. She stepped out onto the gangway.

"Graham."

"Emily, its Chambers."

"Yeah?"

"Are you OK? You sound strange."

"Well, things have been a bit strange here. Where are you?"

"We're here, at the locks."

"Good. You need to come onboard."

"Onboard? They'll let us do that?"

"Well, yeah." Emily paused. "I don't think you're going to hear any complaints."

Chapter 101

Agent Dasilva, Lennie, Chambers, Reyes, Charlie, Frank were standing in the pilot house trying to understand what they needed to do next. It was time for Charlie's shift, but in all the confusion Frank was still sitting in the big chair, driving the boat. A team of Chamber's men had taken the two goons somewhere on shore, and Smitty was down in the galley with the rest of the crew, waiting to be told they could go ashore and head home for a while. Gil Arbel had given each of them a three-month vacation, and a raise.

Emily was standing on the foredeck of the boat, with Susan and the two agents who would take her for formal interviews.

"I just wanted to talk with you for a moment," Emily said, "and give you a message I promised to give."

"A message," Susan said, "from whom?"

"One of your friends in the lab."

"Sasha? You have a message from Sasha? Is she alright?"

Emily glanced down for a moment, to avoid re-seeing the young woman and her burns.

"I'm sorry Susan."

"Oh my God."

"She asked me to tell you that she was sorry. She said that Doctor Shallenger lied to both of you and that she was so sorry."

Susan wept.

"What happened to her?"

"She was in one of the labs during the explosions. She was killed along with Dr. Saenz and a couple of other students."

"No." Susan hesitated. "Sasha introduced me to Doctor Shallenger when I joined the program there. We both believed what he told us; that it was all for..." She drifted off. "Sasha."

"We'll talk more later; I'm so sorry about your friend." Emily nodded to one of the agents, and they guided Susan along the barge to the ladder recessed into the lock wall as Emily walked up to the pilothouse.

"So, at least we won't have any more of those devices to deal with," Lennie said, "that's one good thing, right? Now we can focus on cleaning up the ones already out there."

"Once we figure out how to do that," Reyes said.

"I'm afraid it's not that simple." Everyone turned to Captain Charlie Graff. "You're forgetting that these things are all tied together..."

"We need to find a way to untie them," Reyes said. "It will take a bit of time, but my people will figure it out."

"That's my point, sir," Charlie said. "You don't have the time to do that."

"What do you mean Charlie?" Emily asked.

"Well, you people figured out that the devices are all connected, right?"

"And with the boat, yeah," Chambers said.

"But what I guess you don't know is just how it's tied to the boat."

No one spoke.

"You see, me and my men had an idea for a way we were going to stop the boat ourselves a few nights ago. And for some reason, before we did, Dennis explained to me how everything was tied together, and all somehow linked to the GPS signal of the boat itself. He said that if the boat stops moving for more than one hour, the whole mess would be triggered."

No sound other than a "Shit" from somewhere in the crowded pilothouse.

"Charlie, what did he mean triggered?" Reyes asked.

"Dennis said that if we don't move for an hour, the signal is sent to activate the timers on all of the devices, and they're set for twelve hours. They said it was to give people time to move away from the explosions."

"You're saying that if this boat stands still for more than an hour..."

"The clock starts ticking," Charlie said.

354

Chambers cleared his throat. "Well, I think the obvious question for us at the moment then is, just how long has the Francis B. been sitting here in the lock; without moving?"

Noise and commotion.

"We've actually been stopped for about ten minutes now, I guess," Charlie said. "That's when we got inside the lock."

"So, we have to get the Francis B. Moving again within fifty minutes," Chambers said. "How long will it take to get through the lock?"

"About thirty," Charlie said.

Emily looked around the room and noticed that Lennie and Dasilva were missing. She stepped out the door and started down the stairs. If someone had asked her why, she wouldn't have been able to give them a good reason. She walked down the corridor, down the stairs to the main deck. As she stepped into the corridor, she could hear the voices.

"It's no use denying it; I've got the proof."

"You've got nothing. It's just your word against mine."

Emily tried to match the voices with the man, but the noise from the crew in the galley was too loud.

"I've got it all; the so-called accident, the stupid car bomb, and the pill. And that's just for starters."

"Lies. No one will believe you. It's just a jealous agent trying to make a name for himself."

Who is who? Emily carefully edged closer toward the door to the small room with the computer.

"Listen, you can deny whatever you want to, but I know you've been the mole, and I know you've been communicating with somebody involved in this thing all along. I don't know who it is or how long you've been doing it, but I know for damn sure it's the truth."

Emily stepped through the door and saw Lennie and Dasilva standing and facing each other in the small room, each of them looking like they were braced to kill.

"Em," Lennie said, "I'm glad you're here. I caught our Agent Dasilva trying to mess with the computer. He's been helping them all along; he is our mole."

"That's nonsense," Dasilva said. "Turn that story around and you'll have the truth. Special Agent Ryan here is the snake in the grass, and he knows I can prove it."

Emily stood still, staring at the two men.

Upstairs, the debate continued over the best next step for the boat to take. It had become more interesting as a few more agents and the lock master had joined the group.

"I'm sorry gentlemen," the lock master said, "you can yell at me all you want, but physics is physics and only so much water can flood in and out of this lock at one time. It'll be at least another twenty minutes before we can open the upper gate."

Frank was fidgeting in his captain's seat, looking out the windows at the lock wall.

"That's cutting it pretty damn close," Chambers said.

"You ok there Frank?" Charlie asked. "It's my watch now anyway; why don't you take a break or something?"

"Nah," Frank said, "I'm ok. You help these guys get things figured out."

"So," Reyes said, "it sounds like the only good option we've got is to be ready to move as soon as the gates open and buy us the time for my people to figure out how to disarm things. Are we agreed on that?"

There was conversation around the pilothouse as everyone agreed with Reyes. No one noticed Frank as he leaned forward, reaching a hand toward the throttle levers.

"Em," Lennie said, "you know that Dasilva lied about his trip to Washington, about when he got back. Your friend saw him sitting in a bar talking to some guy. He lied to all of us. And that's just one that we know of."

"Yes I did lie," Dasilva said, "I admit it. I had too. But I wasn't talking to anyone from the boat, or anyone involved with it. I was talking to them about you Graham."

"Me?" Emily said. "What about me?"

"I had information that someone had decided that you needed to be taken out of the loop here; you were finding out things too quickly and had to be either distracted or removed."

"Nice try Dasilva," Lennie said. "Somebody decided that Emily needed to be taken out, yeah, and that person was you."

"Graham," Dasilva said, "I've got proof; evidence to support what I'm saying. You need to look at it." He moved a hand toward his pocket.

Lennie pulled his gun.

"Put the hand back down Dasilva. Your fancy hotshot agent talk isn't going to get you out of this one."

"Put it away Lennie," Dasilva said. "Leaking information is one thing, but killing an agent is something you don't walk away from."

Lennie glanced at Emily.

"Em, how long have we worked together now; eight, nine years? Have I ever lied to you even once during all that time? Have I done anything at all that might cause you to think I'm dirty? And what about Dasilva here. He comes in with his hot shot personality, lying to everyone and sneaking around. You tell me who the best candidate for snake is."

"Graham, ask him about the accident; or the bomb, or the pill. Ask him about those."

"Shut it Dasilva. Emily knows I would never do anything to harm her, or her father. If anyone can tell us anything about that van, or the bomb or the pill; that would be you. Emily, take his gun."

Emily stood for a moment as each man looked at her. One she thought she knew well, and the other not well at all. But something was eating at her inside. A neuron somewhere had fired a spark. The connections began slowly, but built until a full thought reached her consciousness. She looked at Dasilva, then at Lennie.

"Lennie," Emily said, "how did you know it was a van that pulled out in front of me. I never told you that."

"Van?" Lennie smiled, "I don't know, I must have read it in your report or something."

"I haven't written a report about that yet."

"Then I must have heard it from one of your buddies; Chambers, or Reyes; one of them probably told me."

"I never told them either Lennie."

Emily looked him in the eyes.

"Lennie. You? Even my father; how could you?" She reached for her gun as Dasilva did the same.

Lennie smiled, keeping his revolver in front of him.

"It was never personal Em," he said, "you need to know that. It was just business."

No one noticed Frank's hand grip the throttle until they felt the sudden surge as the mighty engines came to life and pushed the Francis B. ahead at full power. Seconds later they felt the force of the impact with the lock gates as it threw them forward in the pilothouse; some landing in heaps on the floor.

"What the hell are you doing Frank?" Charlie shouted as he grabbed the throttle.

"Let's see you open those gates and move north now, you sons a bitches." Frank yelled as Chambers, Reyes and two others wrestle him from the chair and onto the floor.

Charlie crawled into the chair and backed the boat from the gates. As the damage was revealed, the lock master shook his head, "Those gates aren't going to open tonight gentlemen. I'm afraid you have a real problem."

Charlie was numb as he watched them drag Frank out of the pilothouse.

Downstairs, Lennie looked briefly at Emily, then at Dasilva, and then the computer.

"Don't do it!" Dasilva shouted.

Lennie lunged for the computer, pulled a handful of wires, then turned and jumped through the door onto the deck outside. Emily followed him out the door as Dasilva moved to the computer.

The lock walls blocked the evening sunshine, but Emily could make out Lennie's image as he jumped from the boat onto the barge, and ran along the side of the barge toward the ladder on the lock wall. Suddenly, she heard the engines surge and felt the huge boat lunge forward. She grabbed the door frame just as the boat slammed against the gates, throwing her forward again.

As she looked up, she saw Lennie trying to regain his balance from the sudden movement. His street shoes were not made for traction on the slick barge decks, and she watched as he slipped off the side, falling ten feet into the water between the barge and the lock wall. As the boat backed away from the gates, the barges slowly drifted to the left, toward the lock wall. Moments later, one million pounds of Mississippi River towboat rubbed against the solid concrete and steel of the twelve-hundred-foot lock wall, with no space left between them for Agent Lennie Ryan.

"Graham, we've got trouble," Dasilva called from inside.

It may have been Lennie, it may have been Shallenger, it may have been any of a thousand things, but Emily heard herself laughing as she stepped back into the small room.

"The computer is down. That means the connection is broken."

"Twelve hours," Emily said.

"About eleven hours and fifty-six minutes to be exact," Dasilva said.

Chapter 102

Emily and Dasilva stepped into the pilothouse and found it crowded and quiet, with Captain Graff sitting in the chair.

"I'm afraid we have a problem Agent Graham." Charlie said. "We're not getting out of the lock, thanks to Frank, and that means we have less than an hour to..."

"We have twelve hours," Emily said, "or just about that."

Every head in the room popped up.

"What do you mean twelve hours?" Reyes said.

"Lennie disconnected the computer downstairs," Emily said. "He was our mole. The connection is broken, which means the timers have started on all of the devices."

"If we've got twelve hours," Reyes said as he turned to Chambers, "that means your plan just might have time to work."

Reyes punched numbers on his phone.

"Stewart," Reyes said" "tell the team to step it up on that device and see if they can confirm things. Tell them we may have the time to do this if they push it."

Reyes saw the question on Emily's face as he lowered his phone.

"Chambers has an idea for how we can disarm the devices," Reyes said. "You may have just bought us the time we need to pull it off."

"Yeah?"

"Remember when he gave that report at the meeting the other day; about those electromagnetic pulse things? The EMP's?"

"The nukes? You're kidding me."

"No, no, not like that. They've got smaller ones; ones that...hell, you explain it, Bill..."

360

"OK." Chambers said. "They've got the same kind of EM pulse in them, but they're not nuclear, in fact, there's no actual explosion at all; they're more like a giant flashbulb; remember those?"

"No explosion?" Emily said.

"Don't need it. The pulse will essentially fry any electrical circuitry within five to eight feet, quick and simple; if it works."

"If? What do..." Emily began.

"We have to make sure that these things aren't shielded so much that the pulse can't hit everything," Reyes said. "Even if one circuit stays alive, it might be the wrong one. I've got a team tearing the one apart downstairs right now to let us know. Bill," Reyes looked at Chambers, "do you have enough of these things that you can get your hands on? And do you have time to get them out there?"

"They're already moving." Chambers said. "Give us four hours, and you just tell me when to light 'em up."

"Four hours?" Emily said. "That fast?"

"Agent Graham," Chambers said, "this is the kind of thing my people train for every day. Those above me may occasionally have some harebrained ideas, but I guarantee you that the people down the line know exactly what they are doing. Four hours will do it."

"That would give us just under eight hours to do something else if these don't do the job," Dasliva said.

"Well," Reyes said, "if Chamber's idea doesn't work, I'm afraid we'll spend those eight hours trying to move as many people away from the areas as possible. Other than the little flashbulbs here, I'm afraid we're shit out of options."

"If you people will excuse me," Chambers said as he moved to the pilothouse door, "I've got some things to do. Call me if there's anything good on TV."

"Yeah, me too," Reyes said, turning to Emily and Dasilva. "My team is picking up the two guys who've been putting the devices out there for the boat. We'll take them for processing, and then you can have them and see what you can learn from them."

Reye's phone rang, and he lifted it to his ear.

"Yeah?" he listened. "Right. I'll let 'em know. Thanks."

He lowered the phone long enough to punch another button.

"Chambers," he said, "it's a go. My guys say the circuits are vulnerable. Let's do this."

He turned to the two agents.

"Gotta go." And walked out the door.

Charlie and the lock master had gone to view the damage to the lock gate and barge, leaving Emily and Dasilva in the empty pilothouse.

"Well," Dasilva said, "I guess we'd better get up there and talk with some of these people, and see if we can start putting the pieces together."

"Wait," Emily said, "I need to know something."

"Yeah?"

"About Lennie. How did you find out about him? How long have you known?"

"It was when I made the D.C. trip. While I was there, I got a call from someone saying that we needed to talk about what was going on and that he had key information about our mole. That's why I flew back early; so I could meet with him at the bar."

"His name wouldn't have happened to be Steve was it?"

"However did you know that?"

"I'll tell you later. What did he say?"

"Just that he knew we had a mole, and that they believed it was Lennie; whoever they were."

"Yeah, that's Steve."

"So I started looking into things and found that Lennie had been talking with someone outside the firm. He was actually taking orders from someone. That's when I found out about you."

"Me?"

"Lennie was told to get you out of the way. You were putting things together too quickly. They knew they would be stopped at some point, but they wanted to get as far as possible up the river before that happened. So, Lennie was supposed to slow you down."

"By killing me?"

"Or your dad. They figured either one would solve their problem."

"Why didn't you tell me?"

"I couldn't risk doing anything that might tip Lennie off; I needed to have the evidence. So, I called in some people I thought could

362

protect you; you know, kind of follow you around and keep an eye on you. But, they weren't as sharp as I thought they were, so I finally told Steve we needed to do something else. He called Chambers, he showed up in Chester, and you know the rest."

"It's just hard to understand. I mean, Lennie. Why would he do this?"

"I'm afraid it's not all that dramatic. It was money; plain and simple. They gave him a quarter-of-a-million dollars."

"To kill me?"

"For the whole thing. He's apparently been involved in the planning of things since it started; as long as Shallenger anyway. Lennie even helped locate the students to offer scholarships in Shallenger's program."

"Students? What did Lennie know about..."

"He used the company database, and his normal contacts, saying it was all part of some investigation your office was involved in. Nobody gave it a second thought. So, when I saw him leave the pilothouse earlier, I followed him to see what he was up to and caught him logging into the computer. We started arguing, and that's when you came in."

"What about Shallenger?" Emily asked. "What's his part in all of this; other than the obvious."

"I don't know any more than you do about Shallenger," Dasilva said. "Or Dennis. Or this Steve guy. I've chased every lead I can find, but they all fell apart."

"Same for me," Emily said. "But I guess the really good question is where the money came from; and who got Lennie and Shallenger started in the first place."

"That, Agent Graham, is the quarter of a million dollar question. Let's go see if we can learn anything from those two goons you tied up, or Susan, or those fishermen. At this point, they look to be our only hopes."

"Before we go..."

"Yes?"

"Thanks. For, you know, trying to keep me alive."

"Glad to be of service ma'am. Now, do you want to be the good cop or the bad cop?"

Chapter 103

"Thank you all for coming at such short notice," Dasilva said. "I'm assuming you've all read the brief I sent you."

"Damnedest thing I've ever heard," Colonel Goodwin said.

Everyone was connected by phone or computer. Dasilva, Chambers, Reyes and Graham were in St. Louis, Goodwin from the NRC and Nichols from the Corps of Engineers were in New Orleans, Agent Loren Erikson in Louisville, and Agent Carlos Rodriguez in Memphis.

"And who the hell is this Steve guy?" Nichols asked.

"You know as much as we know about him at this point Colonel," Dasilva said. "But we'll chase that rabbit later. Right now we need to let you know what is happening so you can do things that need to be done. Time is short. Colonel Chambers?"

"Thank you." Chambers said. "As you read in Agent Dasilva's brief, we are going to use small EMP units to try and stop the timers on all of the devices. We are confident that this will work, but we need to have steps in place if that outcome is not reached."

"Doesn't sound like we have a lot of steps," Goodwin said.

"I'm afraid you're right Colonel." Chambers said. "That's why my people are making every effort to see that it does exactly what we need it to do."

"Wait a minute," Goodwin said, "I didn't think an EMP would work underwater. The density of the water..."

"That is true for the standard EMP, Colonel," Chambers said. "But we're using something a little different here. The actual physics of the thing is beyond my pay grade, but I assure you that being underwater will not be a problem."

"As Colonel Chambers said," Dasilva continued, "we believe the EMP units will render the devices safe for removal. However, if that does not happen, our only recourse is to get people as far as possible from the areas of risk."

"How much time do we actually have?" Agent Rodriguez asked.

"If we are not able to stop them," Reyes said, "the timers are set to go in about eight hours; at seven-fifty a.m., Central Time."

"That gives us eight hours to get as many people clear as possible." Chambers said.

"Well," Rodriquez said, "that may be well and good for places like Caruthersville, or Helena or Greenville. But for those of us in Memphis, or Baton Rouge, or St. Louis and New Orleans..."

"I fully understand Agent Rodriguez," Dasilva said. "Believe me, I understand. We can just do what we can do. And yes, I'm afraid in some places, that may not be enough."

"Just how far away is far enough?" Rodriguez asked.

"For the detonation itself and immediate risk from radiation," Agent Goodwin said, "a quarter-mile should provide a wide enough perimeter. The real question will be about what comes after the explosion, and that's going to depend on the local wind; the vectors and velocity. Depending on those elements, the best situation for radiation exposure would be three miles downwind in the first hour after detonation, and at least ten miles downwind three hours after detonation. That's radiation. The winds may carry the bio spores further; we just don't know how much further. However..."

"However?" Dasilva asked.

"However, that's all based on conjecture, since we've not actually had time to fully examine one of these things to see what they can really do. The reality is that, if one of them does blow, we'll have to work as fast as we can to find out what it means, and then do what we can to deal with it."

"So, as I sit here in Memphis, with the winds blowing as they are right now, the recommendation is that I need to empty two-thirds of my entire city, and maybe more, in the next seven hours. Is that what I'm hearing?"

"As I said," Chambers began, "we are doing..."

"Please understand Colonel," Rodriguez said, "I have the greatest confidence in your people, but I am just wanting to make sure I understand what you are telling me I may be asked to do here."

"Yes, Agent Rodriguez," Dasilva said, "your understanding is correct."

"Agent Rodriguez?" Goodwin said.

"Yes?" Rodriguez answered.

"I believe if you can secure a perimeter of a quarter mile from the location of the device itself, you will have done your job."

Several moments of silence on the line.

"Colonel," Dasilva said, "how much longer before your team will be ready with the EMP's?"

"Fifteen minutes."

"Very good. While we wait, I will ask Agent Graham to update us on what she has learned since I sent the briefing. She has been interviewing the individuals apprehended this evening."

"Thank you, Agent Dasilva," Emily said. "I'm afraid what we have learned so far is not moving us much further along in the investigation. The students, Susan Handling and Lawrence Abbot, were just that; students. They were two of those apparently recruited by Lennie, by uh, Agent Ryan, and who were caught up in the passions of Dr. Shallenger. They were selected to go on the boat because of their blind worship of the guy, and knew nothing more than the specific tasks they were to carry out."

"What about the other students?" Goodwin asked. "Weren't there others?"

"Yes Colonel Goodwin," Emily said, "there were others. Unfortunately, it appears they all died in the explosions. Lennie was involved there as well, and was quite complete in closing that trail."

A brief silence.

"The two men on the boat with Shallenger were there for muscle. Two guys with minor backgrounds in organized crime. Apparently, Agent Ryan offered them deals in return for their helping Dr. Shallenger, as long as they didn't ask any questions. Some money was involved as well, but they know nothing beyond that."

"Organized crime was involved?" Agent Erikson asked. "Is that the 'they' we keep hearing about?"

"No," Emily said. "These two had minor connections a few years ago and got caught, which is how Agent Ryan found them. They're a

366

couple of small-time hoods who were being paid to do the grunt work and look mean."

Emily paused briefly.

"And it's about the same with the two in the fishing boat. They really are a couple of fishermen from up North who were given a list of bridges, a cell phone and a bag of money to do the job. As they drove up the river, they would get a phone call telling them where to find the canisters and where to put them, and they just did it. They used the money for gas, and meals and such, and whatever they didn't spend, they got to keep. And before anyone asks, the calls came from a different number each time; so nothing has been traceable."

"Do we have any way of finding out where the rest of the canisters are?" Goodwin asked, "The ones for the rest of the bridges?"

"Not at this point, no," Emily said. "So far it's another dead end."

"Anything else Agent Graham?" Dasilva asked.

"No sir," Emily said. "I know that Colonel Goodwin's people at the NRC will do their part to trace the various radiation signatures from the devices once we have them out of the water, so they may be able to offer us some direction there."

"Well do our best," Goodwin said, "I'll guarantee that."

"Agent Dasilva," Chambers said, "I'm told we are ready to go."

"OK then," Dasilva said. "If anyone on the line happens to carry a rabbit's foot in your pocket, now's the time to start rubbing it. Colonel, it's all yours."

Everyone listened as Chambers talked to his people on the radio.

"All stations, this is command. We are go for mission Killing Time. All stations report."

"Crescent City go."

"Huey Long go."

"Hale Boggs go."

"Sunshine go."

"Wilkinson go."

"Baton Rouge go."

"Audubon go."

Emily was mesmerized as she pictured each bridge float by as it reported in.

367

"Natchez go."

"Vicksburg go."

One more chance to stop the ride she had been on for the past week.

"Greenville go."

"Helena go."

One last chance to see that more lives would not be taken by this insanity. That's all it could be: insanity.

"Memphis go."

"Desoto go."

"Caruthersville go."

Were there really this many? It hadn't seemed so big, one at a time.

"Cairo South go."

"Cairo North go."

"Girardeau go."

Screaming wouldn't help.

"Chester go."

"Jefferson Barracks go."

Closer...closer...

"Poplar Street go."

"Eads go."

"King go."

It had to work. But what if...

"Musial go."

McKinley go."

One more. Only one more.

"Merchants go."

Emily stared at her shoes.

"All stations, this is command. We go in three..."

Emily sucked in air.

"Two..."

She closed her eyes.

"One..."

She...

"Go!"

Silence.

Silence.

"All stations, this is command. All stations report."

"Crescent pulse confirmed."

She listened as the entire list was repeated, with each reporting a confirmed pulse from the electromagnetic units in the water.

"Ladies and gentlemen," Chambers said, "now we wait."

"Ok people," Dasilva said. "let's push those perimeters. The National Guard is working with local authorities to help you out. We'll meet again at six-thirty a.m."

Emily sat in her motel room and stared at the phone. She knew the EMP's weren't the end of it, but she had honestly expected to feel a little better after they were used. She was still in St. Louis, or just north of there, in a little motel that was probably safely outside the initial perimeter if she measured it. But at this point, she didn't have the energy to do that. She really wanted a drink, but that meant getting up and leaving the room. That was the same problem with being hungry. She set the alarm on her phone and lay back on her pillow. The vibration stopped her.

"Graham." She offered.

"Emily, its Steve."

Silence.

"Agent Graham? Are you there?"

Silence.

"Agent Graham? Emily?"

She looked at the phone, pressed the button, set the phone on the table, and sat on the beach. She looked at the waves lapping the sand and could see a dozen or so bridges floating out in the water. A photographer was standing next to her chair, popping flashbulbs in her face, and Bear was standing there with that damn look on his face. Jimmy Buffett didn't show up.

Chapter 104

"I'm afraid I can't stay long Ronnie," the older man said as he sat down "things are unfolding quickly this morning."

The grandfather looked older today.

"Things are not going well?" Ronnie asked.

"Oh no, things are where we anticipated they would be. Everyone has performed their roles extremely well."

"Then what?"

"Well Ronnie, you'll have to excuse me if I sound a bit philosophical this morning. We do what we can do to get the results we seek, but we always come to that place where we simply have to sit back and trust that we have done enough. We're at that point this morning."

"With the boat?"

"Yes. I'm confident it will come out as we hope, but I have to admit that these are the times that even those of us who have been doing this for a long time have our moments. It's a good thing, actually. These are the times I am reminded that I am human and that we are just people entrusted with something much bigger than ourselves. I think that's why we have been able to survive for so long; we all understand what would happen if any of us did anything that would cause us to cease existing."

"Silence."

"Plus, it is a reminder that we are able to miss things; important things like this Dr. Shallenger. He should have never become a channel, but we made a mistake. Those mistakes are rare, fortunately, but when they occur, they haunt us forever."

"I'm sorry the plan did not work."

"Oh no, don't misunderstand. Things did not go the way we intended them to go, and the risk and loss were far greater than we intended. But as people learn of what has happened, I believe we will see the kind of response that we were looking for. The opportunity to bring about the changes we need is still here. It is up to us to continue working the channels to make sure they do take place. This is simply one more moment of time that we have invested in our work; we have much more that must be done."

"I must go now. Give my grandchildren a hug when you get home."

"I will grandpa. I will."

Chapter 105

Emily was rinsing her face as her alarm sounded. She had been up for an hour. She had the line open for the call as she heard the others connect.

"Good morning everyone," Dasilva said. "we know why we are here."

A few mumbles on the line.

"Colonel Chambers, are you on yet?"

"I'm here." Chambers said.

"Anything new from you or your team?"

"No."

"Do we have connections from all of the locations?" Dasilva asked.

Each bridge location said they are online.

"Does anyone have anything new for the group this morning?"

Silence.

"Then I guess we wait. Colonel Chambers, Commander Reyes, can you tell us what we should expect?"

"Nothing," Chamber said. "If everything goes well, we should expect nothing at all."

"If no one has anything else we need to deal with," Dasilva said, "I'll let Colonel Chambers take over."

"One thing to let you know." Chambers began. "For those on computers, we've set up a link with split screens showing live video from each of the locations. If you care to make use of that, you will find the link in the message you should have just received."

Emily hesitated, then clicked the link. Her screen displayed twenty small windows, each with a dark video image.

"Because of the hour," Chambers said, "there isn't enough light for a good view, but it should be enough to see if there is...if..."

A pause.

"And you'll see that a couple of streams cover more than one bridge; there in St. Louis and New Orleans, for example."

Silence.

"Thank you for doing this Colonel," Emily said.

"We thought it might be helpful." Chambers said.

Silence.

"Ok," Chambers said, "we don't know the exact moment the timers were triggered, but we are working with a window of three or four minutes. We are confident the timers will go off during that span; I mean if they weren't stopped by the EMP's."

"We've had no indication of any change whatsoever in any of the devices Colonel?" Reyes asked.

"No, sir. There has been no noticeable change."

Silence.

"Ok, we will enter the window in just a few moments...ready in three...two...one. We are in-window."

Silence.

Silence.

Emily stared at the twenty small screens, watching for a flash, or some indication that something is going on.

Silence.

"We are halfway through the window." Chambers said.

Silence.

There is a bright flash in one of the video windows. Emily heard gasps on the line.

"It's OK everyone, it's OK," Goodwin said, "someone in Memphis apparently took a flash photo. I'm not sure who is stupid enough to be that close, or how they got there, though."

"We'll find out," Agent Rodriguez said, "I hope."

Silence.

"We are coming out of the window in a few moments. Again, we have high confidence that if any timers are still active, they will trigger during this period."

Silence.

"The window closes shortly; in three...two...one."

Silence.

"Ladies and gentlemen," Chambers said, "the sound you just heard, was the fat lady singing."

Noise; cheers; laughter; breathing on the line.

"Agent Dasilva," Chambers said, "it's your meeting."

"Thank you Colonel Chambers, and please pass our thanks along to your people, and to yours Commander Reyes. I know we all have things we need to do, so we will schedule a follow-up later today to review clean-up procedures."

Several comments and conversations as the meeting dissolved.

"Agent Graham," Dasilva said, "I would like to speak with you a for a moment before you go if you don't mind."

Silence.

"Agent Graham? Emily?"

Emily was not there.

The surf was calm. The breeze was warm. In her hand was a tall glass with a cute little umbrella sticking out of it. There wasn't a cloud in the sky, and Jimmy Buffett was sitting on the sand next to her, singing "Cheeseburgers in Paradise."

Chapter 106

Three months later:

Special Agent in Charge Emily Graham sat at the table in the conference room next to her new office in New Orleans. It was the first time the group had been in the same room since the Chain of Rocks Lock, so they had spent time catching up. The newspaper lying next to her displayed a small article on the bottom of the front page entitled: Dead Ends Abound: The Search Continues.

They had come together to celebrate Emily's promotion to the lead position in the New Orleans office, and Arturo Dasilva had spent time still trying to convince her to let him take her name up higher to people he knows. He had gotten a nice promotion as well, into a role that kept him visible in lots of places; just the kind of thing he liked.

Commander Reyes was still with the ARG, but in some new office he couldn't talk about, but that he said he enjoyed.

Colonel Goodwin was still with the NRC and was leading the expanded teams still at work on the massive collection of radiation signatures still being analyzed from the devices.

Colonel Chambers had retired from the military and was on contract as part of the ongoing investigation out of his office down the hall from Emily's.

Agents Rodriguez and Erikson weren't at the table but were enjoying their promotions. Erikson was still in Louisville, while Agent Rodriguez had accepted a role in Chicago. He had entered the agency because of his fascination with the stories of Al Capone and Dillinger, and he now spent his free time exploring the sites those guys used to call home.

The other person at the table was Charlie Graff, now retired from the river and working with Gil Arbel in the home office. He grumbled about being a desk jockey but enjoyed being home for dinner and the grandkids' birthday parties.

"OK folks," Emily said, "we'll talk more at dinner, but we'd probably better get some work done here. Let's go around and see what we need to deal with. But before we do, I have a couple of things here you may not have heard about yet. You remember Susan, the grad student with Shallenger; I understand that she is in the hospital with complications from the health issues from her military work; I guess she's not expected to last more than a week."

"That's too bad," Chambers said, "she really didn't know what was going on, did she?"

"No," Emily said, "she didn't."

"I'll also let you know," Charlie said, "that Alma Hendricks just learned that her illness has progressed as well; the same cancer her husband died from; she's still at home, but hospice will start meeting with her soon."

"What did we ever find out about Frank," Reyes asked, "the guy working with you Charlie? Did we ever find out why he was helping them?"

"Yeah," Charlie said, "Frank really caught me by surprise. Emily and Dasilva may know more than me, but I guess it was mostly because of his sister; health issues just like with the rest of the group."

"Yes," Dasilva said, "a younger sister he had helped raise. She apparently had the same kind of insurance problems that kept her from getting treatments that might have saved her life. When all of this started, Lennie was looking for the boat they would use and found Frank. That's how they ended up on the Francis B. in the first place; because that's where Frank was."

"Amazing," Goodwin said.

"Yeah," Emily said. "Colonel Goodwin, what do you have to add this morning?"

"Thanks, Emily, I mean Special Agent in Charge Graham."

Everyone chuckled.

"Unfortunately, I'm not sure I have much for us to sink our teeth into. The signatures we've been able to trace so far come from so many different directions, from every corner of the country and the globe, it's not been possible to identify any patterns or connections between them yet. We've tracked several to instances where a piece of equipment was stolen, but as we chase it, the trails go dark. We find out where they start, and where they end up, but what happens in between is still empty."

"We've seen the same thing Colonel," Reyes said. "We've been through everything we can find about these guys; their communications, their movements, and like you, no patterns or lines that point to anything meaningful. We know they have to be there somewhere, but, as much as I hate to admit it, we can't find them."

"Don't feel bad Reyes," Colonel Chambers said. "It's the same here, as Emily can tell you. I've chased a lot of enemies across a lot of ground, but I've sure as hell never seen anything like this."

The group was quiet for a moment.

"And the media is sure enjoying it too. Did you see the piece on the front page this morning?" Emily said as she lifted up the paper.

"Can't really blame them I guess," Reyes said. "But it's still no fun being made to look like we don't know what we're doing."

"Well," Charlie Graff said, "let me throw one piece of good news in here if I might."

"Please do," Emily said.

"Things are back to normal at Arbel's, and this thing got enough attention that steps are being taken to improve security out there. Gil raised enough hell himself to get them to look at the risk of those unattended barges out there."

"You raised a bit of hell yourself if I recall." Chambers said.

"Yeah," Charlie smiled, "just a bit."

"I think we can also be happy to see that things didn't fall completely apart the way Shallenger and his people wanted them too. There's still a lot of fighting and blaming going on, but not the big split he was going for."

"Yeah," Chamber said, "but I still wish..."

"Emily," a young woman poked her head in the door "there's a call for you."

"Tell them I'm in a meeting Deb, get a number."

"He says it's important, and that he wants to talk with you, and with Colonels Chambers and Goodwin; he's asking for all of you."

Emily looked around the table.

"Put him through Deb, to the conference phone."

"This is Agent Graham," Emily said to the speaker on the table.

"Hello, is this Special Agent in Charge Emily Graham? It's Steve. Is everyone there?"

Emily hesitated briefly.

"Yes, we're all here; we're in a meeting."

"Yes, I know. That's why I'm calling. I thought I might be able to help shed some light on a few things for you."

"That would be appreciated Steve," Emily said. "As you probably know, we're having no luck on our own."

"It's not about luck, Emily."

"By the way Steve," Emily interrupted, "before you go on, I want to apologize for that last time we talked, or I guess didn't talk. You called that morning and I..."

"No apology necessary Emily, truly. Those were difficult days, and I must say that you all handled them extremely well, but we were confident that you would."

"OK," Emily said. "Stop right there; saying that you knew we would handle it. You've said that kind of thing before. Are you going to tell us what that's all about?"

"Emily, as I was saying, this situation was not about luck, or about something just unfolding randomly and everyone sitting back and waiting to see how it turned out. Everyone believes that's how most things happen; but honestly, that is rarely the case. It's just too risky."

"So you're saying that this entire thing was planned by someone?" Chambers said. "That means it would have to be people up high; who had access to..."

"Colonel Chambers," Steve said, "you are a military man, and you understand that there are times in which some things must remain untold; things that need to be left to that place where the conspiracy theory people love to play. Things that may or may not have happened, or that may or may not exist."

"Yes," Chambers said, "I do."

"I don't understand," Emily said. "This whole thing was very real; trust me on that."

"Of course it was Agent Graham," Steve said. "Unfortunately, it was very real. But the event that took place was not the event that was intended; the one that was first put into place. Unfortunately, one of the people involved, Dr. Shallenger, took it upon himself to alter the plan he was asked to participate in, which meant that instead of seeing it through, they had to take the necessary steps to stop it."

"There's that 'they' again." Dasilva said, "Who are they?"

"I'm afraid that must remain one of those unknowns Agent Dasilva. There may or may not be a they. But the project that was originally set in motion was not destructive and would have led to no one being harmed at all. It was the sickness of one individual that changed things. When it was discovered he had changed things, steps were taken to carefully guide things to see that the new action was doomed to fail. That required finding people with the unique abilities to do what needed to be done, and who were in the places to do that. You, those of you around the table, were those people."

"Ok, now just stop there," Emily said. "You are telling us there is a group..."

"No..." Steve began.

"Yeah, that there may or may not be a group, and this group has the ability to..."

"Emily," Steve said, "each of you, all that you really need to understand is that you were called upon to do something extremely important, something that changed the course of history for your country, and you have done that."

"This has to be some kind inter-agency thing," Chambers said. "You're a part of some government thing that involves..."

"Not government; no. Not inter-agency. And I'm not a part of it at all. I have simply been a connection between you and someone else. Even I don't know who, and it doesn't matter. We all did what needed to be done. That is enough."

"This is insane." Chambers said. "It makes no sense at all. We're going to get to the end of this one way or the other."

"It is confusing, yes." Steve said, "And that is the way it must be. And as for getting to the end, well, you are certainly welcome to try.

However, I will let you know that tomorrow morning, you are each going to receive calls with new orders to end your work on this project and focus your energies on more important things."

"That means someone above us knows what is going on."

"No, of course not. All it means is that people are doing their jobs and communicating the information they are given to communicate. Where it began, and by whom; well, that is one of those rabbit trails you've talked about chasing."

Silence, while the faces around the table stared at each other with the same look they might have after watching eight hours of a very bad science fiction movie.

"But listen," Steve said, "I must go. Thank you for your service."

"Wait," Emily said, "I have more questions, when will we talk again Steve?"

"Steve? Steve was never here Emily. There is no Steve."

Click.

Several moments of silence.

"OK, did any of that make sense to anyone at all," Reyes asked

"Well," Chambers said "I don't know about the rest of you people, but I need a drink. A real one, and not one of those might be a drink or might not be a drink things."

"Let's call it a day," Emily said, "I feel like one of Chamber's EMP flashbulb things just went off next to my brain. I suggest we take Chambers' idea and meet for a drink later. Maybe some alcohol will clear things up."

They each collected their materials and left the room. Emily stopped by her office to grab a few things and walked to the parking lot. She got in her car and headed south toward Route 610. Before she went up the ramp, she stopped at a small convenience store to pick up the ice cream she had promised to take him tonight.

PERSONAL NOTE FROM THE AUTHOR

My dad was a towboat captain. That is all he ever needed you to know. If he were to introduce himself to you, it would go like this: "I am a towboat Captain. I am a Captain, and I will BE a Captain until two weeks after I am dead and gone."

I first told him about the idea for this book twenty years ago, and he laughed at it. He said it was silly, it was impossible, and it would simply never happen. In our final conversation last year, two weeks before he died, he asked if I remembered that story I had told him a long time ago. He said it had scared the hell out of him, was absolutely possible, and he just didn't want to think about it while he was still out there. He told me I should write it.

The river and towboats have been a part of my life forever. I am one of the few men on my father's side of the family who did not go to work on the river, and eventually become a towboat Captain. Growing up, I was introduced to 'river rats' he worked with from every walk of life and every part of the country. While no characters in this story are based on any specific person, I am quite sure that each of my characters carries a few pieces of those real men and women I met and admired.

The life of a towboater is a unique one, with unique benefits and pressures on the towboater and his or her family. It is a culture of hard work, loneliness, close friendships, dangerous actions, a forceful sense of humor, and blunt language. I have several friends and family members who are still "out there", continuing a tradition that has defined my family for four generations now. The words and actions of the towboaters you meet in Disruption are offered as a nod of respect and appreciation to those people who helped raise me and taught me how to live a full life.

J. B. Jamison, New Berlin, IL.

ACKNOWLEDGEMENTS

First, a huge thank you to my father, my uncles, cousins and all of the others who, since I was old enough to understand them, filled my mind with stories about life working on the river.

Second, to those who offered their time to read the early manuscript of the story and offer their thoughts. You helped me catch the parts that didn't make sense, or that were just wrong. You helped make the story better than it was.

Third, to E. M. Kaye, my wonderful editor and mentor, who suggested, guided, and sometimes pushed me to see that the final book was far better than I thought was possible.

Finally, to Pat, who made sure I had the time to sit and write, sit and write, sit and write. She helped remove the disruptions from my life so the book could be written.

ABOUT THE AUTHOR

J. B. Jamison is a life-long believer in the power of stories. First as a pastor, then educator, then creator of Centers for Innovation at multiple universities, and finally as the Director of a national Game and Simulation academic degree program, stories have played a central role in his work and have remained a passion throughout his life.

A published author and a long-time gamer, he has consulted with major game development companies and developed a series of learning games for children. Most importantly, John is the proud grandpa of Benjamin William and Emily Grace, the future rulers of the real and virtual universes.

Disruption is his first novel.

CONTACT INFORMATION

Visit J. B. Jamison's website at:
jbjamison.com
Facebook/johnbjamison